The Lost Middy
Being the Secret of the Smugglers' Gap

By

George Manville Fenn

The Lost Middy
Being the Secret of the Smugglers' Gap
by George Manville Fenn

ISBN: 978-93-61151-32-3
Published by

DOUBLE 9 BOOKS
2/13-B, Ansari Road
Daryaganj, New Delhi – 110002
info@double9books.com
www.double9books.com
Tel. 011-40042856

ABOUT THE AUTHOR

George Manville Fenn was a very productive author of novels, a writer, an editor, and an educator from England. He was born on January 3, 1831, in Pimlico, London. He mostly learned on his own; he taught himself Italian, French, and German. During the years 1851–1854, he went to Battersea Training College for Teachers and then became the head of a state school in Alford, Lincolnshire. In the early 1850s, Fenn started to write short stories and pieces for newspapers and magazines. The Old Forest Ranger, his first book, came out in 1856. Afterward, he wrote more than 100 books, many of them for teenagers and young adults. He was one of the most famous writers of his time, and his books were well-liked and read by many people. He also worked as a reporter and writer for Fenn. Among the newspapers and magazines, he worked for was The Boy's Own Paper, which he ran from 1866 to 1874. He worked hard to make children's books better and was a strong supporter of education and reading. The Englishman Fenn passed away on August 26, 1909, in Isleworth.

CONTENTS

Chapter One

There was a loud rattling noise, as if money was being shaken up in a box. A loud crashing bang, as if someone had banged the box down on a table. A rap, as if a knife had been dropped. Then somebody, in a petulant voice full of vexation and irritability, roared out:

"Bother!"

And that's exactly how it was, leaving Aleck Donne, who looked about sixteen or seventeen, scratching vigorously at his crisp hair as he sat back, with his elbows resting upon those of the big wooden arm-chair, staring at the money-box before him.

"I call it foolishness," he said, aloud, talking, of course, to himself, for there was no one else in the comfortable room, the window of which opened out upon the most quaint garden ever seen. "It's all right to save up your money in a box and keep on dropping it through a slit; but how about getting it out? Here, I'll go and smash the stupid old thing up directly on the block in the wood-shed."

But instead of carrying out his threat, he leaned forward, picked up the curved round-ended table-knife he had dashed down, seized the money-box again, shook it with jingling effect, held it upside down above his eyes, and began to operate with the knife-blade through the narrow slit in the centre of the lid.

For a good quarter of an hour by the big old eight-day clock in the corner did the boy work away, shaking the box till some coin or another was over the slit, and then operating with the knife-blade, trying and trying to get the piece of money up on edge so that it would drop through; and again and again, as the reward of his indefatigable perseverance, nearly succeeding, but never quite. For so sure as he pushed it up or tilted it down, the coin made a dash and glided away, making the drops of perspiration start out on the boy's forehead, and forcing him into a struggle with his temper which resulted in his gaining the victory again, till that thin old half-crown was coaxed well into sight and forced flat against the knife-blade. The boy then began to manipulate the knife with extreme caution as he kept on making a soft purring noise, *ah–h–h–h–ha!* full of triumphant satisfaction, while a big curled-up tabby tom-cat, which had taken possession of the fellow chair to that occupied by Aleck, twitched one ear, opened one eye, and then seeing that the purring sound was only a feeble imitation, went off to sleep again.

"Got you at last!" muttered the lad. "Half a crown; just buy all I want, and—bother!" he yelled, and, raising the box on high with both hands, he dashed it down upon the slate hearth with all his might.

Temper had won this time. Aleck had suffered a disastrous defeat, and he sat there with his forehead puckered up, staring at the cat, which at the crash and its accompanying yell made one bound that carried it on to the sideboard, where with glowing eyes, flattened ears, arched back, and bottle-brush tail, it stood staring at the disturber of its rest.

"Well, I am a pretty fool," muttered Aleck, starting out of his chair and listening for a few moments before stealing across the room to open the door cautiously and thrust out his head.

There was no sound to be heard, and the boy re-closed the door and went back to the hearth.

"I wonder uncle didn't hear," he muttered, stooping down. "I've done it now, and no mistake."

As he spoke he picked the remains of the broken box from inside the fender.

"Smashed!" he continued. "Good job too. Shan't have any more of that bother. How much is there? Let's see!"

There was a small fire burning in the old-fashioned grate, and with a grim look the boy finished the destruction of the money-box by tearing it apart at the dovetailings and placing the pieces on the fire, where they caught at once, blazing up, while the lad hunted out and picked up the coins which lay scattered here and there.

"Three—four—five—and sixpence," muttered the boy. "I thought there was more than that. Hullo! Where's that thin old half-crown? Haven't thrown it on the fire, have I? Oh, there you are!" he cried, ferreting it out of the fleeces of the thick dark-dyed sheepskin hearth-rug at his feet. "Eight shillings," he continued, transferring his store to his pocket. "Well, I'm not obliged to spend it all. Money-box! Bother! I'm not a child now. Just as if I couldn't take care of my money in my pocket."

He gave the place a slap, turned to the window, looked out at the soft fleecy clouds gliding overhead, and once more made for the door, crossed the little hall paved with large black slates, and then bounded up the oak stairs two at a time, to pause on the landing and give a sharp knuckle rap on the door before him; then, without waiting for a "Come in," he entered, to stand, door in hand, gazing at the top of a big shaggy grey head, whose owner held it close to the sheets of foolscap paper which he was covering with writing in a bold, clear hand.

"Want me, uncle?"

The head was raised, and a pair of fierce-looking eyes glared at the interrupter of the studies from beneath enormously-produced, thick, white eyebrows, and through a great pair of round tortoise-shell spectacles.

"Want you, boy?" was the reply, as the speaker held up a large white swan-quill pen on a level with his sun-browned and reddened nose. "No, Lick. Be off!"

"I'm going to run over to Rockabie, uncle. Back to dinner. Want anything brought back?"

"No, boy; I've plenty of ink. No.—Yes. Bring me some more of this paper."

The voice sounded very gruff and ill-humoured, and the speaker glared angrily, more than looked, at the boy.

"Here," he continued, "don't drown yourself."

"Oh, no, uncle," said the boy, confidently, "I'll take care of that."

"By running into the first danger you come across."

"Nonsense, uncle. I can sail about now as well as any of the fisher lads."

"Fisher? Bah!" growled the old man, fiercely. "Scoundrels—rascals, who wear a fisher's frock to hide the fact that they are smugglers—were wreckers. Nice sink of iniquity this. Look here, Lick. Take care and don't play that idler's trick of making fast the sheet."

"I'll take care, uncle."

"How's the wind, boy?"

"Just a nice soft breeze, uncle. I can run round the point in about an hour—wind right abaft."

"And dead ahead coming back, eh?"

"Yes; but I can tack, uncle—make good long reaches."

"To take you out into the race and among the skerries. Do you think I want to have you carried out to sea and brought back days hence to be buried, sir?"

"Of course you don't, uncle; but I shan't hurt. Old Dumpus says I can manage a boat as well as he can."

"He's a wooden-legged, wooden-headed old fool for saying so. Look here, Aleck; you'd better stop at home to-day."

"Uncle!" cried the boy, in a voice full of protest.

"The weather's going to change. I can feel it in my old wound; and it will not be safe for a boy like you alone to try and run that boat home round the point."

"Oh, uncle, you treat me as if I were a little boy!"

"So you are; and too light-headed."

"It's such a beautiful morning for a sail, uncle."

"Do just as well to watch the sea from the cliffs, and the carrier can bring what you want from Rockabie next time he goes."

"Uncle! I shall be so disappointed," pleaded the boy.

"Well! What of that? Do you good, boy. Life's all disappointments. Prepare you for what you'll have to endure in the future."

"Very well, uncle, I won't go if you don't wish it."

"Of course you won't, sir. There, run round and get one of the Eilygugg lads to help you with the boat."

"Please, uncle, I'd rather not. I don't like them, and they don't like me."

"Of course you don't like the young scoundrels, sir; but they can manage a boat."

"I'd rather not go now, uncle," said the boy, sadly.

"And I'd rather you did. There, go at once, while the weather's fine, and make that old man-o'-war's man help you to come back?"

"Tom Bodger, uncle? But how's he to get back?"

"I'll give him some shillings, and he can pay one of the smugglers to give him a lift home."

"Thank you, uncle," cried the boy, in an eager way, which showed plainly enough how well satisfied he was with the arrangement.

"Don't worry me. Be off!" said the old man, bending over his writing again.

Aleck needed no further orders, and hurried out into the well-kept garden, where everything looked healthy and flourishing, sheltered as it was from the fierce winds of all quarters by the fact that it lay in a depression formed by the sinking of some two or three acres of land, possibly from the undermining of the sea in far distant ages, at the end of a narrow rift or chasm in the cliffs which guarded the shores, the result being that, save in one spot nearest the sea, the grounds possessed a natural cliff-like wall some fifty or sixty feet high, full of rift and shelf, the nesting-place of innumerable birds. Here all was wild and beautiful; great curtains of ivy draped the natural walls, oak and sycamore flourished gloriously in the shelter as far as the top of the cliff, and there the trees ceased to grow upward and branched horizontally instead, so that from the level land outside it seemed as if Nature had cut all the tops off level, as indeed she had, by means of the sharp cutting winds.

Aleck followed the garden path without looking back at the vine and creeper-clad house in its shelter, and made for one corner of the garden where the walls overlapped, and, passing round one angle, he was directly after in a zigzag rift, shut in by more lofty, natural walls, but with the path sloping downward, with the consequence that the walls grew higher, till at the end of about three hundred yards from the garden they were fully a couple of hundred feet from base to summit, the base being nearly level with the sea. This latter was hidden till the lad had passed round another angle of cliff, when he obtained a glimpse of the deep blue water, flecked here and there with silvery foam, but hidden again directly as he followed the zigzag rift over a flooring of rough stones which had fallen from the towering perpendicular sides, and which were here only some thirty or forty feet apart, and completely shut out the sunshine and a good deal of the light.

Another angle of the zigzag rift was passed, and then the rugged stony flooring gave place to dark, deep water, beautifully transparent—so clear that the many-tinted fronds of bladder-wrack and other weeds could be seen swaying to and fro under the influence of the tide which rose and fell.

Here, in a natural harbour, sheltered from all dangers, lay the boat the boy sought. It was moored in a nook by a rope attached to a great ring; the staple had been sunk in a crack and sealed fast with molten lead, and no matter what storms raged outside, the boat was safely sheltered, and swung in a natural basin at ordinary tides, while at the very lowest it grounded gently in a bed of white sand.

It was well afloat upon this occasion, and skirting round it along a laboriously chipped-out ledge about a foot wide, the boy entered a crack in the rock face, for it could hardly be called a cavern. But it was big enough for its purpose, which was to shelter from the rain and rock drippings a quantity of boat gear, mast, sails, ropes, and tackle generally, which leaned or hung snugly enough about the rock, in company with a small seine, a trammel-net, a spare grapnel or two, some lobster-pots, and buoys with corks and lines.

Aleck was not long about carrying mast, yard, and sail to the boat and shipping them. Then, in obedience to an idea, he placed a couple of fishing-lines, a gaff-hook, a landing-net, and some spare hooks aboard; then, taking a little bucket, he half filled it with the crystal water of the pool, and after placing it aboard took hold of a thin line, one end of which was secured to a ring-bolt in a block of wreck lumber, while the other ran down into the pool.

A pull at the line brought a large closely-worked, spindle-shaped basket to the surface, when a commotion inside announced that the six-inch-wide square of flat cork, which formed a lid, covered something alive.

So it proved; for upon unfastening the lid an opening was laid bare, and upon the "coorge"—as the fishing folk called the basket—being laid across the bucket and turned sidewise, some ten or a dozen silvery eel-shaped fish glided out into the bucket, and began swimming round and round in search of an outlet.

"More bait than I shall want," said Aleck, covering and letting the basket go back into the pool. Then, unfastening the mooring-rope, the boy picked up a boat-hook, and by hooking on to the side rocks here and there he piloted the boat along the devious watery lane, with the mighty walls towering high on either side and whispering or echoing back every sound he produced on his way out to the open sea.

It was beautiful—solemn—grand—all in one, that narrow, gloomy, zigzag way between the perpendicular walls; and a naturalist would have spent hours examining the many-tinted sea anemones that opened their rays and awl-shaped tentacles below the water, or lay adhering and quiescent upon the rocks where the tide had fallen, looking some green, some olive, and many more like bosses of gelatinous coagulated blood.

But these were too common objects of the seashore for Aleck Donne to heed; his eyes were for the most part upon the blue and opalescent picture some two hundred yards before him, where the chasm ended, its sharp edges looking black against the sea and sky as he hooked on here, gave a thrust there, and sent the boat along till rift grew lighter and lighter, and then was left behind, for a final thrust had sent the boat right out into the sunshine, and in full view of three huge skittle-shaped rocks standing up out of the sea, high as the wall-like cliff of which at some time or another they must have been a portion. They were now many yards away and formed the almost secure nesting-places of hundreds upon hundreds of birds, whose necks stood up like so many pegs against the sky, giving the rocks a peculiar bristling appearance. But the sense of security for the young birds was upset by the long flapping wings of a couple of great black-backed gulls which kept on sailing round and round, waiting till the opportunity came to make a hawk-like swoop and carry off some well-fatted, half-feathered young auk. One met its fate, in the midst of a rippling purring cry, just as Aleck laid in his boat-hook and proceeded to step the mast, swaying easily the while with the boat, which was now well afloat on the rising and falling sea.

Chapter Two

"My word! How she does go!" cried Aleck, a short time later. For he had stepped the mast, hooked on the little rudder, and hoisted the sail, the latter filling at once with the breeze which, coming from the sea, struck the bold perpendicular rock face and glanced off again, to catch the boat right astern. One minute it was racing along almost on an even keel; then, like a young horse, it seemed to take the bit in its teeth as it careened over more and more and made the water foam beneath the bows.

Away to Aleck's left was the dazzling stretch of ocean, to his right the cliffs with the stack rocks and a glimpse of the whitewashed group of cottages locally known as Eilygugg, from their overlooking the great isolated, skittle-like, inaccessible stack rocks chosen by those rather rare birds the little auks for their nesting-place year after year.

On and on sped the boat past the precipitous cliffs, which, with the promontory-like point ahead, were the destruction of many a brave vessel in the stormy times; and an inexperienced watcher from the shore would often have suffered from that peculiar sensation known as having the heart in the mouth on seeing the boat career over before some extra strong puff of wind, till it seemed as if the next moment the sail would be flat on the water while the little vessel filled and went down.

But many years of teaching by the fishermen and Tom Bodger, the wooden-legged old man-o'-war's man of Rockabie, had made Aleck, young though he was, an expert manager of a fore and aft sailing boat, and the boy sat fast, rudder in one hand, sheet in the other, ready at the right moment to ease off the rope and by a dexterous touch at the rudder to lessen the pressure upon the canvas so that the boat rose again and raced onward till the great promontory ahead was passed. In due time the land sheltered the young navigator, and he glided swiftly into the little harbour of the fishing town, whose roughly-formed pier curved round like a crescent moon to protect the little fleet of fishing-boats, whose crews leaned over the cliff rail masticating tobacco and gazing out to sea, as they rested from the past night's labour, and talked in a low monotonous growl about the wind and the prospects of the night to come.

Rockabie was a prolific place, as far as boys were concerned. There were doubtless girls to balance them, but the girls were busy at home, while the boys swarmed upon the pier, where they led a charmed life; for though one of them was crowded, or scuffled, or pushed off every day into deep water, when quarrelling, playing, or getting into someone's way when the fish were landed, they seemed as if formed of cork or bladder and wind instead of flesh and blood, for they always came up again, to be pulled out by the rope thrown, or hooked out by a hitcher, if they did not swim round to the rough steps or to the shore. Not one was ever known to be drowned—that was the fate of the full-grown who went out in smack or lugger to sea.

The sight of Aleck Donne's boat coming round the point caused a rush on the part of the boys down to the pier and drew the attention of the fishermen up on the cliff as well. But these latter did not stir, only growled out something about the cap'n's boat from the Den. One man only made the comment that the sail wanted "tannin' agen," and that was all.

But the boys were interested and busy as they swarmed to the edge of the unprotected pier, along which they sat and stood as closely as the upright puffins in their white waistcoats standing in rows along the ledges that towered up above the point. For everybody knew everybody there for miles round, and every boat as well.

There was a good deal of grinning and chattering going on as the boat neared, especially from one old fisherman who lived inside a huge pair of very stiff trousers, these coming right up to his arm-pits, so that only a very short pair of braces, a scrap of blue shirt, and a woollen night-cap were required to complete his costume.

This gentleman smiled, grunted, placed a fresh bit of black tobacco in his cheek, and took notice of the fact that several of the boys had made a rush to the edge of the water by the harbour and come back loaded with decaying fish—scraps of skate, trimmings, especially the tails, heads, and offal—to take their places again, standing behind their sitting companions.

Someone else saw the action too, and began to descend from the cliff by the long slope whose water end was close to the shore end of the pier.

This personage would have been a tall, broad-shouldered man had he been all there; but he was not, for he had left his legs in the West Indies, off the coast of Martinique, when a big round shot from a French battery came skipping over the water and cut them off, as the ship's surgeon said, almost as cleanly as he could have done with the knife and saw he used on the poor fellow after the action was over, the fort taken, and the Frenchmen put to flight.

The result was that Thomas Bodger came back after some months to his native village, quite cured, in the best of health, and wearing a pair of the shortest wooden legs ever worn by crippled man—his pegs, as the boys of Rockabie called them, though he dignified them himself by the name of toes. As to his looks, he was a fine-looking man to just below his hips, and there he had been razed, as he called it to Aleck Donne, while the most peculiar thing about him as he toddled along was what at first sight looked like a prop, which extended from just beneath his head nearly to the ground, as if to enable him to stand, tripod-fashion, steadily on a windy day. But it was nothing of the sort, being only his pigtail carefully bound with ribbon, and the thickest and longest pigtail in the "Ryal Navee."

Tom Bodger, or—as he was generally known by the Rockabie boys—Dumpus, trotted down the slope in a wonderful way, for how he managed to keep his balance over the rough cobbles and on the storm-worn granite stones of the pier was a marvel of equilibrium. But keep upright he did, solely by being always in motion; and he was not long in elbowing his way through the crowd of boys, many of whom overtopped him, and planting himself at the top of the pier steps, where from old experience he knew that Aleck would land.

As soon as he was there he delivered himself of an observation.

"Look here," he growled, in a deep, angry voice, "I've been marking o' you youngsters with my hye, and I gives you doo warning, the fust one on yer as shies any o' that orfull at young Master Donne, or inter his little boat, I marks with what isn't my hye, but this here bit of well-tarred rope's-end as I've got hitched inside my jacket; so look out."

"Yah!" came in a derisive chorus, as the sailor showed the truthfulness of his assertion by drawing out about eighteen inches of stoutish brown rope, drawing it through his left hand and putting it back.

"Yah!" shouted one of the most daring. "Yer can't ketch us. Yah!"

"Not ketch ye, you young swab? Not in a starn chase, p'raps, but I've got a good mem'ry and I can heave-to till yer comes within reach, and then—well, I'm sorry for you, my lad. I know yer;—Davvy, Davvy."

The boy looked uncomfortable, and furtively dropped an unpleasant smelling quid which he had picked up as a weapon of offence, and very offensive it was; but another lad appropriated it instantly and sniffed at it, smiling widely afterwards as if approving hugely of the vile odour. Probably familiarity had begotten contempt, for none of his companions moved away.

Meanwhile Aleck had run his boat close in and lowered his sail. Then, as he rose up, boat-hook in hand, he was greeted with a jeering chorus of shouts, for no other reason than that he was a so-called stranger who did not live there and was well dressed, and belonged to a better class.

Aleck was accustomed to the reception, and gave the little crowd a contemptuous look, before turning to the squat figure beginning to descend the steps to where the boy stood ten feet below.

"What cheer, Tom!" he cried.

"What cheer-ho, Master Aleck!" returned the sailor. "Hearty, my lad, hearty." Then, turning to the boys, he growled out, "Now, then, you heered. So just mind; whether it's fish fresh or fish foul. The one as shies gets my mark."

The voices of the boys rose in a curious way, making a highly pitched jeering snarl, while a number of unpleasant missiles that were held ready were fingered and held behind backs, but from a disinclination to become the victim of the sailor's marking, no lad was venturesome enough to start the shower intended to greet the newcomer. It was held in abeyance for the moment, and then became impossible, for peg, peg, peg, peg, Tom Bodger descended the steps till he was level with the gunwale of Aleck's boat, upon which one extremity was carefully planted, and careful aim taken at the first thwart. The sailor was about to swing himself in, when Aleck held out his hand—

"Catch hold!" he cried.

"Tchah! I don't want to ketch hold o' nothing," grumbled the man. "Stand aside."

As he spoke he spun half round as upon a peg, the second wooden leg lightly touched the thwart, and the next moment, when it seemed as if the poor fellow's wooden appendages must go through the frail bottom of the boat, they came down with a light *tip-tap*, and he was standing up looking smilingly in the young navigator's face.

"Come along tidy quick, my lad?" he said.

"Yes, the wind was lovely. Look here, Tom; I'm going shopping—to get some hooks and things. Mind that young rabble does not throw anything aboard."

"All right, my lad; but I should just like to see one of 'em try."

"I shouldn't," cried Aleck. "But, look here; uncle says as there'll be a good deal of wind dead ahead, and I shall have to tack back again, you're to come with me."

"Course I should," said the sailor, gruffly. "Wants two a day like this."

"And he'll pay you; and you're to get one of the fishermen to pick you up and bring you back."

"Tchah! I don't want no picking up. It's on'y about six mile across from here to the Den, and I can do that easy enough if yer give me time."

"Do as you like, but uncle will pay for the ride."

"And I shall put the money in my pocket and toddle back," said the sailor, chuckling; "do me more good than riding. You look sharp and get back. I'll give her a swab out while you're gone, and we'll take a good reach out to where the bass are playing off the point, and get a few. I see you've brought some sand eels."

"So we will, Tom. I should like to take home a few bass."

"So you shall, my lad," said the sailor, who had stumped forward to the fore-locker to get out a big sponge; and he was rolling up his sleeves over a pair of big, brown, muscular arms ornamented with blue mermaids, initials, a ship in full sail, and a pair of crossed cutlasses surmounted by a crown, as Aleck stepped lightly upon the gunwale, sprang thence on to the steps, and went up, to run the gauntlet of the little crowd of boys, who greeted him with something like a tempest of hoots and jeers.

But the lads fell back as, with a smile full of the contempt he felt, Aleck pressed forward, marched through them with his hands in his pockets, and smiled more broadly as he heard from below a growling shout of warning from the sailor announcing what he would do if the boys didn't mind, the result being that they followed the well-grown lad at a little distance all along the pier, throwing after him not bad fish and fragments, which would, if well-aimed, have sullied the lad's clothes, but what an Irishman would have called dirty words, mingled with threats about what they would give him one of these fine days. The feud was high between the Rockabie boys and the bright active young lad from the Den, for no further reason than has already been stated, and the dislike had increased greatly during the past year, though it had never culminated in any encounter worse than the throwing of foul missiles after the boat when it was pushed off for home.

Perhaps it was something in the air which made the Rockabie boys more pugnacious and their threats more dire. Possibly they may have felt more deeply stung by the contempt of Aleck, who strode carelessly along the rough stone pier, whistling softly, with his hands in his pockets, till he reached the slope and began to ascend towards where the fishermen leaned in a row over the rail, just as if after a soaking night they had hung themselves out in the sun to dry.

And now it was that the boys hung back and Aleck felt that he could afford to pay no heed to the young scrubs who followed him, for there were plenty of hearty hails and friendly smiles to greet him from the rough seamen.

"Morn', Master Aleck."

"Morn', sir. How's the cap'n?" from another.

Then: "Like a flat fish to take back with you, master? I've got a nice brill. I'll put him in your boat."

And directly after a big broad fellow detached himself from the rail to sidle up with: "Say, Master Aleck, would you mind asking the cap'n to let me have another little bottle o' them iles he gives me for my showther? It's getting bad again."

"You shall have it, Joney," cried Aleck.

"Thankye, sir. No hurry, sir. Just put the bottle in yer pocket nex' time you come over, and that'll do."

Aleck went on up town, as it was called, — and the men hung themselves a little more over the rail and growled at the boys who were following the visitor, to "be off," and to "get out of that; now," with the result that they still followed the lad and watched him, flattening their noses against the panes of the fishing-tackle shop window, and following him again when he came out to visit one or two other places of business, till all the lad's self-set commissions were executed, and he turned to retrace his steps to the harbour.

So far every movement had been followed by cutting remarks expressive of the contempt in which the visitor was held. There had been threats, too, of how he would be served one of these times. Remarks were made, too, on his personal appearance and the cut of his clothes, but there was nothing more than petty annoyance till the quarry was on his way back to where he would be under the protection of the redoubtable Dumpus, who did not scruple about "letting 'em have it," to use his own words, it being very unpleasant whatever shape it took. But now the pack began to rouse up and show its rage under the calm, careless, defiant contempt with which it was being treated. Words, epithets, and allusions grew more malicious, caustic, and insulting, and, these producing no effect by the time the top of the slope was reached, bolder tactics were commenced, the boys closing round and starting a kind of horse-play in which one charged another, to give him a thrust so as to drive him — quite willing — against the retiring visitor.

The Lost Middy | 19

This was delightful; the mirth it excited grew more boisterous, and the covert attacks more general.

But Aleck was on the alert and avoided several, till a more vigorous one was attempted by the biggest lad present, a great, hulking, stupid, hobbledehoy of a fellow, who drove a companion against Aleck's shoulder, making him stagger for a moment, while the aggressor burst out into a hoarse laugh which was chorussed by the little crowd, and then stopped.

The spring which set Aleck's machinery in motion had been touched, making him wheel round from the boy who had been driven against him, make a spring at the great, grinning, prime aggressor, and bring his coarse laugh to an end by delivering a stinging blow on the ear which drove him sidewise and made him stand shaking his head and thrusting his finger inside his ear as if to try and get rid of a peculiar buzzing sound which affected him strangely.

There was a roar, and the boy who had been thrust against Aleck sprang at him to inflict condign punishment upon the stranger who had dared to strike his companion.

The attack was vigorous enough, but the attacker was unlucky, for he met Aleck's bony fist on his way before he could use his own. Then he clapped his open hands to his nose and stood staring in wonder, and seemed to be trying to find out whether his nose had been flattened on his face.

There was an ominous silence then, during which Aleck turned and walked on down the slope in a quiet leisurely way, scorning to run, and even slackening his pace to be on his guard as he reached the bottom of the slope, for by that time the boys had recovered from their astonishment, and were in full pursuit.

In another minute Aleck was surrounded by a roughly-formed crowding-in ring, with the two lads who had tested the force of his blows eager to obtain revenge, incited thereto by a score or two of voices urging them to "give it him," "pay him," "let him have it," and the like.

The two biggest lads of the party then came on at Aleck at once; but, to be just, it was from no cowardly spirit, but from each being urged by a sheer vindictive desire to be first to obtain revenge for his blow. Hence they were mastered by passion and came on recklessly against one who was still perfectly cool and able to avoid the bigger fellow's assault while he gave the other a back-handed blow which sent him reeling away quite satisfied for the present and leaving the odds, so to speak, more even in the continuation of the encounter.

Aleck was well on the alert, and, feeling that he was utterly out-matched, he aimed at getting as far as the steps, where he would have Tom Bodger for an ally and the attack would come to an end; but he was soon aware of the fact that to retire was impossible, hedged in as he was by an excited ring of boys, and there was nothing for him but to fight his way back slowly and cautiously. So he kept his head, coolly resisting the attack of the big fellow with whom he was engaged, guarding himself from blows to the best of his ability, and paying little heed to the torrent of abuse which accompanied the blows the big fisher lad tried to shower upon him, and always backing away a few yards, as he could, nearer to the way down to his boat.

By this time the word was passed along the top of the cliff that there was a fight on, and the fishermen began slowly to take themselves off the rail and descend the slope to see the fun, as they called it. They did not hurry themselves in the least, so that there was plenty of time for the encounter to progress, with Aleck still calm and cool, warding off the blows struck at him most skilfully, and mastering his desire to retaliate when he could have delivered others with masterly effect.

But a change was coming on.

Enraged by his inability to close with his skilful, active adversary, the big lad made more and more use of his tongue, the torrent of abuse grew more foul, and Aleck more cool and contemptuous, till all at once his adversary yelled out something which was received with acclamations by the excited ring who surrounded the pair, while it went through Aleck like some poisoned barb. He saw fire for the moment, and his teeth gritted together, as caution and the practice and skill he had displayed were no more, for, to use a schoolboy phrase, his monkey was up and he meant fighting—he meant to use his fists to the best effect in trying to knock the vile slanderous words, uttered against the man he loved and venerated, down the utterer's throat, while his rage against those who crowded around, yelling with delight, took the form of back strokes with his elbow and more than one sharp blow at some intruding head.

But it was against the lout who had spoken that the fire of his rage was principally directed, and the fellow realised at once that all that had gone before on the part of the stranger from the Den was mere sparring and self-defence. Aleck meant fighting now, and he fought, showering down such volleys of blows that, at the end of a couple of minutes, in spite of a brave defence and the planting of nasty cracks about his adversary's unguarded face, the big lad was being knocked here and there, up, down, and round about, till the shouts and cries about him lowered into a dull, dead hum. The pier stones reeled and rose and sank and seemed to imitate the waves that floated in, and when at last, in utter despair, he locked Aleck in his arms and tried to throw him, he received such a stunning blow between the eyes that he loosened his grasp to shake his head, which the next moment was knocked steady and inert, the big fellow going down all of a heap, and the back of his big bullet skull striking the pier stones with a heavy resounding bump.

Chapter Three

In his excitement it seemed to Aleck that the real fight was now about to begin, for the little mob of boys uttered an angry yell upon seeing their champion's downfall, and were crowding in. But he was wrong, for a gruff voice was heard from the fishermen, who had at last bestirred themselves to see more of what they called the fun, and another deep-toned voice, accompanying the pattering of two wooden legs, came from the direction of the steps.

"Here, that'll do, you dogs!" cried the first voice, and—

"Stand fast, Master Aleck, I'm a-coming," cried the other.

The effect on the boys was magical, and they gave way in all directions before the big fisherman who had asked for the "iles" for his shoulders, a medicament he did not seem to require, for his joints worked easily as he threw out his arms with a mowing action, right and left, and with a force that would have laid the inimical lads down in swathes if they had not got out of the way.

"Well done, young Aleck Donne," he cried. "Licked Big Jem, have yer? Hansum too. Do him good. Get up—d'yer hear—before I give yer my boot! I see yer leading the lot on arter the young gent, like a school o' dogfish. Hullo, Tom, you was nigher. Why didn't yer come up and help the young gen'leman afore?"

"'Cause I didn't know what was going on, matey," cried the sailor. "Why didn't yer hail me, Master Aleck?"

"Because I didn't want to be helped," cried the boy, huskily, his voice quivering with indignation. "A set of cowards!"

"So they are, Master Aleck," cried the sailor, joining in the lad's indignation. "On'y wish I'd knowed. I'd ha' come up with the boat-hook."

"Never mind; it arn't wanted," said the big fisherman. "Young Mr Donne's given him a pretty good dressing down, and if this here pack arn't off while their shoes are good we'll let him give it to a few more."

"I want to know what their fathers is about," growled the sailor. "I never see such a set. They're allus up to some mischief."

"Ay, ay, that's a true word," cried another fisherman.

"That's so," growled the sailor, who, as he spoke, kept on brushing Aleck down and using his forearm as a brush to remove the dust and *débris* from the champion's jacket.

"Pity he didn't leather another couple of 'em," cried the big fisherman.

"Ay," growled the sailor. "I don't want to say anything unneighbourly, but it seems a pity that some on 'em don't get swep' up by the next press-gang as lands. A few years aboard a man-o'-war'd be the best physic for some o' them. Look at all this here rubbidge about! I see 'em. Got it ready to fling at the young gent. I know their games."

"Nay, nay," said the big fisherman, as a low, angry murmur arose, and ignoring the allusion to the fish *débris* lying about, "we don't want no press-gangs meddling here."

"Yes, you do," said the sailor, angrily, as he applied a blue cotton neckerchief he had snatched off and shaken out alternately to a cut on Aleck's forehead and to his swollen nose, which was bleeding freely. "Nice game this, arn't it? I know what I'm saying. I was pressed myself when I was twenty, and sarved seven year afore I come home with a pension. It made a man o' me, and never did me no harm."

There was a hoarse roar of laughter at this, several of the fishermen stamping about in their mirth, making the sailor cease his ministrations and stand staring and beginning to mop his hot forehead with the neckerchief.

"What are yer grinning at?" he said, angrily, with the result that the laughter grew louder.

"Have I smudged my face with this here hankychy, Master Aleck?" said the sailor, turning to the boy, who could not now refrain from smiling in turn.

But Aleck was saved the necessity of replying to the question by the big fisherman, who spoke out in a grimly good-humoured way, as he cast his eyes up and down the dwarfed man-o'-war's man:

"Lookye here, Tom, mate," he said, good-humouredly, "I don't know so much about never doing you no harm, old chap."

"What d'yer mean?" growled the sailor.

"What about yer legs, mate?" cried another of the men.

The sailor stared round at the group, and then a change came over him and he bent down and gave his hip a sounding slap.

"I'm blest!" he cried, with the angry looks giving place to a broad smile. "I'm blest! I never thought about my legs!"

There was another roar of laughter now, in which Tom Bodger joined.

"But lookye here, messmates, what's a leg or two? Gone in the service o' the King and country, I says. Here am I, two-and-thirty, with ninepence a day as long as I live, as good a man as ever I was—good man and true. Who says I arn't?"

"Nobody here, Tom, old mate," cried the big fisherman, giving the sailor a hearty slap on the shoulder. "Good mate and true, and as good a neighbour as we've got in Rockabie. Eh, lads?"

"Ay, ay!" came in a hearty chorus.

"There, Tom, so say all of us; but none o' that about no press-gangs, mate," cried the big fisherman. "The King wants men for his ships, but all on us here has our wives and weans. What was all right for a lad o' twenty would be all wrong for such as we."

"Ay, that's true," said the sailor, "and I oughtn't to ha' said it; but look at Master Aleck here. Them boys—"

"Yes, yes, boys is boys, and allus was and allus will be, as long as there's land and sea. Some on 'em'll get a touch o' rope's-end after this game, I dessay. Lookye here, Master Aleck Donne, you come up to my place, and the missus'll find you a tin bowl o' water, a bit o' soap, and a clean towel. You won't hurt after a wash, but be able to go home as proud as a tom rooster. You licked your man, and the captain'll feel proud of you, for Big Jem was too much of a hard nut for such a chap as you. Come on, my lad."

"No, no, thank you," said Aleck, warmly; "I want to get back home now. I don't want to show Mrs Joney a face like this."

"Nay, my lad, she won't mind; and—"

"Tom Bodger's going to sail my boat home," put in the boy, hastily, "and I shall hang over the side and bathe my face as I go. I say, all of you, I'm sorry I got into this bit of trouble, but it wasn't my fault."

"Course it wasn't," said the fisherman. "We all know that, and you've give some on 'em a lesson, my lad. Well, if you won't come, my lad, you won't."

"It's only because I want to get back home," said Aleck, warmly. "It's very kind of you all the same."

A few minutes later the boy was seated in the stern of the boat, while Tom Bodger stood up, looking as if he, too, were sitting, as he thrust the little craft along by means of the boat-hook and the pier walls, while the fishermen walked along level with them to the end, where half a dozen of the boys had gathered.

"Give him a cheer, lads," said the big fisherman, and a hearty valediction was given and responded to by Aleck, who took off and waved his cap.

But just then a hot-blooded and indignant follower of defeated Big Jem let his zeal outrun his discretion. Waiting till the group of fishermen had turned their backs, he ran to the very end of the pier, uttered a savage "Yah!" and hurled the very-far-gone head of a pollock after the boat.

The next minute he was repenting bitterly, for the big fisherman made four giant strides, caught him by the waistband, and the next moment held him over the edge of the pier and would have dropped him, struggling and yelling for mercy, into the sea, but Aleck sprang up and shouted an appeal to his big friend to let the boy go.

"Very well," growled his captor; "but it's lucky for him, Master Aleck, as you spoke. Warmint!" he growled to the boy, lowering him to the rugged stones. "Get home with yer. I'm going on by and by to your father, my lad. Be off."

The boy yelled as he started and ran off, limping, and with good cause, for the boots the fisherman wore were very loose and hung down gaping to his ankles, as if to show how beautifully they were silver-spangled with fish scales, but the soles were very thick and terribly hard, especially about the toe.

Chapter Four

"I didn't get my brill after all, Tom," said Aleck, as the sail filled out and the boat sped along over the little dancing waves.

"Never mind the flat fish, Master Aleck; we'll pick up a few bass as we go along through the race, and they'll be fresher than his brill."

"No, Tom," said Aleck, frowning; "no fishing to-day. I want to get back and have a proper wash and change my shirt and collar."

"Well, you did get a bit knocked about, Master Aleck. You see, he's a hard sort o' boy; awfully thick-headed chap."

"He is, and no mistake," said Aleck. "Look at my knuckles!"

"Ay, you have got 'em a bit chipped; but it'll all grow up again. But what was it he said as made you bile over and get a-fighting that how?"

"Oh, never mind," said the boy, flushing. "It's all over now."

"Yes," said the sailor, knitting his brow, "it's all over now; but," he added, thoughtfully, as he let the sheet slip through his fingers and tightened it again, giving and taking as the sail tugged in answer to the puffs of wind, "but it don't seem like you to get into action like that, Master Aleck. You're generally such a quiet sort o' chap, and don't mind the boys yelping about yer heels any more than as if they was dogs."

"Of course, and I never for a moment thought that anything they could say would put me in such a passion. Oh, Tom, I felt once as if I could kill him!"

"Monkey must ha' been up very much indeed, Master Aleck. I've been a-wondering what he could ha' called you to make you clear the decks and go at him like that. You must have hit out and no mistake."

"Yes, I hit them as hard as ever I could—both of them."

"Both? Did you have two on 'em at yer at once?"

"Yes, part of the time."

"Then I am glad you licked 'em. It was just like a smart frigate licking a couple of two-deckers. What did he call yer?"

"Oh, never mind, Tom; nothing."

"But he must have called yer, as I said afore, something very, very bad indeed. Yer needn't mind telling me, my lad, for I seem to ha' been a sort of sea-father to yer. I've heered a deal o' bad language at sea in my time, and I should like to hear what it was that made you fly out like that. Tell us what it was."

"No, no; don't ask me, Tom."

"Not ast yer, my lad? Well, I won't if yer say as I arn't to. But it must ha' been something very bad indeed."

"It was, Tom, horribly bad; but—but he didn't call me anything. It was something he said made me so angry. I wouldn't have fought like that for anything he had called me."

"Ho!" said the sailor, thoughtfully. "Then it was about somebody else?"

"Yes, Tom," said the lad, frowning, and with his eyes flashing with the remains of his anger.

"Then it must have been something as he called me," said the sailor, naïvely. "Yes, I know he's got his knife into me. So you licked him well for saying what he did, Master Aleck?"

"Yes," said the lad, thoughtfully, and with the frown deepening upon his face.

"Then I says thankye, Master Aleck, and I won't forget it, for it was very hansum on yer."

"What was?" said the lad, starting.

"What was? Why, you licking that big ugly lout, my lad, for calling me names."

"No, no, no," cried Aleck, quickly; "it was not for that."

"Why, you said just now as you did, Master Aleck," said the sailor, blankly.

"Oh, no; you misunderstood me, Tom. It was not for that."

"Ho! Then what for was it, my lad?"

"I can't tell you, Tom," cried the boy, passionately. "Don't worry me. Can't you see I'm all in pain and trouble?"

"All right, sir; I don't want to worry yer. It don't matter. I couldn't help wanting to know why you larruped him; but, as I said afore, it don't matter. You did larrup him, and give it him well, and it strikes me as his father'll give him the rope's-end as well, as soon as he sees him for going back home with such a face as he's got on his front. My word, you did paint him up. His old man won't hardly know him."

"Tom!" cried Aleck, excitedly, as these last words impressed him deeply.

"Ay, ay, sir! Tom it is."

"Look at my face," said the lad, looking up sharply from where he had been leaning over the gunwale scooping up the water in his hand and bathing the injuries he had received in his encounter. "Look at me. Is my face much knocked about?"

The sailor shifted the hands which had held rudder and sheet, afterwards raising that which held the latter and rubbing his mahogany brown nose with the rope.

"Well, why don't you speak, Tom?" said the lad, pettishly.

"'Cause I was 'specting yer like, my lad—smelling yer over like, so as to think out what to say."

"Go on, then; only say something."

"So I will, sir, if yer really wants to hear."

"Why, of course I do. Does my face show much?"

"Well, yes, sir," said the sailor, gravely, as he went on rubbing one side of his nose with the rope. "You've got it pretty tidy."

"Tell me what you can see."

The sailor grunted and hesitated.

"Go on," cried Aleck. "Here, my bottom lip smarts a good deal. It's cut, isn't it?"

"That's right, sir. Cut it is, but I should say as it'll soon grow up together again."

Aleck pressed the kerchief to his lip, and winced with pain.

"Arn't loosened no teeth, have yer, sir?"

Aleck shook his head.

"Go on," he said. "What about my nose? It's swollen, isn't it?"

"Well, yes, sir, it is a bit swelled like. Puffy, as yer might say; but, bless yer 'art, it's nothing to what Big Jem's is. I shouldn't mind about that a bit now, for it have stopped bleeding. There's nothing like cold sea water for that, though it do make yer tingle a bit. I 'member what a lot o' good it used to do when we'd been in action and the lads had got chopped about in boarding the enemy. The Frenchies used to be pretty handy with their cutlasses and boarding-pikes. They used axes too."

"Oh, I don't want to know about that," cried Aleck, pettishly. "There's a scratch or something on my forehead, isn't there?"

"It's 'most too big and long to call it a scratch, sir. I should call that a cut."

"Tut, tut, tut!" ejaculated Aleck.

"That'll soon be all right, sir," continued the sailor, cheerfully. "Bit o' sticking plaster'll soon set that to rights. What I don't like is your eyes."

"My eyes?" cried Aleck. "Yes, they do feel stiff when I wink them. Do they look bad, then?"

The sailor chuckled softly.

"What do you mean by that?" cried the lad, angrily. "Are they swollen too? I'm sure there's nothing to laugh at in that."

The sailor tried to look very serious, but failed. The laughing crinkles were smoothed out of his face, but his eyes sparkled and danced with merriment as he said:

"I didn't mean no harm, Master Aleck, but you wouldn't say what you did if you could see your eyes. They do look so rum."

"Why? How?" cried Aleck, excitedly.

"Did yer see Benny Wiggs's eyes las' year after he took the bee swarm as got all of a lump in Huggins's damsel tree?"

"No, of course I didn't," cried Aleck, impatiently.

"Ah, that's a pity, sir, because yourn looks just like his'n did. You see, they don't look like eyes!"

"Then what do they look like?" cried Aleck.

"Well, sir, I'll tell yer: they looks just like the tops o' bread loaves going to the oven."

"Like what?"

"I mean like the holes the missuses makes in the dough with their fingers. Finishes off by giving a poke in the top with a finger, and that closes up into a crinkly slit with a swelling around."

"Bah!" growled Aleck.

"Well, you would ask me, sir."

"Yes, of course. Something like Big Jem's?"

"Yes, sir; on'y more squeezed in like. Your eyes is allus handsome and bright like, but they arn't now. But, there, don't you mind that, sir. They turn nasty colours like for a bit, but, as I says, don't you mind. Big Jem's face was a reg'lar picter. I don't know what his father'll say when he sees him."

"And I don't know what uncle will say when he sees me," said Aleck, despondently.

"Eh? The captain?" cried the sailor, in a startled tone of voice. "Phe-ew!" he whistled. "I forgot all about him. I say, my lad, he won't like to see you this how."

"No," said Aleck, dismally.

"Arn't got no aunts or relations as you could go and see for a fortnit, have you?"

"No, Tom; I have no relatives but Uncle Donne."

"That's a pity, sir. Well, I dunno what you'd better do."

"Face uncle, and tell him the whole truth."

"To be sure, sir. Of course. That's the way you'd better lay your head — to the wind like. And, look here, sir!"

"I can't look, Tom; my eyes feel closed up, and I can hardly see a bit."

"I mean look here with understanding, sir. I used to be with a skipper who was a downright savage if we got beaten off, and threatened to flog us. But if we won, and boarded a ship and took her, he'd laugh at our hurts and come round and shake hands and call us his brave lads."

"But what has that to do with uncle seeing me in this horrible state?"

"Why, don't you see, sir?" cried the sailor, eagerly. "He's a captain, and a fighting man."

Aleck frowned, but the sailor did not notice it, and went on:

"You ups and tells him that Big Jem and the pack o' blackguard riff-raff come and 'sulted yer and said what you wouldn't tell me. The captain wouldn't want you to put up with that. I know the captain 'most as well as you do. 'Hullo!' he says; 'what ha' you been doing—how did you get in that condition?' he says—just like that. Then you ups and tells him you had it out with Big Jem and the rest. 'What for, sir?' he says—just like that. 'For saying,'—you know what, sir—you says, and tells him right out, though you wouldn't tell me. 'And you let that big, ugly, blackguardly warmint thrash you like that?' he says, in his fierce way—just like that. Then your turn comes, and you ups and says, 'most as chuff as he does: 'No, uncle,' you says, 'I give him the orflest leathering he ever had in his life.' 'Did you, Aleck?' he says, rubbing his hands together, joyful like. 'Well done, my boy,' he says; 'I like that. I wish I'd been there to see. Brayvo!—Now go and wash your face and brush your clothes and 'air.'"

"Think he would, Tom?"

"Sure on it, sir. I wouldn't ha' answered for him if you'd gone back with your tail between your legs, reg'larly whipped; but seeing how you can go back and cry cock-a-doodle-doo!—"

"Like a dog, Tom?" said Aleck, grimly, with a feeling of amusement at the way in which his companion was mixing up his metaphors.

"Like a dog, sir? Tchah! Dogs can't crow. You know what I mean. Seeing how you can go back with your colours flying, the captain'll feel proud on yer, and if he's the gentleman I take him for he'll cut yer a bit o' sticking plaster himself. What you've got to do is to go straight to his cabin and speak out like a man."

"Yes, Tom, I mean to—but, Tom—" continued the lad, in a hesitating way.

"Ay ay, sir; what is it?"

"Did you ever hear any of the fishermen say anything against my uncle?"

"Eh? Oh, I've heered them gawsip and talk together when they've been leaning theirselves over the rail in the sun, gawsiping like, as you may say; but I never took no notice. Fishermen when they're ashore chatter together like old women over the wash-tubs, but I never takes no heed to what they says. The captain's been a good friend to me, and so I shuts my ears when people say nasty things."

"Then you know that they do say nasty things about him?" said Aleck.

"Oh, yes, sir, and 'bout everyone else too. They lets out about me sometimes, I've heered, and about my losing my legs; but I don't mind. I say, though, Master Aleck, sir! Haw—haw—haw! Think o' me forgetting all about 'em and saying that being at sea never did me no harm! It was a rum 'un!"

Aleck was silent and thinking about his own troubles, making his companion glance at him uneasily, waiting for the lad to speak; but as he remained silent the sailor turned the state of affairs over in his own mind till he hit upon what he considered to be a very happy thought.

"I say, Master Aleck."

"Eh? Yes, Tom."

"I've been a-thinking that as a reg'lar thing I'm a bit skeart o' the captain. He's such a fierce, cut-you-off-short sort of a gentleman that I'm always glad to get away when I've been up to the Den to do anything for yer — pitching the boat's bottom or mending holes, or overhauling the tackle; but I tell you what—"

"Well, what, Tom?" said Aleck, for the sailor stopped short and crossed his two dwarf wooden legs in the bottom of the boat, and then, as if not satisfied, crossed them the other way on.

"I was thinking, Master Aleck, that you and me's been messmates like, ever since I come back from sea."

"Yes, Tom."

"I mean in a proper way, sir," cried the man, hurriedly. "I don't mean shoving myself forrard, because well I know you're a young gen'leman and I'm on'y a pensioned-off hulk as has never been anything more than a AB."

"I don't know what you're aiming at, Tom," said Aleck, querulously, as he went on bathing his bruised face again. "Of course we've been like messmates many a time out with the boat, but what has that to do with the trouble I'm in?"

"Well, just this here, sir. Messmates is messmates, and ought to help one another when there's rocks ahead."

"Of course, Tom."

"Well, then, as I've been thinking, suppose I come ashore with yer and follers yer right up to the captain, and lie close by when he begins to sort o' keelhaul yer?"

"What good would that do, Tom?"

"Cheer yer up, my lad. I once went ashore with a messmate to help him like when he was going to have a tooth out as had been jigging horrid for two days. He said it did him no end o' good to have me there. So s'pose I come, sir. It strikes me as the captain won't say half so much to yer p'raps with me standing by."

"Oh, no, no, no, Tom," cried Aleck, quickly.

"It's very good of you, and I'm much obliged, but I'd rather go straight in and face my uncle quite alone. I'm sure he'd think I brought you because I was too cowardly to come alone."

"Would he, sir?"

"I feel sure he would, Tom."

"Well, Master Aleck, I dessay you knows best, but come I will if you'd like me to, sir."

"Yes, I know that, Tom," cried the boy, warmly, "but it would be better for me to go in alone."

"Think so, sir?"

"Yes, I'm sure of it."

"Well, p'raps you're right, sir. It seems more brave British seaman to face the enemy straightforward like. Not as I mean, sir, as the captain's a enemy, but on'y just standing for one till the row's over. D'yer see?"

"Yes, I see, Tom, and I've been thinking, too, that it will be enough for me to go in and face uncle at once, and for you not to wait to be paid for this journey."

"Oh, I don't want no paying, my lad, for a little job like this. Think of the times when you've give me pretty nigh all the fish you've caught!"

"But uncle said you were to be paid, Tom."

"Very well, sir. Let him pay me then nex' time he sees me. That'll be all right. You'll be sending a rock through the boat's planks afore long, and I shall have to come over and put a bit o' noo planking in. The captain will pay me then. I say, it's time we put her about. We can make a good bit this reach. Strikes me that the wind's more abeam than when we started."

"Is it?" said Aleck, drearily, and he felt that it would have been far more satisfactory for it to be dead ahead, or to be blowing so fiercely that they would be compelled to put back to Rockabie, and his return home deferred to another day.

As it was, it became more and more favourable, and an easy passage was made round the great promontory, while the current that rushed round the point and raced outward was so calmed down by the tide being just at the turn that the boat glided round and into smooth water, the stack rocks soon after coming into sight, and, with what seemed to the lad like horrible rapidity, they ran in under the rocks and passed the regular rookery of sea-birds, whose cries were deafening when they were close in.

"Say when," cried the sailor, who had given up the tiller to Aleck and stepped forward ready to lower the sail.

"Now!" cried the lad, dismally, a few minutes later; and down came the sail, while in obedience to the rudder the boat glided in between the two walls of perpendicular rock, running in for some little distance before it became necessary for the sailor to help her along by means of the boat-hook and guide her right into her little haven.

Here Tom Bodger was quite at home, and as active as the boat's owner, stumping about inside, and then hopping off one of the thwarts on to the rocks, ready to take mast, yard, oars, and boat-hook up into their places, securing the boat's painter to the big ring-bolt, and then taking one side while Aleck took the other and swinging her right up on to the rocks.

"There we are, then," said the sailor, a few minutes later; "all ship-shape and snug. Shall I put them baits back in the coorge?"

"No, no, Tom," said Aleck, dismally; "empty the bucket into the sea, and give them a chance for their lives."

"Ay, that's right, Master Aleck, for they begin to look as if they'd been too long in the bucket."

This latter was emptied, and then the couple began to ascend the gap towards the opening into the sunk garden. Tom stopped after getting over the stones like the rock-hopper penguin.

"I'll slip off now, Master Aleck, case the captain may be out in the garden," whispered the sailor.

"Yes, you'd better go now, Tom. Do I look so very bad?"

"Tidy, sir, tidy; but don't you mind that. Go right at him, and let him know as soon as you can that you beat. You'll be all right then. Maybe he'll let out at you at first, but all the time he'll be beginning to feel that you leathered a big hulking chap as is the worst warmint in Rockabie, and you'll come out all right. Day, Master Aleck!"

"Good day, Tom, and thank you. I'll remind uncle about your shillings if he forgets."

"He won't forget, sir; the captain's a gen'leman as never forgets nothing o' that sort. Now then, sir, ram your little head down and lay yourself aboard him. Nothing like getting it over. Head first and out of your misery, same as when I learned you to swim."

Tom Bodger shut one eye, gave the lad a frown and a knowing look, and then away he went up a rugged staircase-like pathway to the top of the cliff, looking every moment, while Aleck watched, as if he would slip off, but never slipping once, and finally turning at the top to take off and wave his hat, and then he was gone.

Chapter Five

"Oh, dear!" groaned Aleck. "How am I to face him?" and he went on till only a few steps divided him from the cultivated garden, where he stopped again. "I wonder where he is. In the study, I suppose—write, write, write, at that great history. Can't I leave it and get into my room with a bad headache? It's only true. It aches horribly. I'll send word by Jane that I'm too poorly to come down. Bah!" muttered the boy. "What nonsense; he'd come up to me directly with something for me to take. I wonder whether he is in his room or out in the garden. He mustn't see me till I've been up into my room and done something to my hair. Perhaps he's in the summer-house and I can get in and upstairs without his seeing me. Oh, if I only—"

"Hullo! Aleck, lad, what are you doing there? Why are you so late? Dinner has been ready quite an hour."

The captain had suddenly appeared from behind a great clump of waving tamarisk, and stood looking down at the lad.

"I was coming to see if you were in sight, and—why, what in the name of wonder is the matter with you? Where have you been? Why, by all that's wonderful, you've been fighting!"

"Yes, uncle," said the lad, with a gasp of relief, for it seemed to him as if, instead of taking the bold plunge, swimming fashion, he had been suddenly dragged in.

"I thought so," cried the captain, angrily. "Here—no, stop; come up to the house, to my room. We can't talk here."

"I don't see why not," thought the lad, dismally. "There's plenty of room, and we could get it over more easily, even if he does get into a furious passion with me."

But the captain had wheeled round at once and began to stump back along over the shell and crunching spar-gravel path, his chin pressed down upon his chest, and not uttering a word, only coughing slightly now and then, as if to clear his voice for the fierce tirade of angry words that was to come.

He did not glance round nor speak, but strode on, evidently growing more and more out of temper, the lad thought, for as he walked he kept on kicking the loose shelly covering of the path over the flower beds, while the silence kept up seemed to Aleck ominous in the extreme.

"But, never mind," he thought; "it must soon be over now. What a sight I must look, though! He seemed to be astonished."

Culprit-like, the lad followed close at his uncle's heels till the side entrance was reached, where, with what seemed to be another sign of his angry perturbation, the old officer stopped short, rested one hand upon the door-post to steady himself, and began to very carefully do what was not the slightest degree necessary, to wit: he scraped his shoes most carefully over and over again—for there was not even a scrap of dust to remove.

"Stand back a moment, sir," cried the captain, suddenly. "Jane has heard us, and is carrying in the dinner. Don't let her see you in that state."

Aleck shrank to one side, and then as a door was heard to close started forward again in obedience to his uncle's order.

"Now in, quick—into the study."

He led the way sharply, and Aleck sprang after him, but the ascent of so many steps gave the maid time to re-open the little dining-room door, from which point of vantage she was able to catch a glimpse of the lad's face, which looked so startling that she uttered an involuntary "Oh, my!" before letting her jaw drop and pausing, her mouth wide open and a pair of staring eyes.

"Come in!" roared the captain, angrily, as Aleck paused to turn for a moment at the door; and instead of entering, stood shaking his head deprecatingly at the maid, while his lips moved without a sound escaping them as he tried to telegraph to one who took much interest in his appearance: "Not hurt much. I couldn't help it!"

He started violently then at his uncle's stern command, uttered like an order to a company of men to step into some deadly breach, and the next moment the door was closed and the old man was scowling at him from the chair into which he had thrown himself, sending it back with the legs, giving forth a sound like a harsh snort as they scraped over the bare oaken floor.

Aleck drew a long deep breath and tried to tighten up his nerves, ready for what he felt was going to be a desperate encounter with the fierce-looking old man whom from long experience he knew to be harsh, stern, and troubled with a terrible temper, which made him morose and strange at times, his fits lasting for days, during which periods he would hardly speak a word to his nephew, leaving him to himself save when he came upon him suddenly to see that he was not wasting time, but going on with one or other of the studies which the old man supervised, or working in the garden.

"I want you, though you lead this lonely life with me, Aleck," he would say, frowning heavily the while, "to grow up fairly learned in what is necessary for a young man's education, so that some day, when I am dead and gone out of this weary world, you may take your place as a gentleman— not an ornamental gentleman, whose sole aim is to find out how he can best amuse himself, but a quiet, straightforward, honourable gentleman, one whom, if people do not admire because his ways are not the same as theirs, they will find themselves bound to respect."

These strange fits of what Aleck, perhaps instigated by Jane, their one servant, called "master's temper," would be followed by weeks of mental blue sky, when the black clouds rolled away and the sun of a genial disposition shone out, and the old man seemed as if he could not lavish enough affection upon his nephew. The result of all this was that the boy's feelings towards the old man, who had always occupied the position of father to him as well as preceptor, were a strange mingling of fear of his harshness, veneration of his learning and power of instructing him in everything he learned, and love. For there were times when Aleck would say, gloomily, to himself, "I'm sure uncle thoroughly hates me and wishes me away," while there were times when he was as happy as the days were long, and ready to feel certain that the old man loved him as much as if he were his own child.

"He must," thought the boy, "or he wouldn't have nursed and coddled me up so when I had that fever and the doctor told Jane that he had done all he could, and that I should die—go out with the tide next day. That's what I like in uncle," he mused, "when he isn't out of temper—he's so clever. Knew ever so much better than the doctor. What did he say then? 'Doctors are all very well, Aleck, but there are times when the nurse is the better man—that is, when it's a cock nurse and not a hen. You had a cock nurse, boy, and I pulled you through.'"

But the love was in abeyance on this particular morning at the Den, as the old man had named his out-of-the-way solitary dwelling, and Aleck felt that the place was rightly named as he stood ready to face the savage-looking denizen of the place, who, after staring him down with a pair of fiercely glowing eyes, suddenly opened upon him with:

"Now, then, sir! So you've been fighting?"

"Yes, uncle," said the boy, meekly.

"Who with?"

"Some of the Rockabie boys, uncle."

"Hah! And in the face of all that I have said and taught you about your being different by your birth and education from the young ragamuffin rout of Rockabie harbour! Cannot you run over there in your boat and do what business you have to carry out without being mixed up in some broil?"

"No, uncle."

"Disgraceful, sir! A gentleman's education should teach him that his weapons are words properly applied, and not tooth and nail, blows and kicks."

"I never bit or kicked, uncle," said Aleck, sullenly.

"Of course not, sir; and don't retort upon me in that insolent way. You know perfectly well that I was speaking metaphorically. Did you for a moment imagine I thought you used your teeth and claws like a savage dog?"

"No, uncle."

"Then don't reply to me like that. Of course I would know you would use your fists. Look at your knuckles!" thundered the old man.

Aleck looked at those parts of his person dismally, and they looked bad. For the skin was damaged in three places, and the nail of his left thumb was split in a painful way.

"Disgusting," said the old man. "I trusted you to go over there, and you come back a disreputable wreck. All my teaching seems to be thrown away upon a pugnacious untrustworthy boy."

"I'm not pugnacious, uncle, if they'd let me alone."

"Bah! You ought to be above noticing the scum of the place."

"I am, uncle, and I don't notice them," pleaded the boy; "it's they who will notice me."

"How, pray?"

"I can't go into the place without their mobbing me and calling me names."

"Contemptible! And pray, sir," cried the old man, in harsh, sarcastic tones, "what do they call you?"

"All sorts of things," replied the boy, confusedly. "I can't recollect now. Yes, I know; sometimes they shout 'Fox' or 'Foxy' after me."

"And pray why?"

"Because they say I've just come out of the Den."

"Rubbish."

"At other times it's 'Spider.'"

"Spider?"

"Yes, uncle; because I've got such long legs."

"Worse and worse," cried the old man. "To fight for that! It is childish."

"Oh, I didn't fight for that, uncle!"

"What for, then, pray, sir?"

"Sometimes they lay wait for me and hide behind a smack or the harbour wall, and pelt me with shells and the nasty offal left about by the fishermen."

"Disgusting! The insolent young dogs! They deserve to be flogged. So that is why you fought this morning?"

"Sometimes they throw pebbles and cobble stones, uncle," said the boy, evasively. "And they're so clever with them; they throw so well. I don't like to be hit and hurt, uncle. I suppose I've got a bad temper. I do keep it under so long as they call me names and throw nasty, soft things, but when a stone hits me and hurts, something inside my chest seems to get loose, and I feel hot and burning. I want to hurt whoever threw as much as he hurt me."

"What!" cried the old man. "Haven't I taught you, sir, that you must be above resenting the attacks of the vulgar herd?"

"Yes, uncle."

"Of course. I have always had to bear those assaults, boy. And so the young ruffians threw stones at you?"

Aleck hesitated.

"It was heads and bits of fish to-day, uncle."

"The scum! The insolent scum! And some of the offal hit you?"

"Well, no; nothing hit me, uncle. They followed me about all through the place, and shouted at me every time I came out of a shop."

"Bah! And because some young ragamuffins were insolent to you, my nephew must lower himself to their level. This is not the first time, sir. You have complained to me before, and you remember what I said to you one day when you came back after engaging in a most degrading scuffle."

"Yes, uncle."

"You promised me that should never occur again, after I had pointed out to you what your conduct ought to be, and how that the more you noticed these young rascals' proceedings the worse it would be."

"Yes, uncle, but I couldn't remember it to-day. You can't tell how bad it was, and how hard to bear."

"I? Not tell? Not know?" cried the old man, passionately. "I not know what it is to be the butt of a few boys? You talk in your ignorance, sir, like a fool talketh. Why, for long years past I have been the mark for the contumely and insult of civilised England. Don't make your paltry excuses to me. I say your conduct has been disgraceful. You were trusted to go. I made no objection, sir, save that for your sake and protection you should have an experienced boatman to help manage your boat on the way back, and you come home in this degraded state—hands and face bruised, your lips cut, and your eyes swollen up ready to turn black with horrible bruises. Aleck, it is blackguardly. You make me feel as if I ought to treat you as you deserve—take down that dusty old riding whip and flog you soundly."

Aleck started violently, and his eyes flashed through the narrow slits of lids.

"But I can't treat you, an educated, thoughtful lad, in such a degrading way. The lash is only for those whose nature is low and vile—whose education has never placed them upon a level with such as you. It would be the right punishment for the lads who continually annoy and assault you. But as for you—Aleck, I am hurt and disappointed. To come back like this because a few boys pelted you!"

"No, uncle, it was not because of that," cried the lad, warmly.

"Then, why was it, sir?"

Aleck was silent, and the sailor's advice suddenly came to mind: "Tell him you won and thrashed your man."

But the words would not come, and while he remained silent Captain Donne spoke again, very sternly now:

"Do you hear me, sir?"

"Yes, uncle," said the boy, desperately.

"Then answer my question. You say it was not because you were pelted and called names. Why, then, did you degrade yourself like this and fight?"

"It was because—no, no, uncle," cried the boy, through his teeth, which were compressed tightly as if he was afraid that the simple truth would escape; "I—I can't tell you."

"Then there is something more?"

"Yes, uncle."

"What is it, then?" cried the old man, whose own temper was rapidly getting the mastery. "Speak out, sir, and let me hear whether you have any decent excuse to offer for your conduct. Do you hear?"

"Yes, uncle," faltered the lad.

"Then speak, sir."

"I—I can't, uncle. Don't ask me, please."

"What! I will and do ask you, sir," cried the old man, furiously: "and what is more, I will be told. I am the proper judge of your conduct. How dare you refuse to speak—how dare you tell me almost to my face that you will not answer my question?"

"I don't tell you that, uncle," cried the boy, passionately. "I only say I can't tell you."

"You obstinate young scoundrel! How dare you!" roared the old man, now almost beside himself with rage. "Tell me this instant. Why, then, did you engage in this disgraceful encounter?"

Aleck darted an imploring look at the old man, which seemed to be begging him piteously not to press for the answer, but in his furious outbreak the old man could not read it aright—could only set it down to stubbornness—and, completely overcome by the passion bubbling up to his brain, he started to his feet and pointed to the door, but only to dash his hand down upon the table the next moment.

"No," he cried, "if you forget your duty to me, Aleck, I will not forget mine to you. I'll not be angry, but quite cool. Now, sir," he cried, with his face looking congested and his heavy grey brows drawn down over his glowing eyes, while his voice sounded hoarse and strange. "Aleck, tell me at once. I'll have an answer before you leave this room. Why did you engage in that disgraceful fight?"

"I can't tell you, uncle," said the boy, in a hoarse whisper.

"Ha! That means, sir, that you are obstinately determined not to speak?"

"It isn't obstinacy, uncle."

"Don't contradict me, sir. I say it is obstinacy. Now, once more, for the last time, will you answer my question?"

Aleck drew in a long, low, hissing breath and stood fast for a few moments, before saying, in a low tone, his voice quivering the while:

"I can't tell you, uncle."

There was a dead silence in the room for a few moments then; so dead was the silence, in fact, that if the proverbial pin had dropped it would have sounded loudly on the polished oaken boards.

Then the old man spoke, in a curiously suppressed tone of voice.

"Very well," he said, huskily; "it is what was bound to come sooner or later. I see I have made another of the mistakes which have blasted my existence. I must have time to think out what I shall do. One thing is very evident—you have rebelled against my rule, Aleck, and are struggling to get away to think and act, sir, for yourself. I have done my best for you, but in my isolation I have doubtless been blind and narrow. It is the natural result of our solitary life here—the young spirit seeking to soar."

"Oh, no, uncle—" began the boy.

"Silence, sir!" thundered the old man. "Hear me out. I say it is so, and I know. You resent my holding the tether longer, but you are too young yet to fly unheld. I have my duty to do for your mother's sake and for yours. I must have time to think out my plans, but in the meantime prepare yourself to go to some school or institution for a year or two before entering upon your profession."

"But, uncle!"

"That will do, sir," said the old man, sternly. "You have struck your blow against my authority, and this painful episode in my life must end."

"If you'd only let me speak, uncle!" cried the boy, passionately.

"I begged of you to speak, sir," said the old man, coldly. "I ordered you to speak; but in each case you refused. Well, now then, tell me simply—I ask again on principle—why did you fight those boys?"

Aleck set his teeth and hung his head.

"That will do," said the old man, in deep, husky tones. "Go to your room and get rid of as much of the traces of your encounter as you can before going down to your dinner. You need not interrupt me here again till I send for you. There—go."

The old man once more raised his hand to point towards the door, and, unable to contain himself longer, Aleck rushed out, made for his room, and shut and bolted himself in.

Chapter Six

It was some time before the boy could do anything but sit with elbows upon knees, chin upon hands, gazing straight before him into vacancy. His head throbbed so that he could not think consistently. In his struggle on the pier he had been a good deal shaken, and that alone was enough to produce a feverish kind of excitement. Then on the way back his brain had been much troubled, while, worst of all, there had been the scene with his uncle.

It was then no wonder that he could not arrange his thoughts so as to sit in judgment upon his acts, especially that last one, in which he had stubbornly, as it seemed, refused or declined to respond to his uncle's question.

He tried, and tried hard, with a curious seething desire working in his brain, to decide upon going straight to the old man and speaking out, giving him frankly his reason for refusing to speak. But this always came to the same conclusion: "I can't—I dare not—I can't."

At last, wearied out and confused more and more by his throbbing brain, the boy rose and walked slowly to the looking-glass, where he started in dismay at the image reflected there. For a few moments it seemed to be part and parcel of some confused dream, but its truth gradually forced itself upon him, and finally he burst out into a mocking, half hysterical laugh.

"I don't wonder at uncle," he cried; "I don't wonder at his being in a rage."

With a weary sigh he went to the washstand and half filled the basin.

"I'd no idea I looked such a sight," he muttered, as he began to bathe his stiff and swollen features. "The brute!" he said, after a few moments. "I wish I'd told uncle, though, that I beat him well. But, oh, dear! what a muddle it all seems! I wish I'd hit him twice as hard," he said, with angry vehemence, half aloud. "Yes?"

For there was a gentle tapping at the door.

"Aren't you coming down to dinner, Master Aleck?"

"No, Jane; not to-day."

"But it's all over-done, my dear—been ready more than an hour. Do, do come, or it'll be spoiled."

"Go and tell uncle then. I'm not coming down."

"But I have been, my dear, and he said I was to come and tell you. He isn't coming down. Do make haste and finish and come down."

"No, not to-day, Jane. I can't come."

"But what is the matter, dear? Is master in a temper because you fell off the cliff and cut your face?"

"I didn't fall off the cliff and cut my face," said Aleck.

"Then, whatever is the matter, my dear?"

"Well, if you must know, Jane, I've been fighting—like a blackguard, I suppose," cried the boy, pettishly.

"And is that what made master so cross?"

"Yes."

"Did it hurt you very much?" came through the door crack in a whisper.

"Yes—no," replied Aleck.

"I don't know what you mean, my dear," sighed Jane.

"Never mind. Go away, please, now. I'm bathing my face."

"But my dinner's all being spoiled, my dear. You won't come, and master won't come. What am I to do?"

"Go and sit down and eat it," cried Aleck, in a passion now; "only don't bother me."

"Well, I'm sure!" cried the captain's maid, tartly. "Master's temper's bad enough to drive anyone away, and now you're beginning too. I don't know what we're coming to in—" *um—um—murmur—murmur—murmur—bang!*

At least that is how it sounded to Aleck as he went on with his bathing, the sharp closing of the passage door bringing all to an end and leaving the boy to continue the bathing and drying of his injuries by degrees, after which he sat down by the open window, to rest his aching head upon his hand and let the soft sea air play upon his temples.

He was very miserable, and in a good deal of bodily pain, but the trouble seemed to be the worse part, and it was just occurring to him that he felt very sick and faint and that a draught of water would do him good, when there was a sharp tap at the door after the handle had been tried.

"Uncle!" thought the lad, and the blood flushed painfully to his face.

Then the tap was repeated.

"Master Aleck, Master Aleck!"

"Yes."

"I've brought you up some dinner on a tray."

"I don't want any—I couldn't eat it," said the boy, bitterly.

"Don't tell me, my dear. You do want something—you must; and you can eat it if you try. Now, do come and open the door, please, or you'll be ill."

Aleck rose with a sigh and crossed the room, and the maid came in with a covered plate of something hot which emitted an appetising odour.

"It's very good of you, Jane," began Aleck; "but—"

"My! You are a sight, Master Aleck! Whatever have you been a-doing to yourself?"

"Fighting, I tell you," said the boy, smiling in the middle-aged maid's homely face.

"Who with, my dear?"

"Oh, some of the fishermen's boys over at the town."

"Then it didn't ought to be allowed. You *are* in a state!"

"Yes; I know without your telling me. What's under that cover?"

"Roast chicken and bacon, my dear."

"Oh, I couldn't touch it, Jane!"

"Now, don't say that, my dear. People must eat and drink even if they are in trouble; because if they don't they're ill. I know what I've brought you isn't as nice as it should be, because it's all dried up, and now it's half cold. So be a good boy, same as you used to be years ago when I first knew you. There was no quarrelling with your bread and butter then, and you were always hungry. But, there, I must go. I wouldn't have master catch me here now for all the millions in the Bank of England. Oh, what a temper he is in, to be sure!"

"Have—have you seen him lately?" asked Aleck, excitedly.

"Seen him? No, my dear. He's shut himself up, like he does sometimes; but I could hear him in the kitchen, walking all over my head, just like a wild beast in a cage, and now and then he began talking to himself quite out loud. It's all your fault, Master Aleck, for he was as good-tempered as could be this morning when I went in to ask him what I was to get ready for dinner, and what time."

Jane closed the door after her with these words and left Aleck with the tray.

"Yes," he said, bitterly, in his pain; "it's all my fault, I suppose, and I'm to go away from everything I like here."

He raised the cover over the plate as he spoke, and a pleasant, appetising odour greeted his nostrils; but he lowered the cover again with a gesture of disgust.

"I couldn't touch it," he said, with a shudder, "even to do me good. Nothing would do me good now. My face feels so stiff, and my eyes are just as if they'd got something dark over them."

He went near the window again to look out in the direction of the sea, with some idea of watching the birds, of which so many floated up into sight above the cliffs that shut in the Den. But it was an effort to look skyward, and he sat down by the window to think, in a dull, heavy, dreamy way, about his uncle's words.

And it seemed to him, knowing how stern and uncompromising the old man was, that it would be a word and a blow. For aught he knew to the contrary letters might have been written by then, making arrangements for him to go to some institution where he would be trained to enter into some pursuit that he might detest. Time back there had been talk about his future, the old man having pleasantly asked him what he would like to be. He had replied. "An officer in the Army," and then stood startled by the change which came over the old man's face.

"No," he had said, scowling, "I could never consent to that, Aleck. I might agree to your going into the Navy, but as a soldier, emphatically no."

"Why doesn't he want me to be a soldier?" mused the boy. "He was a soldier himself. I should like to know the whole truth. It can't be what he said."

Aleck sat wrinkling up his brow and thinking for some little time. Not for long; it made his head ache too much, and he changed from soldiering to sailoring.

"I don't see why I shouldn't," he said, half drowsily, for a strange sensation of weariness came over him. "I should like to be a sailor. Why not go? Tom Bodger would help me to get a ship; and as uncle is going to send me away, talking as if he had quite done with me, I don't see why I shouldn't go."

The drowsy feeling increased, so that the boy to keep it off began to look over his clothes, thinking deeply the while, but in a way that was rather unnatural, for his hurts had not been without the effect of making him a little feverish. And as he thought he began to mutter about what had taken place that afternoon.

"Uncle can't like me," he said. "He has been kind, but he never talked to me like this before. He wants to get rid of me, to send me away somewhere to some place where I shouldn't like to go. I've no father, no mother, to mind my going, so why shouldn't I? He'll be glad I'm gone, or he wouldn't have talked to me like that."

Aleck rested his throbbing head upon his crossed arms and sank into a feverish kind of sleep, during which, in a short half-hour, he went through what seemed like an age of trouble, before he started up, and in an excited, spasmodic way, hardly realising what he was doing in his half-waking, half-sleeping state, but under the influence of his troubled thoughts, he roughly selected a few of his under-things for a change and made them up into a bundle, after which he counted over the money he had left after the morning's disbursement, and told himself it would be enough, and that the sooner he was away from the dear old Den the better.

At last all his preparations were made, even to placing his hat and a favourite old stick given him by his uncle ready upon the chair which held his bundle; and then, with his head throbbing worse than ever, producing a feeling of confusion and unreality that was more than painful, he went once more to the glass to look at his strangely-altered features.

"I can't go like that," he said, shrinking back in horror. But like an answer to his words came from far back in his brain, and as if in a faint whisper: "You must now. You've gone too far. You must go now, unless you're too great a coward."

"Yes," he muttered, confusedly; "I must go now—as soon as it's dark. Not wanted here—Tom Bodger—he'll help me—to a ship."

He had sunk heavily into a chair, right back, with his head nodding forward till his chin rested upon his breast, and the next moment he had sunk into a feverish stupor, in which his head was swimming, and in some unaccountable way he seemed to be once more heavily engaged with Big Jem, whose fists kept up a regular pendulum-like beat upon his head, while in spite of all his efforts he could never get one blow back in return at the malicious, jeering, taunting face, whose lips moved as they kept on saying words which nearly drove him wild with indignation.

And what were the words, repeated quite clearly now?

"Master Aleck, don't be so silly! Wake up, you're pretending to be asleep. Oh, my! what a state your face is in! And your head's as hot as fire."

Chapter Seven

"That you, Jane?"

"Why, of course it is. Were you really asleep?"

"Asleep? No—yes. I don't know, Jane. My head's all gone queer, I think."

"And no wonder, fighting like that, and never touching a bit of the dinner I brought you up. Yes, your head's all in a fever, and your poor swelled-up eyes too. That's better. Now, then, you must take this."

"What is it?" said the lad, drowsily.

"What is it? Why, can't you see?"

"No; my head's all swimming round and round, and my eyes won't open."

"Never mind, poor boy, this'll do you good. I've brought you up a big breakfast-cup of nice, fresh, hot tea, and two rounds of buttered toast. They'll do your head good."

"I say, Jane, where's uncle?"

"In his room. He's had some too. I didn't wait to be asked, but took the tea in."

"What was he doing?" said Aleck.

"Writing."

"His book?"

"No, letters; and as busy as could be. Come, try and drink your tea."

"But isn't it very early for tea—directly after dinner like this?"

"Directly after dinner? Why, bless the boy, it's past seven!"

"Then I must have been asleep," said the boy, speaking more collectedly now.

"I should just think you must, and the best thing for you. Hark! There's master's study bell; he wants more tea. I must go; but promise me you'll take yours?"

"Yes, I'm dreadfully thirsty," said the lad, and as the woman left the room he began to sip the tea and eat pieces of the toast till all was gone, and then, after a weary sigh, he glanced at his bundle and hat upon the chair, reeled towards the bed, held on by the painted post, while he thrust off his boots and then literally rolled upon it, with his face looking scarlet upon the white pillow. The next moment he was breathing heavily in deep, dreamless sleep.

That dreamless sleep lasted till the old eight-day clock on the landing had struck eleven, during which time Jane, who was growing anxious about him, came in three times—the first to take away the tea and dinner things, the other twice to make sure that he was not going into a high fever, as she termed it, and feeling better satisfied each time.

"Nothing like so hot," she said to herself. "It was that cup o' tea that did him good. There's nothing like a hot cup o' tea and a good sleep for a bad headache."

So Jane left and went to bed after a final peep, and, as before said, the sound sleep went on till the clock began to strike, and then he began to dream that his uncle came into the room with a chamber candlestick in his hand, set it down where its light shone full upon his stern, severe old features, and seated himself upon the chair by the bed's head.

Then he began to question him; and it seemed to the boy that in his dream he answered without moving his head or opening his eyes, which appeared strange, for he fancied he could see the old man's angry face all the time.

"Not undressed, Aleck?" said the old man.

"No, uncle."

"Shoes here ready—hat, bundle, and stick on the chair! Does that mean waiting till all is quiet, and then running away from home?"

"Yes, uncle."

"Hah! From one who took you to his heart when you were a little orphan child, just when your widowed mother had closed her eyes for ever on this weary world, and swore to treat you as if you were his own!"

"Yes, uncle."

"And why?"

"Because you are tired of me, uncle, and don't trust me—and are going to send me away."

"Hah! You are not going to try and be taken as a soldier?"

"No, uncle."

"Hah! What then? Going to seek your fortune?"

"No, uncle. I'm going to sea."

Perhaps that *hah*! that ejaculation, was louder than the other words—perhaps Aleck Donne had not been dreaming—perhaps it was all real!

At any rate the sleeper had awakened and with his eyes able to open a little more, and through the two narrow slits he was gazing at the stern, sorrowful face, lit up by one candle, seated there within a yard of the pillow.

"Head better, my lad?"

"Yes, uncle."

"Seems clearer, eh?"

"Yes, uncle."

"Feel feverish?"

"No, uncle, I think not. I'm hardly awake yet."

"I know, my lad. You got a good deal knocked about, then?"

"I don't quite know, uncle. I suppose so. It all seems very dreamy now."

"Consequence of injury to the head. Soldiers are in that condition sometimes after a blow from the butt end of a musket."

"Are they, uncle?" asked Aleck, who was half ready to believe that this was all part of his dream.

The captain nodded, and sat silent for a few moments, before glancing at the bundle, hat, and cane. Then—

"So you've been making up your mind to run away?"

"To go away, uncle; not run."

"Hah! Same thing, my lad."

"No, uncle."

"What! Don't contradict me, sir. Do you want to quarrel again?"

"No, uncle."

"Humph! You prepared those things for running away?"

"I had some such ideas, uncle, when I tied them up," said the lad, firmly; "but I should not have done that."

"Indeed! Then why did you tie them up?"

"To go away, uncle."

"Well, that's what I said, sir."

"That was not quite correct, uncle. If I ran away it would have been without telling you."

"Of course, and that's what you meant to do."

"No, uncle; I feel now that I could not have done that. I should have come to you in the morning to tell you that I felt as if I should be better away, and that I would go to sea at once."

"Humph! And if you went away, sir, what's to become of me?"

"I don't know, uncle, only I feel that you'd be better without such an obstinate, disobedient fellow as I am."

"Oh, you think so, do you? Well, you shouldn't be obstinate then."

"I didn't mean to be, uncle."

"Then, why, in the name of all that's sensible, were you? Why didn't you tell me why you fought and got in such a state?"

"I felt that I couldn't tell you, uncle."

"Why not, sir—why not?"

Aleck was silent once more.

"There you are, you see. As stubborn as a mule."

"No, I'm not, uncle."

"Now, look here, Aleck; I couldn't go to bed without trying to make peace between us. Don't contradict me, sir. I say you are stubborn. There, I'll give you one more chance. Now, then, why did you fight those lads?"

"Don't ask me, uncle, please. I can't tell you."

"But I do ask you, and I will know. Now, sir, why was it? For I'm sure there was some blackguardly reason. Now, then, speak out, or—or—or—I vow I'll never be friends with you again."

"Don't ask me, uncle."

"Once more, I will ask you, sir. Why was it?"

"Because—" began Aleck, and stopped.

"Well, sir—because?" raged out the old man. "Speak, sir. You are my sister's son. I have behaved to you since she died like a father. I am in the place of your father, and I command you to speak."

"Well, uncle, it was because they spoke about you," said the lad, at last, desperately.

"Eh? Ah! Humph!" said the old man, with his florid face growing clay-coloured. "They spoke ill of me, then?"

"Yes, uncle."

"About my past—past life, eh?"

"Yes, uncle."

"Humph! What did they say?"

"Uncle, pray don't ask me," pleaded Aleck.

"Humph! I know. Said I was disgraced and turned out of my regiment, eh? For cowardice?"

"Yes, uncle."

"And you said it wasn't true?"

"Of course, uncle."

"Got yourself knocked into a mummy, then, for defending me?"

"Yes, uncle; but I'm not much hurt."

"Humph!" ejaculated the old man, frowning, and looking at the lad through his half-closed eyes. "Said it was not true, then?"

"Of course, uncle," cried the boy, flushing indignantly.

"Humph! Thankye, my boy; but, you see, it was true."

Aleck's eyes glittered as he stared blankly at the fierce-looking old man. For the declaration sounded horrible. His uncle had been one of the bravest of soldiers in the boy's estimation, and time after time he had sat and gloated over the trophy formed by the old officer's sword and pistols, surmounted by the military cap, hanging in the study. Many a time, too, he had in secret carefully swept away the dust. More than once, too, in his uncle's absence he had taken down and snapped the pistols at some imaginary foe, and felt a thrill of pleasure as the old flints struck off a tiny shower of brilliant stars from the steel pan cover. At other times, too, he had carefully lifted the sword from its hooks and tugged till the bright blade came slowly out of its leathern scabbard, cut and thrust with it to put enemies to flight, and longed to carry it to the tool-shed to treat it to a good whetting with the rubber the gardener used for his scythe, for the rounded edge held out no promise of cutting off a Frenchman's head. And now for the old hero of his belief to tell him calmly and without the slightest hesitation that the charge was true was so staggering, so beyond belief, that the blank look of dismay produced by the assertion gradually gave place to a smile of incredulity, and at last the boy exclaimed:

"Oh, uncle! You are joking!"

The old soldier returned the boy's smile with a cold, stern gaze full of something akin to despair, as he drew a long, deep breath and said, slowly:

"You find it hard to believe, then, Aleck, my boy?"

"Hard to believe, uncle? Of course I do. Nobody could believe such a thing of you."

"You are wrong, my boy," said the old man, with a sigh, "for everyone believed it, and the court-martial sentenced me to be disgraced."

"Uncle! Oh, uncle! But it wasn't—it couldn't be true," cried Aleck, wildly, as he sat up in bed.

"The world said it was true, my boy," replied the old man, whose voice sounded very low and sad.

"But you, uncle—you denied the charge?"

"Of course, my boy."

"Then the people on the court-martial must have been mad," cried the boy, proudly. "I thought the word of an officer and a gentleman was quite sufficient to set aside such a charge."

"Then you don't believe it was true, my lad?"

"I?" cried the boy, proudly; "what nonsense, uncle! Of course not."

"But, knowing now what I have told you, suppose you should hear this charge made against me again, what would you do?"

Aleck's eyes flashed, and, regardless of the pain it gave him, he clenched his injured fists, set his teeth hard, and said, hoarsely:

"The same as I did to-day, uncle. Nobody shall tell such lies about you while I am there."

Captain Lawrence caught his young champion to his breast and held him tightly for a few moments, before, in a husky, quivering voice, he said:

"Yes, Aleck, boy, for they are lies. But the mud thrown at me stuck in spite of all my efforts to wash it away, and the stains remained."

"But, uncle—"

"Don't talk about it, boy," cried the old man, hoarsely. "You are bringing up the past, Aleck, with all its maddening horrors. I can't talk to you and explain. It was at the end of a disastrous day. Our badly led men were put to flight through the mismanagement of our chief—one high in position—and someone had to suffer for his sins, there had to be a scapegoat, and I was the unhappy wretch upon whom the commander-in-chief's sins were piled up. They said that the beating back of my company caused the panic which led to the headlong flight of our little army. Yes, Aleck, they piled up his sins upon my unlucky shoulders, and I was driven out into the wilderness—hounded out of society, a dishonoured, disgraced coward. Aleck, boy," he continued, with his voice growing appealing and piteous, "I was engaged to be married to the young and beautiful girl I loved as soon as the war was over, and I was looking forward to happiness on my return. But for me happiness was dead."

"Oh! but, uncle," cried the boy, excitedly, catching at the old man's arm, "the lady—surely she did not believe it of you?"

"I never saw her again, Aleck," said the old man, slowly. "Six months after my sentence the papers announced her approaching marriage."

"Oh!" cried the lad, indignantly.

"Wait, my boy. No; she never believed it of me. She was forced by her relatives to accept this man. I have her dear letter—yellow and time-stained now—written a week before the appointed wedding-day which never dawned for her, my boy. She died two days before, full of faith in my honour."

Aleck's hands were both resting now upon his uncle's arm, and his eyes looked dim and misty.

"There, my boy, I said I could not explain to you, and I have uncovered the old wound, laying it quite bare. Now you know what it is that has made me the old cankered, harsh, misanthropic being you know—bitter, soured, evil-tempered, and so harsh; so wanting in love for my kind that even you, my boy, my poor dead sister's child, can't bear to live with me any longer."

"Uncle!" panted Aleck. "I didn't know—"

"Let's see," continued the old man, with a resumption of his former fierce manner; "you said you would not run away, only go. To sea, eh?"

"Uncle," cried Aleck, "didn't you hear what I said?"

"Yes, quite plainly," replied the old man, bitterly; "I heard. I don't wonder at a lad of spirit resenting my harsh, saturnine ways. What a life for a lad like you! Well, you've made up your mind, and I'll be just to you, my lad. You shall be started well. When would you like to go?"

"When you drive me away, uncle," cried the boy, passionately. "Oh, uncle, won't you listen to me—won't you believe in me? How can you think me such a coward as to leave you, knowing what I do?"

The old man caught him by the shoulders, held him back at arm's length, and stood gazing fiercely in his eyes for a few moments, and then his own began to soften, and he said, gently:

"Aleck, when I was your age my sister and I were constant companions. You have her voice, boy, and there is a ring in it so like—oh, so like hers! Yes, I heard, and I believe in you. I believe, too, that you will respect my prayers to you that all I have said this night shall be held sacred. I do not wish the world to know our secrets. But, there, there," he said, in a totally changed voice, "what a day this has been for us both! You have suffered cruelly, my boy, for my sake, and I in my blindness and bitterness treated you ill."

"Oh, uncle, pray, pray say no more!" cried the boy, piteously.

"I must—just this, Aleck: I have suffered too, my boy. Another black shadow had come across my darkened life, and in my ignorance I turned against you as I did. Aleck, boy, your uncle asks your forgiveness, and—now no more, my boy; it is nearly midnight, and we must try and rest. Can you go to sleep again?"

"Yes, uncle," cried the boy, eagerly, "I feel as if it will be easy now. Good-night, uncle."

"Good-night, my boy," whispered the old man, huskily, and he hurried out, whispering words of thankfulness to himself; but they were words the nephew did not hear.

As the door closed Aleck sprang off the bed on to his feet, his knuckles smarting as he struck an attitude and tightly clenched his fists, seeing in imagination Big Jem the slanderer standing before him once again.

"You cowardly brute!" he muttered; and then his aspect changed in the dim light shed by the candle, for there was a look of joyous pride in his countenance, disfigured though it was, as he said, hurriedly: "I didn't half tell uncle that I thoroughly whipped him, after all. But old Tom Bodger— he'll be as pleased as Punch."

It was rather a distorted smile on Aleck's lips, as, after undressing, he fell fast asleep, but it was a very happy one all the same, and so thought Captain Lawrence as he stole into the room in the grey dawn to see if his nephew was sleeping free from fever and pain, and then stole out again without making a sound.

Chapter Eight

The breakfast the next morning was rather late, consequent upon Captain Lawrence and his nephew dropping off each into a deep sleep just when it was about time to rise; but it was a very pleasant meal when they did meet, for the removal of a great weight from Aleck's mind allowed some other part of his economy to rise rampant with hints that it had missed the previous day's dinner. There was a pleasant odour, too, pervading the house, suggesting that Jane had been baking bread cakes and then frying fish.

Aleck noticed both scents when he threw open his window to let the perfume of the roses come in from the garden; but the kitchen windows and door were open, and the odour of the roses was regularly ousted by that of the food.

"My word! It does smell good," said the boy to himself, and his lips parted to be smacked, but gave vent to the interjection "O!" instead, for the movement of the articulations just in front of his ears caused a sharp pain.

"That's nice!" muttered Aleck. "How's a fellow to eat with his jaw all stiff like that?"

This reminder of the previous day's encounter brought with it other memories, which took the lad to the looking-glass, and the reflection he saw there made him grin at himself, and then wince again.

"Oh, my!" he said, softly. "How it hurts! My face feels stiff all over. I do look a sight. Can't go down to breakfast like this, I know; I'll stop here, and Jane will bring me some up. One can't stir out like this."

Grasping the fact that it was late, the boy dressed hurriedly, casting glances from time to time at the birds which sailed over from the sea, and at old Dunning, the gardener, who was busy digging a deep trench for celery, and treating the soft earth when he drove in the spade in so slow and tender a way that it seemed as if he was afraid of hurting it.

Aleck noted this, and grinned and hurt himself again.

"Poor old 'Nesimus," he said, feeling wonderfully light-hearted; "he always works as if he thought it must be cruel to kill weeds."

The boy had a good final look at the old man, who wore more the aspect of a rough fisherman than a gardener. In fact he had pursued the former avocation entirely in the past, in company with the speculative growing of fruit and vegetables in his garden patch—not to sell to his neighbours, the fishing folk of the tiny hamlet of Eilygugg, but to "swap" them, as he termed it, for fish. Then the time came when the Den gardener happened to be enjoying himself at Rockabie with a dozen more men, smoking, discussing shoals of fish, the durability of nets, and the like, when they suddenly discovered the fact that a party of men had landed on the shore from His Majesty's ship Conqueror, stolen up to the town in the darkness, and, after surrounding the little inn with a network of men, drawn the said net closer and closer, and ended by trammelling the whole set of guests and carrying them off as pressed men to the big frigate.

That was during the last war, and not a man came back to take up his regular avocation. Consequently there was a vacancy for a gardener at the Den, and it was afterwards filled up by Fisherman Onesimus Dunning, the wrinkled-faced man handling the spade and dealing so tenderly with his Mother Earth when Aleck looked out of the window.

"I wonder old Jane hasn't been up to see how I am," said Aleck, as he handled his comb as gingerly as the gardener did his spade.

"I wonder how Master Aleck is," said Jane, just about the same time. "But I won't disturb him. Nothing like a good long sleep for hurts."

"I know," said Aleck to himself; "I can't call down the stairs, because uncle would hear. I daresay he's asleep. I'll tell old Ness to go round to the kitchen door and say she is to come up. No, I won't; he'd come close up and see my face, and it would make her cross now she's busy frying fish. How good it smells! I *am* hungry! Wish she'd bring some up at once. How *am* I to let her know?"

He had hardly thought this before he started, for there was a sharp rap at the door, the handle rattled, and the old captain came in.

"Getting up, Aleck, boy?" he said. "Ah, that's right—dressed. Come along down. You must be hungry."

"I am, uncle," replied the boy, returning his uncle's warm and impressive grasp; "but I can't come down like this," and the boy made a deprecating gesture towards his battered face.

"Well, you don't look your best, Aleck, lad," said the old man, smiling; "but you are no invalid. Never mind your looks; you'll soon come right."

Nothing loth, the boy followed his uncle downstairs, Jane hurriedly appearing in the little breakfast-room with a hot dish and plates on hearing the steps, and smiling with satisfaction on seeing Aleck.

"Ah, that's right, Jane!" said the captain, cheerfully, making the maid beam again on seeing "master" in such an amiable frame of mind.

"Fried fish?"

"Yes, sir; brill."

"Some of your catching, Aleck?"

"No, sir," put in the maid, eagerly; "that Tom Bodger was over here with it as soon as it was light. He knocked and woke me up. Said Master Aleck forgot it yes'day."

"No wonder," said the captain, smiling at his nephew; "enough to knock anything out of your head, eh, Aleck?"

"Yes, uncle; one of the fishermen said I was to bring it home."

"That's right. Shows you have friends as well as foes in Rockabie."

The breakfast went on, and after the first mouthfuls the boy's jaws worked more easily, and he was enjoying his meal thoroughly, when his uncle suddenly exclaimed:

"What are you going to do to-day, my boy?"

"Go on with those problems, uncle, unless you want me to do anything else."

"I do," said the old man, smiling. "I want you to leave your books to-day—for a few days, I should say, till your face comes round again—I mean less round, boy," he added, laughing. "Have a rest. Go and ramble along the cliffs. Take the little glass and watch the birds till evening, and then you can fish."

Aleck jumped at the proposal, for the thought of books and writing had brought on suggestions of headache and weariness; and soon after breakfast he went up to his uncle's study, to find him sitting looking very thoughtful, and ready to start at the boy's entry.

"I've come for the spy-glass, uncle," said Aleck.

"To be sure, yes. I forgot," said the old man, hastily. "Take it down, my boy; and mind what you're about—recollect you are half blind. Let's have no walking over the cliff or into one of the gullies."

"I'll take care, uncle," said the boy, smiling. "I'll be back to dinner at two."

The captain nodded, and Aleck was moving towards the door, when the old man rose hastily, overtook him, and grasped his hand for a moment or two.

"Just to show you that I have not forgotten yesterday, Aleck, my boy," he said, gravely, and then he turned away.

"Who could forget yesterday?" thought the boy, as he slipped out by the side door and took the path leading round by the far edge of the cliff wall, the part which was left wild, that is, to its natural growth.

For Aleck's intent was to avoid being observed by the old gardener, whom he had last seen at work over the celery trench upon the other side of the house.

"He'd only begin asking questions about my face, and grinning at me like one of the great stupid fisher boys," said Aleck to himself, as he passed the sling strap of the spy-glass over his shoulder and hurried in and out among the bosky shrubs close under the great cliff wall, till, passing suddenly round a great feathery tuft of tamarisk, he came suddenly upon the very man he was trying to avoid, standing in a very peculiar position, his back bowed inward, head thrown backward, and a square black bottle held upside down, the neck to his lips and the bottom pointing to the sky.

Aleck stopped short, vexed and wondering, while the old gardener jerked himself upright, spilling some of the liquid over his chin and neck, and making a movement as if to hide the bottle, but, seeing how impossible it was, standing fast, with an imbecile grin on his countenance.

"Morning, Master Aleck," he said. "Strange hot morning. Been diggin'; and it makes me that thusty I'm obliged to keep a bottle o' water here in the shady part o' the rocks."

"Oh, are you?" said Aleck, quietly, and he could not forbear giving a sniff.

"Ah! nice, arn't it, sir? Flowers do smell out here on a morning like this, what with the roses and the errubs and wile thyme and things. It do make the bees busy. But what yer been eating on, sir? Or have yer slipped down among the nattles? Your face is swelled-up a sight. Here, I know—you've been bathing!"

"Not this morning, Ness; I did yesterday."

"That's it, then, my lad, and you should mind. I know you've had one o' they jelly-fish float up agen yer face, and they sting dreadful sometimes."

"Yes, I know," said Aleck, beginning to move onward past the man; "but it wasn't a jelly-fish that stung my face."

"Wasn't it now? Yer don't mean it was a bee or wops?"

"No, Ness; it was a blackguard's fist."

"Why, yer don't mean to say yer been fighting, do 'ee?"

"Yes, I do, Ness. Going to finish the celery trench?"

"Yes, sir; but the ground's mighty hard. Hot wuck, that it is. But where be going wi' the spy-glass?"

"Over yonder along the cliffs to look at the Eilyguggs."

"Eh?" cried the man, sharply. "'Long yonder, past the houses?"

"Yes."

"Nay, nay, nay, I wouldn't go that away. Go east'ard. It's a deal better and nicer that way, and there's more buds."

"I'll go that way another time," said the boy, surlily, and he hurried on. "A nasty old cheat," he muttered; "does he take me for a child? Water, indeed! Strong water, then. I shouldn't a bit wonder if it was smuggled gin. But, there, I won't tell tales."

"Ahoy there!" shouted the gardener. "Master Aleck, there's a sight more eggs yon other way."

"Yes, I know," cried the boy. "Another time." Then to himself, "Bother his officiousness! Wants to be very civil so that I shan't notice about his being there with that bottle."

The man shouted something back, and upon Aleck looking round he saw to his surprise that he was being followed, the gardener shuffling after him at a pretty good rate.

"Now, why does he want me to go the other way?" thought the boy. "I didn't mind which cliff I went along, but I do now. I'm not going to be dictated to by him. I know, he wants to come with me, just by way of an excuse to leave off digging for an hour or two and chatter and babble and keep on saying things I don't want to hear, as well as question me about yesterday's fight; and I'm not going to give him the chance."

Aleck smiled to himself, and winced again, for the swollen face was stiff and the nerves and muscles about his eyes in no condition for smiles. Then, keeping on for a few yards till he was hidden from his follower by the thick shrubs, he stooped down, ran off to his right, and reached the path on the other side of the depression, well out of the gardener's sight; and reaching a suitable spot he dropped down upon his knees, having the satisfaction of watching the man hurrying along till he came to where the depression narrowed and the pathway along the chasm began.

From here there was a good view downward, and the man stopped short, sheltered his eyes with his right hand to scan the narrow shelf-like declivity for quite a minute, before he took off his hat and began scratching his head, while he looked round and behind before having another scratch and appearing thoroughly puzzled.

"Wondering how I managed to drop out of sight," laughed Aleck to himself.

He was quite right, for he saw Dunning turn to right and left, after looking forward, ending by staring straight up in the air, and then backward, before giving his leg a sounding rap, and taking off his hat to wipe the perspiration from his forehead.

"He doesn't get so hot as that over his work," said Aleck to himself, as he crouched lower, laughing heartily; and he had another good laugh when, after one more careful look, the old gardener shook his head disconsolately and turned to walk back.

"Given it up as a bad job," he said, merrily. "An old stupid! I could have found him. Well, I can go now in peace."

He waited till the coast was clear, and then, stooping low, set off at a trot, getting well down into the gorge-like rift. Striking off gradually to his right, he attacked the great cliff wall in a perfectly familiar fashion, and climbed from ledge to ledge till he reached the top, glanced back to see that the gardener was not in sight, and then strode away over the short, velvety, slippery turf, with the edge of the cliff some fifty yards or so to his left, and the rough, rocky slope that led up to the scattered cottages of the Eilygugg fishermen to his right.

He soon reached a somewhat similar chasm to that which ended in his own boat harbour; but this was far wider, and upon reaching its edge he could look right down it to the sea, where at its mouth a couple of luggers and about half a dozen rowboats of various sizes were moored.

The cottages lay round and about the head of the creek, and partly natural, partly cut and blasted out of the cliff side, ledge after ledge had been formed, giving an easy way down from the cottages to the boats. But there was not a soul in sight, and nothing to indicate that there were people occupying the whitewashed cots, save some patches of white newly-washed clothes which were kept from being blown away by the playful wind by means of big cobble stones—smooth boulders—three or four of which were laid upon the corners of the washing.

There was not even one fisherman hanging about the front of the cottages, where all looked quiet and sleepy in the extreme, so, passing on,

Aleck hurried round the head of the narrow rugged harbour, and was soon after making his way along the piled-up cliffs, keeping well inland so as to avoid the great gashes or splits which ran up into the land and had to be circumvented, where they ended as suddenly as they appeared, in every case being perfectly perpendicular, with the water running right up, looking in some cases black, still, deep and clear, in others floored with foam as the waves rushed in over the black, jagged masses of rock that had in stormy times been torn from the sides.

To a stranger nothing could have appeared more terrible than these zigzag jagged gashes or splits in the stern, rocky coast, for they were turfed to the sharp edge, where an unwary step would have resulted in the visitor plunging downward, to drown in the deep, black water, or be mutilated by the rocks amidst which the waters foamed.

But "familiarity breeds contempt," says one proverb, "use is second nature" another, and there was nothing that appeared terrible to the boy, who walked quickly along close to the edge, glancing perhaps at its fellow, in some cases only a few yards away, and looking so exactly the counterpart of that on the near side that it seemed as if only another convulsion of nature was needed to compress and join the crack again so that it would be possible to walk where death was now lurking.

But there was nothing horrible there to Aleck who in every case turned inland to skirt the chasm, gazing down with interest the while at the nesting-places of the sea-birds which covered nearly every ledge, each one being alive with screaming, clamouring, hungry young, straining their necks to meet the swift-winged auks and puffins that darted to and fro with newly-captured fish in their bills.

Aleck had left the whitewashed cottages behind, along with the last traces of busy human life in the shape of boat, rope, spar, lobster-pot, and net, to reach one of the most rugged and inaccessible parts of the rocky cliffs—a spot all jagged, piled-up rift with the corresponding hollows—and at last selected a place which looked like the beginning of one of the chasms where Nature had commenced a huge gaping crack a good hundred feet in depth, though its darkened wedge-shaped bottom was still quite a hundred feet above where the waves swayed in and out at the bottom, of the cliff. The sides here were not perpendicular, but with just sufficient slope to allow an experienced, cool-headed cliff-climber to descend from ledge to ledge and rock to rock till a nook could be reached, where, securely perched, one who loved cliff-scanning and the beauties of the ever-changing sea and shore, could sit and enjoy the wild wonders of the place.

The spot was exactly suited to Aleck's taste; and as old practice and acquaintance with the coast had made giddiness a trouble he never felt, he was not long in lowering himself down to this coign of vantage. Here he perched himself with a sigh of satisfaction, and watched for a time the great white-breasted gulls which floated down to gaze with curious watchful eyes at the intruder upon their wild domain. The puffins kept darting down from the ledges, with beaks pointed, web feet stretched out behind, and short wings fluttering so rapidly that they were almost invisible, while the singular birds looked like so many animated triangles darting down diagonally to the sea, and gliding over it for some distance before touching the water, into which they plunged like arrow-heads, to disappear and continue their flight under water till they emerged far away with some silvery fish in their beaks.

Some little distance below a few sooty-looking cormorants had taken possession of an out-standing rock upon which the sun beat warmly, and here, their morning fishing over, leaving them absolutely gorged, they sat with wings half open and feathers erect, drying themselves, looking the very images of gluttonous content.

Birds were everywhere—black, black and white, black and grey, and grey and white, with here and there a few that looked black in the distance, but when inspected through the glass proved to be of a deep bronzy metallic green.

But while the air and rocks were alive with objects that delighted the watcher's eye, there was plenty to see beside. Close in where the deep water was nearly still, the jelly-fish floated at every depth, shrinking and expanding like so many opening and shutting bubbles of soap and water, glistening with iridescent hues. Farther out the smooth, vividly-blue water every now and then turned in patches from sapphire to purple, and a patch—a whole acre perhaps in extent—became of the darkest purple or amethyst, all of a fret and work, while silvery flashes played all over it, reflecting the rays of the burning sun. For plenty of shoals of fish were feeding, over which the birds were rising, falling, darting and splashing, as they banqueted upon their silvery prey.

All this was so familiar to Aleck that, though still enjoying it, he satisfied himself with a few glances before, carefully focussing the glass he had brought, he began to sweep the coast wherever he could command it from where he sat.

The opposite side of the rift seemed to take his attention most, and perhaps he was examining some of the deep cavernous hollows seen here and there high up or low down towards the sea; or maybe his attention was riveted upon some quaint puffin, crouching, solemn and big-beaked, watching patiently for the next visit of main or dad; or, again, maybe the lad was looking at a solitary greatly-blotched egg, big at one end, going off to almost nothing at the other, and wanting in the soft curves of ordinary eggs, while he wondered how it was that such an egg should not blow out of its rocky hollow when the wind came, but spin round as upon a pivot instead.

Anyhow, Aleck was watching the other side of the half-made chasm, the great wedge-shaped depression in the coast-line, looking straight across at a spot about a hundred yards distant in the level, though higher up it was too, and going off to nothing at the bottom, where the place looked like the dried-up bed of a river.

All at once he started and nearly dropped the glass, as he wrenched himself right round to gaze back and up, for a gruff voice had suddenly cried:

"Hullo!"

The next moment the boy, was gazing in a fierce pair of very dark eyes belonging to a swarthy, scowling, sea-tanned face, the lower part of which was clothed in a crisp black beard, as black as the short head of hair.

This head of hair of course belonged to a man, but no man was to be seen, nothing but the big round bullet head peering down from the edge of one of the ledges, while on both sides, apparently not heeding the head in the least, dozens of wild fowl sat solemnly together, looking stupid and waiting for the next coming of parent birds.

"Hullo!" cried the head again.

"Hullo!" retorted Aleck, as gruffly as he could, after recovering from his surprise. "That you, Eben Megg?"

"Oh! ay, it's me right enough, youngster. What are you doing there?"

"Now?" said Aleck, coolly. "Looking up at your black face."

"Black face, eh, youngster? Perhaps other people ha' got black faces too. What ha' you been doing of — tumbling off the rocks? Strikes me you're trying it on for another tumble."

Aleck flushed a little at the allusion to his injured face, feeling guilty too, as it struck him that he had brought the allusion upon himself, a Rowland for his Oliver, on the principle that those who play at bowls must expect rubbers.

"No, I haven't had a tumble, and I'm not going to tumble," he said, testily. "I daresay I can climb as well as you."

"P'raps you can, youngster, and p'raps you can't; but, if you do want to break your neck, stop at home and do it, and don't come here."

"What!" cried Aleck, indignantly. "Why not? I've as good a right here as you have, so none of your insolence."

"Oh, no, you haven't. All along here's our egging-ground, and we don't want our birds disturbed."

"Your egging-ground—your birds!" cried Aleck, indignantly. "Why, I do call that cool. You'll be telling me next that the fish in the sea are yours, and that I mustn't whiff or lay a fish-pot or trammel."

"Ay, unless you want to lose your net or other gear. I hev knowed folk as fished on other people's ground finding a hole knocked in the bottoms of their boats."

"What!" cried Aleck. "That's as good as saying that if I fish along here you'll sink my boat."

"Didn't say I would, but it's like enough as some 'un might shove a boat-hook through or drop in a good big boulder stone."

"Then I tell you what it is, Master Eben Megg. If any damage is done to my Seagull you'll have to answer for it before the magistrate."

"Oh! that's your game, is it, my lad? Now, lookye here, don't you get threatening of me or you'll get the worst on it. We folk at Eilygugg never interferes with you and the captain and never interferes about your ketching a bit o' fish or taking a few eggs so long as you are civil; but you're on'y foreigners and intruders and don't belong to these parts, and we do."

"Well, of all the impudence," cried Aleck, "when my uncle bought the whole of the Den estate right down to the sea! Don't you know that you're intruders and trespassers when you come laying your crab-pots under our cliff and shooting your seine on the sandy patch off the little harbour?"

"No, youngster, I don't; but I do know as you're getting a deal too sarcy, and that I'm going to stop it, and my mates too."

"Get out! Who are you?" cried the boy, indignantly. "What do you mean?"

"I mean that if you want to fish off our shore and wants a man to help with your boat you've got to ask some of us to help, and not get bringing none o' your wooden-legged cripples spying and poking about our ground."

"Spy? What is there to spy?" said Aleck, giving the man a peculiar look.

"Never you mind about that. You be off home, and don't you come spying about here with none of your glasses."

Aleck laughed derisively.

"Ah, you may grin, my lad; but I've been a-watching of yer this morning," said the man, fiercely. "You've been busy with that glass, prying and peering about, and I caught yer at it."

Aleck laughed again.

"Oh! that's what you think, is it?" he said.

"Yes, and it's what I says; so be off home."

"I shall do nothing of the kind, Eben," said the boy, hotly. "I've a better right here than you have, and I shall come whenever I please. Spying, eh?"

"Ay, spying, youngster; and I won't have it."

"Then it's all true, eh?" said the boy, mockingly.

"What's true?" snarled the man.

"You know. What have you got hidden away among the caverns—Hollands gin or French brandy? Perhaps it's silk or velvet. No, no; I know. But you can't think that. How do you manage to land the great casks?"

"I dunno what you're talking about, youngster—do you?"

"Thoroughly. But aren't the tobacco casks too big and too heavy to haul up the cliffs?"

"Look here, young fellow," growled the man; "none o' your nonsense. You'd better be off before you get hurt. That's your way back."

"Is it?" said Aleck. "Then I'm not going back till I choose. I say, should you talk like this to one of the Revenue sloop's men if he came ashore?"

"Oh, we know how to talk to that sort if he comes our way," said the man, with a chuckling laugh; "and they knows it, too, and don't come."

"Nor the press-gang either, eh?" said Aleck, mockingly.

Up to that moment the man's fierce face had alone been seen, but at the word press-gang he gave a violent start and rose to his knees, upon which he hobbled close up to the edge of the shelf upon which he had perched himself.

"Oh, that's it, is it, my lad, eh?" he growled, shaking his fist savagely. "Then, look here. If the press-gang—cuss 'em!—ever does come along here we shall know who put 'em up to it, and if they take any of our chaps—mind yer they won't take all, and them behind'll know what to do. I'm not going to threaten, but if someone wasn't sunk in his boat, or had a bit o' rock come tumbling down on him when he was taking up his net under the cliffs, it would be strange to me. D'yer hear that?"

"Oh, yes, I hear that," retorted Aleck. "So you won't threaten, eh? What do you call that?"

"Never you mind what I call it, youngster; and what I says I means. So now you know."

"Yes," said Aleck, coolly; "now I know that what people say about you and your gang up at Eilygugg is quite true."

"What do people say?" shouted the man. "What people?"

"The Rockabie folk."

"And what do they say?"

"That you're a set of smugglers, and, worse still, wreckers when you get a chance, and don't stop at robbery or murder. One of the fishermen—I won't say his name—said you were a regular gang of pirates."

"The Rockabie fishermen are a set o' soft-headed fools," snarled the man. "But what do I care for all they say? Let 'em prove it; and, look here, if we're as bad as that you folk up at the Den aren't safe."

"Which means that you threaten the captain, my uncle," cried Aleck, defiantly.

"Are you going to tell him what I said?"

"Perhaps I am," said Aleck; "perhaps I'm not. I'm going to do just as I please all along this coast, for it's free to everybody, and my uncle has ten times the rights here that you people at the fishermen's cottages have. You've just been talking insolence to me, so let's have no more of it. This comes of the captain, my uncle, being kind and charitable to you people time after time when someone has been ill."

The man growled out something in a muttering way.

"Ah, you know it, Eben Megg! It's quite true."

"Who said it warn't?" growled the man; "but if he'd done ten times as much I'm not going to have you spying and prying about here. What is it you want to know?"

"That's my business," said Aleck, defiantly. "I say, you haven't made a fortune out of smuggling, have you, and bought the estate?"

"You keep your tongue quiet, will yer?" growled the man, fiercely. "What do you know about smuggling?"

"Just as much as you do, Eben Megg," cried the boy, laughing. "Just as much as everyone else does who lives here. Didn't our old maid come in scared one night after a holiday and walking across from Rockabie and go into a fit because she had seen, as she said, a whole regiment of ghosts walking over the moor, leading ghostly horses, which came out of the sea fog and crossed the road without making a sound? Jane said they were the spirits of the old soldiers who were killed in the big fight and buried by the four stones on Black Hill, and that as soon as they were across the stony road they were all swallowed up in a mist. She keeps to it till now, and believes it."

"Well, why shouldn't she?" growled the man. "She arn't the first as has seen a ghost. Why shouldn't she?"

"Because it's so silly, when it was a party of smugglers leading their horses, with kegs slung across their backs and bales on pack saddles."

"Bah!" cried the man. "Horses loaded like that would clatter over the rough stones."

"Yes," said Aleck, "if their hoofs weren't covered over with bits of canvas and a few handfuls of hay."

"What!"

"I found one that a horse had kicked off on the road one morning, Eben," said the boy. "Ah! I see now."

"See—see what?" said the rough, fisherman-like fellow, sharply.

"See why Ness Dunning was so anxious that I shouldn't come along the cliff this side."

"Ness Dunning?" cried the man, scowling. "What did he say?"

"That I'd better go the other way. Behaved just like a silly plover which wants to prove to you that it has no nest on the moor, and sets you looking for it."

"Ness Dunning's an old fool," cried the man, fiercely.

"Yes, he is a thick-headed old noodle, Eben; I wouldn't trust him."

"Then because he did that he made you think there was something hid somewhere and come to hunt for it, did you?" cried the man, angrily.

"No, I didn't think anything of the kind till just this minute, but I see now. You're not much wiser than old Ness, Eben, for you've been trying to throw me off the scent too, and now I know as well as if I could see it that you people have been running a cargo, and you've got it hidden in one of the caves or sunk in one of the holes."

"What yer talking about?"

"Smuggled goods, Eben. I could find it if I tried now."

The man stepped down from the shelf on which he had been standing, and made a great show of being exceedingly ferocious, evidently thinking that the boy would turn and run away. But Aleck stood fast, not even stirring when the man was close up, planting his doubled fists upon his hips and thrusting out his lower jaw in a peculiarly animal-like way.

"So you're going to look and see if you can find something hidden, and when you've found it you're going to send word to the Revenue cutter men to fetch it, are yer?"

"Who says I am?" said Aleck, sharply.

"Who says it? Why, I do, my lad. So that's what you think you're going to do, is it?"

"No," said the lad, coolly enough. "Why should I? It's no business of mine."

"Ho!" growled the man, frowning, and raising one hand to rub his short, crisp, black beard. "No," he said, after a pause, "it arn't no business of yours, is it?"

"Of course not," said the boy, coolly. "I don't want to know where the run cargo's hidden, and I wasn't looking for it. I only came to watch the birds and get a few eggs if I saw any that I hadn't got."

The man made a sudden quick movement and caught Aleck's right wrist tightly, leaning forward as if to pierce his eyes with the fierce look he gave.

"Don't do that—you hurt!" cried Aleck, sharply.

"Yes, I mean to hurt," growled the man. "Now, then, look at me! Is that true?"

"Do you hear, Eben Megg? You hurt me. Let go, or I shall hit out."

"You'll do what?" cried the big fellow, mockingly, as he tightened his grasp to a painful extent, when *spank*! Aleck's left fist flew out, striking the man full on the right cheek, not a heavy blow, but as hard as the boy could deliver, hampered as he was, being dragged close to his assailant's breast.

"Why, you—" roared the man. He did not say what, but flung the arm he had at liberty round the boy's waist and lifted him, kicking and struggling, from the ground, perfectly helpless, with the great muscular arm acting like a band of iron, to do more than try to deliver some ineffective blows, which his assailant easily avoided.

"Ah! Would you?" he growled, fiercely. "You're a nice young game cock chick, you are. Hold still!" he roared, taking a step forward, to stand on the very edge of the shelf. "Keep that hand quiet, or I'll hurl you down among the rocks. You'll look worse then than you do now."

"Do, if you dare," cried the lad, defiantly.

"You tell me what I asked," growled the man; "is what you said true?"

"I won't tell you while you grip my wrist."

"You'd better speak," cried the man. "D'yer see, you're like a feather to me. I could pitch you right out so as you'd go to the bottom yonder."

"You could, but you daren't?" cried Aleck, grinding his teeth and striving hard to bear the pain he suffered.

"Oh, I dare—I could if I liked! Nobody would see out here. It would kill yer, and nobody would know how it happened; but they'd say when they found you that you'd slipped and fell when you was egging. They would, wouldn't they? That's true, arn't it?"

"I suppose so," said the boy, huskily.

"And that's what I'm going to do for hitting me, unless you tell me whether that was true what you said. Now, then, beg me not to hurl yer down."

"I—shan't," ground out the boy through his set teeth, and a grim smile crossed the man's dark face, making it look for the moment open and manly—a smile caused by something akin to admiration.

"Well, you're a nice-tempered sort of a young fellow," growled the man.

"Let go of my wrist."

"Will yer promise not to hit?"

Aleck nodded.

"Nor yet kick?"

The boy nodded again.

"There," said the man, loosening the prisoned wrist. "Now, tell me, is it true?"

"Of course it is," said the boy, haughtily.

"I'll believe yer," growled the man. "There," he continued, dropping the boy to his feet. "Then you won't look for where the stuff's stowed?"

Aleck burst into a hoarse laugh.

"Then there is some stowed?"

The man gave himself a wrench, and his face puckered up again with anger.

"Lookye here," he said, more quietly, "I don't say there is, and I don't say there arn't; but suppose there is, you're going to swear as you won't take no notice."

"No, I'm not," said Aleck, boldly.

"Then you do want me to chuck you down yonder?"

"You've got to catch me first," cried the boy, making a backward bound which took him ten feet downward before he landed and kept his feet, following up his leap by running along the ledge of stony slate he had reached and then beginning to climb rapidly.

The man had followed him at once, leaping boldly, but without Aleck's success, for he slipped, through the stones giving way, and went down quite five-and-twenty feet in a rough scramble before he checked himself and took up the pursuit, which he soon found would be useless, for his young adversary was lighter and far more active, and soon showed that he was leaving him behind.

"There, hold hard, Master Aleck," he growled, looking up at the lad. "I won't hurt yer now."

"Thankye," said the boy, mockingly, as he stopped, holding on by a projecting rock in the stiff slope, and well on his guard to go on climbing if there was the slightest sign of pursuit.

"You made me wild by hitting out at me."

"Serve you right, you great lumbering coward, to serve me like that!"

"I didn't mean to hurt you."

"Yes, you did—brute! You squeezed my wrist as hard as you could."

"Well, I didn't want to hurt you much. But you did make me wild, you know, hitting me like you did."

"Look here," cried Aleck, fiercely, as the man took a step to continue climbing to where the boy stood, some thirty feet above him, "you come another step, and I'll send this big stone down at you—it is loose."

"I don't want to ketch you now, only to talk quiet without having to shout."

"I can hear you plainly enough. Sit down."

The great muscular fellow dropped at once, seating himself upon the slope and digging his heels into the loose screes to keep from sliding down.

"There y'are," he growled.

"Now, then," said Aleck, "what do you want to say?"

"Only about you coming along here to-day. You warn't trying to spy out nowt, was yer?"

"No," cried Aleck; "of course I wasn't. I've known for long enough that you people at Eilygugg do a lot of smuggling. I've stood with the captain, my uncle, of a night and seen you signal with a lanthorn, and then after a bit seen a light shown out at sea."

"You've seen that, youngster?"

"Lots of times; and the boats going and coming and the lights showing up against the cliff. Of course we know what goes on, but my uncle doesn't care to interfere, and I've never tried to find out where you hide the smuggled goods; but I shouldn't be long finding out if I tried."

"Hum!" growled the man, gazing up searchingly. "P'raps you're right, youngster, p'raps you arn't; but there is a deal o' smuggling goes on along this coast."

"Especially about here," said Aleck, with a smile.

"Well, what's the harm, eh? A man must live, and if one didn't do it another would."

"Look here; I don't want to know or hear anything about it," cried Aleck. "Only I shall come along these cliffs, egging or watching the birds, as often as I like."

"Well, I don't know as anyone'll mind, Master Aleck, if I speaks to 'em and says as you says as a young gentleman that you'll never take no notice of anything as you sees or hears—"

"What! How can a gentleman promise anything of the kind about people breaking the law?"

"How? Why, by just saying as he won't."

"A gentleman can't, I tell you. There, I won't promise anything."

The man gave his rough head a vicious scratch, before saying, sharply:

"Then how's a man to trust yer?"

"I don't know," said Aleck, carelessly, "but I'll tell you this. If I'd wanted to I could have found out whether you've got a place to hide your stuff, as you call it, long enough ago."

"I don't know so much about that," said the man, with a grin.

"Well, then, I could have told the Revenue cutter's men where they had better look."

"But you won't, Master Aleck? We are neighbours, you know."

"Neighbours!" said Aleck, scornfully. "Pretty neighbours! There, I'm not going to alter my words. I shall make no promises at all."

"Well, you are a young gentleman, and I'll trust yer," said the man; "for I s'pose I must. But I don't know what some of our lads'll say."

"Then I'd better tell my uncle that if anything happens to me he'd better get the Revenue cutter's men to hunt out the Eilygugg smugglers, because they pushed me off the cliff."

"Nay, don't you go and do that," said the man, anxiously. "I didn't mean it."

"Am I to believe that, Eben?" said the boy, sharply.

The man showed his teeth in a laugh, and put his hands round his neck in a peculiar way.

"Look here, Master Aleck," he said; "man who goes to sea has to take his chance o' being drownded."

"Of course."

"And one who tries to dodge the Revenue sailors has to take his chance of getting a cut from a bit o' steel or a bullet in him."

"I suppose so."

"That's quite bad enough, arn't it?"

"Yes."

"Bad enough for me, sir, so I'm not going to do what might mean being—you know what I mean?"

"What—"

"Yes, that's it. A bit o' smuggling's not got much harm in it, but they call it murder when a man kills a man."

"By pushing him off a cliff, Eben?" said Aleck. "Yes."

Chapter Nine

It was about a fortnight later when Aleck Donne went down the garden directly after breakfast with the full intent, after thinking it over a good deal, of charging old Onesimus Dunning, the gardener, with being leagued with the Eilygugg smugglers.

"If I told uncle," he argued, "he would be sent away at once; but that would be doing the poor fellow a lot of harm and perhaps make him worse. Perhaps, too, it would make him nurse up a feeling of spite against us, and he would set the Eilygugg people against us as well. So I won't do that, but I'm not going to have the nasty old imposter smiling at me and pretending to be so innocent. I just want him to understand that I'm not such a child as to be ignorant of his tricks. I'll let him see that I know why he wanted me not to go along yonder by the west cliff."

Aleck knew exactly where the man was likely to be, for he had been mowing the lawn, sweeping up the fragment result, and wheeling it away.

"He'll be stacking it round the cucumber frame," thought Aleck, "to keep in the heat. By the way, I wonder what became of the beautiful cuke that lay, at the back under the big leaves—we didn't have it indoors! I'm sure he takes some of them away. Uncle never misses anything out of the garden, but I do."

The lad went round to the kitchen garden, which sloped round towards the south, so beautifully sheltered that it was a perfect hot-bed of itself in the summer, and there, sure enough, was the heaped-up barrow of fresh green mowings, and one armful had been piled up to half hide a part of the rough wooden frame.

But no gardener was visible.

"Not here," thought Aleck. "Well, perhaps I was wrong about that cuke."

The next minute he had raised the clumsily-glazed sliding sash, with a hot puff of moist air smelling delicious as it reached his nostrils, while he propped up the glass, reached in, and began turning over the prickly leaves, laying bare the rather curly little specimens of the cool, pleasant fruit; but there was no sign of the big, well-grown vegetable.

"Was I mistaken?" mused the lad. "No, there was one, and there's the remains of the stalk, showing where the cucumber has been cut. What a shame!" he muttered. "I'll tell him of that too. Uncle would be angry if he knew."

Aleck closed the frame again and began to look round.

"What a shame!" he said, again. "Nice sort of a gardener to have—lazy, a smuggler, and little better than a thief. I'll just give him something to think about when I find him. Oh, there he is!"

For just then the boy looked up, to see the old gardener standing on the highest part of the sheltering cliff, his back to him, and shading his eyes as he looked out to sea.

"Ahoy! What are you doing there?" shouted Aleck.

The man started and looked down.

"Ships—men-o'-war—going behind the point," shouted the gardener.

Men-of-war going into Rockabie harbour! That news was sufficient to upset all Aleck's arrangements. He forgot all about the lesson he was going to give the gardener, and rushed indoors, to hurry upstairs and rap sharply at his uncle's study, and, getting no answer he threw open the door to cross the room and seize the glass from where it hung by its sling. Then, dashing out again, he ran downstairs, crossed the garden, mounted the cliff zigzag path, and was soon after focussing the glass upon the men-of-war, which proved to be only a good-sized sloop followed by a trim-looking white-sailed cutter, both vessels with plenty of canvas spread, and gliding steadily over the smooth sunlit sea.

"Oh, I wish I'd known sooner!" groaned the lad, for he had hardly fixed the leading vessel before her bows began to disappear behind the point, and before ten minutes had elapsed the cutter was out of sight as well.

"I don't know that I should much care about going to sea," muttered Aleck, closing the glass, "but the ships do look so beautiful with their sails set, gliding along. What a pity! What a pity! I do wish I had known sooner."

"What are they going to do there?" thought the boy, as he closed the glass and walked back to the cottage, where upon going upstairs to replace the glass he found his uncle in from his morning walk and about to settle down for a few hours' work.

"Well, Aleck, boy," he said; "been scanning the sea?"

"Yes, uncle; two vessels came along into Rockabie, but I only got a glimpse of them."

"Too late, eh? Well, why not run over in the boat? I want something done in the town."

"Do you, uncle? Oh!" cried the boy, half wild with excitement, as he turned and rushed to the little mirror over the chimney-piece to glance in.

"Yes," said the old man, smiling. "There, nothing shows now except that little darkness under your eyes. I'm quite run out of paper, my boy. Go and get me some. But—er—no fighting this time."

"No, uncle," cried the lad, flushing up; and then, quickly: "There's a beautiful soft breeze, dead on to the land, and it will serve going and coming."

"Off with you, then, while it holds. Paper the same as before. Get back in good time."

Aleck wanted no further incitement. The "wigging," as he termed it, that was to be given to Dunning would keep, and he avoided the man as he hurried down into the gorge, stepped the mast and hooked on the rudder, guided the little vessel along the narrow, zigzag, canal-like harbour, and without an eye this time for the birds or beauty of the scene, he was soon after lying back steering and holding the sheet, while the well-filled sail tugged impatiently as if resenting being restrained.

Aleck had fully determined to avoid the boys of Rockabie that morning, and he was half disposed to hug himself with the idea that after the thrashing Big Jem had received they would interfere with him no more. But he was quite wrong, for the port boys were too full of vitality, and always on the look-out for some means of getting rid of the effervescing mischief that bubbled and foamed within them.

The distant sight of the King's vessels heading for the port was quite enough to attract them to the pier, and there they were in force, well on the look-out for something to annoy so as to give themselves employment till the sloop and cutter came in.

There was the something all ready in the person of Tom Bodger, who was seated upon a ship's fender, one of those Brobdingnagian netted balls covered with a network of tarred rope, used to keep the edge of the stone pier from crushing and splintering the sides of the vessel.

This formed a capital cushion, albeit rather sticky in hot weather, and was planted close up to a stone mooring-post, which acted as a back to lean against, while, with his wooden legs stretched straight out, the man employed himself busily in netting, his fingers going rapidly and the meshes seeming to run off the ends of his fingers.

Intent upon his work, active with hands and arms, but rather helpless as to his legs, Tom Bodger was a splendid butt for the exercise of the boys' pertinacious tactics, and with mischief sparkling out of the young rascals' eyes they made their plans of approach and began to buzz round him like flies, calling names, asking questions, laughing and jeering too, all of which had but little effect upon the man, who was an adept at what he called giving "tongue." And so the boys found, for they decidedly got the worst of it.

Soon after, growing bolder, some of the most daring began to make approaches to snatch at the net or the ball of water-cord, but they gained nothing by that. For Tom Bodger never went out without his stick, a weapon he used for offence as well as defence, and there was not a boy there in Rockabie who did not know how hard he could hit.

A few little experiences of this sort of thing were quite enough to make the party draw off and take to the hurling of missiles. But they did not confine themselves to heads, tails, and bones of fish, for they were rather scarce, so they took to the stones which were swept up in ridges by the sea right across the harbour.

But even this was dangerous, for the sailor could "field" the stones thrown at him and return them with a correctness of aim and activity that would have driven a skilful cricketer half mad with envy.

Finally, several of the bigger lads held a kind of conference, but not unseen, for though apparently bending intently over his netting, the sailor was watching them with one eye and asking himself what game they—to wit, the boys—were going, as he put it, to start next.

Old discipline on a man-of-war had made Bodger thoroughly alert, and suspecting a rush he took hold of his ball of net twine, unrolled sufficient to make many meshes, and then put it down again, seizing the opportunity to draw the stout oaken cudgel he generally carried well within reach of his hand.

Then, netting away as skilfully as a woman, he indulged in a hearty laugh, chuckling to himself as he thought of the accuracy and force with which he could send it skimming over the ground, spinning round the while and looking like a star.

"That'll give one on 'em a sore leg for a week if I do have to throw it. On'y wish I could do it with a string tied to it so as to haul it back. Well, why not?" he added, eagerly, and then under cover of his netting he unwound thirty or forty yards of the twine, cut it off, and tied the end to the middle of his cudgel.

"That'll do it," he muttered, and chuckled again with satisfaction. For Tom lived in the days when the Australian boomerang was an unknown weapon; otherwise he would have cut and carved till he had contrived one, and given himself no rest till he could hurl it with unerring aim and the skill that would bring it back to his hand.

The sloop-of-war and the Revenue cutter, its companion, had been lying at anchor some hundred yards from the end of the pier, and every now and then the sailor glanced at the trim vessels with their white sails and the sloop's carefully-squared yards—all "ataunto," as he termed it—and more than one sigh escaped his lips as he thought that never again would he tread the white deck that he helped to holy-stone, let alone show that he was one of the smartest of the crew to go up aloft.

And as he glanced at the vessels from time to time, he, to use his words, "put that and that together," and noticed that, contrary to custom, there was not a single hearty-looking young fisherman lounging upon the rail that overhung the head of the harbour.

"Smells a rat," muttered the old sailor. "Like as not they've dropped anchor here to see if there are any likely-looking lads waiting to be picked up after dark. Why, there's a good dozen that would be worth anything to a skipper, and I could put the press-gang on to their trail as easy as could be; but they're neighbours, and I can't do them such a dirty turn. Now, if they'd on'y take a dozen of these young beauties it would be a blessing to the place; but, no, the skipper wouldn't have them at a gift. But that's what they're after. Hullo, here comes a boat!"

"Oh!" he laughed, as he saw the sloop's cutter lowered down with its crew and a couple of officers in the stern-sheets. "The old game. Coming ashore for fresh meat and vegetables. I know that little game."

Bodger went on netting away, watching the boat out of the corner of one eye as it was rowed smartly up to the harbour steps, where the oars were turned up; and leaving the youth with him in charge of the boat's crew, the officer sprang out with one of the men and hurried up the steps, gave a supercilious glance at the crippled sailor, who touched his hat, and then went along towards the town.

"Yes, that's it," said the sailor to himself. "Having a look round. There'll be a gang landed to-night as sure as my name's Bodger."

The thinker made a few more meshes and then had a glance down on the boat and her crew, his eyes dwelling longest upon the young officer, who had taken out a small glass, through which he began to examine the town.

"Middy," said Bodger. "Smart-looking lad too. What's their game now?" he continued, as the boys drew closer together. "They'll be up to some game or another directly. Shying old fish at that youngster's uniform, or some game or another. Strikes me that if they do they'll find that they've caught a tartar. Just what they'd like to do—shy half a dozen old bakes' tails at his blue and white jacket. I might say a word to him and save it, but if I did I should be saving them young monkeys too, and—look at that now!—if that arn't Master Aleck's boat coming round the pynte! They sees it too—bless 'em! Now they'll be arter him, safe. That'll save the middy, but it won't save Master Aleck. Strikes me I'd better put my netting away and clear the decks for action."

Tom Bodger's clearing for action consisted in turning himself aside so that he could drag a neatly-folded duck bag off the fender, and stuffing his partly-made net and twine, with stirrup, mesh, and needle, inside before tying up the neck with a piece of yarn.

But his eyes were busy the while, and he watched all that went on, Aleck's boat running in fast, the boys whispering together, their leader sending off a couple towards the town end of the pier, and eliciting the mental remark from the sailor:

"Going arter Big Jem for twopence. Are we going to have another fight? Well, if we are he arn't going to tackle two on 'em, for I'm going to see fair with my stick and the crew o' that cutter to look on to form a ring."

By the time he had thought out this observation it was time for him to carefully ascend to the top of one of the great mooring-posts, the flattest-topped one by preference. How it was done was a puzzle, and it drew forth the observations of the cutter's crew, while the midshipman in charge shouted "Bravo!" But somehow or other, by the use of his hands and a peculiar hop, Tom Bodger brought himself up perpendicularly upon the top of the post, steadied himself with his stick, and then held his head aloft.

That was enough. Aleck was near enough in to recognise the figure and comprehend the signal, which in Tom's code read:

"Right and ready, my lad. Steer for here."

Chapter Ten

Aleck ran his boat close in behind the cutter after lowering the sail so close that it touched the midshipman's dignity.

"Hi, you, sir!" he shouted. "Mind where you're going with that boat."

"All right," replied Aleck, coolly enough. "I won't sink you."

"Hang his insolence!" muttered the middy; and as Tom lowered himself from the post and then went, rock-hopper fashion, down the steps and boarded the boat, the young officer gave Aleck a supercilious stare up and down, taking in his rough every-day clothes and swelling himself out a little in his smart blue well-fitting uniform.

Aleck felt nettled, drew himself up, and returned the stare before making a similar inspection of the young naval officer.

"Whose boat's that, boy?" said the latter, haughtily.

"Mine," was Aleck's prompt reply. "What ship's that, middy—I don't mean the cutter, of course?"

"Well, of all the insolence—" began the lad. "Do you know, sir, that you mustn't address one of the King's officers like that?"

"No, I didn't know it," said Aleck, coolly. "I thought you were only a midshipman. Are you the captain?"

"Why, con—"

"Look out!" cried Aleck, giving the speaker a sharp push which nearly sent him backward but saved him from receiving a wet dockfish full on the cheek, the unpleasantly foul object whizzing between the lads' heads, followed by a roar of laughter from a group of the young ruffians on the pier.

"How dare you lay your hands upon a King's officer!" cried the midshipman, furiously.

Aleck shrugged his shoulders and laughed.

"Look out!" he cried. "Here come two or three more," and he dogged aside, while the middy was compelled, metaphorically, to come down from his dignified perch and duck down nearly double to escape the missiles which flew over him.

"Do you see now?" said Aleck, merrily.

"Oh! Ah! Yes! Of course! The insolent young scoundrels! Here, half a dozen of you jump ashore and catch that big boy with the ragged red cap. I'll have him aboard to be flogged."

Six of the boat's crew sprang out on to the steps, but there was no prospect of their catching the principal offender, who uttered a derisive yell and started off to run at a rate which would have soon placed him beyond the reach of the sailors; and he knew it, too, as he turned and made a gesture of contempt, which produced a roar of delight from the other boys who stood looking on.

"After him!" yelled the middy to his men, as he stood stamping one foot in his excitement; and then turning to Aleck: "If the cat don't scratch his back for this my name's not Wrighton."

The communication was made in quite a friendly, confidential way, which brought a response from Aleck:

"He'll be too quick for them. The young dogs are as quick as congers."

"You wait and you'll see. I'll make an example of him."

All this passed quickly enough, while the boy in the red cap, feeling quite confident in his powers of flight, turned again to jeer and shout at the sailors, whom he derided with impudent remarks about their fatness of person, weight of leg, and stupidity generally, till he judged it dangerous to wait any longer, when he went off like a clockwork mouse, skimming over the stones, and from the first strides beginning to leave the sailors behind.

"I told you so," said Aleck. "There he goes. I can run fast, but I couldn't catch him. Ha, ha, ha! Bravo, Tom!" he cried. "Look at that sailor!"

For meanwhile Tom Bodger, stick in hand, had made his way back on to the pier, and just as the boy was going his fastest something followed him faster, in the shape of the wooden-legged sailor's well-aimed cudgel, which spun over the surface of the pier, thrown with all the power of Tom's strong arm, and the next instant it seemed to be tangled up with the boy's legs, when down he went, kicking, yelling, and struggling to get up.

"Hi! Oh, my! Help, help!" he yelled at his comrades; but they only stood staring, while the foremost sailors passed on so as to block the way of escape, and the next instant the offender was hemmed in by a half circle of pursuers, who formed an arc, the chord being the edge of the pier, beneath which was the deep, clear water.

"There," cried the middy, triumphantly. "Got him!" Then to his men: "Bring the young brute here."

Meanwhile, as the boy lay yelping and howling in a very dog-like fashion, the laughing sailors began to close in, and then suddenly made a dart to seize their quarry, but only to stand gazing down into the harbour.

For, in pain before from the contact of the stick and his heavy fall, but in agony now from the dread of being caught, the boy kept up the dog-like character of his actions by going on all fours over two or three yards, and then, as hands were outstretched to seize him, he leaped right off the pier edge, to plunge with a tremendous splash ten feet below, the deep water closing instantly over his head.

"He's gone, sir," said one of the sailors, turning to his officer.

"Well, can't I see he has gone, you stupid, cutter-fingered swab?" cried the middy. "Here, back into the boat and round to the other side of the pier. You'll easily catch him then."

"Not they," said Aleck, quietly; "didn't I tell you he was as quick and slippery as a conger?"

"Look sharp! Be smart, men," cried the middy, angrily.

"What's the good of tiring the lads for nothing?" said Aleck, as the men began to scramble into the cutter. "It will take them nearly ten minutes to get round to where he went off."

"Would it?"

"Of course."

"But, I say," said the middy, anxiously, "mightn't he be drowned?"

"Just about as likely as that dogfish he threw at you. Come and look!"

Aleck led the way up the steps, followed by the young officer, and then as they crossed the pier they came in sight directly of the boy, swimming easily, side stroke, for a group of rocks which formed the starting-point of the pier curve, and beyond which were several places where the boy could land.

"He'll be ashore before we could get near him," said Aleck.

"What! Shall I have to let him go?" cried the middy.

"Of course! He got a tremendous crack on the legs from Tom Bodger's stick—he was nearly frightened to death; and he has had a thorough ducking. Isn't that enough?"

"Well, it will have to be," said the middy, in a disappointed tone. "I meant him to be treed up and flogged."

Aleck looked at him in rather an amused fashion.

"Well, what are you staring at?" said the middy, importantly.

"I was only wondering whether you would be able to order the boy to be flogged."

"Well—er—that is," said the midshipman, flushing a little; "I—er—said I should give him—er—report it to the captain, who would give the orders on my statement. It's the same thing, you know, as if I gave the flogging. 'I'll give a man a flogging' doesn't, of course, mean that I, as an officer, should give it with my own hands. See?"

"Yes, I see," said Aleck, quietly.

"Sit fast there," cried the middy to his men, as he began to descend the steps. "Let the young scoundrel go."

Just then Aleck glanced round and saw that the officer who had gone ashore was returning, followed by the man who had accompanied him, and he turned to Bodger, who stood waiting for orders, before descending again to the boat.

Chapter Eleven

"I say, Tom," said Aleck, "that was cleverly aimed, but you had better mind or you'll be breaking one of the boys' legs."

"Well-aimed, sir? Oh, that was nothing tickler. An easy shot that, sir. No fear o' my breaking no legs. I can tell exactly how much powder to fire with. I give it 'em just strong enough to hurt; that's all."

Just then the officer came back, spoke to the young middy, and went off again with the six men who had been unsuccessful in their chase of the red-capped boy, while Aleck and his companion exchanged glances.

"There, Tom, take away the boat," said Aleck; "I must go and get my uncle's paper."

"Your uncle's paper, sir?"

"Yes, I've run over to get some for him."

"Why, you got some on'y t'other week, sir. Did he have an axdent and burn it?"

"No," said Aleck, laughing. "It's all used up for writing."

"Wond'ful—wond'ful!" muttered the man. "Here's me can't write a word, and him allus going at it. Well, I suppose he was born that way. I'll take care o' your boat all the same, sir."

"What do you mean with your all the same?" asked Aleck, looking puzzled at the man's words.

"All the same, sir, though I can't write a word."

Aleck went off, being saluted by a nod from the middy, who lay back in the stern-sheets of the cutter. It was a nod that might have meant anything—condescension, friendliness, or a hint to keep his distance; but it did not trouble the lad, who trudged along the pier to fulfil his mission, and was soon after in the rugged, ill-paved main street, where he in sight of the naval group from the sloop, evidently busy buying and loading up with fresh provisions from the little shops.

He passed on, and was nearing the place where, in company with toys, grocery, and sweetmeats, the shopkeeper kept up a small supply of paper, for which the captain was his main customer, when a dark-bearded fisherman-like man suddenly turned out of a public-house, caught him by the arm, and hurried him sharply down a narrow alley which ran by the side of the little inn.

The man's sudden action, coupled with the fact that he was the last person in the county he would have expected to see, took away the lad's breath for a moment or two while he gazed up in the fierce searching eyes that seemed to be reading his thoughts.

"You, Eben?" he said at last.

"Me it is, youngster. What game do you call this?"

"I don't call it a game at all. What are you doing here?"

"Never you mind what I'm a-doing here. P'raps I'm watching you. I want to know what your game is."

"I'm playing at no game," cried the boy, speaking rather indignantly. "Let go of my arm."

"When you've told me what you're a-doing of with them sailor chaps."

"I? I'm doing nothing with them. I've come over in my own boat. I'm not along with them."

"I know. I've had my eye on yer, my lad. But let's have the truth. You come over to meet these chaps from the boats lying off there."

"Not I. If you must know, I've come over to fetch some paper for my uncle."

"And what else, my lad?"

"Nothing else," cried Aleck; "but I don't know what right you have to question me."

"You soon will, my lad. You say you're not with these folk. Why, I saw you talking for ever so long to the chaps in the boat that come ashore to lie there by the harbour wall, and afore it had been there long you come into port and run your boat close alongside."

"Of course I did, to get up to the steps and land. Look here; what are you thinking about?"

"Well," said the man, fiercely, "if you want to know over again what you knew before, I'm just going to tell you, so as to let you see that I'm not such a fool as you take me for, and also to let you know that I can see right through you, clever as you think yourself."

"Go on," said Aleck. "Let's have it all then."

"Well, here you are, my lad. I s'pose you know that's a man-o'-war sloop?"

"Yes, I know that, Eben."

"Yes, I s'pose so, my lad, and you know what she's hanging about this coast for?"

"I don't for certain," replied Aleck, "but I shouldn't be a bit surprised if the captain wanted to press a few likely lads, if he could get hold of them."

"Oh, you wouldn't, wouldn't you? I s'pose not," said the man, in a sneering tone.

"Why, anybody would guess that."

"P'raps they would and p'raps they wouldn't, my lad; but, of course, you don't know that there's the little Revenue cutter that's looking out for any little bit of smuggling going on?"

"Why, what nonsense you're talking, Eben! Of course I knew."

"Yes, of course you did, my lad; and you've got a spy-glass, haven't you!"

"No; but I use my uncle's."

"That's right; and when them two vessels come into sight 'smorning you got the glass out to see what they were?"

"Yes; directly."

"And then you went down to your boat-hole and ran over here as fast as you could?"

"Yes; but it wasn't fast, for the wind kept dropping. But how did you know this?"

"Never you mind how I knowed. You knowed that me and four mates came over here last night."

"That I didn't," cried Aleck. "What for—to run a cargo?"

"Never you mind what for, my lad. You knowed we'd come."

"That I didn't. I hadn't the least idea you had. But how did you know I got out the glass to have a look at the vessels? Bah! You couldn't know if you were over here. No one saw me but old Dunning. It's impossible."

"Is it?" said the man, with a sneer. "Then we arn't got a glass at Eilygugg, of course, eh, and nobody left behind to look out for squalls and run across to tell us to look out when they see the wind changing? So, you see, clever as you think yourself, you're found out, my lad. Now do you see?"

"I see that you're on the wrong tack, Eben," said the lad, scornfully, "and let me tell you that you've been talking a lot of nonsense. I don't see why I should tell you. It's absurd to accuse me of being a spy and informer. Do you suppose we up at the Den want to be on bad terms with all the fishermen and—and people about?"

"You mean to say you haven't put the boat's crew yonder up to taking me and my mates?"

"Of course I do. Why, I haven't even spoken to the officer, only to the midshipman."

"Well, it looks very bad," growled the man, gazing at the lad, searchingly.

"If you think a press-gang is likely to come ashore to get hold of you and your mates, why don't you slip off into the hills for a bit?"

The man stared, and his features relaxed a little and a little more, and he caught Aleck by the sleeve.

"Look here, Master Aleck," he said; "the captain yonder's a gentleman, though we arn't very good friends, but he never did anything to get any of us took."

"Of course he didn't."

"Wouldn't like you to, p'raps."

"Why, of course he wouldn't. If the fleet want men they'll get them somehow, and the Revenue cutter will hunt out the smugglers sooner or later; but for you to think that I'm on the look-out always to do you a bad turn—why, it's downright foolishness, Eben."

"Well, I'm beginning to think it is, my lad," said the man, smiling; "but that's just what they thought at home, and my young brother Bill ran across to give us the warning. I put that and that together, and I felt as sure as sure that you'd come over to inform agen us."

"But you don't believe it now?"

"No, my lad, I don't believe it now," said Eben, "and I'm glad on it, because it would be a pity for a smart young chap like you to be in for it."

"In for what?" said Aleck.

"For what? Ah, you'd soon know if you did blow upon us, my lad. But, there, I don't believe it a bit now, and I got some'at else to do but stand talking to you, so I'm off. Only, you know, my lad, as it's the best thing for a chap like you as wants to live peaceable like with his neighbours to keep his mouth shut—*mum*—*plop*."

The two last words were sounds made by slapping the mouth closely shut and half open with the open hand, after doing which Eben Megg stepped down the narrow turning and mysteriously disappeared.

"Bother him and his bullyings and threats," cried Aleck. "Such insolence! But, there, I must see about my paper and get back."

Chapter Twelve

Left alone in the boat, Tom Bodger sat down on one of the thwarts with his wooden pegs stuck straight out before him. Then he brought them close together with a sharp rap and began to rub one over the other gently; but these movements had nothing to do with the thinking, though he more than once told himself that he thought better when he was rubbing his legs together.

As he sat there he naturally enough began to watch the man-o'-war boat with her smart young officer and neat, trim-looking crew, while, continuing his inspection, he ran his eyes over the boat and admired its beautiful lines.

This brought up memories of the time when career and body had both been cut short by that unlucky cannon ball, leaving him a cripple and a pensioner.

"But I dunno," he said to himself, in a way he had of making the best of things, "if I hadn't been hit I might ha' lived on and been drowned, and then there'd ha' been no pension to enj'y as I enj'ys mine; and I don't never have to buy no boots nor shoes, so there arn't much to grumble about, arter all."

So Tom sat rubbing his wooden legs together, watching the sailors in the boat, thinking of how he'd been coxswain of just such a boat as that, and then beginning to feel an intense longing to compare notes with the men left with the middy in charge; but the young officer kept his men in order, and twice over had them busily at work stowing away the vegetables, fresh meat, bacon, and butter that were brought down from time to time and packed well out of the way fore and aft.

Consequently there was no opportunity allowed for him to get up a gossip, the young officer looking fiercely important, and the men making no advance.

"Beautifully clean and smart," said Tom. "Wonder how long Master Aleck'll be."

Then he swept the edge of the pier ten feet above his head in search of inimical boys, letting one hand down by his side to finger his cudgel, and indulging in a chuckle at the skilful way in which he had brought down the young offender a short time before.

"Pretty well scared him away," said Tom to himself; "he won't show himself here again to-day."

But as it happened Tom was wrong, for the boy, after landing in safety, with the water streaming down inside his ragged breeches and escaping at the bottom of the legs when it did not slip out of the holes it encountered on its way, had made his way up the steep cliff and round to the back of the town so as to get up on the moorland, where the sun came down hotly, when he began to drip and dry rapidly.

He could sweep the pier and harbour now easily, looking over the fishing-boats and watching those belonging to the man-o'-war and Aleck Donne, with Tom Bodger sitting with his legs sticking straight out.

And then he called Tom Bodger a very seaside salt and wicked name, in addition to making a vow of what he would do to "sarve him out."

The boy gave another glance round as if in search of coadjutors, but all his comrades had disappeared; so he stood thinking and drying as he turned his thoughts inland, with the result that he had a happy thought, under whose inspiration he set off at a trot round by the back of the little town till he came within view of a group of patches of sandy land roughly fenced in and divided by posts of wreck-wood and rails covered with pitch—rough fragments that had once been boat planks.

He ran a little faster now, and externally did not seem wet, for his hair was cropped so short that no water could find a lodgment, and his worn-old, knitted blue shirt and cloth breeches had ceased to show the moisture they had soaked up.

Once within hearing of the rough fenced-in gardens he put both hands to his mouth and uttered a frightful yell, with the result that a head suddenly shot up from behind one of the fences, and its owner was seen down to the waist, looking as if he were leaning upon an old musket.

But this was only the handle of a hoe, and the holder proved to be Big Jem, occupied in his father's garden, where he had been hoeing and earthing up potatoes in lazy-boy fashion with a chip-chop and a long think, supplemented by a rest at the end of each row to chew tobacco.

A minute later and the boys were lying down side by side, resting upon their elbows and kicking up their heels over their backs, what time the newcomer related what had passed down on the pier, and also what he should like to do.

The narrative seemed to afford Big Jem intense satisfaction, for he uttered a hoarse crowing laugh from time to time and blinked his eyes, squeezing the lids very close and then opening them wide, when sundry signs of black, green and blue bruises became visible.

When the newcomer had finished his narration, Big Jem crowed more hoarsely than ever, and indulged in what looked like an imitation of an expiring fish, for he stretched himself out flat and threw himself over from his face on to his back, beat the ground with his closed legs, and then flopped back again, over and over again, putting ten times the vigour and exertion into his acts that he had bestowed upon the hoeing, and ending by springing up, stooping to secure his hoe, and then tossing it right away to fall and lie hidden in one of the newly-hoed furrows between the potatoes.

"Do, won't it?" cried the new arrival.

"Yes," cried Big Jem, hoarsely. "Sarve 'em both out. Come on!"

No time was lost, the two boys going off at a trot round by the back of the town and aiming for the shore, where by descending a very steep bit of ivy-draped and ragwort-dotted cliff they could get down to a row of black sheds used for fish-drying and the storage of nets, which lay snugly upon a shelf of the cliff.

The place was quite deserted as the boys let themselves slide down a water-formed gully, peered about a bit, and then made for one of several boats moored some fifty yards from the sandy shore.

More or less salt water was nothing to the Rockabie boys, and after a glance along the shore, followed by a sweeping of the pier, which ran out between them and the harbour, they waded a little way out till the water reached their chests, and then began to swim for the outermost boat, into which Big Jem climbed, to hold out a hand, and the next moment his comrade had followed and leaned over, dripping away, to cast loose the rope attached to the buoy, while Big Jem put an oar out over the stern and began to scull.

"Ibney allus leaves one oar in his boat," said Jem, sculling away.

"But we mustn't go yet."

"You hold your mouth," said Big Jem. "I'll show you. You shall see what you shall see. Here, lay hold of the rope and make a hitch round that killick. See?"

The other boy evidently did see, for he knelt down and began to edge a big oval boulder stone from where it lay in company with three more for ballast amidship, worked it right forward into the bows, and then lifted it on to the locker, when he took hold of the boat's painter at the end furthest from the ring-bolt, to which it was secured, and fastened the hempen cord round the boulder with a nautical knot.

By the time this was done and the boy looked round for orders he caught sight of something moving at the shore end of the pier.

"Here comes the sailors back to their boat," he said. "They'll see us."

"Over with the killick, then—easy. Don't splash."

Big Jem drew in his oar, with which he had been making the boat progress by means of a fishtail movement, laid it along the thwarts, and then, as the other boy lifted the stone over the bows into the water, which it kissed without disturbance, it was let go and sank with a wavy movement, sending up a long train of glittering bubbles, running the rope out fast till bottom was reached and the boat swung from its stone anchor.

"Now, then, down with you," said Big Jem, and the next minute the two boys lay in the bottom, each with a great boulder for pillow, quite out of sight, unless their presence had been suspected, when a bit of coarse blue-covered body might have been seen, but then only to be taken for some idle fisher making up for last night's fishing with a nap.

Hence it was that when Tom Bodger swept the pier from where he sat in Aleck's boat lying by the steps in the harbour, he saw nothing but the top of the pier, and his eyes fell again upon the sloop's beautifully clean boat, which he again compared with the one he occupied, with such unfavourable effect to the latter that he muttered to himself a little, took off his jacket, rolled up his sleeves over his tattooed arms, and went in for a general clean up.

Tom was as busy as a bee and, to judge from the latter's usually contented hum, just as much satisfied, for his efforts certainly vastly improved the aspect of Aleck's boat; and he was still hard at work swabbing and drying and laying ropes in coils, when a remark from one of the sailors in the adjacent boat made the midshipman spring up out of a doze in the hot sunshine and give the order to "Be smart!"

In other words, to be ready to help their messmates returning with their officer, well laden with fresh stores, which soon after were handed down into the boat and stowed. Then the men took their places again, while the officers took theirs, the order was given to cast off, there was a thrust or two given by the coxswain, and the boat glided from the steps, leaving Tom Bodger watching the movements, smiling, and thinking of the past.

He smiled again as the oars were poised for a minute and then at a word dropped to starboard and larboard with a splash before beginning to dip with rhythmic regularity, the midshipman seizing the lines and steering her for her run outward to the sloop.

"Well," said the midshipman, in a low voice, "what luck?"

"Pretty good," was the reply. "Not all I should like, but I've seen enough to say that we ought to get a dozen smart fellows easily. There's some game or another on I hear from a man I know—a sort of meeting of fellows from along the coast—and Brown picked up a hint or two."

"A meeting, sir?"

"Well, call it what you like. Brown thinks there's a cargo to be run somewhere and that the men are here to make arrangements for getting it inland."

"What, right under our noses?" said the midshipman.

"Of course; that's a far better way than right under our eyes, my lad. Give way, lads. I want to get aboard, Mr Wrighton, to hear what the captain and the lieutenant of the cutter have to say."

The sloop's boat passed out between the two arms of the little harbour before Tom Bodger recommenced his polishing up in Aleck's boat.

"A pretty cutter," he said. "There arn't anything better worth looking at afloat than a man-o'-war's launch or cutter well manned by a smart crew. Makes me wish I'd got my understandings again and was an AB once more. Not as I grumbles—not me. Rockabie arn't amiss, and things has to be as they is. Here, let's get all ship-shape afore Master Aleck comes. Wish I'd got a bit o' sand here to give them ring-bolts a rub or two. I like to see his boat look a bit smart.

"Wonder what them two's come in for—they arn't lying off here for nothing! Some 'un's been sending 'em word there's a cargo going to be run along the shore, and so they've come in for soft tack and wegetables. Haw! haw! haw!" he laughed, as he bent over his work. "It's well I know that game. Fresh wegetables for the cook, a look round to find out what's what, and as soon as it's dark a couple o' well-armed boats to beat up the quarters and a dozen or so o' men pressed. I know. Well, I s'pose it's right; the King must have men to fight his battles. They ought to volunteer; but some on 'em won't. They don't like going until they're obliged, and then they do, and wouldn't come back on no account. Strikes me there's going to be a landing to-night. Some un must ha' let 'em know. Wonder who could do it, for there's a bit o' fun coming off to-night, I lay my legs. Eben Megg wouldn't be here for nothing, and there's half a dozen more hanging about.

"Well," he added, after a pause. "I'm not going to tell tales about either side. Don't know much, and what I do know I'm going to keep to myself. Smuggling arn't right; no more arn't playing spy and informer—so I stands upon my wooden pegs and looks on. They won't take me. Wouldn't mind, though, if they did. There, that looks quite decent and tidy, that does, and if Master Aleck don't say a word o' praise, why I say it's a shame. Well done; just finished in time. Here you are, then, my lad. Got a load? Why didn't yer let me come and carry it? Hold hard a minute, and I'll fetch it aboard."

For Tom Bodger had heard a step on the pier right above him as he stooped and saw the shadow of him who had made the sound cast right down upon the thwart and flooring of the boat, the maker of the shadow being evidently the bearer of some oblong object, which he carried at arm's length above his head.

Tom was balancing himself upon his wooden legs, and in the attitude of rising from his bent-down position, when he was conscious of a faint sound and an alteration in the shadow cast down, while the next instant there was a tremendous crash.

Chapter Thirteen

A splintering crash as of a heavy mass of stone or metal striking full upon the thwart behind him, while crash again, right upon the first sound, there was a duller and more crushing noise.

"Here, hi! Hullo! Here, what in the name o' thunder! Ahoy! Help!"

Tom Bodger was standing bolt upright as he uttered these last words, fully realising what had happened as he stared down at a rugged hole in the frail planking of the bottom of the boat, up through which the water was rising like a thick, squat, dumpy fountain.

"What game d'yer call this, Master Aleck? Eh, not there? I seed his shadder. He must ha' let it fall. Went through like a sixty-four-pound shot. Master Aleck! Ahoy! Frightened yerself away, my lad? Here, quick; come and lend a hand—the boat's going down!"

Tom Bodger talked and shouted, but he did not confine himself to words, for he saw the extent of the emergency. The boat seemed to be filling rapidly from the salt fount in the middle prior to going down. So, acting promptly, he hopped on to the next thwart, down into the water in the bottom, which came above his stumps, and then on to the next thwart forward and the locker. From here he put one peg on to the bows and swung himself on to the lowest step, where he could seize the boat's painter, fastened to a huge rusty ring in the harbour wall.

It was not many moments' work to cast the rope loose, and then he began to haul the rope rapidly through the ring, just having time to send the boat's head on to one of the steps under water, and hanging on with all his might, while the water rose and rose aft, till, with the bows still resting on the stone step, the after part of the boat was quite submerged.

As a rule there were fishermen hanging over the rail on the top of the cliff a couple of hundred yards or so away, men busy with trawl or seine net on the smacks and luggers, and a score or two of boys playing about somewhere on the pier; but there was, as Tom Bodger had said, something going on in the town, and as soon as those ashore had done watching the man-o'-war's men and seen them row off, there was a steady human current setting away from the harbour, and not a listening ear to catch the sailor's hails and pass the word on for help, as he hung on to the boat's rope with all his might, feeling assured that if he slacked his efforts she would glide off the slimy stone and go to the bottom.

"I arn't got no breath to waste in hollering," he panted. "Why, there's a good fathom and a half or two fathom o' water under her keel, and if I slack out down she'll go. Wants a couple o' boats to back in, one on each side, and get a rope under her thwarts. They could get her ashore then. Oh, dear! oh, dear! oh, dear! For him to leave me in charge, and then come back and find I've sunk her! I warn't asleep, for I was standin' up at work, so I couldn't ha' dreamed I heard him come, and see his shadder cast down. No; it's all true enough. But what could he have had in his hands? I see his shadder plain, with a something held up in his hands. Paper, didn't he say, he'd come to fetch? Well, paper's heavy when it's all tight up in a lump, and he must ha' pitched it down off the pier to save carrying it and to let it come plop, so as to frighten me, not thinking how heavy it was, and then as soon as he see the mischief he'd done he squirms and runs away like a bad dog with his tail between his legs. Why, I wouldn't ha' thought it on him.

"Oh, dear! what a weight she is! If I could only get a turn o' the rope round anywhere I could hold on easy, but if I move an inch down she'll go.

"Can't do it!" he groaned; "it's quite impossible. One hitch round the ring or a catch anywhere else'd do it, but I've got enough to do to hold on, and if I try any other manoover I shall make worse on it. It's no good, Tommy, my lad, that there's your job; bite yer teeth hard and hold on. Bime by it'll be too much for yer, and she'll begin to slide and slither; but don't you mind, it'll be all right—up'll go your hands with the rope, and then in they'll go, fingers first, into the ring. It's big enough to take your pretty little fists as far as yer knuckleses, and then they'll jam and jam more, and the more they jams the tighter they'll hold the rope till some 'un comes. Take the skin off? Well, let it. Sarve it right for not being stuck tighter on to the hones. Have to grow again, that's all. I arn't going to let Master Aleck's boat sink to the bottom if I die for it. But, hub, there! Ahoy! Is everybody dead yonder up town? Why, I'd say bless him now if I could on'y set a hye on the wery wust o' them boys."

The poor fellow hung on desperately, but he knew from his symptoms that he could not hold on much longer. The perspiration stood in huge drops all over his face, and they began to run together and trickle down, while now a queer thought flashed across his brain, bringing hope for the moment, but only for his heart to sink lower directly after.

"No, no," he groaned, "I couldn't do it. If I could it'd be just fine; but who's to hang on with his hands and double hisself up enough to take aim with both his wooden pegs at once so that they could go right into that ring and stopper the rope like a cable going through a hawse hole?

"Can't be done, can't be done; but—ahoy there! Dozens on yer hanging about if yer warn't wanted, and now not a lubber within hail. Ahoy there! Ship ahoy! Is everyone dead, I say? Ship a–a–hoy–y–y–y!" he yelled, in a despairing voice.

"Ahoy there! What's the matter? That you, Tom Bodger?"

"Bodger it is, Master Aleck. Here, quick, or I shall have both my hands off as well as my legs, and you'll have to put me out of my misery then."

"Why, Tom," cried Aleck, wildly. "What ever—oh!"

The lad wasted no more breath, for he grasped the position as soon as he reached the head of the steps.

"Can you hold on a minute?"

"I can't, sir, but my fists will," groaned the man, and then in a hoarse whisper—"Rope!"

"I see," cried Aleck, and he ran back a dozen yards along the pier to where he could see a coil of small rope for throwing aboard vessels in rough weather to bring back their looped cables and pass them over the posts.

He was back again directly, uncoiling it as he came and leaving it trailing, while, end in hand, he reached the top of the steps, went down to where the poor fellow hung on, and shouting out words of encouragement the while, he passed a hand down, got hold of the loose painter below Bodger's, and with the quick deft fingers of one used to the sea and the handling of lines he effected a quick firm knotting of the two ropes.

This done, he made for the next ring hanging from the harbour wall, passed the fresh rope through, and hauled in all the slack.

"Now, Tom," he cried, "both together—ahoy—ahoy!"

He threw all his strength into the hauling, aided by the man-o'-war's man's last remaining force; no little either, for despair gave the poor fellow a spasmodic kind of power, so that the rope passed through the ring and whizzed and quivered, it was so tight. Then another stay was found and a hitch taken twice round that before Aleck fastened off, and, panting heavily, went up a step or two to the assistance of his humble friend.

"You can let go now, Tom. I have her fast."

"Sure, Master Aleck?"

"Yes, certain. Let go; and mind what you're about, or you'll slip overboard."

"It's all right, sir," said the man, in a hoarse whisper. "I've let go now."

"Nonsense! What are you thinking about? You've got hold tight as ever."

"Nay, I arn't, Master Aleck. I let go when you telled me. I'm on'y leaning agen the rope to keep from going down into the water."

"Why, Tom, what's the matter with you?" cried Aleck, wonderingly, as he placed his hands on his companion's. "I tell you that you're holding on as tight as ever."

"Eh?" said the man, feebly. "No, sir, I arn't; 'strue as goodness I arn't."

"But you are," cried Aleck, angrily, as he now grasped the full misfortune to his boat—not the very full, for he was not aware of the hole in her bottom. "Your fingers are clasped tightly round the rope."

"Are they, sir?"

"Yes."

"'Tarn't my doing then, sir. I hoped and prayed as they might hold on to the last, and I s'pose that's how it is. Ah–h!"

He uttered a low groan, his eyelids dropped, and his fingers suddenly became inert, while it needed all the lad's strength to keep the poor fellow from slipping off the wet steps into the deep water of the harbour.

"Tom," he shouted; "rouse up, lad. Do you hear?" he cried, frantically, as he held the man erect, and then in obedience to a sudden flash of thought forced him back into a sitting position on one of the steps.

"Hah!" he panted. "I couldn't have held you much longer. Hold up, man. Can't you hear what I say?"

"Eh? Yes, Master Aleck, on'y don't talk so far off like, and—and—tell 'em to leave off ringing them bells in my ears."

Coupled with the loss of the boat, Aleck's first thought was that the man had been indulging in a sailor's weakness and was the worse for rum; but a second glance at the ghastly face below him opened the lad's eyes to the simple truth, and he spoke more gently:

"Feel faint, Tom?"

"Ay, sir, I s'pose it's that. I feel just as I did after that there cannon ball took off my legs. I'm getting better now you've stopped that ringing o' the bells in my ears."

"That's right, Tom."

"But is the boat safe, sir? Don't let her go right down."

"She's safe enough so long as the rope doesn't part."

"Then look at her knots, sir. I did teach yer proper. Don't say as you've tied one as'll slip."

"The rope's all right, Tom."

"Hah!" groaned the man. "Then if you wouldn't mind, sir, just help me up the other steps and lie me down flat on my back for a minute. I feel as if that would set me right."

"Come on, then," said Aleck; "but you must help, or we shall both go overboard."

"I'm a-going to help, sir," said the man, with his voice beginning to grow stronger. "I think I can keep upright on my pegs again if you'll lend me a hand. No, hold hard a minute like, sir; there's no room for two on these bits o' steps. You've got plenty o' slack line, sir?"

"Yes."

"Then pass the end round under my arms and make fast. Then you go atop and haul, and you can twist the line round a post so as I can't slip."

"Of course," cried Aleck, and following out the poor fellow's instructions he went up to the pier, passed the rope round the nearest post, and hauled steadily, while without rising to his feet the poor fellow hitched himself, after a way he had learned, in a sitting position by means of his hands, right on to the pier, where once landed he rolled over with a groan, and fainted dead away.

Chapter Fourteen

It was quite a minute before Tom Bodger opened his eyes again, to lie staring blankly up at the dazzling blue sky. He looked, for a mahogany and red sun-tanned individual, particularly unwholesome and strange with his fixity of expression, and in his anxiety Aleck forbore to speak to him, but watched for the complete return of his senses, wondering the while that so sturdy a fellow could be affected in a way which he had always understood was peculiar to women.

After staring straight upward for some little time the man began to blink, as if the intense light troubled him. Then his eyes began to roll slowly round, taking a wider and wider circle, till at last they included Aleck in their field of view and remained fixed, staring at him wonderingly.

Aleck's lips parted to ask the natural question, "How are you now?" But before he could utter a word Tom frowned and said, severely:

"What are you up to, my lad?"

"It's what are you up to, Tom? Here, how are you now?"

"Quite well, thankye, Master Aleck. How are you? But, here," he cried, changing his manner, "what does it all mean? Why, what—when—wh-wh-what—ah, I know now, Master Aleck! I say, don't tell me the boat's gone down!"

As he spoke he rose quickly into a sitting position and stared down through the opening where the steps began, uttered a sigh of content, and then said:

"I was afraid you hadn't made them knots fast."

"Oh, they're all right. But has your faintness gone off?"

"Yes, sir, that's gone."

"To think of a big sturdy fellow fainting dead away!"

"Ah, 'tis rum, sir, arn't it? All comes o' having no legs and feet. I never knew what it was till I lost 'em, as I telled yer."

"Well, you're better now. But, I say, Tom, how did you manage to get the boat full of water like this?"

"Oh, come, Master Aleck," cried Tom, indignantly. "I like that! How come you to chuck that great lump o' paper down and make that great hole in her bottom?"

"I do what?" cried Aleck. "Here, wait a bit and rest. You haven't quite come to yet."

"Me, sir? I'm right as a trivet," cried Tom; and to prove it he turned quickly over on his face propped himself up on his hands, with his elbows well bent, and then gave a sharp downward thrust which threw him up so that he stood well balanced once more upon his stout wooden legs.

"That's right," said Aleck, after a glance at the half-submerged boat. "Now, then, how did you manage it?"

"Me manage it, sir? Oh, that's how I allus gets up when I'm down."

"No, no, no," cried Aleck, impatiently. "I mean about the boat. Did some other boat foul her?"

"No–o–o!" cried Tom. "You chucked that great lump of paper down and it went through the bottom."

"Paper? What, the paper I went to fetch?"

"Ay, sir."

The lad went and picked up a small parcel he had dropped on the pier and held it up in the man's sight as he gazed wonderingly at him again, and then said, very severely:

"Look here, Tom, you are mad, or have you been—you know?"

Aleck turned his hand into a drinking vessel and imitated the act of drinking.

"No–o–o–o!" cried Tom, indignantly. "Haven't had a drop of anything but water for a week."

"Then how did you get my boat half full of water?"

"I didn't, sir. You came and chucked that heavy lump of paper down, and it broke the middle thwart, being a weak 'un, because of the hole through for the boat's mast, and went on down through the bottom."

"What! I did nothing of the sort, sir."

"Oh, Master Aleck! Why, I seed yer shadow come right over me with yer hands up holding the lump o' paper, and afore I could straighten myself up down it come, and went right through the bottom."

"You don't mean to tell me that there's a hole right through the bottom of my beautiful Seagull?" cried Aleck, wildly.

"Why, how could she have got full o' water if you hadn't chucked that down? I would ha' come up and fetched it, sir. That comes o' your being so rannish."

"How dare you!" cried Aleck, passionately. "I tell you I did nothing of the sort."

"What's the good o' telling an out-an'-outer about it, Master Aleck, sir, when I see yer quite plain; leastwise, I see yer shadow when yer come to the edge."

"You saw nothing of the sort," cried Aleck, fiercely. "You scoundrel! You've been sailing her about while I've been up the town, and run her on a rock. I did trust you, Tom, and now you try to hoodwink me with a miserable story that wouldn't deceive a child. Tell me the truth at once, sir, or never again do you sail with me."

"I won't," growled Tom, sturdily.

"What! You won't tell me the truth?"

"I didn't say I wouldn't tell you the truth, Master Aleck. I mean I won't say as I took her out and run her on a rock."

"But you did, sir."

"Tell yer I didn't, Master Aleck; she've been tied up ever since you went away, and I've given her a thorough clean up."

"And started a plank or two by jumping down upon her with your wooden legs."

"Nay, I wouldn't be such a fool, sir. Of course if I did I should go through."

"I'd have forgiven you the accident," said Aleck, sternly, "but I can't forgive the lie."

Tom stared up at his young employer, and took off his hat to give his head a thorough good scratch, before saying, quietly:

"Say, Master Aleck, you says to me just now with a sign like as I'd been having a drop o' rum. Well, I arn't; but, you'll scuse me, sir, have you happened to call and see anyone as has given you some cake and wine as was rather too strong for a hot sunny day like this?"

"No!" roared Aleck, in a thorough passion now. "Such insolence! Say again that I threw a weight of paper and broke a hole through her."

"Well, sir, I see your shadder."

"You did not, for I've not been back till just now."

"Then it was somebody else's, sir."

"Somebody else's, sir!" cried Aleck, scornfully. "Own at once that you had an accident with her."

"Me say that?" cried Tom, waxing angry in turn. "I won't. I'd do a deal for you, Master Aleck, and if I'd stove in the boat I'd up and say so; but I arn't a-going to tell an out-an'-out wunner like that to screen you when you've had an accident. Why, if I did you'd never trust me again."

"I never will trust you again, sir. But, there, what's to be done? How am I to get back to the Den? Would a plug of oakum keep the water out?"

"Would a plug o' my grandmother keep the water out?" growled Tom, scornfully. "Why, she couldn't keep it out if we set her in it. I jest got one peep, and then the water hid it, but there's a hole pretty nigh big enough for you to go through."

"My poor boat!" cried Aleck, in agony. "But, there, it's of no use to cry after spilt milk. What's to be done?"

"Well, I've thought it out, sir, and seems to me that what's best to be done is to make her fast between two big boats, run her up on to the beach, get two or three of the fisher lads to turn her over, and then see what I can do with a bit o' thin plank. Patch her up and pitch up the bit where I claps the plaster on, and I dessay she'll be watertight enough for you to run home in. I can mend her up proper when we get her back in the creek."

"How long would it take to put on the patch?"

"I can't say till I sees the hole, sir, but I might get it done by to-night."

"By to-night? How am I to get back in the dark?"

"Oh, I dessay we could steer clear o' the rocks, sir."

"We? No, thank you, sir. I don't want a man with me whom I can't trust."

Tom took his hat off and had a good rub before looking wistfully up in his young employer's face.

"Say, Master Aleck, arn't you a bit hard on a man?" he said.

"No, not half so hard as you deserve. You told me an abominable lie."

"Nay, sir. I see your shadow just as you were going to throw down that there lump o' paper."

"You—did—not, sir!" cried Aleck, fiercely.

"Well, then, it must ha' been somebody else's, sir; that's all I can say."

"Whose, pray?" cried Aleck. "Who would dare to do such a thing as that? Stop!" he cried, as a sudden idea flashed through his brain. "I saw two lads in a boat sculling away from the pier as hard as they could go."

"You see that, Master Aleck?"

"Yes, when I came down from High Street."

"Where was they going, sir?" cried the man, staring hard.

"Towards the curing sheds."

"Could you see who they was, sir?"

"No; they seemed to be two big lads, just about the same as the rest."

"Where was they going from?" asked Tom, excitedly.

"From the pier; there was nowhere else they could be coming from. They wouldn't have been fishing at this time of day."

"Look here, Master Aleck, you mean it, don't you? It wasn't you as pitched something down?"

"Look here, Tom, do you want to put me in a passion?"

"No, sir, course I don't."

"Then don't ask such idiotic questions. Of course I didn't."

"Then it was one of they chaps, Master Aleck."

"Well, it does look like it now, Tom. But, nonsense! It must have been very heavy to go through the boat."

"It weer, sir."

"But why should anyone do that? You don't think that a boy would have been guilty of such a bit of mischief as that?"

"What, Master Aleck?" cried the sailor, bursting into a loud guffaw. "Why, there arn't anything they Rockabie boys wouldn't do. Why, they're himps, sir—reg'lar himps; and mischief arn't half bad enough a word for what they'd do."

"Oh, but this is too bad. Why, the—the—"

"Stone, I should say it were, sir. Bet a halfpenny as it was a ballast cobble as was hev down."

"But it might have come down on you and killed you."

"Shouldn't wonder, sir."

"But you have no one with such a spite against you as to make him do that?"

"Haven't I, Master Aleck? Why, bless your innocence, there's dozens as would! I'd bet another halfpenny as that young beauty as I brought down with my stick this mornin' felt quite sore enough to come and drop a stone on my head. 'Sides, they've got a spite agen you, too, my lad, and like as not Big Jem would try to sarve you out by making a hole through your boat for leathering him as you did a fortnit ago."

"Tom!"

"Ah, you may shout 'Tom!' till you're as hoarse as a bull, Master Aleck, but that seems to be about the bearings of it; and now I think more on it, that's about the course I means to steer. Two on 'em, you says as you saw?"

"Yes, two biggish lads."

"Sculling hard?"

"Yes, the one who stood up in the boat was working the oar as hard as he could."

"Which means as he was in a hurry, sir."

"It did seem like it, Tom."

"On a hot day like this here, sir. Boys, too, as wouldn't work a scull if they warn't obliged. Why, they'd been and done it, and was cutting away as hard as they could."

"It does look likely, Tom."

"That's it, sir. We've got the bearings of it now. It were Big Jem and young Redcap, warn't it?"

"One of the boys had on a red cap, Tom. I remember now."

"Then don't you wherrit your head no more about it, Master Aleck. It was them two as did it, and I shall put it down to their account."

"But we ought to be sure."

"Sure, sir? Why, we are sure, and they'll have to take it."

"Take *it*? Take what?"

"Physic, sir. Never you mind about it any more; you leave it to me. It's physic as they've got to take when the time comes; and all I've got to say is as I hopes they'll like it."

"Well, never mind that now, Tom. What about my boat?"

"Oh, I'll see about her at once. I'll stop and take care of her while you go up to the houses on the cliff yonder, and you says as you have had an accident with your boat and you wants Joney to come with a couple o' mates to help. They'll come fast enough."

"Very well. Let's have a look first, though."

They stepped to the edge of the pier and looked down into the disabled boat, while the water being still and as clear as crystal, they could see through the broken thwart and the splintered jagged hole through the bottom.

Aleck drew a deep breath like a sigh, and Tom nodded his head sagely:

"Stone as big a killick, Master Aleck; that's what did that. Precious big 'un too. Now, then, you be off and get they chaps here while I chews it over a bit about how I'm to manage; but I tell yer this—it's going to be dark afore I gets that done. What d'yer say about walking over to the Den to tell the captain what's happened?"

"I say no, Tom. I'm going to stay here and help you. You won't mind sailing over with me in the dark?"

"Not me, sir, and you needn't wherrit about what to do wi' me. I shall spread a sail over the boat when we've got her moored back in the creek, and creep under and sleep like a top. You'll give me a mug o' milk and a bit o' bacon in the morning afore I start back?"

"Of course, of course, Tom. There, I'll run off at once."

"Hold hard a moment, Master Aleck. Mebbe you'll see them two beauties."

"I shouldn't wonder, Tom."

"Looking as innercent as a pair o' babbies, sir," said Tom, with a knowing wink. "Then what you've got to do, sir, is look innercent too. You arn't going to suspeck them for a minute, cause they wouldn't do such a thing. We're a-going to wait till the right time comes."

"And we're quite sure, Tom?"

"That's it, Master Aleck; and then—physic."

Aleck laughed, in spite of the trouble he was in, for Tom's face was a study of mysterious humour and conspiracy of the most solemn nature. The next minute the lad was going an easy dog-trot along the pier towards the town.

Chapter Fifteen

"Hole in her bottom?" said the friendly fisherman who had presented the brill, in answer to Aleck's application, "and want her brought ashore? Sewerly, my lad, sewerly."

His application to the big fisherman who had taken his part over the fight met with a precisely similar reply, when the lad found the men collected with a number of their fellows outside one of the public-houses, where something mysterious in the way of a discussion was going on, and Aleck noted that their conversation ceased as soon as he appeared, several of the men nudging each other and indulging in sundry nods and winks.

But the lad was too full of his boat trouble to dwell upon the business that seemed to have attracted the men together, and he led the way down to the harbour with his two fishermen acquaintances, finding that all the rest of the party followed them.

Had he wanted fifty helpers instead of three he could have had willing aid at once. As it was, his friends selected four more to help put off their boats, and the rest trudged slowly down the pier to form an audience and look on, while under Tom Bodger's direction the damaged boat was lashed by its thwarts to the fresh corners, and then set free and thrust off the step.

The rest was easy. In a very short time she was rowed ashore, cast loose again, and half a dozen men waded in knee-deep to run her up a few feet at a time, the water escaping through the broken-out hole, till at last she was high and—not dry, but free from water.

Then the mast was unstepped and with the other fittings laid aside, while Tom Bodger had procured a basket of tools and the wood necessary for the repairs, and the little crowd of fishermen formed themselves into a smoking party, sitting upon upturned boats, fish boxes and buckets, to discuss the damage and compare it with that sustained by other boats as far back as they could remember. For Tom required no further help then, save such as was given by Aleck, preferring to work his own way, the idea being to make a temporary patchwork sufficient for safety in getting the boat home.

To this end he measured and cut off, almost as skilfully as a ship's carpenter—consequent upon old experience at home with boats and at sea with the mechanic of a man-o'-war—a piece of board to form a fresh thwart, which was soon nailed tightly on the remains of the old.

Then the hole in the bottom was covered with this boarding, laid crosswise, the necessary fitting taking a great deal of time, so that the afternoon was spent before help was needed, and plenty of willing hands assisted in turning the boat right over, keel uppermost, ready for the laying on of plenty of well-tarred oakum to cover the fresh inside lining, Tom having a kettle of pitch over a wood fire, and paying his work and the caulking liberally as he went on, whistling and chatting away to Aleck the while, only pausing now and then to have a big sniff and to inhale much of the smoke cloud his friends were making.

"I should like to stop and have a pipe mysen, Master Aleck," said Tom, once.

"Well, have one; only don't be long, Tom."

"Nay, sir; I'll have it as we sails over, bime by. I won't stop now. It's a long job, and it'll be quite dark afore I've done."

He fetched the pitch kettle from the little fire a fisherman had been feeding with chips of wreck-wood and adze cuttings from a lugger on the stacks.

"Now then," he said, after carefully stuffing the damaged hole with oakum, "this ought to keep the inside dry, on'y the worst on it is that the pitch won't stick well to where the wood's wet."

"But you're not going to pour all that in?"

"I just am," said Tom, with a chuckle. "I arn't going to spyle a ship for the sake of a ha'porth o' tar. There we are," he continued, spreading the melted pitch all over the patch with a thin piece of wood till, as it cooled, it formed a fairly level surface ready for the pieces of planking intended to form the outside skin.

Tom was a very slow worker, but very sure, and a couple more hours glided by and the sun had long set with the boat still not finished. So slow had the repairing been that at last Aleck expressed his dissatisfaction; but Tom only grinned.

"I know what water is, sir, and how it'll get through holes. I don't want for us to go to the bottom, no more'n I want us both to be allus baling. Didn't I say as it would take me till dark?"

"You did, Tom, but you needn't drive in quite so many nails. This is only temporary work."

"Tempry or not tempry, I want it to last till we gets home."

"Of course," said Aleck, and to calm his impatience he turned to look at the group of fishermen, who sat and stood about, smoking away, and for the first time the lad noticed that the men had ceased to watch Tom Bodger but had their eyes fixed intently upon the sloop-of-war and the cutter, which lay at anchor a couple of miles from the harbour, and were now showing their riding lights.

"'Bout done, arn't yer, Tommy?" said the man who was mending the fire.

"Nay, keep the pitch hot, messmet," said Tom. "I'll just pay her over inside as soon as we've got her turned right again."

"Then that's going to be now, arn't it, matey?" said the big fisherman.

"Yes," said Tom, to Aleck's great satisfaction. "Lend a hand, some on yer."

The words seemed to galvanise the group into action, twice as many men offering to help as were needed, and in another few minutes, to the owner's delight, the boat was turned over, with the iron-plated keel settling down in the fine shingle and the rough inner workmanship showing in the dim twilight.

"Now," cried Tom, "just that drop o' pitch. Power it in, messmet. That's your sort. It'll soon cool. Now, then, I'll just stick a bit or two of board acrorst there, Master Aleck, to protect that pitch; and then we'll say done."

"And time it was done, Tom," said Aleck, impatiently. "Look, you've tired everybody out!"

Tom looked round, and laughed softly.

"Yes," he said, as he noted how to a man the fisher folk had begun to saunter away. "I see. They've been all on the fidget to go for the last half-hour."

"And no wonder; but they might have waited a bit longer, to launch her."

"She arn't ready to launch yet, my lad, and she'll be all the better for waiting till that pitch is well cooled. Besides, in less than an hour the tide'll be up all round her, and we can shove her off oursens."

"Oh, yes, of course; and as we have to go in the dark I suppose it doesn't matter to an hour."

"That's what I've been a-thinking of, Master Aleck. But, I say, do you know why they wanted to be off?"

"Hungry, I suppose."

"Nay! Not them. They're suspicious."

"What of?"

"Why, didn't you see how they kep' one eye on the man-o'-war out yonder?"

"Yes, of course."

"Well, what does that mean? They've made up their minds as boats'll come in from the sloop arter dark just to see in a friendly way if they can't pick up a few likely lads to sarve the King."

"From the smugglers who are hanging about?" said Aleck, eagerly, as he recalled what had passed between him and Eben Megg that afternoon.

"Smugglers, or fishermen, or anyone else. All's fish that comes into a press-gang's net—'cept us, Master Aleck. They wouldn't take a young gent like you, and I should be no good to 'em now, sir," continued the poor fellow, with a ring of sadness in his voice, which gave place to a chuckle as he added, "unless they kep' me aboard the man-o'-war to poke my pins down the scupper holes to keep 'em from being choked. These here two bits o' thin board I'll nail in close together, and then we'll let the water come up all round and harden the pitch. Just you rake them ashes together, Master Aleck, so as not to let the fire go quite out. I shan't be above half an hour now, and then I shall want a light for my pipe, and by the time I've done that you'll be back again."

"Back again? I'm not going away."

"Oh, yes, you are, Master Aleck; you're going up to the little shop yonder to get a noo crusty loaf and a quarter of a pound o' cheese."

"Oh, I can't eat now, Tom," said the lad, impatiently.

"Can't yer, sir?" said Tom, with a grin. "Well, I can—like fun—and if you'll buy what I says I'll teach you how."

"Oh, of course, Tom. How thoughtless of me! I've been so anxious; but, of course, you must be very hungry! I'll go and get some bread and cheese. And you'd like a mug of beer, wouldn't you?"

"Well, Master Aleck, I wouldn't say no to a drop if it was here."

"I'll go at once, Tom, without you want me to hold the boards while you nail them."

"All right, sir. Nay, nay, don't make a blaze. Just rake the ashes together; any little ember will do to light my pipe. I say, Master Aleck, we haven't had a single boy nigh us."

"No, not one. How strange!"

"Not it, sir. Just shows as they all know about the boat, and whose game it was."

Aleck hurried off and obtained the simple provisions needed, and returned to find the last nails being driven triumphantly into the boat.

"There you are, Master Aleck," cried Tom, "and I warrant she won't leak a spoonful. There's the tide just beginning to lap up round the stern, so we'll get the rudder on again, step the mast, and put all ship-shape ready for a start, and if it's all the same to you I'll just light up my pipe at once, and smoke it as we get the tackle back in its place."

"Go on, then," said Aleck, and, after filling the bowl of his pipe, the sailor went to the glowing embers of the fire, one of which he picked up with his hardened thumb and finger, lit the tobacco, and began smoking away.

His first act was to scoop up a little water in the boat's baler and extinguish the fire.

"Too hot as it is, Master Aleck. We can feel the way to our mouths, and I'm allus mortal feared of sparks blowing about among boats and sheds."

The shipping of the rudder, the stepping of the mast, and fastening of the boat's grapnel to the ring-bolt followed. Then oars, boat-hook, and ropes were laid in, and the pair seated themselves in the darkness, to begin discussing their much-needed meal, listening the while to the whispering and lapping of the water, Aleck thinking anxiously of how uneasy his uncle would be.

"How soon shall we be able to start, Tom?" he said.

There was a strange sound which made Aleck start.

"What?" he cried. "What's the matter?"

"Beg pardon, Master Aleck; couldn't say it no better. Mouth was full o' hard crust."

"How long before we start?"

"Good hour, sir. There's a lot o' shallow yonder."

"Oh!" cried Aleck, impatiently. "Let's get some of the fishermen to come and launch us."

"I don't think you'd find anyone as would come, sir. They're all lying low somewhere for fear o' the press-gang."

"Nonsense! Here they come, a lot of them, to get us off."

"Why, so they be," grumbled Tom, in a disappointed way. "Can't see no faces, but—Master Aleck," he whispered, sharply, "it's them!"

"Well, I said so," began Aleck, impatiently; but he got no farther, the words being checked by a feeling of astonishment. For a voice suddenly exclaimed:

"Quick, lads; surround!" and a hand was laid sharply upon the lad's collar, while two men grappled Tom.

"Now, then," he growled, "what is it?"

"Hold your noise, or you'll have a fist in your mouth," said a sharp voice. "Who are you?"

"Name Bodger. AB, King's Navee. Pensioner for wounds. See?"

It was dark, but the shooting out of Tom's wooden legs at right angles to his body from where he sat was plain enough to all of the group of well-armed sailors who surrounded the boat.

"What are you doing here?"

"Eating my supper; been mending our boat."

"Then who is this?" said the same sharp voice.

"My young master. We got a hole in the boat's bottom and had to put in for repairs."

"That's right enough, sir; here's the oakum and tools. Been a fire. Here's the little pitch kettle."

"O' course it's right, messmets. What's yer game—press-gang?"

"Hush!" whispered the commanding voice. "You're an old sailor?"

"Nay, not old, your honour," said Tom. "Thirty-two, all but the legs I lost. They warn't so old by some years."

"A joker, eh? Well, look here, my lad. We're on duty, and it's yours as an ex-Navy man to help. Where are the fishermen? There seem to be none hanging about the cliff."

"I d'know, your honour; up at the publics, p'raps, in the town."

"There's a party of smugglers here to-night?"

"Is there, sir? Running a cargo?"

"You know they are."

"That I don't, your honour. I haven't seen one."

Just at that moment there was the sound of yelling, and a couple of shots were fired. Then more shouts arose, and a shrill whistle was heard.

"Answer that, bo'sun," cried the officer in command of the party, and a shrill chirping sound seemed to cut the night air. "Now, my lads, forward!"

"One minute," cried Aleck. "We want to get afloat. Tell your men to give my boat a shove off."

"Hang your boat!" cried the officer, angrily. "Keep together, my lads. Yes, all right; we're coming."

The party went off after their leader at a run, for another sharp whistle rang out at a distance.

"Well, he might have been civil," said Aleck.

"Haw! haw! haw! Fancy your asking a luff-tenant on duty that, Master Aleck!" said Tom, laughing, and talking with his mouth full, for he had recommended his unfinished meal.

"It wouldn't have hurt him," said Aleck. "Here, leave off eating, Tom, and let's get away from here. I don't want to be mixed up with this horrid business."

"'Tis horrid, sir, to you, but I got used to it," said the man, rolling off the side to begin swaying the boat, Aleck leaping out on the other side.

"No good, sir. She's fast for another half-hour. Tide rises very slowly round here."

"Then we shall have to stop here and listen. Hark, that's glass breaking. People struggling too. I say, Tom, try again; push hard."

"Hard as you tells me, sir; but it's no good—her deep keel's right down in this here fine shingle. We must wait till the tide lifts her."

The sailor stopped short to listen, for the noise which came to them on the still night air increased. Hoarse voices ringing out defiance, savage yells and curses, mingled with the shrieks and appeals of angry women, smote upon the listeners' ears, and Aleck stamped one foot with impatient rage.

"Oh, Tom," he cried, "I can't bear it. I never heard anything of this kind before."

"And don't want to hear it again, sir, o' course. Well, it arn't nice. I didn't like it till I got used to it, and then I didn't seem to mind."

"How brutal!" said Aleck, angrily. "Hark at that!"

"I hear, sir. That's some o' the fishermen's wives letting go."

"Yes; and you speak in that cool way. Aren't you sorry for them?"

"Nay, sir; not me. I'm sorry for the poor sailor boys."

"What!" cried Aleck, angrily. "Tom, I didn't think you could be so brutal."

"You don't understand, sir. That's the women shouting and screaming as they give it to the press-gang. It's the sailors gets hits and scratches and called all sorts o' names, and they're 'bliged to take it all. But, my word, there's getting to be a shindy to-night and no mistake. Let's try again to get the boat off!"

They tried; but she was immovable, save that they could rock her from side to side.

"We'll do it in another ten minutes, Master Aleck, and then we'd better row till we're outside the harbour. Hark at 'em now! That's not the women now; that's the men. I say, I b'lieve there's a good dozen o' the smuggling lot about the town, Master Aleck, but I hadn't seen one. Did you catch sight o' any on 'em?"

"I saw Eben Megg," said the lad.

"And he's about the worst on 'em, Master Aleck. Well, it strikes me his games are up for a bit. He's a wunner to fight, and he'll stick to his mates; but they won't beat the press-gang off, for when they want men and it comes to a fight it's the sailors who win. Well, it'd do young Megg good. He's too much of a bully and rough 'un for me. Fine-looking chap, but thinks too much of hisself. Make a noo man of him to be aboard a man-o'-war for a few years."

"Pst, Tom! Listen! They're fighting up at the back there."

"And no mistake, my lad."

For fresh shouts, orders, and another whistle rang out, followed by what was evidently a fierce struggle, accompanied by blows, the sounds as they came out of the darkness being singularly weird and strange.

"Let's get away, Tom," said Aleck, huskily; "it's horrible to listen to it."

"Yes, sir. Heave away, both together. Now, then, she moves. No, she's as fast as ever."

"Oh!" groaned Aleck, striking both hands down with a loud smack upon the boat's gunwale and then stopping short as if paralysed, for there were quick steps, then a rush, evidently up the nearest narrow way among the sheds.

Then all was silence, and a sharp voice cried:

"Halt there! Surrender, or I fire."

A rush followed the command, and then a pistol shot rang out, Aleck seeing the flash; but the shot did not stop the man who received the command. As far as Aleck in his excitement could make out he rushed at and closed with him who tried to stop him, when a desperate struggle ensued as of two men wrestling upon the cobble stones, their hoarse panting coming strangely to the listeners' ears.

All thought of launching the boat was swept away by the excitement of listening to the struggle, which grew more painful as the voice that had uttered the command rose again in half-stifled tones:

"This way, lads; help!"

A dull thud followed, as of a heavy blow being delivered, followed by a fall and the rush of footsteps again, but this time over the loose shingle, and the next minute a dimly-seen figure approached, running straight for the water.

But instead of the man running into the harbour, he turned sharp to his left on catching sight of the boat and staggered up to it.

"Who's that?" he said, hoarsely. "You, Tom Bodger—Master Aleck? Here, quick, sir; for the love of heaven save a poor fellow! It's the press-gang. Got five on us. Help, sir! Shove off with me. I'm too dead beat to swim."

"I can't help you, Eben. I dare not," cried Aleck. "What could I do?"

"Oh! but, Master Aleck—hark! there's more coming!"

"I tell you I can't. I dare not. They're the King's men, and—"

"Where are you, your honour?" came out of the darkness, to be answered by a groan and a feeble attempt at a whistle.

"This way, lads," rang out, and there was the rush of feet and a deeper groan.

"Eben, you've killed the officer," whispered Aleck, in his horror.

"I was on'y fighting for my liberty, master," whispered the man, hoarsely. "Master Aleck, you don't like me, I know. I'm a bad 'un, I s'pose; but there's my young wife and the little weans yonder waiting for me, and when they know—"

The great rough fellow could say no more, but choked.

"Run for it, then," said Aleck; "wrong or right, we'll try and cover you."

"It's no good, sir," whispered the man; "there's no end of 'em surrounding us, and I'm as weak now as a rat."

He caught Aleck's hand, as the lad thought, to cling to it imploringly, but the next moment he held it to his forehead, and it was snatched away in horror, for the man had evidently been cut down and was bleeding profusely.

"He's wounded badly, Tom," whispered Aleck, excitedly. "We must help him now."

"Ay, ay, sir," said Tom, gruffly.

"Ah, the boat! The boat!" panted the smuggler.

"In with you then," said Aleck.

"Nay, nay," whispered Tom. "She arn't afloat, Eben Megg. Here, lay yer weight on to her if yer can't shove."

"Hi! hallo there!" cried a voice from the direction where the struggle had taken place.

In response there was the sound of the boat's keel grating on the water-covered shingle, and the smuggler pressed close up to Aleck's side.

"Do you hear there?" came from the same quarter. "In the King's name, stand!"

"Lay yer backs into it," grunted Tom. "Shove, my lads, shove!"

"Come on, my lads! We must have them, whoever they are," came from apparently close at hand.

"Ah, look sharp! There's a boat."

"Now for it," whispered Tom, and as he grunted hard the boat began to glide from shingle and water into water alone, while as Aleck thrust with all his might, knee-deep now, he felt the boat give way, and then it seemed to him that the smuggler sank down beside him, making a feeble clutch at his clothes and uttering a low groan.

Aleck's left hand acted as it were upon its own responsibility, closing in the darkness upon Eben's shirt and holding fast, while the lad's right hand held up the boat's gunwale.

The next moment he felt himself drawn off his feet and being dragged through the water, in which the boat was jerking and dancing as if to shake itself free.

It was too dark to see, but this is what was taking place. As the party of three were trying their best to get the little yawl afloat the shingle clung fast to its keel and very little progress was made, although Tom Bodger thrust and jerked at it with all his might, more like a dwarf than ever, for his wooden legs went down in the wet shingle at every movement, right to the socket stumps; but at last, when their efforts began to appear to be in vain, a little soft swell rolled in, just as a rush was being made by the press-gang, the boat lifted astern, and as the water passed under it, literally leaped up forward, shaking itself free of the clinging sand and stones, and, yielding to the three launchers, glided right away.

It was none too soon. Aleck was holding on upon one side nearly amidships, while Tom on the other side let the gunwale glide through his hands till they were close to the bow, and then holding on fast with both hands he made one of his jumps or hops, to add impetus to the boat's way and get his breast over the bow and scramble in.

His bound—if it could be so-called—was very successful, for the next moment he was balanced upon his chest across the gunwale, gripping at the edge of the fore-locker, with his legs sticking out behind, and exulting over the sensation of the boat dancing under him, when he felt himself seized by one of the press-gang party, who had dashed in after the boat and made a grab at the first thing that offered in the dark.

The sailor was unlucky in his hold, but no wonder, for the darkness gave him no opportunity of making any choice, and as it happened he gripped one of Tom's pegs with his right and followed it up by clapping his left hand alongside, trying hard to drag his prisoner out or to stop the boat.

As aforesaid he was unlucky, for he was to suffer an entirely new experience. Had he grasped an ordinary human leg in the black darkness he would only have had a jerking kick or two, and most probably he would have held on, but here it was something very different.

"Got 'em!" he cried, loudly. "Come on!" and then he was smitten with a strange surprise, and also with something else.

For Tom Bodger, as he lay balanced upon the lower part of his chest, half in and half out of the boat, had got his fingers well under the side of the locker and was holding on with all the strength of his horny fingers.

"Ah, would yer!" he roared, as he felt himself seized, and, unable to kick for want of yielding joints, he began to work his stumps, to his holder's horror, like a pair of gigantic shears gone mad. The one that was free struck the sailor a sounding rap on the ear and made him release his hold of the prisoned piece of timber for the moment, and when he splashed after the boat, after recovering from his surprise, and made another grab, the second free peg caught him on the arm like a blow from a constable's truncheon.

The sailor uttered a yell for help, but it was cut short by a blow on each side of his neck as Tom's legs snapped together, and then he fell forward with a splash and was helped out by a couple of his mates, who stood, waist-deep, gazing into the darkness after the boat.

"Where are yer, my lads?" panted Tom, as he progressed over the side like a huge toad.

"Help! Help!" came from his right, and with the boat rocking from side to side he felt about along the gunwale till his hand came in contact with Aleck's fingers, clinging desperately to the edge of the boat.

"Got yer," said Tom, gripping the lad's wrist and hanging over the side to speak. "Can't yer hold on while I get an oar out and move her a bit furder away?"

"No. Help me in," said Aleck, huskily.

"Right, sir. Here, let me get my hands under yer arms, and I'll heave yer in. I say, wheer's Eben Megg?"

"Out here. I've got hold of him."

Tom Bodger whistled softly in his astonishment.

"Hold tight on him, my lad," he growled; and then putting forth his great strength of arm and back, he raised Aleck right over the boat's side, and as Eben was drawn close in, loosened the former and got tight hold of the latter.

"Can yer shift for yourself now, Master Aleck?" he whispered.

"Yes; but have you got Eben?"

"Ay, ay! Got him fast. Out o' my way."

The next minute the smuggler lay perfectly inert at the bottom of the boat and Aleck was passing an oar over the stern and beginning to scull.

"Get another oar out, Tom," he whispered, "or they'll have us yet."

"Ay, ay!" was growled, softly.

But it was too loud, for a voice close at hand shouted:

"Now, then, you in the boat, it's of no use. Surrender, in the King's name!"

The splashing made by the oars ceased, and Tom put his lips close to Aleck's ear.

"You arn't going to surrender, are yer, Master Aleck?"

"No; use your oar as a pole, and get us farther away."

"Do you hear there?" cried another voice. "Heave-to, or I'll fire."

"All gammon, Master Aleck; I know. Don't believe they've got any pistols."

"There was a shot fired," said Aleck.

"Orficer's, p'raps, sir. Here, I can't do no good a-poling; it's getting deeper here."

"Scull then," said Aleck; "and be careful. They've got boats somewhere."

Just then there was a flapping noise, which gave them a turn.

"What's that?" said Aleck, sharply.

"Wind got the sail loose," said Tom. "There's a nice breeze coming on. Shall I shake out a reef or two of the sail, sir?"

"Yes, if you think we can see to steer?"

"Dunno about that, sir. We must go gently, and feel."

The next few minutes were devoted to preparations for spreading a portion of the canvas to the light breeze, as they listened to hail after hail from the shore; and then, as they began to glide softly along, one of the hails from the shore bidding them heave-to was answered from round to their right.

"Ay, ay, sir!"

"Keep a sharp look out for a boat somewhere off here. Three prisoners in her escaping."

"My hye!" muttered Tom Bodger. "That's nice. Resisting the law too. Strikes me as we're going to be in a mess."

Chapter Sixteen

Aleck, in the midst of his excitement in his novel position, had somewhat similar thoughts to those of his rough sailor companion. For what was he doing, he asked himself—resisting the King's men performing a duty— for a duty it was, however objectionable it might be—and helping a man they were trying to impress. Worse still, trying to secure the liberty of a well-known smuggler, one of the leading spirits in as determined a gang as existed on the coast.

It was that appeal for the sake of the wife and children that had turned the scale in Eben's favour, and, as Aleck argued now to himself as they glided steadily over the waters of the outer harbour, what was done was done, and to hang back now would mean capture and no mercy, for he would probably find himself bundled aboard the sloop-of-war and no heed paid to his remonstrances.

"Say, Master Aleck," was suddenly whispered to him, "I hope Eben Megg arn't going to die."

"Die? Oh, Tom, no. I forgot all about his cut head. We must tie it up."

"Tied up it is, sir, wi' my hankychy, but he's got a nasty cut on the head. Ah, it's bad work resisting the law, for lawful it is, I s'pose, to press men."

"Don't talk so loud. Feel Eben's head, and find out whether it has stopped bleeding."

"Did just now, sir, and it about hev. But, I say, Master Aleck, I'm all in a squirm about you."

"About me? Why?"

"You see, we don't know hardly which way to turn, and I expects every minute to be running into one o' the man-o'-war boats."

"Well, if we do we do; but I think we can get right out, and it won't be so dark then."

"I b'lieve there's a fog sattling down, sir, and if there is we shall be ketched as sure as eggs is eggs. I'm sorry for you, my lad, and I s'pose I'm sorry for Eben Megg, though we arn't friends. Bit sorry, too, for myself."

"Oh, they can't hurt you, Tom."

"Can't hurt me, sir? Why, they'll hev me up afore the magistrits, and cut me shorter than I am."

"Nonsense!" said Aleck, with a laugh. "They don't behead people now, and even if they did they wouldn't do it for helping a pressed man to escape."

"Tchah! I don't mean that way, my lad. I mean chop off my pension, and—"

"Pst!"

Unwittingly they had been slowly sailing right for one of the sloop's boats, and their whispers had been heard, for from out of the darkness, and apparently a very little way off, came a hail and an order to stop.

"Shall us stop, sir?" said Tom.

"Stop going that way. Helm down, Tom," whispered Aleck; and the little sail swung over and filled on the other side, the water rippling gently under their bows. Otherwise it was so silent that they could hear whispers away to their right, followed by a softly given order, which was followed by the dip, dip, dip, dip of oars, and they glided so closely by the rowers that Aleck fancied he could see the man-o'-war's boat.

A couple of minutes later they tacked again, and were sailing on, when all at once Aleck whispered, as he leaned over his companion:

"That must be the low line of the fog bank, Tom. Look how black it is!"

"Where, sir?"

"Over where I'm pointing," replied Aleck.

"By jinks!" growled Tom, excitedly, shifting the rudder and throwing the wind out of the sail, which flapped for a bit and then once more filled on the other tack.

"What was it, Tom?"

"What was it, my lad? Why, that warn't no fog bank lying low on the water, but the harbour wall. Why, we should ha' gone smash on it in another jiffy, stove in, and sunk, for there's no getting up the place this side."

"Are you sure it was?"

"Sartain. We're all right, though, now, and it's done us good, for I know where we are, and I think we can get away now unless the boat's headed us once more."

"Keep her away a little more then. Ah! Hark at Eben! He sounds as if he's coming to."

The smuggler was very far from being dead, for he muttered a few words, and then all at once they heard the backs of his hands strike the boat sharply, while to their horror he yelled out the word "Cowards!"

Tom Bodger was active enough, in spite of his misfortune, as he abundantly proved—perhaps never more so than on this occasion—when again, with almost the action of a toad, he leaped right upon the smuggler, driving him back just as he was trying to rise, and covering his face with a broad chest and smothering his next cries.

Then Aleck grew more horrified than ever, for a tremendous struggle began, the smuggler, evidently under the impression that he was in the hands of the press-gang, fighting hard for his liberty, bending himself up and calling to his companions for help. But his voice sounded dull and stifled, and in spite of his strength Tom's position gave him so great an advantage that he was able to keep him down.

"Mind, mind, Tom," whispered Aleck; "you are smothering him."

"And a precious good thing too, Master Aleck. He'll say thankye when he knows. Why, if I let him have his own way he'd—lie still, will yer?— want to have the press-gang down upon us. Lookye here, messmet, if you don't lie quiet I'll make Master Aleck come and sit on yer too."

"But I'm afraid, Tom."

"So'm I, my lad. Pretty sort o' onreasonable beggar. Asts us to save him from the King's men, and when we've got him off, kicking up such a fillaloo as this to show 'em where we are. I arn't got patience with him, that I arn't."

The man struggled again so violently that he got his hand on one side, making the boat rock and Tom Bodger grunt in his efforts to keep his prisoner down.

"It's no good, Master Aleck," he whispered, hoarsely; "if I'd got my legs I could twist 'em round him and keep him still; but there's no grip in a pair of wooden pegs. Come and sit on his knees and help keep him quiet. Lash the helm, sir. She'll run easy enough then."

But at this the smuggler suddenly ceased his desperate efforts to get free, and lay perfectly still.

"He's turned over a noo leaf, Master Aleck, and p'raps I shall manage him now. I say, wish I hadn't put them two pieces o' board over the pitch; he's got it just under his back, and it would have helped to hold him still."

"Who's that?" said the smuggler, hoarsely.

"It's me, what there is left on me," growled Tom. "Great ugly rough 'un. Best thing you can do will be smuggle me a noo blue shirt from Jarsey."

"Tom Bodger?"

"Tom Bodger it is."

"Why are you sitting on me? I thought—"

"You thought," growled Tom, scornfully. "What right's a chap like you to think?"

"But I thought the press-gang had got me."

"Well, I was pressing on yer as hard as I could to keep yer from shouting and flying out of the boat. Here's Master Aleck and me getting oursens into no end o' trouble to keep you out o' the press-gang's hands, and you begins shouting to 'em to come and take you."

"I'm very sorry, mate. I s'pose I was off my head a bit—seemed to wake up out of a bad dream about fighting. Yes, that's it; I recollect now. Where's the gang?"

"Cruising about trying to find us."

"It's so dark. Where are we?"

"Somewheers out beyond the pier head, and it's all as black as the inside of a barrel o' pitch. Keep quiet; don't talk so loud."

"No, mate," said the smuggler, petulantly; "but I'm not quite myself. I got a crack on the head from something; I've been bleeding a bit. But, tell me, are we safe?"

"Dunno yet. Hope so."

"Am I lying in Master Aleck's boat?"

"Yes, on yer back," growled Tom. "Are yer comfy? I put in a nice noo bit o' pine board 'sevening for yer to lie on."

"No; of course I'm not comf'table with you sitting on me."

"Course you arn't. Think I am with that great brass buckle o' yourn sticking in the bottom o' my chest?"

"Is Master Aleck there?" said the smuggler, after a short pause.

"Yes, I'm here, Eben, steering."

"Ah, I can see you now, sir."

"No, yer can't," growled Tom, "so none o' your lies. Just because you want to be civil to the young master."

"I tell you I can see him quite plain. Think I've got eyes like a mole?"

"Look out then, and tell us where we are."

"How can I look out with my head down here?"

"Let him get up, Tom," said Aleck.

"Easy, Master Aleck. Let's make sure first as he won't go off his head again."

"I shan't go off my head again now I'm safe, stoopid," cried the smuggler, angrily. "Master Aleck, sir, thankye kindly for helping a poor desprit fellow. I can't say much, but my poor little wife'll say: 'Gord bless yer for this for the sake of our weans.'"

"There, don't talk about it, Eben; only let it be a lesson to you not to go smuggling any more. Do you hear?"

"Yes, sir, I hear; but this hadn't nothing to do with running a cargo or two. We was unlucky enough to be in Rockabie, and someone has sold us to the press-gang. Warn't you, were it, mate?"

"Get out!" growled Tom; "is it likely?"

"No. Someone did, but I don't believe it was old Double Dot, Master Aleck."

"And you believe I didn't, now?"

"B'lieve yer? Yes, sir; and I'll never forget this night."

"Look here," growled Tom, "hadn't you and him better be quiet, Master Aleck? You're both talking very fine about saving and gettin' free and never forgettin', and all the time there's boats out arter us and they may be clost up for all I can say. It's about the darkest night I was ever out in."

"Let me get up, mate, and have a look round," said the smuggler.

"Think he's safe, Master Aleck?"

"Oh, yes, of course. Let him get up and try if he can make out where we are."

"But I can't get him down again if he goes off his head, sir, and tries to turn us out of the boat."

The smuggler uttered a low, mocking laugh.

"Bit too strong for yer, eh, Tommy?"

"Ay; but you wouldn't be if I was all here. There; get up then."

Tom's legs rattled on the planks of the boat as he rolled himself off and stood up and listened to the smuggler with a low, deep sigh as he sat up, tried to stand, and sat down again in the bottom of the little craft.

"Bit giddy," he said, apologetically; "things seems to swim round."

He had put his hands up to his head as he spoke. Then suddenly:

"Who tied my head up with a hankychy?"

"I did," growled Tom, surlily, "and just you mind as your missus washes it out and irons it flat for you to give it me agen next time you comes to Rockabie."

"I will, mate," said the smuggler, quietly. "There," he added, after drawing a long, deep breath, "I'm beginning to come right again. Yes, it is a bit dark to-night," he added, after staring about him for a minute or two. Then, uttering a sharp ejaculation, "Here, quick, put your helm hard up, Master Aleck. Quick, my lad; can't you see where you're going?"

"No," said Aleck, obeying the order quickly, with the result that the sail began to flap, while, as it filled again and the boat careened in the opposite direction, there was a dull, hissing, washing sound, followed by a slap and a hollow thud, as if a quantity of water had been thrown into a rift.

"Where are we?" said Aleck, who felt startled.

"Running clear now, sir; but in another moment you'd ha' been right on the East Skerries."

"What!" cried Tom.

"Don't holler, mate," said the smuggler, drily. "Mebbe there's one o' the man-o'-war's boats."

"Running right on the East Skerries! Right you are, messmet. That was the tide going into the Marmaid's Kitchen. Here, I feel as if I'd never been to sea and took bearings in my life, Master Aleck!"

"Yes; what is it?"

"Don't you never trust me again."

"But do you mean to say that you can't see those rocks just abeam, Tom Bodger?"

"Not a rock on 'em, messmet; but I can hear the bladder-wrack washing in and out."

"But you, Master Aleck?"

"I can see it looks a little darker there," replied the lad, "and a little lighter lower down."

"Well, it's amazin', sir. I can see 'em quite plain. I s'pose my eyes must be a little better than yourn through being out so much of a night."

"Smuggling, Eben?" said Aleck, quietly.

The man laughed softly, and, standing up now, holding on by one of the stays, he shaded his eyes and looked about him for some time.

"There's the riding lights of the two King's ships," he said, half aloud, "but I can't see the boats. They'd be giving the rocks about here a wide berth, and you pretty well left 'em behind, Master Aleck. Now, sir, what are you going to do?"

"Run home, of course," said Aleck.

"Round outside the point, sir?"

"Of course."

"You'd save a good two miles by running close to shore and inside the big island and the point."

"But the rocks?"

"You could steer clear of them, sir."

"But you mean run through the narrows—through the channel?"

"Of course, sir."

"Oh, it couldn't be done," said Aleck, excitedly.

"Easy enough at high water, sir; and that's what it'll be in another hour."

"Have you ever done it, Eben?"

"Often, sir, and in a bigger boat than this."

"Could you steer us safe through?"

The smuggler laughed.

"My father taught me to do it, sir, when I was a little boy."

"It would save an hour?"

"Quite, sir."

"What do you say, Tom? Would you go?"

"Me, sir? I'd go anywhere as Eben Megg dared to steer."

"But it is so dark," said Aleck, hesitating.

"The breaking water makes it lighter, sir, and the sea brimes to-night out yonder. Look, we're getting to where it flashes, where it breaks!"

"To be sure; it's beginning, too, where the boat cuts the water. Come and take the helm then. But, stop; what about the wind?"

"Westerly, sir, and blowing astern of us all the way through."

"Then we will go, Tom. Why, no man-o'-war boat dare follow us there."

"That they won't, sir," said Tom, decidedly. "I say, messmet, what do you say to a couple o' reefs in the sail?"

"Let her be," said the smuggler, taking his seat by Aleck, who handed him the little tiller. "There, sir, you may say good-bye to the press-gang boats now. I daresay they'll be hanging about on their way to their ship, but we shall hug the rocks in and out all along."

All talking ceased now, and in his new-found confidence in and admiration of the smuggler's knowledge of the intricate ways between the huge rocks that had from time to time become detached from the tremendous cliffs, and stood up forming the stacks and towers frequented by the myriads of sea-birds, the lad sat in silence watching the anchor lights of the men-o'-war, which came into sight and then disappeared again and again. Then, as they approached the wall-like cliffs, it seemed to grow lighter low down where the tide rushed and broke in foam, shedding a pale lambent glow, while deep down beneath them tiny points of light were gliding along as if the whole universe of stars had fallen into the sea and were illumining the dark depths below the boat.

There was a strange fascination, too, in the ride, as without hesitation the smuggler turned the boat's head into channels where the tide rushed like a mill-race close up to towering masses, and round and in and out, threading the smaller skittle-like pieces, whose lower parts had been fretting away beneath the action of the sea till the bottom was not a third of the distance through near the top.

Tom, too, sat very silent for a long time, chewing a piece of pigtail tobacco, evidently feeling perfectly comfortable about the smuggler's knowledge of the coast.

At last, though, he found his tongue:

"I say, messmet, how's that head o' yourn?"

"Very sore, Tommy."

"Ay, it will be. Dessay you lost a lot o' blood."

"I believe I did," said the steersman.

"Well, you're a big, strong fellow, and it'll do you good. But, I say, mind I has that hankychy back!"

"I won't forget, mate," said Eben, quietly. Then to himself, "I shan't forget this night."

"I don't like Eben Megg, and I don't like smugglers in general," Tom Bodger; "but human natur's human natur', even with old King's pensioned men as oughtn't to; but if Eben comes to me with that there hankychy and slips a big wodge of hard Hamsterdam 'bacco and a square bottle o' stuff as hasn't paid dooty into my hands in the dark some night, what am I to do? Say I can't take it? Well, I oughter, but—well, he arn't offered the stuff to me yet."

The other occupants of the boat were thinking deeply during the latter part of the sail. Aleck was wondering what his uncle would say, and Eben Megg thinking of his future, and he was startled from his reverie by Aleck, who suddenly said:

"What about the press-gang, Eben—do you think they will know you again?"

"Hope not, sir; but I'm not very comf'table about it. Someone set 'em on—someone as knows me; and, worse luck, they've got some of our chaps."

"But they haven't caught you."

"Not yet, sir, but there's chaps as don't like me, and if they've been pressed they'll be a-saying to-morrow morning as it arn't fair for them to be took and me to get away. See?"

"Yes; but what difference will that make?" The smuggler laughed aloud.

"Only that they might put the skipper of the man-o'-war cutter up to where he'd find me."

"But you had nothing to do with the cutter's men—that officer was from the sloop?"

"Ay, sir; but they're all working together, and the cutter's skipper has got a black mark against my name."

"Oh!" said Aleck, thoughtfully. "Then I suppose you'll go into hiding?"

"That's right, sir; but I shan't feel safe then. Eh, Tom Bodger?"

"Right, messmet; they'll be ferreting all along the coast arter yer. Tell you what I should do if I was you."

"What?" said the man, eagerly.

"Have a good wash up in the morning, and then jump in a boat and go and board the sloop like a man."

"What!"

"And then, says you, 'I want to see the skipper,' you says, and as soon as he comes on deck, 'Here I am, your honour,' you says. 'I warn't going to let your men take me last night as if I were an enemy or a thief; but if the King wants sailors, here I am, and I'll sarve him like a man.'"

"Well done, Tom!" cried Aleck.

"Think so, Master Aleck?" said the smuggler. "Yes, it sounds very nice, I suppose; but it won't do. I'm the wrong sort. Can't alter now."

"You know your own affairs best, Eben," said Aleck, quietly; "but I expect they'll catch you, and then you'll be obliged to serve."

"I expecks so too, Master Aleck, but I mean to have a fight for it first. There we are. P'raps you'd better take the tiller now and run your boat into the gap. You know the way better than I do. You, too, Tom Bodger."

The latter went forward, to stand boat-hook in hand, while, after passing the tiller to the lad, Eben laid hold of the rope and loosened it from the pin, ready to lower down the yard as soon as Aleck passed the word.

The next minute the boat had been run into the narrow jaws of the great chasm, the sail had been lowered, and after they had glided some distance along, helped by the boat-hook deftly wielded by Tom Bodger, the smuggler suddenly sprang out on to a shelf of rock at the side.

"What are you doing?" cried Aleck. "You can't get up there in the dark."

"Can't I, sir? You wait, and I'll hail you from the top before you get up to your mooring-rings."

The smuggler kept his word, a low farewell shout coming from on high, and echoing in whispers right along the gap.

"Good-night or good morning!" he cried, and then he was gone.

"I couldn't have got up there even in daylight, Tom," said Aleck.

"Nor me nayther, sir. Might ha' done it once upon a time, but wooden legs arn't the best kind o' gear for rock-climbing, sir, any more than they are for manning the yards aboard ship; and that's why I was pensioned-off."

"Yes, Tom; but what about you to-night?"

"Me, sir? I'm a-going to kiver mysen up with the sail and snooze away in the bottom of the boat."

"Very well; and I'll bring you something to eat as soon as I get in."

"Thankye, sir; that's about the right sort for me, as I didn't make much of a business over that there bread and cheese; and here we are!"

"Make her fast, Tom," cried Aleck, springing out. "I want to go and explain to uncle. I wonder what he'll say," the lad continued, to himself, as he hurried up the slope. "He can't be so very cross when he knows all."

There was a candle burning in the kitchen window, evidently placed there to light the wanderer on his return up the gloomy depression; and, after glancing up at his uncle's room, to see that all was dark there, the lad made for the kitchen door.

This was opened, and in a voluble whisper the housekeeper began:

"Oh, Master Aleck, I've been in sech a way about you! I made sure you'd been and drownded yourself, and here have I been sitting hours, fully expecting to see your white ghost coming up the dark path from off the sea."

"Don't be disappointed," said Aleck, merrily; "but, tell me," he whispered, "has uncle gone to bed?"

"Hours ago, my dear."

"Was he very angry because I hadn't come back?"

"He didn't say so, Master Aleck."

"But he asked if I'd come home?"

"Nay, he didn't."

"He went down into the boat harbour?"

"That he didn't, Master Aleck."

"Then he went up on the cliff to look out with the glass?"

"Nay; he's been writing his eyes out of his head almost, Master Aleck. Wouldn't come down to his dinner nor yet to his tea, and I had to take him up something on a tray, or else he wouldn't ha' eat a mossle. I shall be glad when he's writ his book."

"Then he didn't know I hadn't come?"

"No, I don't believe he thought about you a bit."

"Hah!" sighed Aleck.

"But what have you been a-doing of, Master Aleck? Not fighting again, have you?"

"You don't see any marks, do you?"

"Nay, I don't see no marks; but whatever did make you so late, Master Aleck?"

"Someone broke a hole in the boat, and we had to mend it, that's all. Now cut me some bread and ham for Tom Bodger down at the boat-shelter; he's nearly starved."

The provender was willingly out and carried down, and soon after Aleck lay dreaming over the adventures of the day.

Chapter Seventeen

The next morning one of the first things that saluted Aleck's eyes on making his way up to the look-out on the cliff, was the sloop-of-war about a couple of miles out, sailing very slowly along, followed at a short distance by the Revenue cutter, and the lad had not been watching five minutes before he became aware of the fact that Ness Dunning's work in the garden was at a standstill, that individual being laid flat upon his chest watching the vessels' movements through a piece of pipe.

Away to the right on the cliffs, dotted about which lay Eilygugg, there was a white speck here and a blue speck there, and a little more intent gazing proved to the lad that there was another speck upon the edge of the farthest cliff in view.

"Women on the look-out to give warning to the smugglers," thought Aleck, and he hurried back to see if his uncle was down, and if he were not to return to the cliff-top with the glass.

But the captain was just descending, and his first words were:

"That's right, my boy; let's have breakfast. By the way, did you get my paper?"

This started the lad, who was crammed with his news, which he hurriedly made known.

"Humph!" said the old man. "Rather a lively experience for you, my lad; but you must be careful, for I don't want to have you in trouble over helping smugglers to escape."

"No, uncle, of course not," said Aleck; "but do you think I did wrong?"

"Certainly, my boy. This fellow—ill-conditioned fellow Megg—was fighting against the law. He was doubtless there on some business connected with smuggling, and nearly got caught by the press-gang—an institution I do not admire, but those in authority consider it a necessity for the supply of the Navy. Keep away from all these worries, and as much as possible from Rockabie and its young ruffians."

"Yes, uncle; but I really did not seek to be amongst all that business in Rockabie yesterday," pleaded Aleck.

"Of course not, my boy, and you need not look so penitent. The law's the law, of course, but I'm afraid if I had been appealed to as you were last night I should have done the same, and given the scoundrel a good talking to as I brought him away. There, have no more to do with it, and keep out of sight if there are boats landed, as there most probably will be, to make a search."

"But suppose the officers land and know me again, uncle?"

"There, there, I'm just in the midst of a tiresomely intricate chapter of my book, and don't want to have my attention taken off."

"No, uncle, of course not; but if the officers and men know me again?"

"Why, let them, my lad. You were doing no harm, and they can do you none. Now let's finish our breakfast."

"Shall I stay in, uncle?" said Aleck. "Tom Bodger slept down in the boat last night, and I wanted to take him some breakfast."

"Go and take it then, of course."

"And then stay in?"

"No, no; nonsense. Now don't bother me any more."

"I won't get into any trouble," Aleck said to himself, as he hurried out, armed with two huge sandwiches and a mug of well-sweetened coffee, with which he got on pretty well going through the garden, hardly spilling a drop, till he was startled by the voice of the gardener, saying, from the other side, in anticipation:

"Thankye, Master Aleck. That's very good of yer."

That startling made the lad half stop, and about a tablespoonful of the hot preparation flew out on to the path. But Aleck paid no attention, not even turning his head, but increasing his pace, with the mug troubling him a good deal in his efforts to preserve the liquid in a state of equilibrium in a rapidly descending and very slippery and uneven rocky path.

"I daresay you'd like it," muttered Aleck, as he hurried on, followed directly after by:

"I'm over here, Master Aleck."

"Thank you for the information, Ness, but they say none are so deaf as those who will not hear."

At the next zigzag of the path he was out of sight and hearing, and a few minutes later close upon the niche devoted to his boat, with the big sandwiches complete, and quite three parts of the coffee in the mug.

"Sorry to have been so long, Tom," he cried, breathlessly, "but here you—"

Aleck was going to say *are*, but he felt that it would not be correct, for Tom was not there, nor anywhere within sight down the narrow waterway in the direction of the sea. He had left tokens of his presence in the shape of tidy touches, for the boat tackle had all been taken out and stowed away in the overhanging cavernous part, and the boat lay ready for any amount of necessary repairs, for, in spite of the sailor's declaration the previous evening, she had been leaking to such an extent during the night since she had been tied up, that she was one quarter full of water.

"Why, he ought to have stopped to mend the hole properly. Seen the men-o'-war coming, I suppose, and gone back to Rockabie so as not to be found if the sailors come searching here. But how stupid! What am I to do with this coffee and bacon?"

A moment was sufficient for his decision, and he turned and hurried back, made straight for the tool-house, where he placed the mug on the bench, with the sandwiches carefully balanced across. Then, carefully keeping out of the gardener's sight till the last minute, he turned down a path which led him near, and then, putting his hands to his lips, he shouted:

"Ness!"

"Yes, Master Aleck," came directly from where the man was making believe to have been busy for hours.

"I've put some coffee and something to eat in the tool-shed," bellowed Aleck. "Let him think what he likes," he muttered, as he ran back indoors, obtained the glass, and was off again to make for the cliff and watch the proceedings of the men-o'-war.

Their proceedings seemed to be nil, for both vessels were hove to, and after watching them for a few minutes by means of the glass, Aleck closed it, and hung about, undecided what to do.

A minute later he had made up his mind, for the cave in which the smugglers' boats lay drawn up attracted him, and he was level with the cottages and preparing to descend when it occurred to him that he had better not go, for if Eben had been suspicious of his visit and ready to think him guilty of giving information to the press-gang people and Revenue men, it was quite possible that others there might be the same, while doubtless the women who had lost son, husband, or father during the past night would be in no pleasant temper to encounter.

So instead of descending, Aleck went on in the direction of the great gap in the cliff where he had had so exciting an encounter with the smuggler, intending to make for the shelf again so as to sit down and watch the sloop and cutter, but only to find when he reached the place, that the view in that direction was cut off by towering rocks.

Consequently he climbed back, went round the head of the deep combe, and crept round to the other side, mounted to the top, and then stood looking down into another of the great rifts in the coast-line, one which had perpendicular sides, the haunt of wild fowl, going sheer down to the water, which here came several hundred yards right into the land.

There were plenty of capital places here where a strong-headed person could go and perch and excite no more notice than a sea-bird. They were what ordinary inshore folk would have called "terribly dangerous," but such an idea never occurred to Aleck, who selected one of the most risky, in a spot where the vast wall where he stood was gashed by a great crack, which allowed of a descent of some thirty feet to a broad ledge littered by the preenings of the sea-birds, which seemed, though none were present, to have made it their home.

It was a delightful spot for anyone who could climb to it without growing giddy; but there was no going farther, for the angle of the ledge was quite straight, and when the lad peered over he was looking straight into the gurgling, foaming and fretting water a hundred feet below.

"What a boat cove that would have made," he thought, "if there were not so many sharp rocks rising from the bottom! I shouldn't like to try and take my kittiwake in there, big as it is."

The gloomy place, with its black shadowy niches and caves at the surface of the water, had a strange fascination for him. In fact, with its solemn twilight and irregular crag, arch and hollow, it looked quite an ideal entrance to some mermaid city such as is described by the poets who deal in fable.

But there were the two little men-o'-war to watch, and Aleck drew back a step or two from the edge to select a comfortable seat, where the colour of the rock which rose up behind was likely to assimilate with his garments and not throw him up as a plainly-seen watcher if a telescope were directed shoreward from one of the vessels.

"I wonder whether the smugglers ever come here," thought Aleck, as he looked at the face of the rock in a spot that just suited his purpose; and then he laughed to himself and felt no doubt at all, for there, just level with his face, and about eighteen inches within a crack in the rock, a shabby old horn lanthorn was wedged, and just below it was a tinder-box and a square wide-mouthed bottle, well corked, evidently to protect its contents from the spray which would come rushing up from below in a storm, the contents being so many thin slips of wood, whose sharply-pointed ends had been dipped in molten brimstone.

"One of their look-outs," he said to himself, as he turned again to sit down, but only to start and crouch upon his knees in surprise; for close up to the rock wall, half hidden by a tuft of sea-pink and grey sea holly, was a very old ragged black silk neckerchief, folded and creased as if lately torn off, and bearing strange rusty dark stains, dry and unpleasant-looking, and with very little consideration Aleck settled in his own mind that, if it were not the kerchief Tom had torn from his neck to wind round the smuggler's wound, it was as like it as could be.

It did not look a nice thing to take up and handle, but the lad bent lower, before rising up to say, decisively:

"It must be, I'm sure, for I almost seem to know the holes. Then Eben must have been here this morning watching for the press-gang people."

Another thought flashed across the lad's brain directly:

"Perhaps he's close by somewhere, watching me."

This thought produced a very uncomfortable feeling, and Aleck was divided between two forces which pulled different ways. One was to—as Tom Bodger called it—look out for squalls, the other to sit down quite calm and unconcerned to watch the vessels.

"I can't help it if Eben does fancy I'm watching his proceedings; he must feel that I should be longing to know what is going on. No, after last night I'm sure he won't think I should make signals to the ships. Why should I? There's nothing to signal about."

He focussed and re-focussed the glass, and held its larger end towards the sloop and placed one eye at the little orifice; but the left would not close and the right would not look at the sloop, but persisted in rolling about in every direction in search of Eben, who, the boy felt certain now, must be crouching back in one of the rugged clefts watching every movement he made.

Aleck did the best he could to look calm and unconcerned, but anyone who had seen him from near at hand would have pronounced it as being a dismal failure.

Then all at once he started. Down went the glass, and he craned forward towards the edge of the shelf to look down, for all at once there was a hoarse rumbling sound and a tremendous plash and crash as if a mass of rock had fallen from somewhere beneath him right into the rock-strewn gully below.

He could not resist the desire to lie down upon his breast and edge himself forward till his face was over the edge and he could look right down into the water, which was all in motion, swaying and eddying, foaming round the half-submerged blocks of weed-hung stone, and behaving generally according to its custom as the tide went and came, for these chasms displayed little change, the water being very deep and never leaving any part of the bottom bare.

There was nothing fresh to see, and after a time the lad drew back, to resume his old attitude with the glass to his eye.

But he had hardly settled down again before he experienced a slight quivering sensation, as if the cliff had suddenly received a blow, while directly after there was a deep roar as of stones falling along some vast slope. Then once more silence, with the water whispering and gurgling far below.

"Part of the cliff given way," thought Aleck, as he called to mind places here and there where masses of the rocky rampart which guarded the western shores had evidently fallen, and about which he had heard traditionary stories. But these falls had taken place in far distant times. No one that he had heard speak of them could go farther back than chronicling the event as something of which "my grandfather heered tell."

Aleck thought no more of the sounds and went on watching the two vessels, till suddenly they seemed to be doing something in the way of action. A boat was lowered from each, and the lad's glass was powerful enough to enable him to make out the faces of the officers in the stern-sheets, one of whom was the midshipman who had charge of the boat at Rockabie pier.

Aleck watched the boats rowing shoreward and separating after a time, one of the sloop's making for the Eilygugg cove, the other rowing in the direction of the gap which led up to the depression in which lay the Den.

Feeling that he would like to be at home if the boat entered their private chasm, as the lad dubbed it, he turned back along the cliff and reached the garden so as to descend to the mooring-place just in time to see the cutter's boat framed in the opening, the dark rocks round and above, and the little craft floating upon a background of opalescent sea and sky.

"They can't have come right in," thought Aleck, and after a time he made for the cliff again to get near the edge and look down, in time to see that both boats were being rowed back to their respective vessels.

An hour after they were slowly gliding away in the direction of Rockabie, their examination having been of the most perfunctory kind.

Chapter Eighteen

"No, Master Aleck, not gone, as you may say, right off," replied Tom Bodger, a few days later, as he adzed and planed and hammered away at the kittiwake down in front of the natural boat-house. "They're a-dodging of it, strikes me. King's skippers is artful when they wants men. They just got enough of that smuggling lot aboard the sloop to make the cap'n hungry for more, and, you mark my words, he'll keep away so as to make the likely ones think they're safe, and then there'll come a night when they'll find they arn't."

"Oh, I don't think so, Tom," said Aleck, opening a fresh packet of glistening golden-hued copper nails. "I don't believe the press-gang will come again."

"All right, Master Aleck, you go on thinking they won't, and I'll go on thinking they will, and let's see who's right."

"But what makes you suspicious, Tom?"

"Old sperience, sir," said the man, with a grim smile. "I 'member how we used to pick 'em up aboard the Hajax—'our Jacks,' as the lads used to call her. That's just how our old skipper used to work it; and if I were Eben Megg and didn't want to go to sea I should give up smuggling and take to an inland job, where he warn't known, and then he'd be safe. Ha! Them's the sort," he said, taking the fresh nails. "No rusting about them coppery nails."

"No; but uncle says you're to be careful and not use so many, for they're expensive, and you do seem to like to drive in as many as you can."

"Now, you lookye here, Master Aleck," said the sailor, solemnly; "a copper nail may mean a man's life. You put in a hiron one and after a bit the sea water eats it all away. Soon as the nail's eat away up starts a plank, in goes the water, and before you knows where you are down goes your boat and a man's drowned. Copper nail costs a ha'penny, p'raps, and if it's a big 'un, a penny. Well, arn't a man's life worth more'n that?"

"Of course; but how long shall you be before you've done?"

"Finish this week, sir; and then she'll last for years. You know how it was; soon as I ripped off that patch we found that a lot of her streaks under the pitch was rotten, and there was nothing for it but to cut a lot away and make a good job of it. Well, sir, we're making a good job of it, and she'll be like a noo boat when I've done."

"Of course," said Aleck; "and uncle said you were to do it thoroughly."

"And thorough it is," said Tom. "I've took a lot o' time, but there's been every bit to make good. Let's see; this makes a week and three days I've been coming over reg'lar."

"Yes, Tom," said Aleck, laughing; "and what do you think Ness says?"

"Dunno, Master Aleck," said the sailor, passing his hand, as if lovingly, over the well-smoothed sweet-smelling wood he was putting into the boat. "Wants some beer?"

"Oh, of course," said Aleck; "but he said he could have mended the boat up in half the time."

"Ah, he would," said Tom, drily. "Done it in two days, maybe, and first time she was out in bad weather the sea would undo all his work in quarter the time. Won't do, Master Aleck; boat-building's boat-building, and it's all the same as ship-building—it means men's lives, and them who scamps work like this ought to be flogged. Our old chips aboard the Hajax, as I worked with as mate, used to say precious ugly things about bad boat-building, and he'd say what he'd do to him as risked men's lives by bad work. He taught me, Master Aleck, and I feel like him. I'd rather be paid a score o' shillings for doing a fortnight's good work than have it for doing a week's; and I'm going to drive in as many o' these here best copper nails as I thinks'll be good for the boat, and you're going to hold my big hammer agen their heads while I clinch 'em. Then I shall feel as the boat's as safe as hands can make it. And, as I said afore, if I was Eben Megg, I'd drop the smuggling and go inland for a bit. That there sloop'll come into harbour some night when she arn't expected; you see if she don't! They was fine young men the skipper got the other night, and I say he'll try for another haul."

"And I say," cried Aleck, "that if he does send his men he'll be disappointed, for Eben and the other smugglers will be too foxy to let themselves be surrounded as the men were at Rockabie the other night."

"Well, Master Aleck, so much the better for them."

Then Tom began hammering and clinching the soft copper nails as if he loved his work, and as soon as the sun went down started off to trudge across the moor to Rockabie, taking his time over the task and looking as cheerful at the end as he did at the beginning of the long day.

Aleck had worked pretty hard, too, in the hot sun, and he was so drowsy that night that he was glad enough to see his uncle, wearied out with the writing, which seemed as if it would never come to an end, begin to nod and doze, and suddenly rise up and say:

"Let's go to bed!"

Aleck hardly knew how he got undressed, but he did afterwards recall going to the fully-open window and looking out at the dull night, as he drank in the soft cool air, which seemed so welcome after a still, sultry day.

Then he was asleep, dreaming of nothing, till about midnight, when his brain became active and he fancied that he was back in the darkness by the unlaunched boat at Rockabie, growing wildly excited as he listened to the shouting and scuffling up one of the narrow lanes, followed by firing and what seemed to be either an order or a cry for help.

The next moment the sleeper was wide awake, listening to what was undoubtedly a shout, and it was followed by another, both far away, but sounding clear on the night air, while from time to time came a dull murmur as of several voices together.

"They're landing a cargo," thought Aleck, and with his mind full of luggers lying off the coast, with boats going to and fro to fetch kegs, chests and bales, he hurried on his clothes, dropped from his bedroom window, hurried down the garden to the cliff path, and began to climb up the zigzag.

The landing-place would no doubt be away to the west and below Eilygugg, where the smugglers' fishing-boats lay, and as soon as he was up out of the depression on to the level down, Aleck went off at a trot to get right at the edge of the cliff, where, unseen, he calculated upon getting a good view of what was going on by the light of, as he expected, many lanthorns.

Before he was half way to the edge a thrill ran through him, for a wild shrieking arose, beginning with one voice, and turning to that of several.

"Oh, it's a wreck!" cried the lad, wildly, and he hurried on, hoping to reach the way down to the boats and be of some use before it was too late.

But as he ran on with throbbing heart and his breath growing short it gradually dawned upon him that the shrieks were those of angry women raging and storming, and this was soon confirmed, for there was the gruff burr of men's voices in the distance, followed by a shout or two, which sounded like the orders he had heard in his dream.

"Why, it's a fight," he cried, half aloud. "Tom Bodger's right; the press-gang has landed again, but, instead of going to Rockabie, they've come here."

He was as right as Tom Bodger, for at last when he made his way to the edge of the cliff it was to look down on the lanthorns carried by three boats, which were close up to the shingly patch of beach from which the fishing craft put off.

As far as he could make out in the darkness, badly illumined by the lanthorns, there was a desperate struggle going on in the shallow water lying between the shingle and the boats.

For the first few moments it seemed to Aleck in his excitement that the press-gang was being beaten off by the smugglers. Then he was puzzled, for he could hear hoarse shouts and laughter, mingled with shrieks and what seemed to be loud abuse in women's voices, followed by splashing in the water as of struggles going on again and again.

After the last of these encounters the lights began to move outward in obedience to an order given loudly from one of the boats; the regular *dip-dip* of oars came up, and then there was a rushing sound and a wild passionate chorus of cries from the shore.

"I know," panted Aleck, with a feeling of angry indignation attacking him. "They've taken and are carrying off some of the men, and the women have been fighting to try and rescue them. Poor things, how horrible, but how brave!"

He had confirmation of his surmises directly after, for there now rose up to his ears a burst of sobbing cries in a woman's voice, followed by confused eager talk from quite a party, who seemed to be trying to comfort the weeping woman.

For a few moments there was a pause, during which in the deep silence there was the regular dip of oars, and the lanthorns gently rose and fell upon the smooth rollers of the tide. Then there was a cry which went straight to Aleck's heart, so piteous and wailing were its tones:

"Oh, Eben! Eben! Come back, dear; come back!"

It reached him for whom it was intended, and was answered directly from one of the boats in words which reached Aleck more clearly perhaps then the listeners below him on the shore.

"All right, lass. Cheer up!"

The order had its effect, for a cheer given heartily in women's voices was the result; but the lad's thoughts were active.

"Cheer up!" he said to himself. "How can the woman be cheerful with her husband dragged away like that?"

The lights in the boats gradually grew more distant, while Aleck lay thinking what he had better do, for the low eager murmur of voices down below raised a feeling of commiseration in his breast, which made him feel disposed to go down and try to say a few words of comfort to the bereaved women, who had evidently been trying hard to save their husbands. But he felt that he would only be able to act in a poor bungling way and that the smugglers' people might look upon him as an intruder and a spy. For though the Den was so short a distance from Eilygugg, there had been very little intercourse, and that merely at times when the help of the captain was sought in connection with some injury or disease.

"They would likely enough turn on and begin fiercely at me," he thought. "I can do no good;" and he lay still, wanting to get away, but afraid to stir lest he should be heard.

"They'll go soon," he thought; and he waited patiently, watching the lights gradually getting fainter and fainter as their distance from the shore increased.

But the poor women seemed to have seated themselves just beyond reach of the lapping waves, which kept on breaking regularly in the little cove, and they, too, were watching the boat-lights till the last gleam had died away and all was darkness as far as they could see.

Then a low sobbing was heard, half drowned at times by many voices raised in angry protest, and mingled with threats.

This went on and on, rising, falling, and quite dying out at times, but only to break out again, having a strange effect upon Aleck, who would have given anything to get away unnoticed; but every now and then the silence was so perfect that he felt confident of being heard if he made the slightest movement, and consequently lay still.

"They'd be sure to look upon me as an intruder," he muttered, "and be ready to resent my being here."

At last though the silence was broken by the trampling of feet amongst the loose shingle, accompanied by a low murmured conversation, which was continued up the gap and died out finally high up towards the cottages, leaving the way for the listener clear.

Aleck took advantage of this, and, sad at heart, he was going slowly back towards the Den, when suddenly became aware of steps coming from the direction of the smugglers' scattered patch of cottages.

Whoever it was had approached so near and had come upon him so suddenly that he obeyed his first impulse, which was to say, sharply:

"Who's that?"

"Eh? That you, Master Aleck?"

"Yes, it is I, Ness. What are you doing out here at this time of night?"

"Mornin', arn't it, sir? Same as you, I s'pose. Who was to stop in bed with press-gangs coming and dragging folkses off to sea?"

"Then you heard them?"

"Heerd 'em, yes, sir! I was that feared o' being took myself that I got into hiding."

"You were not fighting, then?"

"Me? Fight? Not me! I lay low and listened."

"The press-gang landed and surprised the smugglers, then?"

"Yes, sir, and they've nabbed Eben Megg and six of his mates. Did yer hear the women giving it to the sailors?"

"I heard something of it."

"They was fighting savage like to save their men, and the sailor chaps was glad enough to get back to their boats; but they took Eben Megg and half a dozen more along with 'em."

"You seem to know all about it, Ness," said Aleck, suspiciously.

"Me, Master Aleck? Well, you see, being such near neighbours like I can't help hearing a deal. But it's bad work smuggling, and I keep as clear of the folk as I can. Going home to bed?"

"Yes."

"That's right, sir. Best place, too, of a night. But how did you know the press-gang was coming?"

"I didn't know they were coming."

"But you were theer?" said the old gardener, suspiciously.

"I was there?" said Aleck, "because the noise woke me, coming through my open window."

"Oh!" said the gardener. "I see."

The next minute their ways diverged, and Aleck soon after climbed up to his bedroom window, to drop off into a sleep disturbed by fights with press-gangs and smugglers all mixed up into a strange confusion, from which he was glad to awaken and find that he had hardly time to get dressed before his uncle would be down.

Chapter Nineteen

Captain Lawrence listened with knitted brows to his nephew's narration of all that had taken place in the night, and shook his head.

"It's miserable work, my boy," he said; "so piteous for the poor women. Well, perhaps good will come out of evil, and it may be the breaking up of a notorious smuggling gang."

It was just as Aleck was finishing his third cup of coffee, which he set down sharply in the saucer, startled by the sudden rush of the gardener to the open window, through which he thrust his head without ceremony.

"Here's—" he began, excitedly. "Oh!"

For a big heavy hand appeared upon his shoulder, clutching him hard and snatching him away.

"What is the meaning of this, boy?" cried the captain.

Aleck's head was already out of the window, and he drew it back again to answer:

"A lot of sailors, uncle, and their officer."

The lad's words were followed by the appearance of Jane, whose eyes were wide open and staring, her mouth following suit to some extent, so that she had to close her lips before saying:

"Plee, sir, orficer, sir. To see you, sir."

The captain nodded shortly and rose to go, followed by Aleck, out into the little ball, at whose door a naval officer and a boat's crew of men were waiting.

"Good morning," said the officer, shortly; and then turning upon Aleck, "Hallo, young man, I've seen you before!"

"Yes, in Rockabie harbour," said the lad, looking at him wonderingly, while his heart began to beat fast as he glanced at the party of sturdy sailors.

"Ah, to be sure," said the officer; then to the captain again, "You are aware, I suppose, that we made a descent last night upon your nest of smugglers here."

"I have just learned, sir, what took place," said the captain, coldly.

"Of course. Well, sir, in the struggle and after trouble with the women, who resented the taking away of the men, the young officer of the second boat was missed."

"Not the midshipman who was with your boat the other day?" said Aleck, eagerly.

"Eh? Yes," cried the officer. "What do you know about him?"

"Only that we had a few words together."

"And you know that he was missed?"

"I did not know till you told me," said Aleck.

"Didn't know, I suppose, that there was that struggle over yonder by the cove last night, eh?"

"Yes," said Aleck, frankly; "I saw some of it."

"Ah! Then you were with the smugglers, eh?"

"No," replied Aleck; and he briefly related his experience, including his being awakened by shots.

"Ah, to be sure," said the officer; "they're a nice daring set of scoundrels—fired on the King's men; but we got the rascals who did. Well, sir, what's become of our officer?"

"How should I know?" said Aleck, staring.

"You must have seen something of what went on after we started back."

"No," said Aleck. "There seemed to be no one there but the women."

"But you saw them and heard what they said? You heard them talking about him?"

"No, I did not go near the women."

"Why?" said the officer, sharply.

"Because I was afraid they would think I had something to do with the press-gang coming."

"Well, he must be found. He's here somewhere."

"Is there any possibility of the poor young fellow having been knocked overboard during the struggle?"

"Not the slightest," replied the officer, shortly. "He may have been knocked down somewhere on the way between the cottages, where we pounced upon the men, and the landing-place. Well, he must be found."

"Of course," said the captain, quietly. "You will go up, then, and search the smugglers' cottages—fishermen they call themselves?"

"We have searched them thoroughly," said the officer, "and we've come across now, sir, to search your place—what do they call it?—the Den."

Aleck glanced at his uncle's face, and could see the blood gathering in his cheeks.

"Search my house, sir?" he said. "Are you so mad as to suppose that I should entrap one of the King's officers?"

"Possibly, sir," replied the visitor, "on the *quid pro quo* principle, to hold on ransom. We've got some of your friends; you have snatched at one of ours."

"This is the first time, sir, that I've been led to suppose that I was a friend to the smugglers. Eh, Aleck?"

"What nonsense, uncle!" cried the lad, indignantly.

"Oh, indeed, young gentleman!" said the officer, turning upon him sharply. "No friends of yours neither?"

"Certainly not," cried Aleck.

"Ho! Then, perhaps you will be good enough to explain how it is that the gardener here is the smugglers' chief assistant in signalling, spying, and warning them?"

"He isn't," said Aleck, sharply.

"He is," said the officer. "What is more, I found that cargoes are run down here in a cove or rift upon your coast, where a handy boat is kept."

"We've got a boat down the rift," said Aleck.

"Exactly; one that runs to and fro between here and Rockabie."

"Yes," said Aleck, mockingly; "to fetch fishing-tackle and grocery—and writing paper; eh, uncle?"

The captain nodded, while the young lieutenant went on:

"And to take messages from here to Rockabie."

"No," cried Aleck; but the officer went on, quietly:

"Look here, sir, I am credibly informed that it was your boat that rescued one of the most daring of the smugglers on the night of an encounter we had there—a man whom I was holding with my own hands till I was savagely struck down. It is quite likely that this may be examined into later on, but my business now is to find my messmate. Look here, it will save a good deal of trouble, and make things much easier for you, if you put me up to the place where the prisoner is hidden."

"Perhaps it would," said Aleck, firmly now; "but I tell you I know nothing whatever about your young midshipman. If you think he is hidden somewhere here you are quite wrong."

"Perhaps so," said the officer, sternly, "but we shall see."

Then, turning to the captain, he said, shortly:

"I shall have to search your place, sir," and then rather jeeringly, as if suggesting that it would not matter in the least if the captain objected, he added: "I presume that you will not put difficulties in my way?"

"None whatever, sir," said the captain. "And as an old commissioned officer in his Majesty's service should feel it my duty to help in any way I could."

"Eh? Oh, thank you," said the officer, changing his manner. "I beg your pardon. I heard the people called you captain, but I supposed that you were captain of some fishing or trading boat."

The captain bowed coldly.

"Aleck," he said, "do you know anything about Dunning being intimate with the smugglers?"

"Yes, uncle; I have been suspecting it lately."

"Oh, Master Aleck!" came from outside. "Me? How can you say such a word! When did you ever know me smuggle anything? Oh, my dear lad, tell the truth; when did you—whenever did you know me smuggle anything?"

"Often," said Aleck, bluntly.

"What; tea and sperrits and 'bacco and silk?"

"No," said Aleck; "but fruit."

"Oh, fruit!" said the gardener, contemptuously. "What's a bit of fruit?"

"Perhaps you will have my house and grounds searched at once, sir," said the captain, waving the gardener back. "The house is small, and—"

"Stop a moment, sir," said the young lieutenant, for such he proved to be; "will you give me your word of honour as an officer and a gentleman that my brother officer is not concealed about your premises?"

"Certainly," said the captain. "I give you my word of honour that he is not; and I add to it that I have never had any dealings with the smugglers."

"That is enough, sir. Now, will you tell me where we are to find their hiding-places, for they must have some stowages for the goods they run."

"I assure you, sir, that I have not the slightest knowledge of any such places. I have often suspected the existence of a cave or caves. Aleck, my boy, do you know of any?"

Aleck turned sharply to speak, and as he did so he caught the gardener's eyes fixed upon him with a peculiar glare that might have been threatening or imploring, the lad could not tell which; but he spoke out frankly at once:

"No, uncle. I've often wondered whether there was a smuggler's cave, but I never found one."

"Humph! That seems strange," said the officer. "You have a boat?"

"Yes, I have a boat."

"And go coasting and fishing about close in. Do you mean to tell me you never found anything of the kind?"

"Yes."

"And you never saw a cargo being landed — I mean a cargo of smuggled goods?"

"Never," said Aleck.

"Then you must have been very unobservant, young gentleman. I presume that you have seen smugglers about here?"

Aleck's face lit up, and he once more caught Ness's eyes fixed upon him as he spoke.

"Oh, yes," he said; "several."

"And you could direct us to their cottages?"

"I could," said Aleck, "but I'm not going to."

"Well done, Master Aleck!" shouted the gardener.

"Silence, sir," said the captain, sternly. "Go on, Aleck."

"I've no more to say, uncle," replied the lad, "only that I'm not going to lead people to take and press men by force for sailors. Besides, the lieutenant does not need showing — he has been to the men's cottages, and taken some of them."

"To be sure," said the officer, good-humouredly; "and I don't want to be hard on you. It is not the thing to ask a gentleman to do. But please understand, sir, that I am not seeking for men to press now, but to find my brother officer who is missing. Can you help me in that?"

"I'm afraid I can't," said Aleck, frankly; "but I will do all I can."

"Thank you; that's right," said the officer. "Come, Captain Lawrence, we are making some progress after all."

"I'm glad of it, sir," replied the captain; "but, tell me, you pressed some men last night?"

"Yes, we got seven sturdy fellows to the boats, in spite of a vigorous resistance."

"Seven?" said the captain. "Well, surely that must be quite as many as we have living in the little cluster of cliff cottages! Of course there are their wives and children!"

"Yes," said the lieutenant, drily; "we learned to our cost that they had wives, and strapping daughters too."

"Then how can it be possible that your brother officer can be here? There is no one to keep him a prisoner."

"Well, it doesn't seem likely," said the officer, in a disappointed tone. "Unless," he added, "these viragoes of women are keeping him, out of spite."

"There's not the slightest probability of that," said the captain. "I'm afraid, sir, that you will find an accident has befallen him."

The lieutenant shook his head, and then turned to Aleck.

"You have a boat and a wonderfully retired nook where you keep her! Where is it—down below here?"

"Your men came to the mouth of it last time you were here."

"What, last night?"

"No, no; a fortnight ago."

"Ah, yes, I remember. You mean that narrow split in the rock; but surely no boat could go in there?"

"Mine goes in, and out too," said Aleck; "and it's nearly as big as yours. But what of that?"

"Is it likely that my brother officer, finding himself left behind, may have hidden himself there?"

"Not a bit likely," said Aleck; "but, let's go and see!"

"By all means," said the captain; and Aleck led them off at once through the sunken garden and down to the slope which led into the chasm.

"My word, what a place!" said the officer, in his admiration. "Wonderful! And this is your boat-house, eh?" he added, when, followed by his boat's crew, they reached sea level and gazed into the great niche in which the kittiwake was securely moored.

"Not a bad place," said Aleck; "and it's easy enough to get in and out when you know how."

"One moment," said the officer; "here are plenty of cracks and crevices in the sides of this rift or cave, or whatever you call it, where a fellow might hide. Here, my lads, give a good loud hail or two! Raven—ahoy!"

The hail rang out, the men shouting together, their powerful voices raising up a broadside of echoes as if the shout ran along zigzag to the mouth of the place before the hail passed out to sea, while at the first roar a multitude of sea-birds flung themselves off the shelf and flew up to the surface and away over the cliffs, shrieking and screaming in hundreds to add to the din.

The men shouted again, and as soon as the echoes had died out sent forth a louder roar than ever; but there was no answering cry, and the lieutenant turned disappointed away.

"He is evidently not here," he said. "Forward, my lads, back up to the house. We're on the wrong tack, squire," he continued, speaking to Aleck. "Look here; I'm going back to our boat in the smugglers' cove to coast along each way as close in as we can get for the rocks. He may have gone off a rock into deep water during one of the scuffles and then swum to some nook or cavern, out of which he can't get on account of deep water."

"That seems likely," said Aleck. "Like me to come and show you some of the caves?"

"Smugglers' caves?"

"Oh, no; little places where you couldn't row in, but where anyone might hide."

"Ah, that's better," said the officer. "You'll do that?"

"Of course I will," said Aleck; and after a short visit to the house Aleck led the boat's crew and their leader across the cliff and down the rough descent, feeling greatly relieved on finding that there was not a fisherman's wife in sight, for he was pretty certain that his appearance in company with their enemies might prove to be a very uncomfortable thing.

In due time the beach was reached, and the keepers of the sloop's boat backed in to allow the officer and crew to get aboard, after which there was an order or two given, and then they rowed out a short distance and, keeping in as close as possible, visited cave and crevice for about half a mile, landing wherever it was possible, sometimes climbing over weed-hung slimy rocks, sometimes wading, and then returning to continue the search in the opposite direction far past the entrance to the Den, before rowing back after an exhaustive search.

The officer gave the word to stop as the entrance to Aleck's boat haven was reached, and, under guidance, rowed and poled up till he could land.

"Thank you for all you've done, youngster," said the lieutenant; "it has been a barren search, but I shall give up for to-day. Maybe I shall look you up again. Meantime I hope you'll keep your ears open, and if you can pick up anything worth having hoist a white tablecloth or sheet on your boat's mast on the top of the cliff, if it's by day, and if it's night, burn one of the blue lights I'll leave with you. Neither of these things will be fighting against your neighbours the smugglers, but only helping us to find our midshipman and making more friends than you know. You'll do this for us?"

"Of course," said Aleck, eagerly.

"Hand out three of those blue lights, coxswain! Next time we come, squire, I'll bring you a rocket or two. There; thankye, and good day!"

"Good day," said Aleck; "but can you make your way out?"

"My lads will, never fear," said the lieutenant, and Aleck stood with the blue lights in his hand, watching the boat till it passed round one of the angles and was out of sight, when he turned round, to find that he was not alone.

"You here, Tom?" he said to the sailor, who was standing in the shadow of the boat haven, close up to the dark rocks.

"Me it is, sir."

"What is it—any news?"

"Me, sir? No; on'y what I got when I come across to see what was going on about the press-gang coming here. Say, Master Aleck, I told yer so."

"Yes, Tom, you told me so," replied the lad, warmly. "There, I'm fagged out; let's get up to the house. I want some dinner. You want some too, don't you?"

"Oh, I dunno, sir! I had my braxfus."

"So did I, Tom, hours and hours ago. What time is it?"

"'Bout four, sir."

"Late as that? Come and have some dinner with me. It's a horrible business about that poor midshipman."

"Ay, 'tis, sir. Smart lad as ever I see."

"Where do you think he can be?"

"Carried out by the tide, I should say, sir."

"Oh! Horrible! Then you don't think the smugglers can have taken him prisoner?"

"Tchah! What could they do with prisoners, Master Aleck? May have given him a crack on the head and knocked him into the water. Easy done in a scrimmage, and nobody none the wiser."

"But mightn't he be hid in the smugglers' cave?"

"Well, he might be, sir, if there is one. If he is he's shut up tight and they've took away them as knows how to get in."

"Yes," said Aleck, as they reached the garden and caught sight of the gardener watching them. "I say, Tom, there must be a big cavern somewhere."

"Very like, sir."

"You don't know where it is?"

"Not me, sir."

"Don't look that way, but tell me what you think. Isn't old Ness likely to know?"

"Very likely, sir; but if he did know he wouldn't tell."

"Then you think he is mixed up with the smuggling gang?"

"That's so, sir."

"Then I'll make him tell me," said Aleck, between his teeth.

"Do, sir, for I should like us to find the young gen'leman, he being an officer and me an old Navy man. Make old Ness tell yer. You are good friends with him, arn't yer?"

"Yes, of course," said Aleck. "No, of course not," he cried, angrily, for like a flash came the recollection of the scene that morning, when the gardener had protested against being suspected of having any dealings with such outlawed men. "Oh, Tom, what an unlucky fellow I am!"

"Feel like that, sir?"

"Yes."

"That's because you wants yer dinner very bad, Master Aleck. You get indoors and have your salt beef and biscuit, or whatever your Jane has stowed away, and you'll feel like a noo man."

Chapter Twenty

The party from the sloop-of-war came twice, led by the lieutenant, and had long and patient searches with Aleck in their boat ready to follow or lead the men into one or other of the openings in the rocks where the waves ran in with a peculiarly hollow echoing rush at low water, but which were covered deeply at half tide. These chasms were examined diligently, for the lieutenant had noted that the tide was very low when the attack was made. But nothing was discovered.

Aleck noted that the young officer looked very despondent on the second occasion, and the next morning when the lad went down to the smugglers' cove to meet the boat, which he had sighted from his look-out place on the cliff, where with Tom's help he had set up a spar ready for signalling, he found another officer in command of a fresh set of men.

The lad met them as a matter of course, feeling that his services would be welcome, but encountered a short, sharp rebuff in the shape of an enquiry as to who he was, and, upon explaining, he was told sharply to go about his business.

"Look here, sir," said the officer, "I don't want any natives to lead me on a false scent."

"Very well," said Aleck, quietly, and he climbed up the cliff again, and after noting which way the boat's head was turned he went off beyond the smugglers' cove and reached the great gap, where he descended to the shelf where he had found the lanthorn and tinder-box.

He had just reached it, when a figure started up and began to hurry inland, just giving him a glimpse of her face before she disappeared among the rocks, and he recognised Eben Megg's wife.

"Been looking out to sea, poor thing!" thought Aleck. "I'm afraid she'll watch for a long time before she sees him coming back."

He forgot the woman again directly in the business of watching the boat, which kept on coming into sight far below and disappearing again, drawing forth the mental remark from Aleck, "Labour in vain," for he felt that all the openings below where he stood had been thoroughly searched.

Aleck hung about till the afternoon, and saw the boat shoot off from beyond one of the points in the direction of the sloop lying at anchor, and then went home.

The next morning, when he went up to his signalling spar to direct the glass at the sloop, she was not there; but the cutter, which had been absent, lay in about the same place, and after a time the lad made out another boat coming towards the smugglers' cove.

"A fresh party," he said to himself. "Well, I should like to help them find the poor fellow, but if they want help they must come and ask me; I'm not going to be snubbed again."

He closed his glass and struck off by the shortest way across the head of the smugglers' cove, making once more for the high ground beyond, for it commanded the coast in two directions. But long before he reached his favourite spot he again caught sight of the fluttering blue petticoat of a woman, and saw her hurrying inland.

"Poor woman!" thought Aleck. "She needn't be afraid of me."

He kept an eye upon her till she disappeared, and then went on to the niche in the rock face, settled himself down with his glass, and watched the cutter's boat, which was steadily pulling in. The birds meanwhile kept on flitting down from where they sat in rows along the inaccessible shelves, skimmed over the water, dived, and came up again with small fishes in their beaks, to return to feed the young, which often enough had been carried off by some great gull, one of the many which glided here and there, uttering their peculiarly querulous, mournful cries, so different in tone from the sharp, hearty calls of the larger inland birds.

There were a good many sailing about overhead, Aleck noted, and they were more noisy than usual, and this, judging from old lore which he had picked up from Tom Bodger and the fishermen, he attributed to a coming change in the weather, wind perhaps, when the sea, instead of being soft blue and calm, might be lashed by a storm to send the waves thundering in upon the rocks, to break up into cataracts of broken water and send the glittering foam whirling aloft in clouds.

"No more hunts then," thought Aleck; and then aloud to a great white-breasted gull which floated overhead, watching him curiously, "Well, what are you looking at? I've not come egging now."

The gull uttered a mournful cry and glided off seaward, to dive down directly after beyond the cliff, its cry sounding distant and faint.

The boat came on nearer and nearer till it, too, disappeared, being hidden by the great bluff to his left.

Then half a dozen more gulls rose up and came skimming along the rugged trough-like depression towards where he sat, with bird-covered ledges to left and right. When they caught sight of him they rose higher with a graceful curve, and began wheeling round, uttering their discordant cries, some of the more daring coming nearer and nearer upon their widespread spotless wings, white almost as snow, till a sway would send one wing down, the other up, giving the looker-on a glimpse of the soft bluish grey of their backs, save in the cases of the larger birds—the great thieves and pirates among the young—which were often black.

There was no boat to watch now, so Aleck, after sweeping the horizon in search of the sloop-of-war, gradually turned the end of his glass inland over the sweep of down and wild moor, till, just as he was in the act of lowering it, he caught sight, some distance off and directly inland, of some object which looked like a short, pudgy, black and white bird sitting upon a rock.

"What's that?" he said, steadying the glass which had given him the glimpse in passing over it; but, try he would, he could not catch the object again.

"Couldn't have been a rabbit," he muttered. "Fancy, perhaps," and he lowered the glass, to begin closing it as he trusted to his unaided vision and looked in the direction of the grey weathered rocks.

"Why, there it is!" he cried. "It's a black bird with a white breast. It must be some big kind of puffin sitting with its feathers stuck-up to dry."

He began to focus the glass once more, and raised it to his eye; but he could not get the object in the field of the glass again, nor yet when he lowered it catch a glimpse of that which he sought with his naked eye.

Turning away to look down the deep depression, he began to watch the birds again, when he was impressed by the cry of one which seemed to have settled, after passing overhead, somewhere on the open beyond the ridge in which lay the niche containing the old lanthorn.

"Ahoy-oy-oy!" he cried, softly, trying to imitate, but with very poor success, the gull's querulous cry.

"Tah! tah! That's a jackdaw," said Aleck, half aloud. "Plain enough; but that mournful wail! It must be a different kind of gull. Black-backed perhaps, with a bad cold through getting wet. I wonder whether a gull could be taught to talk! I don't see why not. Let's see, parrots can be taught, of course, and cockatoos learn to say a few words. So do jackdaws and starlings, but very few. Oh, yes! then there's the raven. Uncle said he knew of one at an old country inn that used to say 'Coming, sir,' whenever anyone called for the ostler. Then there are those Indian birds they call Mynahs. Uncle says that some of them talk beautifully. Hallo! There he goes again! It's just like 'Ahoy–oy–oy–oy!' Plain enough to deceive anyone if it came off the sea. I'll wait till I catch sight of the gull that makes that noise, and next nesting-time I'll watch for some of the same kind and get two or three of the young ones to bring up. If they can say what sounds something like 'Ahoy!' so plainly it ought to be possible to teach one to say more."

Aleck sat and mused again, running over in his mind such gulls as he knew, and coming to the conclusion that unless it was some unusual specimen, of great vocal powers, it could not be the black-backed nor the lesser black-backed, nor the black-headed herring gull or kittiwake.

"I don't know what it is," he said, "but, whatever it may be, it's a good one to talk," and as he listened he heard the peculiar, weird, wailing cry again, sounding something like "Ahoy!"

"Gone now," said Aleck, half aloud, as he keenly watched in the direction of the cry, which had now ceased. "It might as well have flown over this way instead of down over the cliff. Hooray! There it goes!"

He shaded his eyes to follow the steady regular course of a large bronze black bird flying close down the trough-like depression, as close to the bottom as it could keep clear of the rocks, till it reached the end, where it dipped down towards the sea and disappeared.

"Well, I'm a clever one," cried the lad, with a scornful laugh; "lived ever since I can remember close to the sea, and been told the name of every bird that comes here in the winter and in the summer to nest, and didn't know the cry of an old shag. Well, say that cry, for it was very different from the regular croak I know. He had been fishing, having a regular gorge, and ended by swallowing a weevil. The little wretch set up its spines, I suppose, as it was going down and stuck, making the old shag come up there to sit and cough to get rid of it. If ever I'm along with anyone who hears that noise and wants to know what it is I can tell him it's a shag or a cormorant suffering from sore throat."

Aleck began to use the glass again, for the cutter's boat came into sight for a few minutes, before gliding along close in once more, to be hidden by the perpendicular cliffs.

"Gone," he said to himself. "Well, they will not find the poor fellow, for I don't believe they can search any better than we did. It's very dreadful. Nice, good-looking chap; as clever as clever. Cocky and stuck-up; but what of that? Fellow gets into a uniform and has a cocked hat and a sword, it makes him feel that he is someone of consequence. How horrible, though! Comes along with the boat ashore over that press-gang kidnapping business, and the boat goes back without him. I wonder whether he was better off than I am, with a father and mother! They'll have to know soon, and then I wonder what they'll say!"

Aleck gave another look round, sweeping the sea, and carrying his gaze round to the land, and then starting.

"There it is again!" he said, eagerly, as his eyes rested upon the distant black and white object inland. "Come, I can get a shot at you this time," he muttered, as, carefully keeping his eyes fixed upon the squat-looking object amongst the rocks, he slowly raised the glass. "I believe it must be a black and white rabbit. There are brown and white ones sometimes, for I've seen them, so I don't see why there shouldn't be black and white. Got you at last, my fine fellow. Ha, ha, ha," he laughed. "How absurd! Why, it's Eben Megg's wife; just her face with the patch of black hair showing above that bit of rock she's hiding behind. Why, she must be watching me. I know; poor thing, she's watching for me to go away so that she can come and look out to sea again for poor Eben."

Aleck closed his glass and rose to make his way back along the cliff and leave the place clear, a feeling of gentlemanly delicacy urging him to go right off and not intrude his presence upon one who must be suffering terribly from anxiety and pain.

"It seems so dreadful," he mused, as he went right on without once turning his head in the woman's direction; "but somehow it only seems fair that both sides should suffer. She's all in misery because her husband has been dragged away. Yes, he said he'd come back to her, but it's a great chance if she ever sees him again, and it's as great a chance whether that poor young middy's friends ever see him again. I don't like it, and it's a great pity there's so much trouble in the world. Look at poor uncle! Why, I don't know what real trouble is. I might have gone off to sea all in a huff after what uncle said, and then might have come back as badly off as poor old Double Dot. Well, I'm very, very sorry for poor Eben's wife, and—there I go again with my poor Eben. Why should I talk like that about a man who has the character of being a wrecker as well as a smuggler? He was never friendly to me and I quite hate him. But whether the King wants men or whether he doesn't, I just hate Eben so much that if he wanted to escape back to his wife and asked me to help him I'd do it; and just the same, if the smugglers had caught that young middy and were going to ill-use him — kill him perhaps — why, I'd help him too. It's very stupid to be like that perhaps, sort of Jack o' both sides, but I suppose it's how I was made, and it isn't my fault. Why, I say, it must be near dinner-time. How hungry I do feel!"

The coast was clear for Eben Megg's wife, and as soon as the lad was out of sight she once more made her way towards the cliff.

Chapter Twenty One

Aleck went along the cliff the next day to look out for the boat, fully intending to turn back if he caught sight of Eben's wife; but as far as he could make out she was nowhere in that direction. Still he concluded that she might possibly come to the place she affected, so he determined to keep on his own side of the depression, lowering himself down to the shelf in which was the niche or crack, in the belief that he could get a fair view over the sea from among the scattered masses of rock while being quite out of the woman's sight if she should come after all.

He swung himself down till he stood upon the shelf, and gave one hasty look round, to come to the conclusion directly after that if the poor woman sought his favourite look-out spot he could not have chosen a worse place, for he would be in full view, no matter where he crouched.

"I know," he said to himself; "I can get over here and lie down in the crack on the other side."

He began to climb, after making for the hole where the lanthorn and tinder-box still lay tucked tightly in beyond the reach of the wind; and the next minute, after making his way diagonally upward, he came upon the beginning of a steep narrow gully, going right down more and more deeply, so that forty or fifty yards away he could not see the bottom, the place having the appearance of being a vast crack formed by a sudden subsidence of the rocky cliff.

He was now out of sight from the other side of the great depression, and was just congratulating himself upon his selection of a hiding-place and look-out combined, when he recalled the sounds he had heard during a former visit.

"Why, it must have been caused by something falling down here," he argued, and he looked outward, to see that this was one of the narrowest, deepest and most savage-looking gullies he had seen, the place being giddy to look down and impressing him with the belief that the greatest care was necessary for anyone to move about; and as he dropped down upon his knees it was with a feeling of relief and safety, for accustomed though he was to climbing about upon the cliffs, this one particular spot looked giddy and wild.

To his great satisfaction he found that he could follow the crack right down to the sea and obtain a good view without being seen, unless anyone had followed his example and climbed; but what most took his attention was that though he had been climbing about the place often in search of the eggs of rare birds, he had never been there before, or noted the existence of such a deeply-split cavity in the cliffs.

"I must have been able to see it from off the sea," he argued, but gave himself up to the thought directly after that ridges and hollows had a completely different aspect when seen from below.

"I should know it now directly if I were sailing by and looked up, of course. I fancy I can recollect this steep wall-like bit down below where I'm sitting."

He started the next moment, for a great gull had come gliding up from behind and passed so closely over his head that he was startled by the faint whizz of its outspread wings, while the bird itself was so startled that it uttered a hoarse cry of alarm and plunged down head foremost like a stone.

"Why, that must have been the kind that made that cry like a hail," cried Aleck, as the bird disappeared into the depths of the gully, while he had hardly realised the thought before there rose from below a faint, hoarse cry.

"I thought so," he said; "those birds have different cries and they sound strange, according to where you are."

He did not finish his words, for all at once the peculiar cry arose again, and this time it seemed to come from out of the deep jagged hollow, and certainly from the other side.

"How strange!" said the lad, with a feeling akin to dread running through him. "That can't be a bird."

He listened again, waiting for some minutes in the midst of the silence of the great wilderness in which he crouched.

Then "Ahoy!" came up, so clearly that there was no room for doubt, and Aleck's heart began to beat fast as thought after thought flashed through his brain.

"It must be someone calling," he felt and when after a few minutes the cry arose again, the thought struck him that it must come from somewhere beneath his feet, from an opening in the wall of the crack and then strike against the opposite wall, from which it was reflected, so that it seemed to come from that side, and from some distance away.

Aleck waited till the cry came across again, and then shouted in answer:

"Hallo there! What is it?"

There was no response. Then after a pause came "Ahoy!" once more.

"Where are you?" shouted Aleck, but there was no reply, and the result was the same when he tried over and over again.

"Whoever it is, he can't hear me," thought the lad, and growing excited now as he concluded that some fisherman, or perhaps a strange wanderer, had slipped, fallen, and perhaps broken a limb, he began to set about finding him and affording help.

Coming to the belief more fully that the sound came from beneath him, Aleck lay down upon his chest with his head over the brink of the rocky gash, and, holding on tightly, strained out as far as he could to look down. But he could see nothing, and rose up again to look to his left for the dying out in the solid cliff of the top end of the gorge.

That meaning a difficult climb, he made up his mind, to lower himself down over the edge, and setting his teeth, he began to lower himself over; but a slip at the outset so upset his nerves that he scrambled back, panting as if he had been running a mile.

"Nearly went down," he muttered. "That's not the way to help anyone who has just fallen."

He paused for a few moments to think about getting help from Eilygugg.

"There are no smugglers at home now," he said to himself, and his thoughts turned homeward.

"Uncle couldn't climb up here and handle ropes," he muttered; "and as for Ness—bah! he's a stupid muddling old woman.

"I must get right round somehow and see where the opening is," said the lad, at last. "But when I have found it, what then? I must get back here again; and then? Yes, I must have help and a rope. Oh, what a lonely old place this is when you want anything done! Bah! What a grumbler you are," he cried, the next moment. "You forgot all about Tom. He's sure to be over to-day, and I'll bring him with a rope."

This thought heartened the lad up, and he set off cautiously and quickly to get round by the head of the great rocky gash to the other side.

The journey was very dangerous and bad, but he was a good climber, and at the end of a dozen yards he was stopped by a great block which lay across his path with the portion to his right overhanging the gulf, forcing him to go round by the other end.

This he passed with ease, and he uttered a cry of astonishment the next moment, for he found himself at the narrow head of a transverse gash which stopped further progress in the way he intended, but offered apparently, as it curved round and down, an easy descent to the very part he wished to reach. And so it proved, for proceeding cautiously, he began to descend by a narrow ledge or shelf, with the overhanging wall on his right and a sheer fall of twenty feet on his left.

A few yards further it was forty feet, and again a few yards placed him in a position that cut off all view of the bottom.

"Won't do to be giddy here," he said to himself. "Who'd have thought of finding such a place?"

He moved along cautiously, holding on by the rock on his right, and found that it was singularly cracked and riven, but it afforded good hold. Directly after a short pause and peer forward and downward to try if he could see any signs of the poor fellow who had called for help, he stepped on again slowly and cautiously, anchoring himself, as it were, by thrusting his arm to the elbow in a perpendicular crack, so that he could hang outward and get a better view down.

"Hullo!" he ejaculated, in wonder. "How strange!" and he began to sniff, as a cool dank puff of air saluted his nostrils and he recognised the peculiar odour of decaying seaweed.

"This narrow crack must go right down to the sea somewhere," he said to himself. "Well, why not? Rocks do split all sorts of ways. There, I'm right," he added, for there was another moist puff of cool air, and in company with it a peculiar far-off whispering sound, one which he well knew, for he had heard it thousands of times, it being the soft rattling of pebbles running back over one another after being cast up by a wave.

"This is queer," he muttered, and, withdrawing his arm, he took another step or two along the ledge, which curved more round to his right, so that he could not see above a couple of yards, while upon getting to the end of these he found that he had to pass an angle in the rock face which brought him to where the ledge widened out considerably.

"I must be just under where I lay down to look over," he said to himself, and having plenty of room now he turned to look upward, and then stopped short as if turned to stone, for from somewhere just beyond where he stood came the soft hollow rush and hiss of shingle following a retiring wave, and with it a distant hollow-sounding "*Ahoy!*"

The Lost Middy | 163

But Aleck did not start forward to peer down some deep chasm leading through the huge cliffs to the sea, but, as has been said, stood fast, looking upward, as if turned to stone, his attention having been seized upon by the rattling, rustling sound made by something above his head, and the next moment a pair of feet came into sight so close to him that he could have touched them where they hung on a level with his eyes.

They stopped short, with the toes resting for a few moments upon a projecting stone, and then a man dropped lightly upon the broad ledge with a panting ejaculation of relief.

Chapter Twenty Two

There was another ejaculation uttered upon that rough ledge of rock, and it was uttered by Aleck, in the form of the one word:

"Eben!"

The man gave forth a hoarse cry, sprang upon him, and pinned him by the shoulders against the rock, panting breathlessly the while as if exhausted by previous exertions, while his lips were drawn back from his white teeth and he wore generally the aspect of some savage bunted beast at bay.

"Don't!" cried Aleck, angrily, dragging at the man's wrists as he noted his fierce looks; "you hurt. Let go. Why, I thought the press-gang had taken you right away?"

"Did yer?" growled the man, breathlessly, through his set teeth, while his dark eyes seemed to glitter. "Then you see they haven't. What are you doing here?"

"Having the skin rubbed off the back of my head, I think," cried Aleck, struggling to get free. "Be quiet! Are you mad?"

"'Most," panted the man, tightening his grasp.

"But you'll have me off the ledge here if you don't mind."

"Yes, and then you'll tell no tales," growled the man, in a hoarse whisper, for he was recovering his breath.

"What about?" said Aleck, uneasily, for the man's manner was terrible in its intensity.

"What about?" snarled Eben.

"Yes; I don't understand you. I say, Eben, have you escaped?"

The man glared at him, and the look which met his—a look full of enquiry and perfectly fearless—seemed to disarm him somewhat.

"No," he said, "I won't think it was your doing, my lad."

"What?" asked Aleck.

"Putting the gang on to us the other night."

"Mine? No; I was fast asleep in bed when the shots woke me, and I went up the cliff to see."

"Ah! I s'pose so," said the smuggler, in a hoarse whisper. "I've escaped for a bit, but they're after me. I s'pose they felt I should come back to the missus. I say," he continued, eagerly, "is she all right, Master Aleck?"

"Yes. I've seen her two or three times right up the cliff."

"What for?" said the smuggler, sharply, and his eyes glittered fiercely again.

"To look and see if you were coming, of course."

"Yes, of course," said the man, in a peculiar manner, and a curious smile dawned upon his lip.

"But how did you manage to escape?"

"Jumped overboard and swam for it."

"From the cutter's boat?"

"No, from the sloop's port-hole, my lad. But what about the cutter's boat?" he added, with a sharply questioning look.

"She came across to the cove this morning, and I saw her not long ago."

"Looking for me?"

"No; for the young middy who is missing. Tell me, Eben, did you know anything about him?"

"Me? Hush, don't talk! The cutter's men have been hunting me this last half-hour, and they're out yonder among the gullies now. They see me, I think. So you've found it then?" he said, with a savagely malicious grin.

"Yes; I never knew there was a way down here."

"Been often, I s'pose?"

"Been often? Why, I'd just got here when I heard you coming."

"Ahoy!" came faintly from somewhere in front. "There it is again, Eben," cried Aleck, forgetting everything else now in the excitement of his discovery. "You heard it?"

"Yes, I heard it," said the man, grimly.

"I heard it yesterday too," continued Aleck. "Some poor fellow has fallen down the cliff somewhere about here, and I was trying to get down to him."

The man looked at him curiously and as if he was trying to read him through and through.

"What for?" he said, hoarsely.

"What for? Don't I tell you I've heard him before, crying for help? He must have broken an arm or a leg, or he would have climbed back."

"If he could," said the smuggler, grimly. "Here, hold hard a minute. Don't you stir, on yer life."

"Oh, I'm not going to run any risks!" said Aleck, coolly. "I know it's dangerous."

"Very," said the hunted man, in a peculiar tone and with a peculiar look. "You stand fast, my lad."

He had for some time released his hold of the lad, and turned to remount the rock.

"What are you going to do?" said Aleck.

"Hush! Don't shout like that, youngster. Don't I tell you the cutter's men saw me and are after me?"

"Oh, yes; of course," said Aleck, coolly; "but, look here; you hide a bit, and I'll call them."

"What!" gasped the smuggler, in his astonishment. "What for? To take me?"

"No, no! They could help to find the poor fellow lying somewhere below there."

"No, they couldn't," said the man, fiercely. "You be quiet there, I say."

"Well, of course you don't want to be taken, and I don't want them to take you, Eben."

"Say that again, lad," cried the man, excitedly.

"What for? I say I don't want the press-gang to drag you away, even if you are a smuggler."

"Why?" cried the man, excitedly.

"Because it seems so hard on your poor wife."

"Hah–ah–ah!" ejaculated the man, softly, as he turned away his face and spoke more gently. "You keep quiet here, Master Aleck, while I go and see what the cutter's men are about. I won't be long, and when they've gone I'll help you to find the poor fellow for saying that."

"For saying what?"

"Your words about my poor lass. Master Aleck, I'm a bad 'un, but she don't think so, and if I don't get back to her it'll be the death of the poor gal. Now, after my saying that soft stuff will you go and split upon me?"

"Betray you? No, you know I won't."

"Yes, I know you won't, my lad. You allus was a gentleman, Master Aleck. There, I'm off. I shan't be long, and when I come back I'll help you to find the poor chap as is hurt."

"Thank you, Eben; but mind the men don't take you."

"I'll mind, my lad; but if there's an accident and I don't come back you wait till the cutter's men have rowed me away, and then you go and tell the missus. Say she's to help you find the poor chap as is hurt and get him away."

"But she couldn't climb about here, Eben."

"Better than you can, my lad."

"Very well, then. Thank you," said Aleck, feeling a bit puzzled at the man's words. "In the meantime I'll go on looking for him. He must be somewhere close by."

"No, he isn't," said the man, grimly.

"How do you know?"

"'Cause I do," was the reply, and then, actively as a goat, the smuggler sprang up the rocks and was gone.

Chapter Twenty Three

Eben Megg had only just disappeared when the faint, monotonous cry of "Ahoy!" rose once more from below, setting the thoughts buzzing and throbbing about in Aleck's brain in a most extraordinary way. For the lad felt utterly puzzled—he knew not why. He felt that there was something he ought to know, and yet he did not know it, and he failed to grasp the reason why he could not understand it. There was some mystery that he ought to clear up, he felt; but, all the same, simple as it was, he could not find it out.

Like the children playing at a nursery game, he was so close that he was burning, and at one moment he was on the point of being as wise as the smuggler, but just then a loud piercing whistle rang out, followed by answering shouts, and he did grasp at once from whence they came, and waited anxiously, fully expecting to hear more shouts, some of a triumphant character, telling that the fugitive was in view or perhaps caught.

"I oughtn't to mind, of course," he muttered, as he strained his ears to catch the next sound; "but somehow I do, and, as I said, for that poor woman's sake. Ah! They've caught him now. No; it was only an order shouted. Why, they're coming right up here—I can hear them plainly!"

The lad listened excitedly, for though he could see nothing of the sailors he could follow them by the sounds they made and tell that they had spread out over a good deal of ground in their hunt for the escaped man.

Nearer and nearer they came till Aleck felt that they must have reached the ledge from which he had watched the rippling sea, while directly after they were so near to the hiding-place that he could catch a good deal of what was said, the voices ascending and then seeming to curl over and drop down the steep rockside where he stood.

"They haven't caught him yet," thought Aleck, after some few minutes' beating of the cliff-top and slopes had taken place. "Perhaps they won't catch him, after all, for he must be as cunning as a fox about hiding-places. Why, they must be coming here!" he thought, excitedly, as the voices began to come nearer and nearer. "They'll find me, for certain, and then—

"Well, what then?" he thought, as he came to a sudden stop. "Suppose they do catch me and ask me why I'm here! Why, I can tell them I came to try and find someone whom I heard calling for help; and I can't help what Eben says, I must let the sailors help me then."

He listened, and felt certain that the sailors and their leader came along as far as the great piece of rock he had been obliged to circumvent, and once round that the men were bound to find him.

"Ahoy!" came faintly again.

"Ahoy yourself!" said a voice. "Who's that so far off? Some fellow has wandered right away and lost himself. Idiot! Why didn't he keep within touch of his messmates? Ahoy, there! Ahoy! Ahoy!"

The cry was answered, and in a few minutes Aleck was able to detect the fact from the dying-away of the voices that the search party were growing more distant, so that the next mournful "Ahoy!" fell upon his ears alone, sounding so despairing that the desire to go in search of the appealer for help was stronger than he could restrain.

Glancing back and upward then at the spot where Eben had disappeared, he went cautiously forward for a few yards, to find to his astonishment that from being fairly broad the rugged shelf along which he was proceeding rapidly narrowed till progress grew risky, while at the end of another dozen feet or so it ceased, and he came to a dead stand, looking in vain for a way forward and a sight of some crack or passage along which he could descend towards the sea.

Then he listened for a repetition of the call for help as a guide to his next proceedings; but all was still save the querulous cry of a gull.

"I can't understand it a bit," he said, looking about him in a more perplexed way than ever. "Eben Megg spoke as if he knew about someone being in trouble; yes, and that if he did not return I was to go to his wife. Why, what nonsense it seems! How could he who has been away for days know anything about—about—oh! Was there ever such a dense, wooden-headed idiot as I am!" he raged out. "Why, of course! I can see now as clear as clear. It's that young middy—what's his name?—calling for help. They must have trapped him during the struggle, and there is a regular smugglers' cave somewhere, after all. The poor fellow must be shut up in it; and that explains why Eben looked so furiously at me when he found me here. He thought I had discovered the secret hiding-place that he was making for. Oh, my word, how plain and easy it all is when you know how! Yes, that's it," he said aloud, excitedly, "and the cutter's people are gone, so I'm not going to hold myself bound by anything I have said to Eben. That poor fellow must have been left to starve in some dark hole, and—no, he hasn't. 'Go to my wife,' he said. Of course! Because she knew where the prisoner was hid, and—to be sure, she wasn't going to watch for Eben, as I thought, but to take the prisoner something to eat and drink. Talk about wiping the dust out of one's eyes! I've got mine clear now, and that poor fellow has to be found, while, what is more, he must be somewhere down below where I stand."

Aleck's brow ran into lines and puckers as he stood looking about him for a few minutes before hurrying back to the perpendicular crevice he had discovered, and upon reaching it there was the hissing rush of the pebbles and a suggestion of a slapping sound as if water had struck against the rock, but evidently far, far down, while the damp seaweedy odour came cooler and fresher than ever to his nostrils.

"I could get down here," he muttered, "if I were no bigger than a rabbit; but of course this isn't the way. There must be just such a place as this, only many times as big, and I've got to find it."

"Ahoy!" came faintly the next minute, but not up the cavity, and the lad stood puzzled and wondering for a few moments longer, before placing his face as far in as he could, and, breathing in the soft, salt, moist air, he shouted back down the hole, "Ahoy!" as loudly as he could.

Then he stood listening, for "Ahoy!" came from quite a different direction, and then there was a reply from somewhere else, closely followed by a shrill whistle.

"That's not from the prisoner," said Aleck, growing more excited. "The sailors are coming back. Are they coming here, after all? Well, I'm sorry for Eben, but that poor fellow must be rescued, and I shall have to—"

Aleck did not say what, but hurried along the shelf again, startled by the sound of falling stones, and the next minute he caught sight of the smuggler's descending feet, and then the fierce-looking fellow dropped lightly before him and caught him by the arm.

"They saw me," he panted, breathlessly, "and have been hot on my track—I couldn't dodge them anyhow—quite surrounded. Look here, Master Aleck—you know what it means if they get me—flogging now for escaping! You don't want me to be took?"

"No, Eben; but—"

"Don't talk, my lad. I'm hard set. You're a gentleman, and won't betray a poor fellow?"

"No, but I won't help to keep that poor young officer a prisoner."

"Ah, you've found out then—you know where he is?"

"Then it is true that you've got him shut up somewhere?"

"Somewhere?" cried the man, sharply, in a hoarse whisper. "Then you haven't found the place?"

"No," said Aleck, frankly, "only guessed that he is somewhere hidden, and keeps calling out."

"Look here, Master Aleck, it is true, and if I swear that as soon as all is safe I'll help you to set him free and put him where he can get back to his ship, will you swear, too, that you'll never tell where our stores are?"

"I'm not going to swear anything, Eben."

The man made a fierce gesture, and the lad felt that he was at the fellow's mercy, where a sharp thrust of the hand would send him headlong down, most likely to his death. But he did not shrink.

"I promise you I won't betray you, Eben," he said, "if you give me your word to set the poor young fellow free."

"Come on, then—if there's time," said the smuggler, hoarsely. "I can hear 'em coming on fast. Now, then, I'm going to show you what all us chaps have sworn on our lives never to let out. Quick! I know you've got plenty of game in you, my lad. I'm going to jump down there."

He pointed down over the edge of the shelf as he spoke.

"Are you mad?" said Aleck, hoarsely, feeling that the man must be to propose what seemed to be like a leap into the next world.

"Not me, my lad. Look! I trust you to come after me sharp—before the cutter's men see you. Come, you won't shrink now?"

"He came along this way, I'll swear," came from overhead, quite loudly, and a whistle rang out again.

Eben Megg seized Aleck's arm with his left hand, and with his right caught the lad's fingers for a moment in a firm grip.

"Jump just as I do. I'll be ready to catch you."

Aleck nodded, and then felt ready to shut his eyes, for the man gave one glance upward where a loud murmur of voices could be heard, and then stepped close to the edge of the shelf, placed his feet close together, drew himself up stiffly, and then made a little jump, just sufficient to let himself drop, as it were, clear of the rock, his back being visible just for a moment, and then there was a slight pat coming from below.

Aleck stood with his heart seeming to rise to his throat as if to choke him, while he listened intently for the sound of a falling body loosening a little avalanche of stones.

But all was still below, while above there was the trampling of feet, and a voice said, loudly:

"Are you sure he came this way?"

"Quite, sir. He must have dodged round by that great block of stone."

"Forward then," cried the first voice, while from below where he stood came a low, hoarse whisper:

"Now, then, jump!"

For a moment Aleck felt that it was too much. Coward or no coward, he dared not make such a leap in the dark as that. Then, setting his teeth, he stepped close to the edge of the shelf, placed his feet exactly as he had seen the smuggler prepare to drop, and then, with his elbows pressed close to his sides and his open hands raised to a level with his chest, he took the little leap, with the opposite side of the rift seeming to rush upward past his staring eyes, while he dropped what seemed, from the time it lasted, to his overstrained nerves and imagination a tremendous depth—in reality about seven feet—before his feet came flat upon the rock and a strong arm caught him across the chest like a living protecting bar.

Aleck's eyes turned dim, and the rock face in front spun round before him as he felt himself pressed backward—a few feet beneath what seemed to be a rugged stone eave, which protected him and his companion from being seen by anyone who should peer over the edge, while the next moment the smuggler's lips were close to his ear and the breath came hot as the man whispered:

"I never knowed a lad before who dared to jump like that. Come on, Master Aleck; I'd trust you with anything now."

Chapter Twenty Four

Aleck resigned himself to the smuggler's guiding hand, which gripped his arm tightly, and as the giddy sensation began to pass off and he saw more clearly, he grasped the position in which he stood — to wit, that he was upon another ledge of rock, apparently another stratum of the great slowly-built-up masses which formed the mighty cliffs, one, however, which had been eaten away more by the action of time, so that it was much more deeply indented, while the upper stratum from which he had dropped overlapped considerably, save in one place, where this lower shelf projected in a rocky tongue, which resembled a huge bracket, and a cold shiver ran through the lad as he saw now fully the perilous nature of his leap.

"Haven't found out the way yet," said Eben, coolly; "but when they do they won't find out which way we've come. What do you say, sir?"

"Oh, no!" said Aleck, trying to conceal a shiver. "But what a horrible leap!"

"Nothing when you're used to it, sir. All right if you keep your head, and safe from being found out."

"But suppose anyone were on the opposite side?"

"No good to suppose that, master. Nothing ever comes there but the gulls and mews, with a few sea parrots. Nobody could get there without being let down by a line, and the birds never nest there, so it's quite safe. Now, then, if you're ready we'll go down."

"Go down?"

"Yes, my lad; this is the way down to the shore."

"With an opening to the sea?" said Aleck, eagerly, for his curiosity was beginning to overcome the tension caused by the shock his nerves had suffered.

The smuggler laughed.

"Well, you're asking a good deal, youngster," he said, "but it's of no use for me to play at hide-and-seek with you now. Yes; there's a way open to the sea just for 'bout an hour at some tides. Then it's shut up again by the water, and that's what makes it so safe."

Half a dozen more questions were bubbling up towards his lips, but the smuggler made a movement and Aleck felt that the best way to satisfy his curiosity would be to remain silent and use his eyes as much as he could.

He was gazing sharply round, to see nothing that suggested a way down to the sea but the great gully beneath his feet, when he became aware of the fact that Eben was watching him quietly with a dry, amused look in his eyes.

"Well," he said, "can you find it now?" Aleck shook his head.

"Come along, then."

The smuggler took a few steps along beside the great wall on their right, and Aleck followed closely, till his companion stopped short and faced him.

"Well," he said, "see it now?"

"No," said Aleck.

"Look back, then."

The lad turned, and found that without noticing it he had passed a spot where a great piece of rock terminated in a sharp edge, which overlapped a portion of the wall, and as he looked in the direction from which he had come there was a wide opening, quite six feet in height, looking as if a portion of the rock had scaled off the main mass, forming an opening some three feet wide, and remained fixed. Into this the lad stepped at once, shutting out a portion of the light, and for a few moments it seemed to him that the place ended some seven or eight feet from the entrance; but as he ran his left hand along the wall for safety and guidance, he found that instead of its being solid wall upon his left, he had been touching a mere sheet of stone, which screened another opening leading back to the original direction. Upon holding tight and peering round a sharp corner Aleck found that he was gazing into black darkness; but a breath of cool, moist air and the peculiar odour told their own tale of what was beyond, and to endorse this came the soft, sighing, whispering rush of waves sweeping over pebbles far enough below.

"Now you know the way down, my lad," said Eben.

"Yes, I suppose I do."

"But even if you'd found it all by yourself I suppose you wouldn't have ventured down."

"What, into that horrible cavern?"

"'Tarn't a horrible cavern, my lad, only a sort of a dark passage going straight down for a bit. Had enough, or will you come further?"

"I'll come, of course," said the lad, firmly.

"All right, then. That's right; there's nothing to be afraid of. You do as I do."

It was a faint twilight now where the pair were standing, with a dark forbidding chasm just in front, and Aleck was longing for a lanthorn, which he half expected to see the smuggler produce. But instead of doing so he stepped suddenly into the darkness.

"Now, then," he said, "you'll do as I do. It's nothing to what you did just now in jumping, for there's no danger; only that looked better, for it was in the light. This is in the darkness. That was straight down; this is only a slope, and you'll hear me slide. I'll tell you when to come after me."

"I understand," said Aleck; and then suddenly, "What's that?"

"What's what, my lad?"

"It felt as if something soft had come right up in my face."

"Wind," said the smuggler.

"But it's blowing the back of my head now, just as if something touched me," said Aleck, in a husky voice.

"Yes, I know," said the smuggler. "It's just as if little soft snaky fingers were feeling about your head."

"Yes, just like that," said Aleck, in a husky whisper. "I don't think it could be the wind."

"Yes, it is. That's right; only the wind, my lad. The cave's sucking because the sea keeps on opening and shutting the mouth at this time of the tide, and one minute the air's rushing in here and the next it's rushing out. Now do you see?"

"Yes, I think so," said Aleck.

"Then here goes."

Through the dim light the boy now saw his companion's face for a few moments, and then the smuggler turned round, took another step, spread out his arms to grasp the rocky sides, and the next minute there was a low rustling sound and a puff of wind struck the lad in the face, followed by silence.

"Are you there, Eben?" said Aleck, softly.

"Right, my lad. Now, then, you don't want no more teaching. Do as I did, and come down."

"How far is it?" said Aleck, hesitating.

"Eight or nine fathom, my lad. Never measured it. Ready?"

"Yes," said the lad, and setting his teeth hard he pressed his hands against the wall on either side, felt about with one foot, drew the other up to it, and then let go and began to slide down a steep slope, the passage taking away his breath, so that he was panting hard when his heels met with a sudden check and the smuggler's voice, sounding like a hollow whisper, said:

"Bottom o' this bit."

"What, is there any more?" faltered Aleck.

"Lots," said the man, laughing. "It's only a great ziggery-zag crack running right through the rock from top to bottom. There's nothing to mind, as you'd see if we'd got the lanthorn. They were so close after me that I hadn't time to get the one I left up yonder in the cliffs. Now, then, I'm going down again. It's quite dry, and worn smooth with all sorts of things coming up and folk like us going down. Just the same as before, my lad. I calls it Jacob's Ladder. Natur' made a good deal on it, and my grandfathers, fathers, and us lot finished it a bit at a time and made it what it is."

There was a rushing sound directly after, and the smuggler's voice next time he spoke came from a lower stage.

Aleck followed again with more confidence that he would not plunge into some horrible well-like hole full of water with he knew not what horrible, eel-like creatures waiting to attack him. This time the slide down felt comparatively easy, while at another angle of the zigzag, as he followed his unseen guide, Aleck actually began to think that such a way of progression must be bad for the clothes.

"You'll have to ease yourself down this next one," said Eben, as he was starting for the next descent; "it's a bit steeper. Let your hands run along the wall over your head, just touching it, and that'll be enough. Don't shove hard, or you'll be taking the skin off."

"I'll mind," said Aleck, rather hoarsely.

"What's the matter?" said the man.

"I've hurt my head a little against the roof."

"Humph!" grunted the smuggler. "Forgot to tell you about that bit. It's the only place where you can touch the top, and you run agen it. Hurt yerself much?"

"No."

"Then come on."

The rather swift descent was accomplished more easily than Aleck anticipated, and he slid down into a pair of hands.

"Now, then, the next bit's diff'rent," said the smuggler. "You'll sit down on your heels like to slide, but it arn't steep, and every now and then you'll have to give yerself a bit of a shove to help yer down to the next bit, and that's worse still."

"Worse?" said Aleck, trying to suppress a catching of the breath; but the smuggler detected it.

"Not what you think bad," he said, with a hoarse chuckle, "but what we call bad. You have to walk all the way."

"And there are no side places where you might slip into?"

"Not half o' one, my lad. There was a nasty hole at the bottom of the next but one, that seemed to go right down to the end of the world. P'raps it did, but we brought up big bits o' rock till some on 'em caught and got wedged into niches, and then we kept on till we filled it up level, and you wouldn't know it's there. Now, then, let's get down."

"Stop a moment," said Aleck. "I don't feel the wind coming and going now. Have we got below where it comes in?"

"Not us. The tide's up above the mouth now, and there'll be no wind to feel till next tide. Here's off."

The rustling began, and the two next portions of the strange zigzag series of cleft were passed down easily enough, while, as he descended a couple more, Aleck felt how smoothly floor and sides were worn and carved, and began to dwell upon the time that must have elapsed and the industry bestowed upon the curious passage by the smugglers, who had by virtue of their oaths and their interest in the place kept it a secret for generations.

"I wonder how many more there are," Aleck was thinking as he glided down, when all at once Eben said, loudly:

"Bottom! Stand fast, my lad, while I get a light."

"That you, you scoundrel?" came in a strange echoing voice from a distance.

"Ay, ay, this is me," replied the smuggler. "I'll be there soon."

There was silence, for, though eager to speak to the prisoner, Aleck concluded that he had better wait, and not commence his first meeting with the prisoner in the character of one of his enemies.

The next minute there was the rattle of iron or tin, and then a short, sharp, nicking sound began, accompanied by a display of flowery little sparks. At the end of a minute the frowning face of the smuggler was lit up as he blew softly at the tinder, into which a spark had fallen and caught; the light increased, and as a brimstone match was applied to the incandescent tinder, the brimstone melted, bubbled, and began to turn blue. Then the splint of wood beneath began to burn, and at last emitted a blaze, which was communicated to the wick of the candle. This, too, began to burn, and then the door of the lanthorn was closed.

"There we are," said the smuggler. "Now let's go and see our bird."

Aleck made no reply, for his eyes were wandering over all that the feeble light of the dim horn lanthorn threw up; and very little though this was at a time, it was enough to fill the lad with wonder. For as far as he could make out, they were in a vast cavern, whose floor about where they stood supported stacks of kegs and piles of boxes and bales. There was also a tremendous collection of wood, the most part being evidently the gatherings of wrecks, and in addition there were the fittings of vessel after vessel, so various in fact that Aleck hurriedly turned away his eyes, to gaze with something like a shiver at the reflection of the lanthorn in a far-stretching mirror of intense blackness which lay smooth and undisturbed, save in one part away to his left, where it was blurred and dimmed, rising and falling as if moved by some undercurrent.

"Water," he said, at last, as the smuggler raised up his lanthorn and smiled.

"Yes, and plenty of it."

"But where's the mouth of the cave?"

"Over yonder," said the man, pointing towards where the surface was in motion.

"Let's walk towards it with the lanthorn," said Aleck.

"Why, my lad?"

"I want to see the daylight again."

"But we couldn't get far along there with the tide up, and even if we could you wouldn't see the mouth of the cave."

"Why not?" asked Aleck.

"Because it's under water."

"Never mind; hold up the lanthorn, and let me see what I can."

"Then I'd better hide it or shut it," said Eben, and, setting the lanthorn down upon the rocky floor, he slipped off his rough jacket and covered the lanthorn so that not a ray of light could be seen escaping through the panes of thinly-scraped horn.

To the lad's wonderment, no sooner was the lanthorn hidden than instead of the place being intensely dark, it was lit up by a soft translucent twilight, which seemed to rise out of the water where it was disturbed. This light, where the water was wreathing and swaying softly, was of a delicious, transparent blue, and by degrees, as he gazed in awe and wonder, a low archway could be made out spanning a considerable space, but beautifully indistinct, festooned as it was by filaments and ribands of seaweed and wrack, all apparently of a jetty black, seen through water of a wondrous blue. But the whole archway was in motion, as it seemed, and constantly changing its shape, while the sea growth swayed and curved and undulated, and at times lay out straight, as if swept by some swift current.

"Is it always like this?" said Aleck, in a whisper, though he could not have explained why he spoke in such awe-stricken tones.

"Oh, no, my lad; it's a deal darker than that when the tide's high."

"Tide—high?" said Aleck, in a startled voice. "Does the water ever fill the cavern? No, no, of course not," he said, hastily. "I can see it never comes up to those stacks of bales and things."

"That's right," said the smuggler.

"And the tide lays the mouth quite open?"

"Not very often," said the smuggler. "Just at certain tides."

"But I must have seen the mouth from outside sometimes."

"Like enough; my lad, but I don't s'pose you were ever there when a boat could come in."

"Then a boat could come in?"

"Yes," said the smuggler, meaningly, "it could come in then. Want to know exactly?" he added, with a laugh.

"No, I don't know that I do," said Aleck, shortly. "Now, then, I didn't come to see how beautiful the place looked. I want to see and talk to that poor fellow you've got shut up here."

"Um!" grunted the smuggler. "I don't know about 'poor fellow.' He has been better off, I daresay, than I was while they kept me a prisoner. Better fed and all. Nothing the matter, only he couldn't get out."

"But why did you make a prisoner of him?"

"I didn't," said the smuggler, contemptuously; "it was the silly women."

"What for?"

"They got the silly idea in their heads that they could make the press-gang officer exchange—give the pressed men back—if they held on to the lad."

"But you'll set him free at once?" said Aleck, quickly.

"I don't know, my lad," was the reply. "It's rather a mess, I'm afraid, taking a King's officer like that; and it seems to me it will be a worse one to let him go."

"Oh, but you must let him go. The punishment will be very serious for keeping him."

"So it will for breaking loose and swimming ashore after being pressed for a sailor."

"Yes," cried Aleck; "but—"

"Yes, sir; but," said the smuggler, with a bitter laugh, "it's all one-sided like. I didn't begin on them—they began on me, to rob a poor fellow of his liberty. Now, I know it was a foolish thing for those women to get hold of that boy, half smother him, and shut him up here; and I don't want to keep him."

"Of course not."

"But what am I to do? If I let him go, and say 'Run for it,' he'll be back before I know where I am with another boat's crew to take me; and of course, being a man, I shall have to stand fire for everybody. 'Sides which it'll be making known to the Revenue officers where our lair is, and that'll be ruin to everybody."

"Then you must escape, Eben, for that poor fellow must be set free."

"Don't see it yet, Master Aleck," said the man, stubbornly. "It wants thinking about. Simplest way seems to me to be that I should put him out of his misery."

"What! Kill him?"

"Something of that sort, sir."

"Bah! You're laughing at me," cried Aleck. "Come, no nonsense—take me to him; and he must be set at liberty directly."

"Well, don't be in quite such a hurry, Master Aleck," said the man. "You ought to play fair after what has passed 'twixt us two."

"And so I will, Eben. I have promised you that I will not tell anyone about this place."

"That's right enough, sir. So you say I must let him out?"

"Of course."

"Well, don't you think I ought to have my chance to get away?"

"Certainly."

"Very well, then, sir, you must wait a bit. You know what it'll be if he's let out now."

"No, I don't."

"Very well, then, I'll tell you, sir. He'll forget all about being treated well and all that sort o' thing, and go and get help to try and catch me. Then he'll come directly upon the party who've been hunting me, and I shall be took at once."

"Then you must have a few hours to escape, and then I will set him free."

"I must have two or three days, or I shall be taken again. But you wait a bit; he can't be set loose yet. Come and see him now if you like, or would you rather stay away?"

"I'd rather go to him, poor fellow; he must be in a horrible state."

"Not he," said the smuggler, coolly. "He's had plenty to eat and drink, and a lot of canvas for a bed. He hasn't hurt."

"You didn't hear his cries for help," said Aleck.

"No, or I should have come down to quiet him if I'd been near," said the smuggler, gruffly. "Come on."

He led the way farther in away from the mouth of the cavern, and in and out amongst rocks which lay about the rugged floor, the course being beside the water, which now began to grow of a jetty black, while from time to time Aleck caught a gleam of something bright overhead, showing that here and there the roof came lower. He saw, too, that the winding, canal-like channel of water gradually grew narrower, till the lanthorn illumined the place sufficiently for the lad to see that they could easily cross to the other side by stepping from rock to rock, which rose above the shallow water.

"We'll go over here," said the smuggler, "but by and by the water will be right over there, and you have to go right to the end and climb along the ledge. Can you see where to step?"

"Yes. Go on."

"Mind how you come; the stones here are slippery with the wet seaweed."

"I can manage," said Aleck, and he carefully stepped across and stood on the other side. "Now, where is he?"

"Yonder, half way up that side! There's a snug hole there, plenty big enough for him. I've slept there lots of times when we've been busy."

Aleck did not enquire what the business was, but he surmised as he followed the guide, with the light from the lanthorn enabling him to see where to put his feet.

They were now going back towards the submerged mouth of the vast cavern, and Aleck felt a strange sensation of relief even at this, for thoughts would keep crowding into his brain about what would be the consequence if a greater tide than usual flooded the place, a thought so horrible that the perspiration stood out upon his forehead, though it might have been caused by the exertion of stepping over the rugged floor and the heat of the place.

"Isn't he very quiet?" whispered Aleck.

"Yes, but he's watching us," said the man, in a hoarse whisper, while Aleck looked in vain for a likely place to be the young officer's prison, "over yonder" being a very vague indication.

Just then the smuggler began to step up a steep slope of moderate-sized rocks piled one upon the other, to stop short about ten feet above where his companion was standing.

He held the lanthorn down low for the lad to see, and as Aleck stood beside him he raised the light as high as he could, so that the dim rays fell upon the angry staring eyes of the young officer, who lay upon a thick cushion composed of many folds of sail-cloth, the bolt ropes and reef points in which showed plainly that it had been in use possibly in connection with some unfortunate vessel wrecked upon the rocks of the iron-bound coast.

The face was familiar enough to Aleck as the midshipman hitched himself up a little higher upon the elbow which supported him, and his new visitor saw that the fierce eyes were not directed at him, but at the smuggler who bore the lanthorn.

"Then you've come at last?" he said, fiercely. "Now, then, no more of this tomfool acting; unlock this iron and take me out into the fresh air, or as sure as you stand there, you great, black-muzzled, piratical-looking scoundrel, I'll say such things about you to the captain that he'll hang you to the yard-arm, and serve you right."

"What!" growled the smuggler. "Not got tame yet?"

"Tame, you miserable ruffian! How dare you speak to an officer in His Majesty's Navy like that? There never was such an outrage before. Unfasten these irons, I say, and take me out!"

"Why, skipper," said the smuggler, mockingly, "your temper gets worse and worse."

"My temper, you dog!" cried the midshipman, furiously. "How dare you treat me like this?"

"And how dare you come with your gang, knocking honest men on the head and dragging them off to sea?" retorted Eben. "You'd think nothing of putting them in irons because they wouldn't take to the sea. How do you like it, my young springold?"

"I'm not going to argue with you, you ruffian, about that," cried the midshipman. "Now, look here, that woman who brought me the wretched food said she dare not and could not unlock that iron I've got round my ankle, but that when her husband came I was to ask him. Now, then, you're the husband, aren't you?"

"Oh, yes, I'm the husband, safe enough," growled the smuggler.

"Then I order you in the King's name to take these irons off."

"You wait a bit, captain," said the smuggler; "all in good time. Here, take it coolly for a bit longer; I've brought you some company."

"Ah, who's that with you? I thought I saw someone and heard whispering."

The smuggler held the lanthorn lower and opened the door, so that the candle light shone full on Aleck's face.

"You?" cried the midshipman, excitedly. "Then I was right; I thought you were one of the smuggling gang."

"Then you thought wrong," said Aleck, shortly.

"What do you want here?" cried the prisoner, wildly, for the fit of rage and command into which he had forced himself was fast dying down into misery and despair.

"I've come to help you, middy," cried Aleck, warmly, and he sank upon one knee and caught the poor fellow's hand.

"To—to—to help me?" he gasped.

"Yes, and to have you out into the daylight again. You, Eben Megg, take off the chain directly!" cried Aleck. "How dare you chain an officer and a gentleman as if he were a thief or a dog?"

"Oh!" cried the prisoner, and the ejaculation sounded wildly hysterical and passionate as that of a girl. "Oh—oh! Don't—don't speak to me—don't! Oh, you—I can't bear it! I'm not a coward, but I've been shut up down here in the horrible darkness of this place till I've been half mad at times, and—and I'm half mad now. It's the loneliness—the being alone down here night and day."

"Of course it is," cried Aleck, feeling half choked as he spoke; and holding the lad's hand tightly between his own, he kept pressing it hard, and ended by shaking it more and more warmly as he spoke. "Of course, of course it is. It would have driven me quite mad; but you shan't feel the loneliness again, for I'll stop with you till you're out, happen what may."

"Hah! Thank you, thank you!" whispered the prisoner. "I couldn't help breaking down. I did try so very hard. I didn't think that I should behave like a girl."

"Hush!" whispered Aleck, who had interposed between the prisoner and the gaoler with his lanthorn. "Hold up; don't let him see. There, it's going to be all right now. There's a boat's crew and an officer from the cutter somewhere above on the cliff, trying to find you."

"What!" cried the midshipman, holding on to Aleck now with both hands. "Is that true, or are you saying it to keep up my spirits?"

"It's as true as true," cried Aleck.

"Then I'll hail again. Oh, how I have hailed! Do you think they could hear me now the water's up?"

"Perhaps," said Aleck. "I heard you, and I've been hunting for long enough to find the way down."

"What!" cried the middy, who was beginning to master the emotion from which he had suffered. "Then you didn't know the way?"

"No, not till just now."

"But you knew of this horrible cave?"

"No; though it isn't above a mile from where I live."

"I—I thought you were mixed up with these smugglers, and—and—I beg your pardon."

"There's nothing to beg pardon about," said Aleck, cheerfully. "There, I'm going to have you out of this. Now, then, Eben, bring the light closer. Where did these fetters come from?"

"Out of a King's ship as was wrecked off Black Point, Master Aleck. We got dozens out of the sands. They're what they use when they put men in irons."

"Nonsense."

"I tell you they are, sir. You ask Tom Bodger if they arn't."

"Yes, they're the regular irons," said the midshipman, huskily; and Aleck, who still held his hand, felt that he was all of a tremble.

"So, you see, Master Aleck, it's on'y fair. Tit for tat, you know."

"That will do, sir," cried the lad, sharply. "Don't be a coward as well as cruel to this gentleman. Now, then, set down the lanthorn on one of the stones and unlock this fetter, or whatever it is."

"Can't, sir," said the man, gruffly.

"What! I order you to do it."

"Yes, sir, I hear you, but the chain's locked round his ankle."

"Well, I know that. Unlock it."

"Well, I would, sir, as it's come to this, but I arn't got the key."

"What!" cried Aleck, with a chill of despair running through him. "Where is it, then?"

"My missus or one of the other women's got it."

"But you said there were a lot of these irons; there must be more than one key."

"I never saw but one, sir, and that we had up at home. It was my old woman's idee to chain him up like this. You see, it's three or four of them irons locked together, and one end's about his ankle and the other's locked to the ring there that we let into the rock and fixed with melted lead so as to fix tackle to when we wanted to haul in casks or moor a boat."

"Then you must go and find your wife, and get it," said Aleck, firmly.

"Go up on the cliff, young gentleman, and walk right into the hands of the boat's crew hunting for me, eh?"

"I don't care; I will have this gentleman set free. You may not meet any of the sailors," cried Aleck, and almost at every word of his brave standing up for the prisoner he felt himself rewarded by a warm pressure of the hand.

"That's all right enough, Master Aleck Donne, but you know what I've told you 'bout being made prisoner and having to nearly lose my life in swimming for my liberty?"

"Yes, perfectly well; but I must have him cast free, even if he has to wait a bit before he goes out of the cave."

"But you heard, too, what he said, sir, and I shouldn't be a bit surprised if, when they caught me, they did hang me to the yard-arm of one of their ships."

"Yes, yes, I know," said Aleck; "but—"

"But you arn't reasonable, Master Aleck. My life's as much to me as another man's is to him, whether he's a poor fellow or a gentleman. Now, look here, you know yourself it arn't safe for me to go out of the cave now, is it?"

"Well, I'm afraid it is not just yet, Eben; but—"

"Wait a minute, Master Aleck. Give a man a chance. Look here; as soon as it's dark I'll go up on to the cliff and try and get to my cottage, and as soon as I can get the key I'll come back and let your orficer here go loose if he'll swear as he won't show his people the way down here."

"No," cried the midshipman, firmly; "I can't promise that."

"Not to get free, squire?" said Eben, grimly.

"N–no, I can't do that. It's my duty to help clear out this place. I can't; don't ask me. I can't promise that."

"Look here," said Aleck, smiling; "could you lead a party down here?"

The midshipman started, and was silent.

"How did you come down here?"

"Come down? I didn't come down. I was half stunned, and then thrown into a boat. I can just recollect feeling myself dragged out again, and then I lay sick and giddy, just as if I was in a horrible dream, till I awoke in the darkness to find that I was chained up here."

"Then he could not lead a party here, Eben," said Aleck; "and you could get him out of here so that he would never know how he was taken out."

"Ah!" said the middy, sharply. "Then you two didn't come in a boat?"

"Never you mind how we came or how we didn't, my lad," said the smuggler, "we're here; and as the game's up, Master Aleck, and all I want to do is to keep out of the clutches of the press-gang and the law, I'll do as I said, go up by and by and try to get the key, and if I can't get the key I'll bring down a file."

"That will do, Eben—I'll trust you; and as you're going to do your best now I don't think Mr—Mr—"

"Wrighton," said the middy.

"Mr Wrighton will want to be hard on a man who wants to escape from being pressed. How long will it be before it's safe to go up?"

"I daren't go till it's midnight, my lad. I've been run too close before, and as it is I'm not sure but what they'll be waiting for me about my home; but anyhow I'll try."

"And I must wait till then?" said the middy, with a break in his voice.

"Yes," said Aleck; "but I shall keep my word—I'll stick by you till you're free."

"Ah!" ejaculated the lad, and his voice sounded more natural, as he added, in a low tone to Aleck: "Don't think me a coward, please. You don't know what it is to be shut up in a place like this."

"No," said Aleck; "but if I were I should feel and act just as you have, and I hope be quite as brave."

A pressure of the hand conveyed the midshipman's thanks, and directly after the two lads awoke to the fact that the smuggler was doing something which could mean nothing else but the providing of something to eat and drink.

For upon raising the lanthorn to look around, he came upon a basket, and beside it a good-sized bottle, both of which he examined.

"Why, skipper," he said, "you haven't eat your dinner!"

"How could I eat at a time like this?" said the midshipman, angrily.

"Well, I s'pose it didn't give you much hankering arter eating tackle," said the smuggler, grimly. "I took nowt but water when I was aboard your ship; but you ought to eat and drink now you ye got to the end of your troubles, thanks to Master Aleck here. Why, you've got two lots. What's in the bottles?"

The speaker screwed out the corks of two bottles, one after the other, and smelt the contents.

"Ha! Water. Want anything stronger?" he said, with a grin. "Plenty o' Right Nantes yonder," he added, with a jerk of his thumb over the right shoulder.

"No, no, I don't want anything," said the midshipman, impatiently.

"Well, sir, I do," said Eben. "I'm down faint, and if you don't mind—what do you say, Master Aleck?"

"I never thought of it," replied Aleck; "but now you talk about eating and drinking you make me feel ready. Let's have something, Mr Wrighton; it will help to pass away the time."

The result was that the contents of the basket were spread between them, and from forcing down a mouthful or two of food the prisoner's appetite began to return, and a good meal was made, Aleck and the smuggler naturally playing the most vigorous part.

Chapter Twenty Five

Aleck ate heartily, for the state of affairs began to look bright, but as he played his part his eyes were busy, and he noted that the beautiful effect of light which came through the transparent water beneath the submerged arch grew less and less striking till the colour had nearly faded out, while the water had evidently risen a good deal in the long canal-like pool, and was still rising, and where the cavern's weird configuration had in one part appeared through a dim shadowy twilight all was black darkness.

There had been a little talking during the consumption of the meal, but when it was ended silence had fallen upon the group. The smuggler had proceeded to fill a black pipe which he had lit at the lanthorn, and then drawn back a little, leaving the two youths to themselves; but very little was said, conversation in the man's presence seeming to be impossible.

The pipe was smoked to the very last, and then, after tapping out the hot ashes, the smuggler coughed and turned to the others.

"Look here, gen'lemen," he said; "I think we understand one another a bit now, which means I'm going to trust you two and you're going to trust me?"

"Yes," said Aleck.

"That's right, then. Of course, all I want to do is to get safe away so as to bring back the key of them irons, or a file, and as soon as we've got them off you're going to give me till to-morrow about this time before you come out?"

"We can't stay in this horrible hole all night," cried Aleck, impetuously.

"Don't see as it's much of a horrible hole, master," said the man; "there's plenty to eat and drink, and a good roof over your heads. I've slept here times enough. There arn't nothing to worry you—no old bogies. Wust thing I ever see here was a seal, which come in one night, splashing about; and he did scare me a bit till I knowed what it was. But that's the bargain, gentlemen, and there's no running back. There's the lanthorn, and there's a box yonder with plenty of candles, and a tinder-box with flint, steel, and matches, so you never need be in the dark. Plenty of bread and bacon, cheese, and butter too, so you'll be all right; so there's no call to say no more about that. Now, then, I'm going uppards to try if I can find out what's going on outside. I shall keep coming down to tell you till I think my chance of getting home has come, and then I shall run off and you'll wait till I come back."

"Very well," said Aleck, who found that he had all the talking to do, and after a time the smuggler rose.

"There," he said, "I'm going now. Say good luck to me."

"Well," replied Aleck, "good luck to you! Be as quick as you can. But what are you going to do about a light?"

"What for?" said the man, gruffly.

"To find your way to the zigzag slopes."

The smuggler laughed softly.

"I don't want any light to go about this place, squire. There arn't an inch I don't know by heart."

"I suppose not," said Aleck, thoughtfully. "But, look here; what about that place?"

"What about it, sir?"

"The getting up. Of course it was easy enough to slide down, but how about getting up?"

"Didn't I tell you? No, of course, I didn't. Look here, sir; it's all smooth in the middle, but if you keep close up to the left you'll find nicks cut in the stone just big enough for your toes, and as close together as steps. You'll find it easy enough."

"I understand," said Aleck, and the next minute they were listening to the faintly-echoing steps, for the moment the man stepped out of the faint yellow glow made by the lanthorn he plunged into intense black darkness. But from what he had so far gleaned of the configuration of the place the lad was pretty well able to trace the smuggler by his footsteps, till all at once there was a faint rustling, and then the gloom around was made more impressive by the silence which endured for a couple of minutes or so, to be succeeded by a faint, peculiar, echoing, scraping sound.

"What's that?" asked the midshipman, excitedly.

Aleck explained that it was evidently the noise made by the scraping of the smuggler's boots against the stone, as he ascended the zigzag crack to the surface.

This lasted for about a minute, to be succeeded by a peculiar harsh noise as of stone being drawn upon stone, after which there was another peculiar sound, also in some way connected with stone jarring against stone; but Aleck could give no explanation to his companion as to what that might be, feeling puzzled himself. Another stone seemed to be moved then, and it struck the listener that it might be somehow connected with the more level of the zigzag passages, though why he should have thought that he could not have explained.

Probably not more than three minutes were taken up altogether before the last faint sound had died completely away, and then Aleck found himself called upon to explain the configuration of the natural staircase by which ascent could be made and exit found. For it never occurred to the lad that he was in any way breaking the confidence placed in him in making the prisoner as familiar with the peculiarities of the cavern as he was himself. The midshipman, his companion in the strange adventure, had asked him about the shape and position of his prison, and he had explained what he knew. That was all.

The account took some time, for the prisoner's interest seemed to increase with what he learned, and his questions succeeded one another pretty quickly, with the result that in his explanations Aleck had to include a good deal of his own personal life, after which he did not scruple to ask his companion a little about his own on board ship.

"I say," said Aleck, at last, "isn't it droll?"

"Droll!" groaned the midshipman. "What, being shut up here?"

"No, no; our meeting as we did in Rockabie harbour, and what took place with the boys. I never expected to see you again, and now here have I found you out, a prisoner, chained by the leg, and in ever so short a time you and I have grown to be quite friends."

"Yes," said the midshipman, drawing a deep breath. "I didn't like you the first time we met."

"And I didn't like you," said Aleck, laughing. "I thought you were stuck-up and consequential. I say, I wish Tom Bodger were here!"

"What, that wooden-legged rasé sailor?"

"Yes."

"What good could he do—a cripple like that?"

"Cripple! Oh, I never thought of him as a cripple. He's as clever as clever. There isn't anything he won't try to do. I was thinking that if he were here he'd be scheming some plan or another to get rid of the chain about your leg."

"Hah!" sighed the midshipman, "but he isn't here. I say!"

"Well?"

"Hadn't you better have another candle to light—that one's nearly burned down?"

"I've got one quite ready, lying out here on the stone."

"Hah! That's right," said the prisoner. "It's so horrible to be in the dark."

"Oh, no; not when you've got company."

"But be quite ready. It might go out quickly."

"Well, if it did, I know where the flint and steel are."

"You couldn't find them in the dark."

"Oh, couldn't I? I kept an eye on everything Master Eben did."

"I say, do you think he will come back?"

"Yes; he's sure to, unless some of the cutter's men catch him and carry him off."

"Ah! and you think, then, that he wouldn't speak, out of spite, and leave us here to starve?" cried the middy, excitedly.

"No, I don't," said Aleck; "I don't think anything of the sort. Don't you be ready to take fright."

"I've been shut up in this place so long," said the middy, apologetically, "and it has made me as weak and nervous as a girl."

"Well, try not to be," said Aleck. "Look here; there's nothing like seeing the worst of things and treating them in a common-sense way. Now, suppose such a thing did happen as that Eben Megg did not come back— what then?"

"We should be starved to death."

"No, we shouldn't, for I daresay there's a good store here of biscuits and corned beef out of some ship, as well as smuggled goods, that we could eat."

"Till all was finished," said the middy, sadly.

"What of that? We could get out, couldn't we? I know the way."

"Oh, yes. I had forgotten that. But was there any door to the way down—trap-door?" "Door? No," said Aleck, laughing. "It's all the natural stone, just chipped a little here and there to make it easier."

"That's right," said the midshipman, sadly. "But it is a terrible place to be shut up in. Hasn't he been very long?"

"Oh, no. I daresay he'll be a long time yet. Come, cheer up. Let's watch the water there. I wish I knew what the time was. Can't we tell? When the water looks blackest it ought to be high water. I wonder whether we shall see the arch quite cleared and the light shining through. Have you noticed it?"

"Don't!" said the young sailor, rather piteously. "I know what it means—you are talking like this to keep up my spirits."

"Well, suppose I am?"

"Don't try; it only makes me more weak and miserable. You can't think of the horrors I've suffered."

"But—"

"Yes, I know what you're going to say—that I ought to have been firmer, and fought against the dread and horror, and mastered the feelings."

"Something of the sort," said Aleck.

"Well, I did at first, but I gradually got weaker and weaker, till in the darkness and silence something happened which scared me ten times more than the being here alone."

"Something happened? What?" said Aleck, wonderingly.

"I suddenly felt frightened of myself."

"I don't understand you."

"I was afraid that I was losing my senses."

"Well, then, don't be afraid like that any more, for you're not going to lose them."

"Men have lost their wits by being shut up alone," said the middy, piteously.

"Perhaps. But you're not going to, for you're not alone, and all you've got to do is to lie there patiently and wait. I say, aren't you tired?"

"Oh, horribly. I couldn't sleep for the horror I felt."

"Well, you could now. Go to sleep, and I'll wake you when Eben Megg comes back."

"No," said the middy; "I couldn't sleep now. Suppose I awoke at last and found that you had gone!"

"Ah, you're going to imagine all sorts of things," said Aleck, who felt that he must do something to keep his companion from brooding over his position.

"Look here; suppose I go up the passage and see if I can make out anything about Eben!"

Before he had finished speaking he became aware of how terribly the poor fellow had been shaken by his confinement. For the lad caught him spasmodically by the arm with both hands.

"No, no," he panted. "Don't leave me—pray don't leave me."

"Very well, then, I'll stay," said Aleck; "but I do hope the poor fellow will not be caught by the cutter's men."

Aleck felt sorry as soon as he had said these words, for his companion gave another start.

"You feel that he won't come back?"

"I feel," said Aleck, quietly, "that we seem to be wasting time. Have you got a knife?"

"Yes, of course."

"So have I. Well, mine has a small blade; has yours?"

"Yes. Why?"

"One small blade would not be strong enough, but if two were thrust into the back of those irons together we might be able to open them. I believe all these fetters are opened by a square key, and I'm going to try."

"Ah, yes; do."

"Once get you free, we could pass the time climbing up the natural staircase, and get a look out from the top at the fresh green trees and clear sky."

Aleck's attempt to take his companion's attention was successful, inasmuch as after the production of the knives, and the changing the position of the opened lanthorn so that the dim light should do its best in illuminating the rusty anklet and chain, the midshipman began to take some feeble interest in the proceedings.

Aleck knew as much about handcuffs and fetters as he did about the binomial theorem, but he was one of those lads who are always ready to "have a try" at anything, and, after examining the square deeply-set holes which secured the anklets, he placed the two pen-blades of the knives together, forced them in as far as they would go, and tried to turn them.

The first effort resulted in a sharp clicking sound.

"There goes the edge of one blade," said the lad, coolly. "I hope it's your knife, and not mine. Hullo! Hooray! It turns!"

For the blades held fast, jammed as they were into the angles of the orifice, and the operator was able to turn the knives half way, and then all the way round.

"Now try," said the midshipman, beginning to take deep interest in the attempt.

"I have," said Aleck, gloomily; "the blades turn the inside, but the thing's as fast as ever."

"But you are not doing it right," said the middy.

"I suppose not; you try."

"No, no; go on. But you haven't turned enough."

"It wants the proper key," said Aleck.

"No, I think those knives will do, after all. I saw a sailor put in irons once for striking his superior officer, and I think that part wants not only turning like a key in a lock, but turning round and round, as if you were taking out a screw."

"Oh, I see," cried Aleck, with renewed eagerness, and he turned and turned till, to his great delight, the anklet fell open like an unclasped bracelet, and then dropped on to the folded sail-cloth which formed the prisoner's couch.

"Hooray!" shouted Aleck again.

"Hurrah! Hurrah!" cried the young officer, with a decision in his voice that brought up their first meeting in the harbour.

"There, it's all right," cried Aleck, as the young officer caught him by the hands; "nothing like patience and a good try."

"I—I can't thank you enough," said the middy, in a half suffocated voice.

"Well, who wants thanks, sailor?" cried Aleck. "Don't go on like that. It's all right. I'm as glad as you are. Now, then—oh, I say, your being shut up here has pulled you down!"

"Yes, more than I knew, old fellow," said the middy. "There, I'm better now. You can't tell what an effect it had upon one. There were times in the night when, after dragging and dragging at that miserable iron, I grew half wild and ready to gnaw at my leg to get it free. Why, if you know the way out we can escape now."

"Yes, but let's play fair by Eben Megg. He has gone to try and get the key to open this thing, and I promised that I would wait till he came back."

"But he will not come back, I feel sure. He's only a smuggler, and ready to promise anything."

"Oh, no," said Aleck, "I don't think that. If he is not taken by the men from the boat he'll come back, I feel sure. So let's wait till the morning."

"I can't—I tell you I can't," cried the midshipman, half wild with hysterical excitement. "I must get out now at any cost. I couldn't bear another night in this place."

"Nonsense," cried Aleck, good-humouredly. "You bore it when you felt almost hopeless as a prisoner; surely now that you are as good as free you can manage to bear one more night!"

"No, I cannot and I will not," cried the young officer. "See to that lanthorn at once, and let's get out of this living tomb."

Aleck lit a fresh candle and secured it in the sconce, watching the midshipman the while as he sat up rubbing the freshly-freed leg, and then stood up and stamped his foot as if the leg were stiff. Then, as if satisfied that he could get along pretty well, he turned to his companion.

"It's rather bad," he said, excitedly; "but—I can manage now. Jump up and come along."

Aleck remained silent.

"Do you hear?" cried the middy.

"Yes. It's time now that we had something more to eat," said the lad, quietly.

"Eat? Eat? Who's going to think of eating now? I want to get out and breathe the cool, soft air. I feel just as if I were coming to life after having been buried. Here, pick up the lanthorn and let's start."

"If Eben Megg does not come back by the morning," said Aleck, coldly.

"What! Do you mean to tell me that you are going to stay here all night when the way's open?"

"The way is not open," said Aleck, coldly.

"Not open? You told me there was no door or fastening at all."

"There is neither, but it's shut up by the promise I gave that man."

"You tell me really that you mean to stop here all night waiting for him?"

"Yes," said Aleck; "I was quite ready to stop here all night to keep you company when you were a prisoner chained to that wall."

The midshipman stood staring down at his companion as if half stunned, till better thoughts prevailed.

"Yes," he said, at last, in a quieter way. "So you were; and you would have done it, wouldn't you?"

"Of course I would," said Aleck.

"And it wouldn't be fair to break your word, eh?"

"That's what I feel," was the reply.

"Yes, and I suppose it's right, Aleck—that's what they call you?"

"Yes, that's what they call me," said the lad, coldly.

"Yes—yes," said the middy, slowly. "I say, you're not an officer, but you're a jolly deal more of a gentleman than I am. You see, I've been a prisoner so long, and I want to get out."

"Of course; it's only natural."

"Well, then, you're going to show me the way out?"

"To-morrow morning, when I feel satisfied that Eben Megg will not come."

"No, no, to-night—if it is to-night yet. Come!"

"No," said Aleck, firmly. "I gave him my word that I'd wait, and I'll stay even if he doesn't come back; but I have no right to try and stop you."

"No, that you haven't; but I'm not going to behave worse than you do. Now, once more, are you going to show me the way out?"

"No," said Aleck.

To his intense astonishment the midshipman threw himself back upon his rough couch again.

"All right," he said; "I know what it means when you're all alone in the stillness here and your brain's at work conjuring up all sorts of horrible things. You've behaved very handsomely to me, old fellow, and I'm not going to be such a miserable beggar as to go and leave you in the lurch. If you stay, I stay too, and there's an end of it. Now, then, snuff the candle and hunt out some prog. I've been so that everything I put into my mouth tasted like sawdust, but I feel now as if I could eat like anything. Look sharp."

"Do you mean this?" cried Aleck, turning to his companion, excitedly.

"Of course I do," said the middy, merrily. "Think you're the only gentleman in the world?"

It was Aleck's turn to feel slightly husky in the throat, but he turned away to the rough basket and began to hand out its contents, joining his companion in eating hungrily, both working away in silence for a time.

Then the ex-prisoner opened the conversation, beginning to talk in a boisterous, careless way.

"I say, Aleck, we shall have plenty of time before lying down to sleep. Let's light two or three candles and have a jolly good rummage of the smugglers' stores."

"We will," cried the lad addressed.

"I shouldn't wonder if we find all sorts of things. Treasure, perhaps, from wrecked vessels. I wouldn't bet that these people hadn't been pirates in their time. That Eben, as you call him—I say, it ought to be Ebony—he looks a regular Blackbeard, skull-and-crossbones sort of a customer. We'll collar anything that seems particularly good. I'm just in the humour to say I've as good a right to what there is as anybody else; but we'll share—fair halves. I say!"

"What?"

"Old Blackbeard will stare when he finds that we've opened the irons. My word, I must go and see Mrs Ebony again. Nice woman she is, and no mistake."

"Did she fasten the iron ring on your ankle?"

"Well, no; I think it was an ugly old woman of the party; but I couldn't be sure, for they half killed me—smothered me, you know—and when I came the half way back to life the job was done."

Aleck entered into the spirit of the rummage, as his companion called it, and their search proved interesting enough; but after finding a vast store of spirits, tobacco, and undressed Italian silks, the principal things in the cavern were ship's stores—the flotsam and jetsam of wrecks, over which they bent till weariness supervened.

"Tired out," said Aleck, at last.

"So am I," was the reply, as they threw themselves side by side on the rough bed, after extinguishing all the candles they had stuck about the rock and confining themselves to a fresh one newly set up in the lanthorn.

"Shall we let it burn?" said Aleck, in deference to his comrade's feelings.

"Oh, hang it, no!" was the reply. "It might gutter down and set us on fire."

"Then you don't mind being in the dark?"

"Not a bit with you here. Do you mind?"

"I feel the same as you."

Five minutes later they were both sleeping quietly and enjoying as refreshing a slumber as ever fell to the lot of man or boy.

Chapter Twenty Six

Aleck woke up wondering, for he felt as if he had had a good night's rest and that it ought to be morning, whereas it was very dark.

This was puzzling, and what was more curious was the fact that on moving he found that he had his clothes on.

Naturally enough he moved, and turned upon his other side, to find that it was not so dark now, for he was looking at what seemed to be a beautifully blue dawn. Then someone yawned, and the lad was fully awake to his position.

"Sailor!" he said, loudly.

"Eh? My watch? My—my—I'll—here, Aleck, that you?"

"Yes, it's morning; rouse up. I fancy it must be late."

"Looks to me as if it is dreadfully early. I fancied I was being roused up to go on deck. What are you doing?"

"Going to get a light."

This Aleck did after the customary nicking and blowing. The candle in the lanthorn was lit, and the lads, after cautiously testing the depth of the water, indulged in a good bathe, gaining confidence as they swam, and finally dried themselves upon an exceedingly harsh towel formed of a piece of canvas, one of many hanging where they had been thrown over pieces of rock.

As they dressed they could see that it was getting lighter inside the arch, which gradually showed more plainly, and as the water grew lower during the time that they partook of the meal which formed their breakfast, the twilight had broadened, so that both became hopeful of seeing the tide sink beneath the crown of the arch so as to give them a glance at the sunlit surface of the sea.

"How long are you going to wait for the smuggler?" asked the middy, suddenly.

"Not long," was the reply. "It is not fair to you. But I should like to give him a little law. What do you say to waiting here till the tide has got to its lowest, and as soon as it turns we'll start?"

"Very well, I agree," said the midshipman, "for I don't think that we shall have long to wait. I was expecting it to go down so low that I should see the full daylight yesterday, but before I got the slightest peep it began to rise again."

"But it came lighter than this?" said Aleck.

"No; I don't think it was so light as this. I believe it is just about turning now."

The sailor proved to be right; and as soon as Aleck felt quite sure he turned to his companion and proposed that they should start.

"I don't know what my uncle will say," he said. "You'd better come home with me. He will be astonished when he sees that I have found you."

"Did he know that I was lost?"

"Of course. Your fellow officer came straight to our place to search it, thinking we knew where you were. Well, uncle will be very glad. Come along. I shall take the lanthorn with us to see our way up the zigzag. I think I could manage in the dark, as I came down and know something of the place, but it would be awkward for you."

"Oh, yes; let's have all the light we can," said the midshipman. "I'm quite ready. Shall we start?"

"Yes, come on," was the reply, and, holding the lanthorn well down, Aleck led the way along by the waterside till the rocks which had acted as stepping-stones were reached, and which were now quite bare.

These were passed in safety, but not without two or three slips; and then after a walk back towards the twilight, somewhere about equal to the distance they had come, Aleck struck off up a slope and in and out among the blocks that had fallen from the roof to where he easily found the lowest slope of the zigzag, which they prepared to mount, the light from the lanthorn showing the nicks cut in the stone at the side.

"It's much harder work climbing up than sliding down," said Aleck.

"Of course," replied the midshipman, who toiled on steadily in the rear; "but it's very glorious to have one's leg free, and to know that before long one will be up in the glorious light of day. I say, are you counting how many of these slopes we have come up?"

"No," said Aleck, "I lost count; but I think we must be half way up."

"Bravo! But, I say, these smugglers are no fools. Who'd ever expect to find such a place as this? It must have taken them years to make."

"They were making it or improving it for years," said Aleck; "but they found the crack already made—it was natural."

"Think so?"

"Yes; the rock split just like a flash of lightning. Mind how you come—the roof is lower down here. Let's see, this must be where I hit my head in coming down. No, it can't be, for that was somewhere about the middle of one of the slopes, I think, and this is the end, just where it turns back and forms another slope."

Aleck ceased speaking and raised the lanthorn so as to examine the rock above and around him more attentively.

"Nice work this for a fellow's uniform. What with the climbing and sleeping in it I shall be in rags. But why don't you go on?" said the midshipman.

"I—I don't quite know," said Aleck, hesitating. "It seems different here to what it was when I came down."

"But you said you came down in the dark?"

"I did, and I suppose that's why it seems different."

"Well, never mind. Go on. It hurts my feet standing so long resting in this nick."

Aleck was still busy with the lanthorn, and remained silent, making his companion more impatient still.

"I say, go on," he said. "Why do you stop?"

"Because it seems to me as if I had come the wrong way, taken a wrong turning that I did not know of—one, I suppose, that I passed in the dark."

"But this must be right," said the midshipman; "it goes up. Here are all the nicks for one's feet, and the part in the middle is all ground out as if things were dragged up. Go on, old chap; you must be right."

"So I think," said Aleck; "but I can't go on. It seems to me as if the place comes to an end here, and I can get no farther."

"That's a nice sort of a story. But you carried the light; have you taken a wrong turning?"

"I didn't know that there were any turnings."

"Have another good look, and make sure."

Aleck peered in all directions by the aid of the lanthorn—a very short task, seeing how they were shut in—and then carefully felt the stones.

"Well?" said the midshipman.

"I'm regularly puzzled," said Aleck. "Of course, it's very different coming in the other direction, and by candlelight instead of the darkness."

"Then you're regularly at fault."

"Quite."

"Try back, then. You light me and I'll lead."

They slid down to the bottom of the slope and stopped.

"I say," cried the midshipman; "you'll have to take me to your place and find me some clothes, for I shan't have a rag on if we're going to do much of this sort of thing."

"This must be right," said Aleck, without heeding the remark. "I can shut my eyes here and be sure of it by the feel."

"Then it's of no use to go down any farther?"

"Not a bit," said Aleck, firmly. "Look for yourself. Here are the foot nicks at the side, and the floor is all worn smooth. We must be right."

"Then forward once more. You must have missed something."

Aleck toiled up the slope again, reached the top, where the crack should have run in a fresh direction and at a different inclination, and carefully examined the place with his light, while his heart began to beat faster and faster from the excitement that was growing upon him rapidly. For as he ran his hands over the rock in front, which completely blocked his way, he noted that there were three great pieces—one which ran right into the angle, where the pathway should have made its turn; a second, which lay between it and the smooth wall at the bend; and another smaller piece, which lay over both, jammed tightly in between the two other stones and the roof, and carrying conviction to Aleck's mind as he now recalled the peculiar grating sounds he had heard soon after the smuggler left them the previous day.

He was brought out of his musings by his companion, who suddenly exclaimed:

"I say, look here; I'm not a puffin."

"Eh? No, of course not. What made you say that?"

"Because you seemed to think I was, keeping me perched up on a piece of rock like this. Now, then, are you going on?"

Aleck was silent, for he had not the heart to say that which was within.

"Are you going dumb? If you've lost your way say so, and let's begin again."

"It's worse than that," said Aleck.

"Worse? What do you mean?"

"Look here," said Aleck, holding the lanthorn up high with one hand, and pointing with the other.

"Well, I'm looking, and I can see nothing but stone—rough stone."

"Neither can I. We can go no farther."

"What! You don't mean to say that the roof has fallen in?"

"No; it's worse than that."

"Can't be," cried the middy.

"Yes, it is, for we could have dug the fallen stones away. Sailor, I'm obliged to say it—we're regularly trapped!"

"What! Who by? Oh, nonsense!"

"It's true enough, I'm afraid. The smuggler would not do as we did. We trusted him, but he would not trust us."

"You don't mean to say he has blocked us in?"

"I'm obliged to say so. I heard him forcing down the stones after he'd gone. Look for yourself. I can't move one."

"No," said the midshipman, quietly, as he reached past Aleck and tried to give the top one a shake. "He has been too clever for us. Think we can move these lumps? No; their own weight will keep them down. That's it, Aleck; the things here are too good to lose, and he has got us safe."

To Aleck's astonishment he had begun to whistle a dismal old air in a minor key after propping himself across the rough crack so that he could not slip.

"What's to be done?" said Aleck, at last.

"Done, eh?" was the reply. "Well, I'm afraid if I had been alone and found this out, I should have lain down, let myself slide to the bottom, and then set to and howled; but the old saying goes, 'Two's company, even if you're going to be hanged,' and you're pretty good company, so let's go back to the cave. We can breathe there. The heat here is awful. This shows that it doesn't do to be too cocksure of anything. Come on down."

"But we must have a thoroughly good try to move the stones," said Aleck, angrily.

"Not a bit of use. That brute has wedged them in and jumped upon them. Why, we may push and heave till we're black in the face and do no good. We're fixed up safe."

"And you're going to give up like that?"

"Not I," said the midshipman, calmly. "Show me what I can do, and if it's likely to be any good I'll work as long as you like; but it's of no use to make ourselves more miserable than we are. Come on down."

The young sailor spoke in so commanding a tone that Aleck yielded, and, following his comrade's example, he slid down slope after slope, and finally stood in the great open cavern, breathing in long deep breaths of the fresh soft air.

"Hah! That's better," said the midshipman. "I felt stifled up in that hole. Now I don't bear malice against anybody, but I think I should like to see that smuggling ruffian shut up here for a few days. Look here, Aleck; all he said was pretence—he never meant us to get out again."

"Oh, I don't know," said Aleck, passionately. "He might, or he might not. Now, then, what's to be done—try and find some tools, and then get to work to chip those stones to pieces?"

"No, it would only mean try and try in vain."

"Here, what has come to you?" cried Aleck. "You take it all as coolly as if it were of no consequence at all. I don't believe you can understand yet how bad it all is."

"Oh, yes, I can," said the midshipman, coolly; "but I've got no more miserables left in me. I used 'em all up when I was chained up by myself in the dark. I feel now quite jolly compared to what I was."

"Nonsense. You can't grasp what a terrible strait we're in."

"Oh, yes, I can. We're buried alive."

"Well, isn't that horrible?" said Aleck.

"Pretty tidy, but not half so bad as being buried dead. It would be all over then; but as we're buried alive perhaps we shall be able to unbury ourselves."

"You must be half mad," said Aleck, angrily, "or you'd never talk so lightly."

"Lightly? I don't talk lightly. I'm as serious as a judge."

"But what are we to do?"

"Wait a bit and let's think. We can live down here for ever so long; that is, as long as the rations last. Then we shall have to try some other way out."

"Yes; but what way?"

The midshipman pointed towards the dimly-seen submerged arch.

"Can you swim?" he said.

"Of course. Pretty well."

"And dive?"

"Yes."

"Then my notion is that we take it as coolly as we can till we think it's a suitable time. Then we'll strip, make a couple of bundles of our clothes, go in as near to that arch as we can, and then try to dive under and out to the daylight."

Aleck raised the lanthorn to bring its dim light full upon his companion's face, gazing at him hard as if in doubt of his sanity. For the words were spoken as calmly and coolly as if he had been proposing some ordinary jump into clear water at a bathing-place.

But he only saw that the speaker's countenance was perfectly unruffled, and his next words convinced him that he was speaking in all seriousness.

"Well, don't look so horrified," he said, half laughingly. "You haven't been bragging, have you? Don't say you can't swim?"

"Oh, I can swim easily enough," said Aleck, impatiently; "but suppose one rose too soon, right up amongst those rugged rocks, with the sea-wrack hanging down in long strips ready to strangle us?"

"I'm not going to suppose anything of the sort," said the midshipman. "Why should you suppose such horrors? I might just as well say: suppose a great shark should rush in open-mouthed to swallow me down and then grab you by the leg, throw you over on to his back, and carry you about till he felt hungry again?"

"But you don't see the danger?" cried Aleck.

"And don't want to see it. I daresay it is dangerous, but nearly everything is if you look at it in that way. Well, what now? Why do you look at me like that?"

"Because I don't understand you," said Aleck. "Yesterday you seemed as weak as a girl, while now you are proposing impossible things, and seem to be trying to brag as if to make me feel that you are not so weak as you were then."

"Perhaps so," said the middy, laughing good-humouredly. "I was as weak as a girl yesterday, but I don't feel so now; and though you are partly right, and I don't want you to think me such a molly, I really am ready to make a dash at it if you will."

"I'll do anything that I think is possible," said Aleck, gravely, "but I don't want to be rash."

"Then you think it would be rash to try and dive out under that archway?"

"Horribly," said Aleck, with a shudder; and at that moment the candle, which, unnoticed through the dull horn, had burned down and begun flickering in the socket, suddenly flashed up brightly, flickered for a moment or two, and went out.

Chapter Twenty Seven

"Ugh!" ejaculated the midshipman. "I don't feel half so brave now, and I don't believe I dare go in here in the darkness, set aside make a dive. Where's the tinder-box? For goodness' sake, strike a light and let's have another candle. Oh, you oughtn't to have let that out!"

"Come along," replied Aleck. "I think I can find the way to the place again. Mind how you come; there are so many stones. I say, why is it that one feels so shrinking in the dark and frightened of all sorts of things that we never dream of in the light?"

"I don't know, and don't want to talk about it now. Let's have a light first. I say, we must do something before the candles are all burnt out."

"Mind!" cried Aleck, for his companion caught his foot against one of the pieces of projecting rock against which he had been warned, and but for the throwing out of a friendly hand he would have gone head first into the water.

"Ugh!" he panted, as he clung, trembling now violently. "I wonder how deep the water is just there! How horrible! I say, don't let go of my hand. What are you doing?"

"I'm feeling for the lanthorn."

"What!" cried the midshipman, aghast. "Don't say you've lost that?"

"I wasn't going to," said Aleck, rather gruffly, as he thought that his companion was about the strangest compound of bravery and cowardice he had ever met. "But didn't you hear it go down crash?"

"No, I heard nothing. Here, what's this against my foot?"

Aleck stooped down and found that it was the missing lanthorn.

"It's lucky it did not roll into the water. Now, then, all right. Keep hold of hands, and let's feel our way to where I left the tinder-box. Hold up; don't stumble again."

"I can't help it," said the middy, with his teeth chattering. "It feels as if all the strength had gone out of my legs. Here, Aleck, it's of no use to be a sham; hold on tightly by my hand and help me along. I'm afraid that was all brag about making the dive. I suppose I must be a horrible coward, after all."

"I'm afraid I am too," said Aleck bitterly, as he held the other's hand tightly and tried to progress cautiously in the dark. "I feel horrible, and as if the next step I take will send us both into the water."

"Ugh! Don't say that," whispered the middy, huskily. "I remember what that fellow said about the seals; but it's my belief that a dark piece of water like this must swarm with all kinds of terrible creatures."

"And yet you wanted to dive into it for a swim?"

"Yes, when the candle was alight."

"I didn't feel anything attack us when we bathed," said Aleck, quietly.

"Oh, don't talk about it," said the middy, shuddering. "I bathed then, but I don't feel as if, feeling what I do, I could risk another plunge in."

Aleck felt no disposition whatever to talk about the venture his companion in misfortune had proposed, for he was intent upon getting to the spot where the light-producing implement had been bestowed, and twice over he nearly lost his calmness, for the horrible idea attacked him that he had wandered quite away from the spot in the darkness.

It was an ugly thought, bringing up others of a strangely confusing nature, but at last, just when he was ready to confess to this fresh trouble, he came upon candle and tinder-box, over which his trembling fingers played for some minutes before the welcome spark appeared in the tinder and suffered itself to be blown up into a glow instead of dying out.

Hot and tired, the two lads made for the resting-place, and were thankful to cast themselves down, to lie in silence for close upon an hour before either of them ventured to advert to their position; but at last the midshipman declared that he knew it from the first, and that they were a pair of idiots to trust the word of a smuggler.

"I don't see it," said Aleck, who felt ready to give the man credit for having met with some mishap.

"Well, I do. It was a deeply-laid scheme to trap us—shut us up here and leave us to die while he escaped."

"Nonsense," cried Aleck. "Why, it would be a horrible murder!"

"Yes; horrible—diabolical—shocking."

"I don't believe Eben Megg would be such a wretch," said Aleck, stoutly.

"What, not a smuggler? They're the greatest villains under the sun."

"Are they?" said Aleck, drily.

"Yes, I know that," cried the middy angrily; "but I'll let the brute see. I'll have him hung at the yard-arm for this. He shall find out he made a mistake."

"When we get out," said Aleck, smiling in spite of their trouble, for his companion's peppery way of expressing himself was amusing.

"Yes, when we get out, of course. You don't suppose I'm going to settle myself quietly down here, do you?"

"Of course not," said Aleck; and then an idea occurred to him which made him check his companion just as he was about to burst into a tirade about what he would do.

"I say," cried Aleck, "it must be easy to get out of this if we wait till the time when the boats can come in."

"But do they ever come in?"

"Of course. How else could the smugglers have landed all this stuff?"

"It must be at a spring tide then," said the middy.

"To be sure. When's the next?"

"I don't know," said the middy. "You do, of course?"

"Not I. You're a pretty sort of a sailor not to know when the next spring tide is."

"And you're a pretty sort of a fellow who lives by the shore and don't know. You seem to know nothing."

"Bother the spring tides," said Aleck, testily. "I know there are spring tides, and that sometimes you can walk dry-shod half way down our gully; but I can't tell the times. Tom Bodger would know."

"What, that wooden-legged sailor?"

"Yes."

"Then you'd better go and fetch him here."

"I wish I could," said Aleck, sadly. "What's the good of wishing? Here, I'm hungry. Let's have something to eat."

"No, we mustn't do that," said Aleck. "We had better eat as little as we can so as to make the food last as long as possible."

"No, we hadn't," replied the middy, roughly. "We may just as well eat while we can. There's plenty to keep us alive; but if we can't get out we shan't be able to live all the same."

"Why?"

The middy was silent for a few moments before he could master himself sufficiently, the horror that he as a sailor foresaw not having been grasped by his shore-going companion.

"You haven't been to sea?" he said, at last, in quite a different tone.

"Only about in my boat."

"In sight of land, when you could put ashore at any time."

"Yes; but what do you mean?"

"I mean, the first thing a sailor, thinks about is his supply of fresh water."

"To be sure," said Aleck. "I always take a little keg from our spring when I go for a long day's fishing."

"Pity you didn't bring it here," said the middy, dismally.

"Eh? What do you mean?"

"I want to know what we're going to do for water as soon as those bottles are empty?"

It was Aleck's turn to be silent now, and in turn he was some moments before he spoke.

"I never thought of that," he said, and he felt as if a cold chill was running through him, to give place to a hot feverish sensation, accompanied by thirst.

Then he recovered his boyish elasticity.

"Here," he cried, "never say die! I'm not going to give up like this. Look here; we've got a spring at home where the water trickles out of a crack in the rock and flows down into a great stone tank like a well. It only comes in drops, but it's always dropping, and so we have enough for our wants."

"Pity you didn't bring your tank here," said the middy. "What's the good of telling me that?"

"Because the cliff all along here for miles has places where the water trickles out, and I shouldn't be a bit surprised if we were to find that the smugglers have something in the shape of a tank here in this place. They must have wanted water here, and they would be sure to have saved any that trickled in."

"Then you'd better find it," said the middy.

"Come along, then; let's search. This place is very big."

"You can if you like. I've had such a dose this morning, just when I felt I was going to get out, that I'm going to lie down and try to forget it."

"What! Go to sleep?" cried Aleck.

"Yes."

"That you're not. You're going to help me search the cavern."

"I'm not."

"You are," cried Aleck, firmly.

"Look here; do you want to make it a fight?"

"No, and you don't either. Come on; we'll light another candle and stick it upon a piece of stone or slate. Then we'll have a good hunt."

"Oh, very well," said the middy, rising. "Come on, then; but I'm sure we're only going to tire ourselves for nothing."

"Never mind, it will keep us from thinking."

There was no difficulty in picking up a flat piece of slate, and then a fresh candle was cut free from the bunch, its end melted, and stuck on to the stone, and then the lads looked at one another.

"Look here," said the middy; "I wish I wasn't such an awful beast."

Aleck laughed.

"You don't look one," he said.

"No, but I feel one. Fellows in trouble ought to be like brothers, and I keep on having fits of the grumps. Here, I mean to work with you now."

"I know you do," said Aleck, frankly, "but it's enough to make anyone feel savage."

"Now, then, where are we going to look for water?"

"Right up at the narrowest end of the cave."

"Why?"

"Because what there is always seems to make for the sea."

"That's right," said the middy; and, taking the lead, he began to pick his way along by the side of the canal-like pool, whose clear waters reflected the lights as if it were a river.

"Water's higher now," said Aleck.

"Yes, and it looks good enough to drink; but it's salter than the sea, I suppose. I say!"

"Well?" said Aleck.

"This place gets narrower. It seems to me that if the roof fell in it would make another of those caves you have all along this coast. I shouldn't wonder if in time all the top of this comes in and opens the mouth so that the waves can rush in and wash it bigger and bigger."

"Very likely," said Aleck. "Look here!"

He held down the candle to show that they had come to the end of the deep water, which was continued farther in by a series of pools, which were probably only joined into one lane of water at very high tides.

The middy said something of the kind, and then pointed out, as they progressed slowly, that the pools grew smaller and smaller till they came to an end, where the cavern had grown very narrow and seemed to be closing in, and where a huge mass of stone blocked the way.

"How are we to go now? Climb right over that big lump? I don't believe there's room to crawl between that and the roof."

"I say," replied Aleck, excitedly, "it's wet right up."

"All the worse for our clothes," was the reply; "but is it any use to go any farther?"

Aleck's answer took the shape of action, for he sank upon his knees, set the piece of slate which formed his candlestick upon the rock floor, and going down upon his chest reached out and scooped up some of the water of the pool in his palm and raised it to his lips.

"Don't swallow it," said his companion; "it will only make you horribly thirsty."

"No," cried Aleck, exultantly, "it's all right—fresh and sweet. Look here; you can see how there's water trickling very slowly down."

"So there is," cried the middy. "You were all right about that."

"Yes," said Aleck, "and I believe we shall find ships' stores enough amongst those barrels to last us for months."

"Let's see!" said the middy. "Oh! this is getting too jolly," he added. "Let's open some of the boxes too. Why, the next thing will be that I shall be finding a new uniform all ready for putting on, but—oh, dear!" he added, dolefully.

"Well, of all the fellows," cried Aleck. "Here have we just found out that things aren't half so bad as they seemed, and now you're breaking out again. What is the matter now?"

"I was thinking about the uniform, been lying here perhaps for months; it's sure to be too damp to put on."

"Bah!" cried Aleck. "Dip it right into the big pool and make it salt. It won't hurt you then."

"Right," shouted the middy. "Now, then, what next? I believe if we keep on we shall find a fresh way out."

"Like enough. Let's try."

They tried, but tried in vain. The middy held the light, and Aleck climbed up the wet face of the huge mass which blocked the way, and then began to crawl on beneath the roof.

"How do you get on?"

"Splendid. It goes upward, and I could almost stand."

"How are you getting on?" said the middy, after listening to the scrambling noise made by the climber.

"Middling. Just room to crawl now." Five minutes later the middy shouted again:

"Look here; hadn't I better come up now?"

"Yes, if you like."

"Is there plenty of room?"

"No."

"Then what's the use of my coming?"

"Only to keep me company. Better still, come and give a pull at my heels."

"Pull at your heels?"

"Yes, it's like a chimney laid on its side, and I'm quite stuck fast."

"Oh!" cried the middy; and then, "All right, I'm coming."

"No, no, don't!" came to him in smothered tones, as he began to climb; "I've got room again. Coming back."

There was a good deal of shuffling and scraping, and then Aleck's feet came into the light over the top of the block. The next minute he was on his feet beside his companion, hot, panting, and with the front of his clothes wet.

"There's a tiny stream comes trickling in there," he said, brushing himself down softly; "but there isn't room for a rat to get any further than I did. My word, it was tight! I felt as if the water had made me swell out, and it didn't seem as if I was going to get back."

"Phew!" whistled the middy. "We should have been worse off then. I say, Aleck, you'd have had to starve for a few days to get thin, and then I could have pulled you out. Here, I say, though, old fellow, I'm not going on the grump any more; things might be worse, eh?"

"Ever so much," said Aleck, cheerfully. "Let's have a good drink now, and then go and examine some of those barrels. If one of them turns out salt beef or pork we'll go back and finish our stores, for we shall be all right for provisions."

"Without counting the fish I mean to catch. I'm sure there'll be some come in with the tide."

"Very foolish of them if they do," said Aleck, wiping his mouth after lying down to take a long deep draught, in which action he was imitated by his companion. "Now, then, I want to be satisfied about flour and meat."

Within half an hour he was satisfied, for a little examination proved to the prisoners that some unfortunate vessel had gone to pieces outside and its stores had been run in by the smugglers.

"Yes," said the middy, as they returned to their resting-place, to begin making a hearty meal, "things do look a bit more rosy, but you mustn't be too chuff over it. I'll bet sixpence, if you like, that the tackle in those tubs is as salt as brine."

"I'm afraid so," said Aleck, "and all the outside of the flour mouldy."

"Very likely," said the middy. "But never mind; if the outside's bad we'll eat the in."

"Look at the crack over yonder now!" cried Aleck, after a time, during which the only sounds heard were those of two people eating.

"What for?"

"It look's so light; just as if the sun was shining upon it outside. I must try if I can't dive down and swim out."

"With a rope round your waist," said the middy, eagerly, "so that if you stuck—"

"You could pull me back," said Aleck.

"And if you got through safely—" cried the middy.

"You would tie the other end round you," said Aleck, "ready for me to haul and help you out in turn."

"Oh! What's the good of a fellow being grumpy?" cried the middy. "Why, we're enjoying ourselves. This is one big adventurous game. I'm getting to be glad those women took me prisoner. I don't believe there ever were two who dropped in for such an adventure as this. But, I say, I don't think we'll try the diving trick to-day. We ought to be rested and fresh."

"Yes," replied Aleck, "and we ought to have another good try up the zigzag first."

"Yes, it might be as well. I say, just ring for the people to clear away. I want to have a nap now. What time is it?"

"Oh, I don't know. Why?"

"Because I want to know what to call it. You see, I don't know whether I'm going to have a siesta or a genuine snooze."

"Have both," said Aleck, laughing, "and I'll do the same."

"And it doesn't matter, does it, for night and day seem to be about the same? Put out that candle, and mind where the tinder-box is."

"Here, you see where it lies," was the reply, and then there was silence, both lying thinking deeply before once more dropping fast asleep, many hours having been taken up by the hard toil and suffering they had gone through.

Chapter Twenty Eight

The next morning, as it seemed from the beautiful limpid appearance of dawn that rose from the surface of the waters, to become diffused in the soft gloom overhead, the lads lit a candle and set off manfully to try as to the possibility of making their way out through the zigzag passage, Aleck trying first and dragging and pushing at the stones which blocked his way, till, utterly exhausted and dripping with perspiration, he made way for his comrade to have a try.

The latter toiled hard in turn, and did not desist till he found that his fingers were bleeding and growing painful.

"It's of no good," he said, gloomily; "that scoundrel has done his work too well. Let's get down to where we can breathe. I say, though," he added, cheerily, "I've learned one thing."

"What?" asked Aleck.

"That I was never cut out for a chimney-sweep. This is bad enough; I don't know what it would be if there was the soot."

They slid down, and as soon as they were back in the comparatively cheerful cavern, where they could breathe freely, Aleck proposed that they should look out amongst the sails and ships' stores for a suitable rope for their purpose.

There was coil upon coil of rope, but for the most part they were too thick, and it seemed as if they would be reduced to venturing upon their dive untrammelled, when, raising the lanthorn for another glance round, Aleck caught sight of the very piece he required, hanging from a wooden peg driven in between two blocks of stone.

"Looks old and worn," said the middy, passing the frayed line through his fingers. "Let's try it."

The means adopted was to tie one end round a projection of the rocky side, run the line out to its full length, and then drag and jerk it together with all their might.

Satisfied with the effects of this test, the rope was untied, the other end made fast, and the dragging and snatching repeated without the tough fibres of the hemp yielding in the least.

"Looks very old," said the middy, "but wear has only made it soft. If it stands all that tugging with the weight of both of us on the end it will bear one of us being dragged through the water, where one isn't so heavy. Now, then, are we going to try this way?"

"Certainly," said Aleck.

"Very well; who's to go first?"

"I will," said Aleck.

"I don't know about that," replied the middy. "You're only a shore-going fellow, while I'm a sailor. I think I ought to go first."

"It doesn't much matter who goes first, but I spoke first and I'll go."

"Look here," cried the middy; "if I give way and let you have first try, will you play fair?"

"Of course. But what do you mean?"

"You won't brag and chuck it in my face afterwards that you got us out of the hole?"

"Do you think I should be such a donkey?" cried Aleck. "Why, look here, I'm going to try and chance it, but I don't believe I shall get through. Never mind about who's to be first. Let's do all we can to make sure of escaping. Now, then, shall we try now, or wait till the water's at its lowest? It's going down now."

"If we wait till the tide's at its lowest it will be slack water, and we shall get no help. It's running out now, and we can see the shape of the arch."

"Yes, and how rugged and weed-hung it is. I say, I don't like the look of it. You'd better go first."

"Very well," said the middy, promptly, and he began taking off his jacket.

"Hold hard," cried Aleck, hurriedly stripping off his own. "Come along."

He led the way to the edge of the water where, though not the nearest, the best leap off seemed to present itself, and then stood perfectly still, gazing down into the softly illuminated water, quivering and wreathing as it ran softly out, and looking dim and blurred through being kept so much in motion by the retiring waves.

"Then you still mean to go?" said the middy.

"Of course. But what shall I do—strip, or try in my clothes?"

"Strip, decidedly," cried the middy.

"I shall get scratched and scraped going under the rocks."

"You'll get caught by them and hung up if you keep your clothes on. Have 'em all off, man; you'll slip through the water then like a seal."

"Yes," said Aleck, calmly, "I suppose it will be best."

It did not take him long to prepare, and as soon as he was ready his companion made the rope fast just round beneath the arm-pits with a knot that would neither slip nor tighten.

"There!" said the middy, as he finished his preparations by laying out the rope in rings and curves of various shapes, such as would easily run out. "I say, you are perfectly black when I look at you from behind, but in front you seem like a white image on a black ground. Now, then, what do you mean to do?"

"Dive in from here and try to keep right down and swim as deeply as I can for the mouth."

"Try to swallow the job at one mouthful?"

"Yes."

"Won't do," said the middy, authoritatively. "You couldn't do it. You must slip in gently here and swim to that rock that's just out of the water."

"What! That one that seems just to the left of the arch?"

"That's the one. Get out on it, wait a few moments, and then take a long, deep breath and dive."

Aleck pondered for a few moments.

"Yes," he said, "I think you're right. I should have had to swim so far first if I started from here."

"To be sure you would. The less diving you have the better."

"I see," said Aleck. "Now, then, let the rope run out easily through your fingers till I give it a sharp jerk. That means pull me back as fast as you can."

"Yes, because you can go no further."

"If I pull twice it means I am safe through, and then—"

"I shall tie my end of the rope round my chest and come too. You need not pull, only just draw in the line, unless it stops, because that would mean I had got into difficulties. Do we both understand? I do."

"So do I," said Aleck, "so let's get it over. If I wait much longer I shall be afraid to go."

"Don't believe you," said the middy, bluntly. "Now, then—ready?"

"Yes."

The word was no sooner uttered than Aleck slipped down into the water and began to swim, with the rope being carefully paid out by his comrade, and in a minute he was fairly started. He was at first invisible, but very soon began to look like a black object making its way over a surface that grew transparent.

Then all at once the rope ceased to run.

"What is it?" cried the middy, anxiously.

"Got to the rock."

"Is the water deep?"

"Very."

"Well, get up, ready for your dive."

"It's all seaweed, and horribly slippery."

"Never mind; up with you."

A peculiar splashing sound arose, and the middy could just make out the dim shape of his companion climbing, or rather dragging, himself on to the slimy rock, whose top was about a foot above the surface of the water.

"Stop a minute or two first," said the middy, "so as to take—"

He was going to say "breath," but before the word could be uttered Aleck, who had drawn himself up to stand erect, felt his feet gliding from under him, and it was only by a violent effort that he escaped falling heavily upon the weed-covered rock. As it was he came down with a tremendous splash into the water, going head first in a sharp incline down and down, while, obeying his first impulse, he struck out sharply.

The middy was about to obey his first impulse too, and that was not to pay out, but begin to haul his comrade back. His hands tightened round the line, but as he awoke to the fact that it was gliding through his hands in obedience to the regular pulsation of the movements of a swimmer, he felt that all must be right, and waited while, foot by foot, the rope glided on and the transparent water grew more and more agitated and strange to see.

Once he fancied he could clearly make out Aleck's steadily swimming figure, but directly after he knew it was a great, waving, flag-like mass of weed fronds, and he uttered an impatient gasp and turned cold.

"He couldn't have got his breath for the dive," he said to himself, "and the current must be taking him helplessly away. Half the line must have run out, and perhaps he's insensible. No; that means swimming, for it goes in jerks, and—he has stopped. He must be through. Hooray! Well done, old—oh, that's the signal to pull him back!"

It was surely enough, and the middy began at once to haul in, and then the cold feeling became a chill of horror, for he had drawn the rope quite tight at the second haul, and it was perfectly evident that the swimmer had signalled because in some way he was caught fast.

What to do?

The middy was energetic enough, and in those perilous moments, full of horror for his companion's sake, he hauled till he dared pull no more for fear that the rope should part, and, obeying now a sudden thought, he relaxed the strain, and the rope seemed to be snatched back towards Aleck.

"That can't be a signal," he said to himself, in despair; but he began to haul again, recovered the line lost, and to his intense delight he found that the swimmer was once more free, and that he was drawing him rapidly back to where he stood. The lad's action was as rapid now as he could pass hand over hand, and in a very short space of time he had the poor fellow close up to the rock edge, and then, taking hold of the rope where it passed round Aleck's chest, he dragged him out, half insensible, upon the rocks.

Another half minute or so might have been fatal, but Aleck had some little energy left, and, after a strangling fit of coughing, he was able to sit up.

"Take—the rope off!" he panted.

This was done, and in a few minutes he was breathing freely and able to talk.

"I didn't get a fair start," he said, hoarsely. "I slipped, and went in before I was ready; but I got on all right for a bit till I seemed to be sucked in between two pieces of rock, and felt myself going into black darkness. Then I signalled to you."

"I hauled directly."

"Yes, and it seemed to drag me crosswise so that I couldn't pass through between the two rocks again. How did you manage then?"

"I did nothing, only let go so as to make a fresh start."

"Did you?" said Aleck, quietly. "Ah, I didn't know anything about that. I only knew that it was very horrible, and I thought it was all over. It was very near, wasn't it?"

"Oh, I don't know," said the middy, coolly. "You say that you didn't have a fair start?"

"No; it was that fall. But it's queer work. You can't make out where you are going, and the current grinds your head up against the weedy rock."

"But you got nearly through, didn't you?"

"I suppose so, but I don't know. It was all one horrible confusion."

"Yes; but another few yards, I expect, and you would have been safe, and could have pulled me through, or helped me as I swam."

"Perhaps," said Aleck, rather slowly, for he felt confused still. "But what are you doing?"

"Peeling off my clothes."

"What for?" said Aleck, speaking now with more animation.

"To do my turn, and see how I get on."

"No, no, no!" cried Aleck, excitedly. "You mustn't try. It's too horrible."

"Horrible? Nonsense. It's only a swim in the dark. I like diving."

"I tell you it can't be done, sailor," cried Aleck, angrily. "The risk is too great. I should have been drowned if you had not hauled me out."

"Well, and if I'm going to be drowned you'll haul me out. You're strong enough now, aren't you?"

"Oh, yes; but you mustn't risk it."

"You wait till I get these things off, my lad, and I'll show you. Why, you'd have done it splendidly if you had dived off the rock instead of going in flip-flap like a sole out of a basket. I'll show you how to do it."

"You'd better take my word for it that it can't be done. Let's wait till the tide's low enough, and then swim out in daylight."

"You wait till I get out of my uniform," said the middy, stubbornly, "I'll show you, my fine fellow. I've practised diving a good deal. Some day, if we get to the right place in the ocean, I mean to have a go down with the sponge divers, and if I'm ever in the South Seas I mean to try diving for pearl shell."

"Well," said Aleck, rather sadly, "I've warned you, and I suppose it is of no use for me to say any more?"

"Not a bit," said the middy, dragging off his second stocking. "You make fast the dry end of the line round my noble chest. Not too tight, mind, and a knot that won't slip."

The young sailor possessed the greater will power now, for Aleck was yet half stunned by what he had gone through. He obeyed every order he received, and carefully knotted on the rope.

"Now, are you ready?" said the middy. "Feel up to hauling me back if I don't get through?"

"Yes."

"And, mind, when I am through I shall not drag you. No, no, don't untie your end of the rope; you'll want that. Now, do you understand?"

"Yes."

"Very well, then, as soon as I'm through I shall get on a dry rock and signal to you to come. Then you'll slip in and swim to the rock again, and take a header off it. Don't bungle it this time, and when you feel my touch at the rope, mind it's not meant to haul, only to guide you to where I'm sitting."

"But what about our clothes?" said Aleck, drearily.

"Bother our clothes! We want to save our skins and not our clothes. Now, then, ready?"

"Yes, if you will go."

"Will go? Look here!"

The lad sprang, feet foremost, into the water, and rose directly from out of the depths, to strike out, and as Aleck tried hard to follow his movements, he heard him reach the weedy rock, drag himself out, and the rope was gently drawn more and more through his hands as the middy succeeded in getting erect upon the stone, close to its edge.

"See that?" he shouted.

"Yes."

"That's what you ought to have done. Now, then, slacken the line well. I'm taking a long, deep breath, ready for you know what. That's it. Ready— ho!"

The middy sprang into the air, and very dimly Aleck saw that he curved himself over, and the next moment his hands divided the water, and he plunged in for his dive almost without a splash, while as the rope ran swiftly through his hands Aleck felt a flash of energy run through him, and stood ready for any emergency that might befall.

Then a feeling akin to jealousy came over him, as he found the rope drawn out vigorously, and it seemed to him that the midshipman was a far better swimmer and diver than he.

"But he hasn't come to the difficult part yet," he thought, the next moment. "He'll find that he can't keep down deep, and that while he is trying to beat the tangling wrack to right and left something like a current sucks him upward and forces him against the rocks that form the arch."

Then, full of eagerness so as to be ready to help the diver when his time of extremity came, Aleck held the rope attached to him with both hands gingerly enough to let it pass easily through as wanted, but at the same time, in the most guarded way, ready to let it fall against his right shoulder when, as he intended, he turned sharply to walk swiftly back into the interior of the cavern and draw his companion back to the water's edge.

Then a curious thought struck him, consequent upon the rope beginning to run out faster and faster.

"Why, he's getting through," he cried, mentally, with a suggestion of disappointment in his brain at his comrade's better success. "He's getting through, and he'll run out all the line quickly now and draw me in.

"Well, so much the better," he thought. "If he can pass through I can, and perhaps in a few moments we shall both have escaped.

"Wish I'd done something about our clothes," he muttered then. "We shall want them, of course. But, I know; we can hide somewhere about the mouth of the cave till it gets dark, and then I can take him up to the Den, and—"

Aleck did not finish the plan he was thinking out, for the rope had seemed to him to be running out to a far greater extent than he had taken it himself; but in reality it had gone away at about the same rate, so that something like the same quantity had been drawn through his hands when it suddenly ceased to glide, and directly after a spasm shot through the lad's brain, for it had stopped, and directly after the signal was given sharply, sending a thrill through him.

He responded directly by clutching the rope tightly and beginning to run.

It was only a beginning, for he was brought up short on the instant, and so sharply that he was jerked backwards.

"Just the same as I must have been," he said to himself, excitedly, after bearing hard against the rope and finding it quite fast. "It's like conger fishing," he thought, "and I must give him line."

Slackening out at once, he waited for a moment or two, and then tightened again, when to his great delight he found that he was no longer dragging at something set hard, but at a yielding body, which he drew easily to the edge of the pool by means of his long coil, before dropping it and running to seize and repeat the middy's performance upon himself.

"He's quite insensible," he gasped, as he drew the dripping lad right out on to the driest part.

"That I'm not," panted the middy; "but another minute would have done it."

He remained silent then, panting hard and struggling to recover his breath, while Aleck untied the line and set his chest at liberty to act as it should.

Then for some minutes nothing was said, the only sound heard being the middy's hoarse breathing as he laboured hard to recover his regular inspirations.

At last he spoke in an unpleasantly harsh, ill-humoured way.

"Well, aren't you going to have another try? It's lovely. Only wants plenty of perseverance."

"Not I," replied Aleck. "You don't seem to have got on so very well."

"Got on as well as you did," snarled the middy. "Ugh! It was horrid. Just as if, when I felt that I could hold my breath no longer, I was suddenly seized and sucked into a great sink-hole, only the water was running up instead of down."

"Yes, that's just how I felt," said Aleck.

"You couldn't have felt so bad as I did," said the lad, irritably and speaking in the most inconsistent way. "I got my head rasped, too, against the stones overhead, and it's bleeding fast. Look at it, will you?"

Aleck examined the place, after opening the door of the lanthorn.

"It isn't bleeding," he said.

"Don't talk nonsense," cried the middy, irritably. "It smarts horribly, and I can feel the blood trickling down the back of my neck."

"That's water out of your hair."

"Are you sure?"

"Yes, certain. I can't even see a mark on your head."

"Well, there ought to be," grumbled the lad. "Aren't you going to have another try?"

"No. Are you?"

"Not if I know it," replied the middy. "Once is quite enough for a trip of that kind."

"I don't think it's possible to get out by swimming."

"Well, it doesn't seem like it; but the smugglers get in."

"Yes, at certain times."

"Then this is an uncertain time, I suppose!" said the middy, beginning to dress.

"Hadn't we better get round and have a good rub with a bit of sail?" asked Aleck.

"No; we can't carry our clothes without getting them wet, and if we don't take them it means coming all the way round here again. Let's dress as we are; the salt water will soon dry."

"Very well," said Aleck, and he followed his companion's example with much satisfaction to his feelings, listening the while to the middy's plaints and grumblings, for he had been under water long enough to make him feel something like resuscitated people, exceedingly discontented and ill-humoured.

Every now and then he burst out with some disagreeable remark. One minute it was against his shirt for sticking to his wet back; another time it was at Aleck for getting on so fast with his dressing consequent upon his being drier; and then he began to abuse Eben Megg.

"A beast; that's what he is. It's just as bad as murdering us with a knife or chopper, that it is."

They were dressed at something like the same time, Aleck having achieved his task quietly, the middy with a sort of accompaniment of grumbles and unpleasant remarks.

"There," he said, at last; "that seems to have done me a lot of good. There's nothing like a good growl."

"Got rid of a lot of ill temper, eh?" said Aleck, smiling to himself.

"Yes, I suppose that's it. But, I say, we're not going to try that way out again! I say it's perfectly impossible."

"So do I," said Aleck.

"We should both have been drowned if it hadn't been for the rope."

"That we should, for a certainty," replied Aleck. "Well, there's nothing to be done but to wait patiently for the coming of that low tide when a boat could come in, as Eben Megg said, and as it's plain it does, or else all these stores couldn't have been brought in."

"And when it does come?" said the middy.

"We shall swim or wade out, of course," said Aleck.

The Lost Middy | 227

"No, we shan't," grumbled the middy. "You see if it doesn't come in the night, when we're asleep."

"We must be too much on the look-out for that," said Aleck.

"It will not come all at once, but by degrees—lower and lower tides, till we get the one we want; and till then we shall have to be patient."

"Hark at him!" said the midshipman. "Who's to be patient at a time like this? Well, I'm beginning to feel warm and dry again; what do you say to getting back and having dinner, or whatever you like to call it? Oh, dear! Eating and drinking's bad enough on ship board, but it's all feasts and banquets compared to this."

"We must try to improve it," said Aleck. "I don't see why we shouldn't be able to catch fish."

"What? You don't suppose fish would be such scaly idiots as to come into a hole like this?"

"Perhaps not, but I believe they'd be shelly idiots enough. I shouldn't be a bit surprised, if we had a lobster or crab pot thrown out here, if we caught some fine ones."

"Set one, then," said the midshipman, sourly. "Perhaps there is one."

"Not likely," replied Aleck. "Never mind, let's make the best of what we've got and be thankful."

"No, that I won't," cried his companion. "I'll make the best of what we've got as much as you like, but I must draw the line somewhere—I won't be thankful."

"I will," said Aleck, good-temperedly; "thankful enough for both."

"Come on," said the midshipman, gruffly.

"Wait a moment till I've coiled up the line loosely. We may want it, and it must be hung up to dry."

This was done, and then after noting that the water was growing deeper in the direction of the sea entrance, the pair made their way right round by the head, stopped at the spring to have a hearty drink, and then pressed on, lanthorn in hand, to their resting-place, where, thoroughly upset by his adventure, the midshipman grumbled at everything till Aleck burst into a hearty laugh.

"Hallo!" cried his companion, eagerly; "let's have it. Got a bright idea as to how to get out?"

"No," said Aleck, "I was laughing at the comic way in which you keep on finding fault."

"Humph! Well, I have been going it rather, haven't I?"

"Doing nothing else but growl."

"That's the worst of having a nasty temper. Don't do a bit of good either, does it?"

"Not a bit," said Aleck. "Makes things still worse."

"Think so?"

Aleck nodded.

"Yes, I suppose you're right. I'll drop it then. Now, then, what do you say to having a good long snooze?"

"I'm willing," said Aleck, "for I'm thoroughly tired out."

"Put out the light then. My word, what a good thing sleep is!" said the midshipman, after they had lain in silence for a few minutes. "Makes you able to forget all your troubles."

There was a pause, and then the midshipman began:

"I say it makes you able to forget all your troubles, doesn't it?"

Still silence.

"Don't you hear what I say?"

No answer.

"Hanged if he isn't asleep! How a fellow can be such a dormouse-headed animal at a time like this I don't know."

He ought to have known, a minute later, for he was lying upon his back, fast asleep and breathing hard, dreaming of all kinds of pleasant things, some of which had to do with being feasted after getting free.

Chapter Twenty Nine

The next day the two lads could only think of their attempt with a shudder, for their efforts, though they did not quite grasp the narrowness of their escape from death, had resulted in a peculiar shock to their system, one effect of which was to make then disinclined to do anything more than sit and lie in the darkness watching the faint suggestion of dawn in the direction of the submerged archway. Then, too, they slept a good deal, while even on the following day they both suffered a good deal from want of energy.

Towards evening, though, Aleck roused up.

"Look here, sailor," he said, "this will not do. We ought to be doing something."

"What?" said the middy, sadly. "Try again to drown ourselves?"

"Oh, no; that was a bit of madness. We mustn't try that again."

"What then? It seems to me that we may as well keep going to sleep till we don't wake again."

"What!" shouted Aleck, his companion's words fully rousing him from his lethargic state. "Well, of all the cowardly things for a fellow to say!"

"Cowardly!" cried the middy, literally galvanised into action by the sound of that word. "You want to quarrel, then, do you? You want to fight, eh? Very well, I'm your man. Let's light the lanthorn and have it out at once."

"Oh, very well," cried Aleck. "There's a nice soft bit of sand yonder that will just do."

The middy snorted like an angry animal and began to breathe hard, while Aleck, feeling regularly angry now, felt for the tinder-box and matches, and began to send the sparks flying in showers.

The tinder was soon glowing, the match well alight, and a fresh candle stuck in its place, the lanthorn being set upon a flat stone, with the door open, after which the two lads slipped off their jackets and rolled up their sleeves.

"Shut the lanthorn door, stupid," cried the middy.

"What for?"

"What for? To keep the candle from tumbling out the first time I knock you up against that stone."

"I should like to catch you at it," said Aleck. "If I shut the door how am I to see to hit you on the nose?"

"You hit me on the nose? Ha, ha!" cried the middy. "Why, I shall have you calling out that you've had enough long before you get there."

"We shall see," said Aleck. "Don't you think that you're going to frighten me with a lot of bounce. Now, then, are you ready?"

"Yes, I'm ready enough. I'll show you whether I'm a coward or not. Here, hold out your hand."

"What for?"

"To shake hands, of course, and show that we mean fair play."

"I never stopped for that when I had a fight with the Rockabie boys, but there you are."

Hands were grasped, and the midshipman was about to withdraw his, but it was held tightly, and somehow or another his own fingers began to respond in a tight clench.

And thus they stood for quite a minute, while some subtle fluid like common-sense in a gaseous form seemed to run up their arms through their shoulders, and then divide, for part to feed their brains and the other part to make their hearts beat more calmly.

At last Aleck spoke.

"I say," he said, "aren't we going to make fools of ourselves?"

"I don't know," was the reply, "but I'll show you I'm not a coward."

"I never thought you were a coward, but you'd say I was one if I told you that I didn't want to fight."

"No, I shouldn't," said the middy, "because I can't help feeling that it is stupid, and I don't want to fight either."

"Then, why should we fight?"

"Oh," said the middy, "there are times when a gentleman's bound to stand upon his honour. We ought to fight now with pistols; but as we have none why, of course, it has to be fists. Besides, I don't suppose you could use a pistol, and it wouldn't be fair for me to shoot you."

"I daresay I know as much about pistols as you do," said Aleck. "I've shot at a mark with my uncle. But we needn't argue about that."

"No, we've got our fists, so let's get it done."

But they did not begin, for the idea that they really were about to make fools of themselves grew stronger, and as they dropped their hands to raise them again as fists, neither liked to strike the first blow.

Suddenly an idea struck Aleck as he glanced sidewise to see their shadows stretched out in a horribly grotesque, distorted form upon the dark water, and he smiled to himself as he saw his fists elongated into clubs, while he said, suddenly:

"I say, I don't want, you to think me a coward."

"Very well, then, you had better show you are not by fighting hard to keep me from giving you an awful licking."

"You can't do it," said Aleck; "but I say I don't want to fight."

"Perhaps not; but you'll soon find you'll have to, or I shall call you the greatest coward I ever saw."

"But it seems so stupid when we are in such trouble to make things worse by knocking one another about."

"Well, yes, perhaps it does," replied the middy.

"Suppose, then, I do something brave than fighting you," said Aleck.

"What could you do?"

"Put the rope round me again and try to swim out. That would be doing some good."

"You daren't do it?"

"Yes, I dare," cried Aleck, "and I will if you'll say that it's as brave as fighting you."

"I don't know whether it's as brave," said the middy, "but I'd sooner fight than try the other. Ugh! I wouldn't try that again for anything."

"Very well, then, I will," said Aleck, stoutly. "You must own now that it's a braver thing to do than to begin trying to knock you about. There, put down your hands, I'm not going to fight."

"You're beaten then."

"Not a bit of it. I'm going to show you that I'm not a coward."

"No, you're not," said the middy, after a few minutes' pause, during which Aleck ran to the rock and brought back the now dry rope in its loose coil.

To his surprise the middy took a step forward and caught hold of it tightly to try and jerk it away.

"What are you going to do?" said Aleck, in wonder.

"Put it back," said the middy.

"Why?"

"Because you're trying to make me seem a coward now."

"I don't understand you."

"Do you think I'm going to be such a coward as to let you do what I'm afraid to do myself?"

"Then you would be afraid to go again?"

"Yes, of course I should be. So would you."

"Yes, I can't help feeling horribly afraid; but I'll do it," said Aleck.

"To show you're not a coward?"

"Partly that, and partly because I fancy that perhaps I could swim out this time."

"And I'm sure you couldn't," said the middy, "and I shan't let you go."

"You can't stop me?"

"Yes, I can; I won't hold the rope."

"Then I'll go without."

"Why, there'll be no one to pull you back if you get stuck."

"I don't care; I'll go all the same."

"Then you are a coward," cried the middy, triumphantly.

"Mind what you're about," said Aleck, hotly. "Don't you say that again."

"Yes, I will. You're a coward, for you're going to try and swim out, and leave your comrade, who daren't do it, alone here to die."

"Didn't think of that," said Aleck. "There, I won't try to go now; so don't be frightened."

"What!"

Aleck burst out laughing.

"I say," he cried, "what tempers we have both got into! Let's go and do something sensible to try and work it off."

"But there's nothing we can do," said the middy, despondently.

"Yes, there is. As the lanthorn's alight, let's go and have a try at the zigzag."

The middy followed his companion without a word, and they both climbed up wearily and hopelessly to have another desperate try to dislodge the stones, but only to prove that it was an impossible task.

Literally wearied out, they descended, after being compelled to desist by the candle gradually failing, while it had gone right out in the socket before they reached the cave.

But their utter despondency was a little checked by the sight of the soft pale light which seemed to rise from the water more clearly than ever before; and Aleck said so, but the middy was of the opposite opinion.

"No," he said. "It only seems so after the horrible darkness of that hole."

"I don't know," said Aleck; "it certainly looks brighter to me. See how clear the arch looks with the seaweed waving about! I say, sailor, I've a great mind to have another try."

"No, you haven't," growled the middy, wearily. "I can't spare you. I'm not going to stop here and die all alone."

"You wouldn't, for I should drag you out after me."

"Couldn't do it after you were drowned."

"I shouldn't be drowned," said Aleck, slowly and thoughtfully.

"Be quiet—don't bother—I'm so tired—regularly beat out after all that trying up yonder; and so are you. I say, Aleck, I'm beginning to be afraid that we shall never see the sunshine again."

Aleck said nothing, but lay gazing sadly at the dimly-seen arch in the water, and followed the waving to and fro of the great fronds of sea-wrack, till he shuddered once or twice and seemed to feel them clinging round his head and neck, making it dark, but somehow without causing the horrible, strangling, helpless sensation he had suffered from before. In fact, it seemed to be pleasant and restful, and by degrees produced a sensation of coolness that was most welcome after the stifling heat at the top of the zigzag, which had been made worse by the odour of the burning candle.

Then Aleck ceased to think, but lay in the cool, soft darkness, till all at once he started up sitting and wondering.

"Why, I've been asleep," he said to himself. "Here, sailor."

"Yes; what was that?"

"I don't know. I seemed to hear something."

"Have you been asleep?"

"Yes; have you?"

"I think so," said the middy. "We must have been. But, I say, it really is much lighter this time."

"So I thought," said Aleck. "And, I say, I can smell the fresh seaweed. Is the arch going to be open at last?"

Phee-ew! came a low, plaintive whistle.

"Hear that?" cried Aleck, wildly.

"Yes, I heard it in my sleep. The place is getting open then. There it goes again. It must be a gull."

"No, no, no!" cried Aleck, wildly, his voice sounding cracked and broken from the overpowering joy that seemed to choke him. "Don't you know what it is?"

"A seagull, I tell you."

"No, no, no! It's Tom Bodger's whistle. You listen now."

There was a dead silence in the cavern, save that both lads felt or heard the throbbing in their breasts.

"I can't hear anything," said the middy, at last. "What was it?"

"Nothing," gasped Aleck. "I can't—can't whistle now."

But he made another effort to control his quivering tips, mastered them into a state of rigidity, and produced a repetition of the same low, plaintive note that had reached their ears.

Directly after, the whistle was repeated from outside, and, as Aleck produced it once more in trembling tones, the lads leaped to their feet, for, coming as it were right along the surface of the water, as if through some invisible opening, there came the welcome sound:

"Ship ahoy! Master Aleck—a—" *suck—suck—flop—flop*—a whisper, and then something like a sigh.

"It is Tom Bodger!" cried Aleck, in a voice he did not know for his own, and something seemed to clutch him about the throat, and he knelt there muttering something inaudible to himself.

Chapter Thirty

Phee-ew! Phee-ew! The peculiar gull-like whistle once more, to run in a softened series of echoes right up into the farthest part of the cavern. Then there came the peculiar sucking, ploshing sound as of water filling up an opening. A minute later "Ship ahoy!" from outside.

"Tom! Ahoy!" yelled Aleck, wildly.

"Ahoy, my lad! Ahoy!" and something else was cut off by the soft sucking splash of water again, while to make the lads' position more painful in their efforts to reply, twice over they were conscious of the fact that when they replied with a shout their cries did not pass through the orifice, which the water had closed.

But the tide was ebbing steadily, and the tiny arc of the rocks which showed the way in was growing more open, so that at the end of a few minutes they heard plainly:

"Where'bouts are yer, my lad?"

"In here!" shouted Aleck, but only in face of a dull *plosh.*

Another minute and the question was repeated, but from whence the lads could hardly tell, for instead of coming from the cavern mouth the words seemed to come from far up the cavern, to be followed by another splash. It was quite half a minute before, taught by experience, Aleck shouted:

"Shut in here! Cave!"

There was another plosh, but they had proof soon after that the words had been heard, for the hail now came:

"Are yer 'live, my lad?"

"Ye-es," cried Aleck. "Quite!" and then he could in his excitement hardly control a hysterical laugh at the absurdity of the question and answer.

"Thought yer was dead and gone, my lad," came now, in company with a fainter splashing.

"Tom Bodger!"

"Hullo!" came quickly.

"We're shut in by the water."

"Who's 'we'?"

"The cutter's midshipman and I."

"Wha–a–at! Then there arn't nayther on yer dead and drownded, my lad?"

"No–o–o–o!"

"Then I say hooray! hooray! But can't you swim out?"

"No. We've tried."

"Ho!" came back. "Wait a bit."

"What for? Can't you get help for us, Tom?"

"Ay, ay, my lad," came back. "But jest you wait."

Then there was silence, and the prisoners joined hands, to kneel, waiting and listening.

"He has gone for help," said the middy.

"Yes, and before he gets back that little hole that let his words in will be shut up again."

"Never mind," said the middy, sagely; "he knows we're here."

"Oh, but why didn't I think to tell him of the zigzag path? I daresay they could get the stones out from above where they were pushed in."

"Perhaps he hasn't gone," said the middy. "Ahoy there!"

There was a peculiar sound as of the water rising up and gurgling along a channel, while a lapping sound at their feet told that the water inside was being put in motion.

"Why, he has dived down," cried Aleck, suddenly, "so as to try and get to us."

"Tchah! Nonsense. That squat little wooden-legged man couldn't swim."

But at the end of what seemed to be a long period they heard a louder splash, followed by another, and the illuminated water began to dance and a curious ebullition to be faintly seen.

Then there was a panting sigh, and a familiar voice cried:

"Where'bouts are yer?"

"Here, here!" cried the lads, in a breath, and the next minute they were conscious of something swimming towards them, which took shape more and more till they saw that it was a man swimming on his back.

"What cheer-ho!" came now, in the midst of a lot of splashing. "Lend us a hand, my lads, for I'm all at sea here. Thanky! Steady! Let's get soundings for my legs. Mind bringing that lanthorn a bit forrarder? That's right; now I can see where I go."

Tom Bodger had managed to find a hold for his stumps, and stood shaking himself as well as he could for the fact that he had a lad holding tightly on to each hand.

"Well, yer don't feel like ghostses, my lads!" cried the sailor. "This here's solid flesh and bone, and it's rayther disappynting like."

"Disappointing, Tom?"

"Yes, Master Aleck. Yer see, your uncle says: 'You find the poor lad's remains, Bodger,'—remains, that's what he called it—'and I'll give yer a ten-pound Bank o' Hengland note,' he says."

"Oh!" cried Aleck, passionately.

"And the orficer there from the Revenoo cutter, he says: 'You find the body o' young Mr Wrighton of the man-o'-war sloop, and there'll be the same reward for that.'"

"Humph! I should have thought I was worth more than that," said the midshipman.

"Ay, ay, sir!" cried Tom Bodger, who was squeezing his shirt and breeches as he talked. "So says I, sir; but it's disappynting, for I arn't found no corpses, on'y you young gents all as live-ho as fish; and what's to come o' my rewards?"

"Oh, bother the rewards, Tom! How did you get in?"

"Dove, sir, and swimmed on my back with my flippers going like one o' the seals I've seen come in here."

"But we tried to do that, both of us, and we couldn't do it."

"Dessay not, sir. Didn't try on the right tide."

"Nearly got drowned, both of us, my lad," said the midshipman. "But don't let's lose time. You show the way, and we'll follow you."

"No hurry, sir; plenty o' time. Be easier bimeby. Tide's got another hour o' ebb yet. But how in the name o' oakum did you two gents manage to get in here? I knowed there was a hole here where the seals dove in, and I did mean to come sploring like at some time or other; but it's on'y once in a way as you can row in."

Aleck told him in a few words, and the man whistled.

"Well, I'll be blessed!" he said. "I allus knowed that Eben Megg and his mates must have a store hole somewhere, and p'raps if I'd ha' lay out to sarch for it I might ha' found it out. But I didn't want to go spying about and get a crack o' the head for my pains. The Revenoo lads'll find out for theirselves some day; and so you young gents have been the first?"

"Stop a minute," said Aleck. "What about Eben Megg?"

"Oh, they cotched him days ago, sir—cutter's men dropped upon him while they was hunting for this young gent's corpus, and he's aboard your ship, sir, I expect, along with the other pressed men."

"But haven't they been looking for me any more?" said the middy.

"No, sir; they give it up arter they'd caught Eben; and, as I told yer, there was a reward offered for to find yer dead as they couldn't find yer living."

"So that's why Eben didn't come back, sailor," said Aleck, quietly.

"Yes," said the middy, "but why didn't he tell the cutter's officer that we were shut up here?"

"Too bitter about his capture, perhaps, or he might not have had a chance to speak while he was ashore."

"I don't believe it was that," said the middy. "I believe he wouldn't tell where their storehouse was."

"And so this here's the smugglers' cave, is it?" said Tom Bodger, looking about. "But where's t'other way out, sir?"

Aleck explained that the smuggler had closed the way up.

"Well, sir, it's a wery artful sort o' place, I will say that. Lot o' good things stored up here, I s'pose?"

"Plenty."

"Hah! Is there now? Well, it means some prize money, Mr Wrighton, sir, and enough to get a big share."

"And I deserve it, my man," said the middy, with something of his old consequential way; "but let's get out into the daylight. I'm afraid—I'm— that is, I shouldn't like to be shut in again."

"No fear, sir. You trust me. Lot more time yet. 'Sides, the tide'll fall lower to-morrow morning; but I'll get you out as soon as I can, for your poor uncle's quite took to his bed, Master Aleck."

"Uncle has?"

"Yes, sir. Chuffy sharp-spoken gent as he always was, blest if he didn't say quite soft to me, with the big tears a-standing in his eyes: 'It's all over, Bodger, my man,' he says, 'and you may have the poor boy's boat, for I know if he could speak now he would say, "Give it to poor old Tom."'"

"Poor old uncle!" said Aleck, huskily. "Then you're cheated again, Tom, and have lost your boat?"

"And hearty glad on it, too, Master Aleck, say I. A-mussy me, my lad, what would the Den ha' been without you there? The captain wouldn't ha' wanted me. I don't wonder as I couldn't rest, but come over here every morning and stayed till dark, climbing about the rocks and cliffs, with the birds a-shouting at me and thinking all the time that I'd come arter their young 'uns—bubblins, as we calls 'em, 'cause they're so fat."

"And so they haven't been looking for me any more?" said the middy, in a disappointed tone.

"No, sir; not since they telled me to keep on looking for yer. You see, everybody said as you must ha' gone overboard and been washed out to sea, same as the captain felt that you'd slipped off the cliff somewhere, Master Aleck, and been drowned. But I kep' on thinking as both on yer might ha' been washed into some crivissy place and stuck there, and that's why I kep' on peeking and peering about, hoping I might come upon one of you if I didn't find both; and sure enough, here you are. I don't know what you gents think on it, but I call it a right-down good morning's work for such a man as me."

"But you did not walk over from Rockabie this morning, my man?" said the middy.

"Not walk over, sir? Oh, yes, I did."

"You must be very tired?"

"Not me, sir. My legs never get tired; and yet the queerest thing about it is that they allus feel stiff."

"Don't talk any more, Tom," said Aleck. "I want to get to business. Now, then, don't you think we might get out now?"

"Well, yes, sir; p'raps we might. It's a good deal lighter, you see, since I come, but she's far from low water yet, and it'll come much easier when tide's right down. But can't I have a bit of a look round, Master Aleck?"

"Of course," was the reply, and the sailor grinned and chuckled as he ran his eyes over what he looked upon as a regular treasure house for anyone whose dealings were on the sea with boats.

The cavern was lighter now than the two prisoners had ever seen it, so that Tom was able to have a good look; and he finished off by trotting down as near to the mouth of the great place as he could, and then turning to Aleck.

"There," he said, "I think we might venture out now. You can swim out now without having to dive. What do you say, Mr Wrighton, sir?"

"I think we ought to go at once."

"Come on, then, gen'lemen. You'll get a bit wet, but there's a long climb arterwards up the hot rocks in the sunshine, and you'll be 'most dry 'fore you get home."

"Oh, never mind the water," cried the middy. "My uniform's spoilt. I'm ready to do anything to get out of here."

"Will you go first, sir?" cried Tom Bodger.

"No, you found the way in," was the reply, "so lead the way out."

"Right, sir. Ready?"

"Then come on."

The man took three or four of his queer steps, to stand for a moment on the edge of the deep pool, and then went in sidewise to swim like a seal for the low archway, whose weed-hung edges were only a few inches above the surface of the water, and as he reached it to pass under he laid his head sidewise so that the dripping shell-covered weed wiped his cheek.

There had been no hesitation on the part of the prisoners. Aleck sprang in as soon as their guide was a few feet away, and the middy followed, both finding their task delightfully easy as they swam some fifty yards through a low tunnel, whose roof was for the most part so close to the surface that more than once, as the smooth water heaved, Aleck's face just touched the impending smoothly-worn stone.

But there were two places, only a few yards in, where the arch was broken into a yawning crack, from which the water dripped in a heavy shower.

"Look up as you come along here," cried Aleck to his companion, and then he shuddered, for his voice raised a peculiar echo, suggesting weird hollows and tunnels, while as he increased his strokes to get past and the middy came under in turn, he shouted again after his leader:

"Why, Tom, that must be where the water snatched us up and nearly drowned us."

Five minutes later all three were swimming for a rough natural pier, and Tom Bodger gave his head a sidewise wag towards another low cavernous arch.

"'Nother way in there," he said. "Jynes the one we came out of. You must have seen how the waves dance and splash there in rough weather, Master Aleck?"

"No," was the reply. "I've only seen that it's a terribly rough bit of coast. I never came down here, and of course I was never out in my boat when it was rough."

"Course not, sir. It is a coarse bit. I had no end of a job to get down, and I spect that it's going to be a bit worse going up agen. What do you say to sitting up yonder in the sunshine on that there shelf? The birds'll soon go. You can make yourselves comf'able and get dry while I go up and get a rope. Dessay I can be back in an hour or so."

"No," cried the lads, in a breath. "We'll climb it if you can."

Climb up the dangerous cliff they did by helping one another, and with several halts to look down at the still falling tide; and in one of these intervals Aleck exclaimed:

"But I still can't see how the smugglers could run a boat up and row into that cavern."

"Course they couldn't row, sir," replied Tom, "on'y shove her in. But don't you see what a beautiful deep cut there is? Bound to say that at the right time they'd run a big lugger close in. Look yonder! It's just like the way into a dock, and sheltered lovely. Ah, they're an artful lot, smugglers! You never know what they're after."

It was about an hour later that, without passing a soul on their solitary way, the party reached the cliff path down into the Den garden, where no Dunning was visible, and a chill came over Aleck like a warning of something fresh in the way of disaster that he was to encounter.

It came suddenly, but it was as suddenly chased away by his hearing the voice of Jane crooning over the words of some doleful old West Country ballad, not of a cheering nature certainly, but sufficient to prove that someone was at the house.

"Wait here," he whispered to his companions. "Let me go and see my uncle first."

He crept in unheard, glanced round to see that the lower room was empty, and then went softly up the stairs, his well-soaked boots making as little noise as if they had been of indiarubber.

The study door yielded to a touch, and he stood gazing at the figure of his uncle, seated in his usual place, but with pen, ink and papers thrust aside so that he could bow his grey head down upon his clasped hands.

"Asleep, uncle?" said the lad, softly.

"Aleck, my boy!" cried the old man, springing up to catch the lost one in his arms. "Heaven be thanked! I was mourning for you as dead."

Chapter Thirty One

Comfortably settled down at the Den as Aleck's guest and made most welcome, the middy felt not the slightest inclination to stir; but all through life there is to all of us the call of duty, and the lad was ready to recommence his, and eager to report to headquarters his discovery of the notorious smugglers' cave.

Enquiries at Rockabie proved that the sloop and cutter had both sailed, so a letter had to convey some of the information—"a despatch," the young officer called it; and after it was sent he constituted himself guardian of the smugglers' treasure and headed a little expedition, composed of Aleck and Tom Bodger, to examine the land way down into the cave, which they approached by a rope provided by Tom, who said he didn't "keer" about jumping down from that there shelf, because his legs were so stiff.

Then a descent was made by the sloping zigzag paths, till the corner was reached, about half way down, where the way was blocked.

"Only fancy," said Aleck. "How we did fight to get out from below, and it's all as simple as can be from up here."

And so it was, for three stones had been drawn down the slope, one partly over the other and the other fitting nicely to either, but only requiring a little effort to pull them back, *after*—

Yes, it was after one smaller wedge-shaped piece had been lifted out by Tom Bodger, this wedge being like a key stone or bolt to hold the others in place so tightly that it was impossible so shift them from below.

Tom Bodger had just removed the last stone into a big recess, which had probably been formed by the smugglers to hold them, when the middy turned round sharply upon a dark figure which had, unseen before, been following them.

"Hallo!" he cried. "Who are you?"

"It's me, sir—Dunning, sir—the captain's gardener, sir. Come to see, sir, if I could be of any help."

"No," cried Aleck, sharply, "you've come to play the spy, you deceitful old rascal."

"Oh, Master Aleck, sir!" whined the man, "how can you say such a thing?"

"Because I know you by heart. You've been hand and glove with the smugglers all through."

"Master Aleck, sir!"

"That will do," cried the lad, indignantly. "I've never told my uncle what I've seen or heard, but I must now, and you know what to expect."

"Master Aleck!"

"That's it, is it?" said the middy. "He's one of the gang, and of course I shall make him a prisoner as soon as we get out. Here, you, Bodger, I order you in the King's name to take that man prisoner."

"Ay, ay, sir," cried Tom, and he made a move towards the gardener.

But it was ineffective, for the man suddenly thrust out a foot and hooked one of the pensioner's wooden legs off the stone floor of the slope, giving him a sharp thrust in the chest at the same time.

There is a game called skittles, or, more properly, ninepins, in which if you strike one of the pins deftly it carries on the blow to the next, which follows suit, and so on, till the blow given to number one has resulted in all nine being laid low.

"Jes' like ninepins, Master Aleck," said Tom, "only there's nobbut three on us. I beg your pardon, sir; I couldn't help it."

"No, no, no, no, no!" roared Aleck, each utterance being a part of a hearty laugh, for the gardener had knocked Tom over, Tom had upset him, and the blow he carried on to the midshipman had sent the latter rolling down the slope, to come raging up as soon as he could gain his feet and climb back.

"What are you laughing at?" he shouted.

"It was so comic," panted Aleck, wiping his eyes.

"Shall I go arter him, sir?" said Tom.

"No, no. He is half way to the top by now."

"Yes, yes," cried the middy; "and look sharp, or perhaps he'll be trying to shut us up again."

"Not he," said Aleck; "he won't stop till he is safe. I don't believe we shall see the lazy old scoundrel again."

Aleck's words proved to be true.

Later on he and his party made their way up to the smugglers' cottages, to find them deserted by everyone save Eben Megg's wife, with three pretty little dark-eyed children.

The woman looked frightened, and burst into tears as she recognised the young officer, who began at her at once.

"You're a nice woman, you are," he said. "What have you got to say for yourself for keeping me a prisoner below there?"

"I—I only did what I was told, sir," faltered the woman.

"Were you told to fasten us down there to starve?" cried the middy.

"Fasten?—to starve? Were you left down there, sir, when my Eben was knocked down and carried away?"

"Of course we were."

"I didn't know, sir," sobbed the woman. "If I had, though I was in such trouble, I'd have come and brought you all I could, same as I did before, sir. Indeed I would."

"Humph!" grunted the middy. "Well, you did feed me as well as you could. So you've lost your husband, then?"

The woman tried to answer, but only sobbed more loudly.

"There, don't cry," said the middy, more gently. "We shall make an honest man of him."

"And what's to become of my poor weans, Master Aleck? We shall all be turned out of the cottage."

"I don't think you will," said Aleck. "I daresay uncle won't let anyone interfere with you."

There were busy days during the next week, with men from the sloop and cutter, brought back by the middy's "despatch," going up and down the zigzag like so many ants, bringing up the principal treasures of the cave, the sailors working with all their might over the greatest haul they had ever made, and chuckling over the amount of prize money they would have to draw.

There was a fair amount of work done and much recovering of valuable gear during two days of the next spring tide, when Aleck and his companion were rowed in one of the sloop's boats along a narrow channel of deep water right up the cavern. They were poled in, and found so much to interest them that they stayed too long and were nearly shut in once more, for the tide rose fast, and the men had to lie down in the boat and work her out with their hands, and then a wave came in and lifted her, jamming the gunwale against the slimy rock and weeds, threatening a more terrible imprisonment still; but just as matters were very serious and the lives of the party in imminent danger, the water sank a few inches and enabled the men to thrust the boat on into daylight.

That was the last time a boat entered that cave, for during a terrific storm in the ensuing winter the waves must have loosened and torn up some of the supporting stones of the archway, letting down hundreds of tons of rock in a land slide, so that where the cave had lain like a secret, the waves played regularly at high water, working more and more at every tide to lay bare the gloomy recesses to the light of day.

Aleck saw no more of Willie Wrighton, midshipman, for two years, and then he came on a visit to the Den.

The next morning the two young men went for a stroll along the cliffs to have a look at the rocky chaos which had once formed the cave.

As they came near they caught sight of a solitary figure down towards where the archway submerged had lain, and Aleck made put that it was a big, well-built man-o'-war's man.

"Is that one of your fellows, sailor?" said Aleck, with the appellation he had used when they were prisoners together.

"Yes, he came over with me from Rockabie. Capital fellow he is too. Don't you know him again?"

"No," said Aleck, shading his eyes. "Yes, I do. How he is changed! Why, Eben Megg, I hardly knew you again without your beard."

"Glad to see you, Master Aleck," said the man, warmly. "Mr Wrighton here was good enough to bring me along with him to see the old place. I'm coming to make a long stay, sir, as soon as we're paid off, and—and—there, I arn't good at talking—about them things," continued the man, huskily, "but God bless you and the captain, sir, for all you've done for my poor wife and bairns."

"Oh, nonsense! Don't talk about it, Eben," said Aleck, huskily; "but, I say, young man, you nearly made an end of us by not coming back after you'd shut us in. What did you do it for—to kill us?"

"To kill you both, sir? Not me! I on'y wanted to make sure of you for an hour or two till I'd been home and scraped a few things together to take away with me. When I come back the cutter's lads dropped upon me, and I showed fight till a crack on the head knocked all the say out of me for about a fortnit. When I could speak they told me you'd both been found."

"Ahoy!" cried the middy, excitedly. "Here comes your rasé chap, old wooden pegs. I'd nearly forgotten him. Does he live here?"

"Oh, yes, he's our gardener and odd man; been with us ever since Dunning ran away. Capital gardener he makes, sailor—digs a patch and then walks down it, making holes with his wooden legs to drop in the potatoes or cabbage plants, before standing on one leg and covering in the earth with the other. Hallo, Tom, what is it?"

"Sarvant, sir," said Tom, pulling his forelock, man-o'-war fashion, to the young officer. "Been showing Eben Megg how the cave was busted up, sir, in the storm. I beg pardon, sir; I've been scouring and swabbing out the boat 'smorning in case you and the luff-tenant wanted to go for a sail."

"To be sure," cried Aleck, eagerly. "Here, we'll go for a run to Rockabie and back, Eben; come and take the helm and show Mr Wrighton how the smugglers could run a boat close in among the rocks. You know; the same as you did that night."

"Ay, ay, sir. Come along, Tom. Shall we go round to the Den gully and fetch her, sir? We could run in up the channel below here, and pick you up? Bodger says the channel's quite clear."

"Do you think you could find your way in, Eben?" said Aleck, with a merry look.

"Find my way in, sir? Ay, sir, if it was black as ink, or with my eyes shut."